CAVALIER
CHRISTOPHER HEPWORTH

Publishing and Marketing Consultant: Lama Jabr
Website: https://xanapublishingandmarketing.com
Sydney, Australia

Connect with Christopher Hepworth
Website: https://christopherhepworth.com
Email: christopherhepworth15@gmail.com

This book is dedicated to three special people who are part of the rich History of Red House:

Major Tony Gordon and **Mrs Jill Gordon** (headmaster and matron of Red House from 1975 to 2001) who were loved and respected by a generation of students fortunate to have been in their care. Tony sadly passed away in 2018 while Jill still runs Red House Estate with her family.

Stephen Heptinstall (head prefect of Red House 1974), my much-loved brother and life-long friend who was eagerly anticipating the publication of Cavalier but passed away unexpectedly in November 2023.

CHRISTOPHER HEPWORTH

PART ONE

"The only thing necessary for the triumph of evil is for good men to do nothing."

— **Edmund Burke**

CHAPTER 1

The Tower of London,
8th June 1658

'You have twenty-five minutes before we take Slingsby to the block,' the guard said as he unlocked the heavy wooden door of the cell for the condemned. Samuel Fauconberg removed his broad felt hat and stepped into the cramped but tidy cell that had been the last abode of many of England's most notorious traitors.

He waited while the man he loved as a father, Sir Henry Slingsby, knelt beside the small wooden desk and concluded reciting the final verse of the twenty-third psalm.

'... and I shall dwell in the house of the Lord forever.' The condemned man's gaunt face assumed a serene expression, as if his imminent execution was to be the beginning of a journey to a better place rather than the brutal ending of his earthly existence.

'Amen,' Fauconberg said to attract Sir Henry's attention. Slingsby turned and his face lit up with joy as he recognised his young steward. His arthritic knees clicked as he rose from the cold, hard floor to greet the former stable lad. He rested his hands on Fauconberg's shoulders and stared at the young man's face in wonder. Slingsby kissed him on both cheeks, and then brushed a small tear from the corner of one eye.

'My dear Samuel! Each time I see you, you become ever more agreeable in appearance and impressive in stature. My sole regret in this temporal life is that I was too arrogant to adopt you as a son when you came into my care.'

It had been three years since Sir Henry Slingsby had been arrested for his part in the failed Penruddock Uprising. In that time, his demeanour had deteriorated from that of a sprightly middle-aged knight of the realm, to a shuffling old man. His hair had greyed and his eyes had a sunken and watery appearance. Yet his humble nature, his dignified presence and his defiant spirit remained undaunted.

Fauconberg gazed at Sir Henry through veiled tears. He owed everything he had in life to this man and his late wife.

Fauconberg had been the illegitimate child of an indiscreet affair between a parlour maid, who had died in childbirth, and an unknown Yorkshire nobleman. He had been farmed out to a succession of judgemental and uncaring relatives, until Baronet Slingsby and his wife had taken pity on him and set him to work as an apprentice stable lad on Slingsby's sprawling estate. When Slingsby rode off to war in 1642, the fifteen-year-old stable lad followed him into battle as his squire. Whereas Slingsby had been a reluctant and awkward soldier, the young Fauconberg had blossomed into an accomplished cavalryman with an aptitude for warfare. Fauconberg had risen through the royalist ranks to the position of colonel of the much-feared Northern Horse cavalry regiment.

'Grieve not for me, my beloved Samuel, for I have reconciled with God. My conscience is clear, and my soul is resolved.' Slingsby took Fauconberg by the arm and led him to the edge of his neat little bed. 'Sit down, for we have much to discuss before the appointed hour. Tell me, what news of my children, Tom, Harry and Rebecca?'

Fauconberg knew he must be strong for Sir Henry. He drew a deep breath and composed himself. 'Tom and Harry have been exiled to the court of Prince Charles in The Hague.'

'Why so? They have committed no act of treason.'

'The Puritan elders of the City of York issued a warrant for their arrest when you were sentenced to a traitor's death.'

'On what charge?'

'Like you, they refuse to swear Cromwell's oaths. But they are safe in Holland. They send you their love and they lament they could not be with you today.'

'Perhaps it is for the best,' Slingsby said sadly. 'And what of my beloved daughter, Rebecca? Is she still the exiled Prince Charles's favourite?'

Fauconberg swallowed hard. 'Indeed she is. She has returned to Red House with twin boys.'

'I am a grandfather?'

'Indeed you are, sir.'

Slingsby's forehead creased with worry. 'Then why in the name of God did she return to Red House with the children?'

'I could not stop her. The elders of York are plotting to seize your estate and sell it to your neighbour Benedict Bourcher.

They are claiming the house has been abandoned by the Slingsby family and hence your property is to be forfeited to the Commonwealth. She is the only one without a warrant for her arrest and so has returned to protect your estate.'

'She must return to Holland for the sake of the children,' Slingsby insisted.

'She will not go, sir. She will not abandon the house.'

'Tell her it is my dying wish.'

'Then the house will be lost and as your steward, I know not how to discharge my duty to your family.'

'You are to protect Red House from the Puritans at all costs. That is my last command to you.'

'The Slingsby family is so stubborn,' Fauconberg said, exasperated. 'How can I protect both your daughter and the house?'

'Trust in God. He will find a way.'

Fauconberg knew better than to argue with Sir Henry.

'Has Rebecca spoken of taking marriage vows with the prince? She would not give herself so freely to him if she were not betrothed. My daughter is a woman of honour.'

'She will not tell me, sir; it being a matter of national politics. The prince could not openly marry the daughter of an English baronet while he is seeking to procure foreign troops from the courts of Europe. Their terms may include his acceptance of a foreign princess of their choosing.' Fauconberg did not mention that Rebecca was one of several mistresses Prince Charles had entertained at The Hague, and each one had ambitions to be the future Queen of England.

'Of course. You are correct.' Slingsby relaxed his grip on Fauconberg's arm, and his serene demeanour returned. 'Now, tell me about Red House. Has the pulpit been delivered to the chapel?'

'Yes, sir. The chapel is complete, but the grounds are in sore need of repair and the roof leaks like an old bucket.'

'It was ever thus. What of the livestock?'

'The horses are breeding well, and the cows are fat. This season the estate turned its first profit since the Civil War ended.'

Slingsby's eyes were closed in silent rapture. Since the death of his wife ten years before, Red House had become the centre of his existence.

'Yet the situation at Red House remains precarious,' Fauconberg continued.

'Because of Benedict Bourcher, our neighbour?'

'Indeed, the very same. He is covetous of both your house and your daughter. Since he learned of your death sentence, he feels himself entitled to both. He knows not of Rebecca's relationship with the prince or the birth of the twins.'

'The man is a scurvy knave as well as a poor excuse for a gentleman farmer. He shall never have my daughter's hand while she is promised to a prince. It was he who spotted me walking in my orchard and reported me to the aldermen of York.' Slingsby sighed. 'You must protect Rebecca from this evil man, Samuel. Hence why she must return to Holland.'

'It shall be so, Sir Henry.'

Slingsby looked with sadness into Fauconberg's deep-blue eyes. 'I know you love my daughter with all the passion Adam had for Eve. And that is natural, for she has the fairest countenance ever blessed by nature. Yet once I accepted you into my house, she was forbidden to you. The future prosperity of the Slingsby family depends upon her securing a favourable match with a noble family, if it is not to be the exiled prince.'

'I understand, sir. I will forever be in the debt of the Slingsby family for providing me with a home, a gentleman's lifestyle, and a Cambridge education.'

'You have been like a son to me, Samuel. However, your sworn duty is to protect and serve Rebecca and her two younger brothers, till the odious Oliver Cromwell and his regime is overthrown. Do you understand?'

'Yes, sir.'

'If you can fulfil that duty, then you may consider your debt of honour to the Slingsby family repaid and you may make your own fortune in the world. God knows, you have earned it.'

'Thank you, sir. But there is one last favour I beg of you.'

'Ask away, my dear Samuel.'

'I need to know the name of my natural father. The lack of this knowledge eats at my heart.'

'I promised your father I would never reveal his name to you. That was the condition on which I was granted custody of you. As a man of honour, I cannot break my word.'

Fauconberg sighed in exasperation. 'You are indeed a man of

honour, sir, and that is why you are in a cell awaiting execution. Had you sworn loyalty to parliament and signed their oath of allegiance, you would be a free man. It is not what you sign under duress that defines you as a man, but the purity of your heart, and of that there can be no doubt.'

'The one makes me renounce my allegiance to my sovereign, and the other my religion. I cannot sign either and face death as an honest man.'

'And because of your pride, your offspring will be without a father in two hours hence.'

'Rebecca has your protection and my sons are safe in Holland. I can die in peace.'

'Rebecca will be labelled a traitor's daughter.'

'Let no man say I was a traitor. I was held by Cromwell as a prisoner of war and as such, under English law I cannot commit treason against my declared enemy. Had I been tried by an English jury and not by Cromwell's cronies, I would be on my way back to Red House as a free man. I expect you to explain those facts to my family and friends.'

'Yes, sir. But surely you will not take the secret of my father's identity to the grave?'

Slingsby sighed deeply. 'I spent a small fortune on your education, and the answer you seek is clear to all but the meanest village idiot. Why do you think you can strut free among your enemies like a cavalier peacock without fear of arrest?'

Fauconberg considered the matter. 'Perhaps my natural father is an eminent parliamentarian?'

'Precisely. And where do you think your astonishing gifts on the field of battle came from? Certainly, they did not come from me.'

'Then might I be the son of a military leader?'

'Now think, boy. Your late mother was a servant in a nearby estate when you were born. Why would my wife take pity on you and bestow her family name of Fauconberg on you unless she felt the burden of family loyalty towards you?'

'So, my father was a parliamentarian general related to your wife?'

'And how many such men are there?'

'But your wife's family are all royalists.'

'Except one, who for reasons known only to himself, sided

with the Roundheads.'

Fauconberg stroked his sandy beard as he considered the matter. 'General Fairfax? I cannot be his son. That is absurd.'

Slingsby allowed himself a small chuckle. Slingsby unconsciously touched the little bible that lay at the foot of his bed. 'As you have worked out the identity of your illustrious natural father for yourself, I can meet our Saviour in heaven without breaking my promise.'

'I almost killed Sir Thomas with a musket ball at Selby. You should have told me before the battle.'

'If your loyalties had been divided, you would not have become the most feared cavalry officer in the land.'

'Why did Fairfax not raise me as his son?'

'Thomas Fairfax was a frequent enough visitor to Red House before the Civil War and bestowed many treasures on you. But alas he was only sixteen years old when you were born, and the scandal would have ruined him.'

'Would Sir Thomas reconcile with me now?'

'He may. He is a man of good character, unlike our cruel and devious Lord Protector, Oliver Cromwell. But I suspect your presence may cause Cousin Fairfax some embarrassment even today. You may forsake the silent protection he has afforded you since the Civil War ended.'

The sound of guards marching on the cobbled stones of the Tower courtyard below reminded Slingsby his time was drawing close. 'Come. I must prepare for the guards. Did you bring the clothes I requested for my final reckoning?'

'Yes, sir. They are in the bag.'

'Then while I change, gather the documents from the desk and keep them safe. There is my last will and testament to Tom, Harry and Rebecca. There is also my diary and correspondence from my dear friends who have supported me through these difficult times.' Slingsby withdrew a gold locket from his pocket. 'This locket has been a great comfort to me while I have been in this prison.'

'Why so?'

'Inside the locket is a portrait of my dear daughter, painted when she was but eighteen years of age. On the other side is a portrait of you, Samuel, which I had painted when you attained your colonelcy of the Northern Horse. Please give the locket to Rebecca. The rest of my affairs ...' he indicated the piles of paperwork, 'I place in your care.'

'They will be safe with me.'

'Good. Then we will pray together for safe deliverance of my soul to our merciful Lord, and that our poor country may see an end to the misery and division that has afflicted it these past fifteen years.'

***

Slingsby's place of execution, Tower Hill, London

'You will do me one last favour to ease my final journey, my beloved Samuel?' said Slingsby as he placed his foot on the first of the scaffold steps.

'Anything, sir.' Fauconberg was amazed at Slingsby's calm demeanour, which contrasted with the circus atmosphere that pervaded Tower Hill. Over a thousand morbid onlookers had gathered to watch the gruesome spectacle. Many were drunk despite the early hour. Insults were hurled at Sir Henry Slingsby and the official execution party in equal measures. But as Slingsby continued to mount the scaffold steps, it was clear the mob was quietening as if affected by his dignity and humility. Pamphlets were circling among the crowd suggesting Slingsby's execution was a last act of spite from a decaying regime.

'Would you position yourself in the front row of the crowd, so I might look into your eyes as the axe falls? It would be a great comfort to me.'

'It shall be so,' replied Fauconberg.

The mob hissed as the common executioner of London, Richard Brandon, approached the scaffold. He was running late and paused to put on his black leather hood. The crowd jeered as he did so. Brandon shook his fist at the crowd then picked up his axe and ran his thumb over the keen edge of its blade. He nodded in satisfaction as a trickle of blood pooled onto his thumb.

'Oi! You boy!' Brandon said, looking down at Fauconberg. 'Are you the traitor's whelp?'

'Baronet Slingsby is no traitor, but I am indeed acting as his earthly representative.'

'The lord lieutenant of the Tower ain't paid me no gold for me trouble,' he said, holding his hand out to Fauconberg.

'I gave Colonel Barkstead a silver half-crown to pass on to you,' Fauconberg replied.

'Ain't seen it.'

Fauconberg sighed. Executioners had been known to botch their death blow if they were not well rewarded. He fished out three gold sovereign coins from his leather pouch and placed them in Brandon's filthy hands. The amount was sufficient to feed a large family for half a year, but Brandon looked at the gold coins with contempt. 'I've got a sore shoulder. Know what I mean? Could make things messy, like.'

'How many heads have you severed with the axe, Brandon?'

'Dozens, me lord. I'm the best there is.'

'You are mistaken. My sword, Enlightener, has severed more Puritan heads from their filthy shoulders on the battlefields of England than you will ever behead in a lifetime on the scaffold. Sir Henry will die a clean, painless death from one blow or, God help me, the next head to roll will be yours. Do we understand each other?' he said, staring into the eye slits of Brandon's hood.

'Well, if you put it like that … yes, yes, it will be a clean blow.'

Sam nodded as he walked towards the front row of the mob, where he could make eye contact with Sir Henry. A woman in a dirty black dress and tattered bonnet cursed him as he asked her to make room for him, then reluctantly she shuffled to her left.

As Sir Henry dropped to his knees to recite the Lord's Prayer, a respectful hush descended on the crowd. When he had finished, he stood up and turned to Sheriff Robinson, whose duty it was to keep public order during the execution.

'Have you any last words to say to the assembled witnesses?' Sheriff Robinson asked. He had difficulty meeting Slingsby's gaze.

Slingsby was a man of few words, but he turned towards the crowd and straightened his posture. Then in a low but clear voice he uttered his last words:

'My Lord Cromwell has condemned me to die for being an honest man, and for that I am very glad, for Cromwell himself shall not be entitled to the same blessing when his time draws near.'

Slingsby anxiously scanned the assembled throng, looking for Fauconberg, then relaxed as he spotted him in the crowd. As their eyes met, he smiled and mouthed the words '*My beloved son*'.

Fauconberg struggled to contain his emotions. Slingsby had never referred to him with this endearment before. He needed to appear strong in front of Sir Henry in this desperate moment. He straightened his back, put his right fist across his heart and nodded his head in acknowledgement. Slingsby smiled in the manner of a man who was at peace. He knelt in front of the wooden block and mumbled one last prayer. As he did so, the woman to Fauconberg's left fainted. A baby cried out and the sound of soft weeping filled the air. Still maintaining eye contact with Fauconberg, Slingsby laid his head on the block. He pulled down the collar of his shirt and moved the hair from around his neck. He stretched out his arms either side of the block and took one last, deep breath. When he was settled, he signalled with his right hand that he was ready to receive the axe.

Sheriff Robinson nodded towards the executioner and the axe came crashing down.

CHAPTER 2

Red House,
three months later

Slingsby had successfully eluded Cromwell's militia for eighteen months, even as they spent weeks at a time ransacking his home in their quest to find him. The Roundheads had never discovered the network of priest holes and hidden passageways that riddled his imposing, ivy-covered red-brick house.

Slingsby had intended to wait out Cromwell's Protectorate until either Cromwell died, or the public rebelled against his oppressive regime. But he had grown restless with his self-imposed confinement. He had taken to walking in his orchard at dusk for exercise, and surveying his estate from the roof of Red House. One fateful day he had been spotted by his neighbour Benedict Bourcher, a fanatical Puritan, who had alerted the commissioners of York to his presence. The commissioners had set a trap in the orchard and Slingsby had been arrested and subsequently found guilty of treason.

His faithful young steward, Samuel Fauconberg, had taken the required oaths of allegiance to Cromwell so he could manage the financial affairs of the Slingsby family and tend to the running of the estate. Yet the Puritan commissioners still interfered in every aspect of his life, as if they resented Fauconberg's battlefield successes during the Civil War.

Fauconberg had received a tip-off from the housemaid, Helen, that a delegation of civic and religious commissioners was planning to search the chapel for religious icons and other symbols of 'popery'. While he awaited their arrival, he took the opportunity to hide Sir Henry's few remaining treasures into a chamber-sized priest hole beneath the chapel.

As Fauconberg fixed the pew that hid the entrance to the priest hole back into place, he heard a horse and carriage accompanied by six mounted soldiers pull up on the gravel outside the main entrance of Red House. He sighed, then made one last check of the chapel that had been Slingsby's pride and joy. The floor was paved in black and white, chessboard-patterned marble, and the wood panelling that lined the sides was of sturdy English oak.

A magnificent stained-glass window behind the altar displayed the Slingsby crest and those of his many illustrious relatives and ancestors. At each of the four corners of the chapel corresponding to the points of the compass was a wooden plaque. Each was inscribed in elaborate gold lettering with one of the four Latin words of the Slingsby family motto: '*Benignitas, pietas, fides et audacia*', meaning 'kindness, piety, loyalty and courage'.

At length, Fauconberg strode out of the chapel to greet the officials from York. Their horses were skittish and blowing hard from the journey. It was raining, and the four men struggled against the wind as they climbed out of the carriage, assisted by the maid and footman. He nodded with satisfaction as his stable lad ushered the six bellicose soldiers away from the main house and towards the stable yard, where they would be plied with strong ale and a hearty broth to keep them pliant.

'Ah, Mister Bourcher,' Fauconberg shouted over the wind to his neighbour as he emerged from the carriage. 'I see you are in eminent company. Pray, come to my withdrawing room where you can warm yourself in front of the fireplace and introduce me to your friends.'

Benedict Bourcher was a tall man with powerful, broad shoulders, a face scarred from smallpox and close-cropped jet-black hair. He exuded Puritan malevolence. Bourcher's father had been one of the fifty-nine regicides who had signed King Charles's death warrant ten years before. Unlike Sir Henry Slingsby, Bourcher had proven to be an ineffective farmer, beset with bad luck compounded by his refusal to move with the times. He had become embittered and jealous that Slingsby's crops, livestock and horses were thriving, while the Bourcher estate was neglected and run down.

Fauconberg recognised Alderman Watson of the York Council, but the other two men, one a priest and the other, who was dressed like a vagrant, were strangers and they muttered to each other in a thick east-country accent that he struggled to understand.

Fauconberg led the four men through the grand entrance and into the marbled hall. They turned right and walked along a narrow passage decorated with terracotta floor tiles, then into the withdrawing room, where tastefully upholstered furniture and a welcoming open fire awaited them.

Fauconberg sensed the open hostility of his visitors and noticed Bourcher's covetous glances at his furnishings, but etiquette demanded he treat them as honoured guests.

'You are aware of the impoverished circumstances of our household since the death of Sir Henry,' Fauconberg said. 'But while I was in London, I chanced upon a few ounces of the new drink from the Orient they call tea. Would you gentlemen care to join me for a cup?'

His guests nodded as they warmed themselves by the fire and Fauconberg rang a small bell to summon the maid. 'Would you be so kind as to boil up a pot of tea for our esteemed guests?' he asked Helen when she arrived.

'Yes, Master Samuel.' The maid curtseyed to the guests and left the room.

'And to what do I owe the pleasure of your company, gentlemen?' Fauconberg asked.

'The late Sir Henry promised me the hand of the Lady Slingsby in marriage,' Bourcher said. 'Charity demands I save her from the shame of being a traitor's daughter.'

'You are aware she has given birth to twins?'

Bourcher reeled at the news, but then recovered his wits.

'With whom?'

'That is not your concern.'

'Then one can only assume she has fallen into sin and the children are bastards.'

'As I said, that is not your concern.'

'Then where is she now? I demand to see her.'

'That is not possible. She has returned to Holland so the children can live in safety. These are dangerous times since the Lord Protector, Oliver Cromwell, died.'

Bourcher's face reddened with anger. 'Why was I not told this? She was promised to me.'

'Sir Henry made no mention of such an arrangement when I attended him at the Tower, yet he was meticulous in all other matters of personal significance.'

'It matters not what a deceased traitor of the realm did or did not desire,' said Alderman Watson. The alderman was a small, rotund man who had been appointed to the role of Commissioner for Moral Affairs. He moved away from the fire and sat in one of the upholstered chairs. 'Lady Slingsby is in need of a firm, guiding hand and Mr Bourcher is a man of upstanding reputation, no small means and a strict disciplinarian.'

'May I ask why you allowed her to abscond to Holland?' said the priest in his strange East Anglian accent. 'That place is a viper's nest of royalist exiles. And besides, the Dutch are of an ill conversation and full of many loathsome diseases.'

'And who might you be?' asked Fauconberg.

'William Dowsing.'

A shudder ran up Fauconberg's spine. Dowsing was a famous iconoclast. He was dressed in Puritan black except for his oversized white collar. His head was bald apart from thick tufts of grey hair that sprouted over his protruding ears. It was well known he had rampaged through dozens of churches and royalist houses, destroying any object of religious imagery.

'I do not control Lady Slingsby. In fact, as the Slingsby family steward, it is I who serve her and her younger brothers.'

'That is preposterous! It is against the laws of nature and God for an ex-colonel, even one who rode with the infamous royalist Northern Horse, to serve a woman,'

'Lady Slingsby is descended from a long line of nobles, Mr Dowsing. Her father, Sir Henry, was gracious enough to accept me into his family when I was orphaned, and I am sworn to protect her.'

'It is still against God's law, and she is a fallen woman,' said Dowsing. He hissed the words like a venomous snake.

Helen arrived with the tea. She glared at Dowsing, then stirred the porcelain pot. She poured out five cups and retreated from the room.

Dowsing stared at his tea and took a sip. 'The local parishioners of All Saints Church in Moor Monkton tell me you have not attended church since April. What say you to that charge, young man? Be thou a secret papist?'

'Red House has its own chapel. Why would I need to travel to Moor Monkton?'

'Then I must inspect your chapel for superstitious and idolatrous images.'

'I presume you already checked All Saints and found it agreeable?'

'Of course. It is a fine, godly building.'

'Then you will also find the chapel of Red House agreeable.

Sir Henry Slingsby renovated the one and built the other. You have no grounds to search his chapel.'

They were interrupted by the fourth man. 'What be this foul China drink?' he said in a similar East Anglian accent. He wore a tall black Puritan hat with a large rim. His long white beard accentuated his snarl, and his eyes had a fanatical glint. 'Be this the devil's brew?'

Fauconberg finally recognised the man from a woodcut engraving he had seen on a London pamphlet, and shuddered. It was John Stearne, one-time associate of Matthew Hopkins, the notorious Witchfinder General. The two men had hanged more witches during the recent war than had been hanged in England's entire history. Fauconberg realised he was sharing a room with four of England's most infamous and evil men.

Stearne stared at the decorations on his blue porcelain teacup. Two stylised Chinese warriors on horses were hunting rabbits. The eyes of the hunters were narrow, their beards pointed. At the top of the cup, Chinese patterns and characters gave the cups a pleasing visual appeal. They were Rebecca's favourite possessions and had cost her a small fortune. Stearne's face contorted in rage as he looked at the Chinese images, then he threw the delicate cup and its contents onto the fire. The fire hissed as the cup shattered into fragments.

'The devil's horsemen!' he raged. 'Thou darest serve me this foul witch's brew in an idolator's cup?' he accused Fauconberg in his strange East Anglian accent.

Fauconberg rounded on Stearne. 'Even your former master, Oliver Cromwell, drank tea from such cups. I demand that while you are my guest, you do not abuse my hospitality. And pray, may I ask what is your business here in Yorkshire?'

'Alderman Watson and Mr Bourcher invited me hence to York. Mr Bourcher hath been beset by unnatural calamities and bewitched by some foul hag.'

'What calamities would those be?'

Stearne turned to Alderman Watson. 'This impertinent fellow speaketh like a young peacock from London. He doth not respect the tongue of our forefathers.'

'I regret that most young men have long eschewed the language of King James' Bible,' lamented Watson. 'It will not be long before only those of pure faith shall speak according to the custom of the good book.'

'My crops have failed and five of my cows have perished since the summer solstice. Yet your horses and cattle are the picture of health,' said Bourcher, pointing an accusing finger at Fauconberg. 'I tell you I am bewitched and I mean to find out who is responsible.'

'Perhaps you offended God in some manner?' countered Fauconberg.

'And his two daughters have lately experienced strange convulsions,' added Watson.

'Pardon my impudence,' replied Fauconberg, 'but there are rumours Mr Bourcher takes a leather strap to his son and a wooden paddle to his two daughters each Sabbath. Perhaps their convulsions have a natural rather than a diabolic cause?'

'If Lady Rebecca had not been spared the rod, she would not be in the predicament she now finds herself,' said Watson.

'The fact that Mr Bourcher is neither a good father nor a competent farmer does not suggest the existence of witches in this district,' replied Fauconberg.

'So say you, but York has suffered six months of high winds that have no earthly cause.'

'The winds are in the hands of God, not the devil, surely?'

'You may rationalise these malevolent manifestations as much as you like, Mr Fauconberg,' said Watson, 'but there is evil afoot, and the aldermen of York mean to root out this malfeasance. Mr Stearne and Mr Dowsing have been commissioned to hunt down the evildoers responsible for these diabolical events and they will begin their activities right here at Red House.'

'If these two charlatans from the dark and uncivilised counties of East Anglia dare to persecute the innocent women of this estate, then it will be they, not the women, who will suffer the consequences.'

'I must warn you, Mr Fauconberg, there are six soldiers waiting outside with orders to escort you to York Castle gaol, should it be my will,' said Watson.

Fauconberg strode towards the fireplace and picked up an iron poker. He spun it in his hands before adding another log to the fire and stoking it high. 'Do not try to intimidate me, gentlemen, for it is a waste of good breath,' he said in a menacing tone.

'There is one more thing before we take our leave, Mr

Fauconberg,' said Watson.

'Please make it quick, for I am losing patience.'

'There is the delicate matter of Red House.'

'And what of it?'

'As Sir Henry and his sons refused to sign the Oath of Loyalty to Parliament, the Committee for Compounding with Delinquents has sequestered Red House and the rest of his estate.'

'Not so. The Lady Slingsby signed the oath before she left for Holland, so under the law of the land, the house still belongs to the Slingsby family,' Fauconberg replied.

'But you just informed us Rebecca has abandoned the house, therefore it reverts to the City of York.' Alderman Watson folded his arms around his chest and smiled triumphantly.

'You call yourself a godly man, yet you scheme to dispossess a woman and her two newborn children of their home. Do you not feel shame burning your soul?' Fauconberg pointed the smoking poker in the alderman's direction before replacing it the bracket by the fireplace.

'We are not unreasonable men. If she agrees to consider Bourcher's offer of marriage she may return to Red House.'

'Yet I checked the records in the law courts this morning and no transfer of ownership has taken place.'

'Ah, you are mistaken. The council put Red House up for auction last week and Mr Bourcher submitted a sealed bid to the committee only this morning. I was both his financial sponsor and the alderman responsible for the sale of the property. I closed the bidding once Mr Bourcher's bid had been received. We only needed proof that Lady Slingsby has vacated the property to transfer the ownership of Red House to Mr Bourcher, and you have just provided it. Thus, you are required to vacate Red House within the week, but Lady Rebecca may return here to consider Mr Bourcher's offer of marriage.'

'You did not think to inform anyone else of this so-called auction other than Mr Bourcher?'

'Why would I? Mr Bourcher's offer of five thousand pounds was a most generous one.'

'The estate is worth over twelve thousand pounds.'

Bourcher and Watson looked at each other conspiratorially. Buying up ex-royalist property on the cheap was a lucrative business.

'You are well informed about the value, Mr Fauconberg,' Watson conceded.

'I am well informed because Mr Simms, the committee clerk, asked for my valuation before you put it up for auction.'

'Then you should congratulate Mr Bourcher on his good fortune.'

'As I suggested earlier, Mr Bourcher must have offended God, as once again fortune has deserted him.'

'What do you mean?' said Bourcher, his face contorted in anger.

'Mr Bourcher was not the sole bidder.'

Bourcher and Alderman Watson looked at each other in confusion.

'Had you not been in such a hurry to cheat the Slingsby family of their rightful home, you would have checked with Mr Simms that there had been no other bids,' said Fauconberg. 'I too put in a sealed bid this morning, but mine was for eleven thousand, two hundred pounds.'

'You lie,' accused Bourcher. 'You lack a fortune of such magnitude. You are the impoverished and illegitimate son of a parlour maid.'

'That is true,' replied Fauconberg. 'But Sir Henry had family connections with many noble houses in Yorkshire and beyond. When I informed them about the council's connivance to steal his estate, they were most insistent they did not want to see his children made destitute. Hence, they raised the sum required and appointed me as their trustee to bid on behalf of Sir Henry's heirs. Now, if you would be so kind, I have important things to do and I bid you gentlemen good day.'

CHAPTER 3

Red House,
October 1658

Fauconberg spurred his thoroughbred stallion towards the large paddock of horses, where the River Ouse bordered the extensive Red House grounds. He stopped by the jetty known as Red House Landing, which he had repaired the previous week, and waited for Lady Rebecca Slingsby to join him.

'Good day, my brave cavalier colonel,' she said as she manoeuvred her black mare close to his chestnut stallion. He felt the touch of her riding boots against his own as she settled her horse down. Fauconberg smiled fondly at her. She had returned from Holland two weeks before and looked more beautiful than ever, he thought, as he admired her high cheekbones, deep emerald-green eyes, and a mouth that was always at the point of breaking into a smile. Her chestnut coloured hair was tucked into her broad-brimmed riding hat and her skin glowed with the lustre of recent motherhood. She had brought her twins home to Red House with her and had taken to her role as mistress of the estate with confidence and obvious happiness.

'The horses are well nourished and will fetch a good price at the market,' Fauconberg said. 'If the farm continues to prosper, and if the estate's tenants pay their rent in good time, we will soon clear Sir Henry's debts.' He glanced once more at Rebecca, stirring feelings of fondness and desire.

'My brothers send their affection and gratitude to you, Samuel, as do I.'

'Your father asked me if you had married the prince while you were in Holland?'

Rebecca laughed. 'Are you jealous, my dear Samuel? Many ambitious young women have claimed the honour of marrying the prince, but I will not be one of those who indulges in such gossip.'

Fauconberg could not hide his love for the woman he had adored since he had first entered the Slingsby household. 'I am concerned only for your welfare and reputation, my lady. If the father is not the prince, will you not at least tell me his name?'

'You will not prise his name from my lips, no matter how hard you try. There are reasons of state why such things must remain secret. But that does not diminish the affection I have always felt for you.'

'Do you love this man?'

'Of course, but in a different way. I do not feel the same when I am with him as I do when I am with you ... but I admire and respect him very much.'

'Then why have you returned England without him?'

'Because he will be preoccupied with affairs of state for six months. Maybe much longer. I cannot bear to be alone at The Hague for all that time.'

'Does he know I resent him for taking you away from me?'

Rebecca leaned over and laid a hand on his arm. 'He knows you are my bold cavalier colonel and protector, and the Puritans would never dare harm me while I am with you. He also knows you gave my father your word you would not take me as your own.'

'The passion I displayed on the field of battle was but a design to impress your father sufficiently to release me from that oath, yet he remained unmoveable to the last.'

'And to impress me?' Rebecca's eyes sparkled with good humour.

'Always, my lady.' Fauconberg stared in the direction of York. His brow furrowed as he considered her safety. 'Oliver Cromwell may have died last month, and the aldermen of York may have promised you safe passage, but I fear England will descend into anarchy once more. Cromwell's son Richard is a weakling, and Yorkshire's Major General Lambert covets the office of Lord Protector.'

'Then perhaps His Majesty Prince Charles will return from exile to resume his rightful place on the throne of Great Britain and Ireland, and thus avert further anarchy.'

'Be careful of such talk, Rebecca. It cost your father his head.'

'It must come to pass. The people of England can no longer tolerate a state of affairs where brother is set against brother or mother against daughter. The return of Charles will see the end to religious bigotry and the return of the arts.'

Fauconberg was distracted by an acrid smell carried on the breeze. He turned to look south and saw a column of smoke rising from one of the barns that bordered Bourcher's property.

'We must ride like the wind, Rebecca,' he said, 'before the fire can take hold.' He turned his horse around and raced towards the plough shed. They galloped past the shed, their horses' hooves kicking up clods of black earth, and through the swaying fields of golden corn that was almost ready for harvesting. They approached the rear of Red House, skirted around its eastern edge and through the narrow gap between the house and the chapel. At last they emerged onto the lush green lawns, surrounded by neat symmetrical walls, and then vaulted over the low gate that barred the entrance to the deer park.

Rebecca whooped with excitement as her black mare overtook Fauconberg's stallion. The nearby deer scattered at the sound of the approaching hooves. Fauconberg laughed as he took up the challenge and narrowed the gap between the two horses.

As they approached the smoking barn in the paddock they knew as Mary's Field, Fauconberg touched her arm and pointed to a retreating figure heading towards the bushes at the extremity of the property.

'The fire is but cinders and kindling,' Rebecca said. 'I can dowse it with a wet sack while you hunt the vagabond in the bushes.'

Fauconberg nodded and veered towards the spot where he had seen the man disappear into the thicket that marked the boundary between the Red House Estate and Bourcher's farm. He dismounted and unsheathed his short-bladed hunting sword attached to his saddle. Peering into the shrubbery, he saw the outline of a tall, powerful-looking man attempting to conceal himself, but his bulk made the attempt futile.

'I mean you no harm,' Fauconberg said, 'but if you do not show yourself, I will run you through with my sword.'

The figure in the bushes remained as still as a statue.

Fauconberg sighed loudly. 'You give me no choice but to cut you out from your hiding place.'

The bushes swayed and branches snapped as the large, broad-shouldered man emerged with twigs and leaves stuck to his black jacket and knee-length breeches. He hastily hid his soot-covered hands behind his back.

Fauconberg stepped back in surprise as he recognised the arsonist. 'Mr Bourcher! This is most unseemly,' he said as he replaced the hunting sword into its scabbard. 'May I ask what folly is this?'

'I was chasing away a rogue who was setting fire to your barn.'

'I beg you not to take me for a fool, Mr Bourcher. We may have our political and religious quarrels, but must I now assume we can no longer live harmoniously alongside each other?'

Bourcher looked at Fauconberg with poorly concealed fury. His pock-marked face turned an angry red. 'Some scoundrel has killed two more of my cows and there was nary a mark on them.'

'I am sorry to hear of your misfortune, but it does not give you leave to burn your neighbour's barn.'

'And yesterday Doctor Fryars diagnosed me with the French pox, yet I have not slept with a wench these past three weeks. 'Tis witchcraft, I tell thee.'

Both men looked up as Rebecca rode towards them on her black mare. She was smiling in satisfaction after extinguishing a smouldering bale of hay, using water from a nearby trough. She gazed down at her neighbour with an expression of mild amusement.

'Why, Mr Bourcher! How blessed we are that you have come to pay us a visit. But I beseech you, next time please come by way of the front door rather than through the thicket.'

'Mr Bourcher was telling me he has lost two more cows,' said Fauconberg.

'That is most unfortunate, but I can assure you they are not in the thicket,' said Rebecca.

Bourcher stared open-mouthed at the sight of Rebecca's long legs clad in tight-fitting riding breeches. It felt like an eternity before he could respond.

'My Lady Rebecca. I ventured here to say how delighted I am that God has brought you safely back from Holland.' He removed his broad-brimmed conical hat and clutched it to his chest. 'Did not your unworthy steward pass on the news of my marriage proposal to you?' He glared at Fauconberg, and then dropped to one knee in front of her horse. 'Since the death of my good wife from scurvy three years since, I have thought of naught else but you. Such is my love for you, I will accept your two infants, even though they be not mine own and must bring disgrace upon the Bourcher name. What say you, my lady?' As he rose from his arthritic knee, his joints clicked like the cocking of two flintlock pistols.

'Do you still beat your son and daughters, Mr Bourcher?' Rebecca asked.

'I beat them once a week,' he confessed, 'but it gives me little pleasure. If it be an impediment to our proposed marriage, I can reduce the number of the beatings.'

'And would you beat me?'

'Perish the thought, Lady Slingsby. Of course not,' he said hurriedly. 'Umm … unless you were to speak to another man without my consent or contradict me on a matter of religion,' he mumbled.

Fauconberg could contain himself no longer. 'It has not gone unnoticed that you entered this property with malfeasance in your heart. As my lady's protector, I could not agree to such an ill-conceived match.'

Bourcher rounded on Fauconberg and they stood toe to toe. 'I see you desire the wench for yourself, yet you are the bastard son of a parlour maid, unworthy of her noble touches.' He struck out with the flat of his hand and slapped Fauconberg hard across the face. Bourcher was a powerful man with broad shoulders and Fauconberg reeled backwards from the blow.

Bourcher appealed once more to Rebecca. 'Do you not see the benefit of merging our two estates? It would make me … umm, you and I … the largest landholders betwixt York and Knaresborough.'

'I see you are a man of quick temper and obvious greed, Mr Bourcher,' said Rebecca. 'I thank you for being so explicit about your true nature. My maid, Helen, will give you my answer in three days hence. But for now, I wish you good day.

CHAPTER 4

Red House,
one year later,
October 1659

Fauconberg stared out of the library's French windows, and sighed. 'Major General Lambert and his Army of the North have come to arrest me at last,' he said. 'My word, there must be over two thousand of them. Would you mind handing me my sword?' He tore his eyes from the spectacle to look at Rebecca.

'Surely you would not fight two thousand men with only your sword?' Rebecca replied with alarm.

'No, but they will respect one of their own, even though I was once their sworn enemy.'

'Then I will fetch your old regimental jacket and boots from the wardrobe, for there can be no more exhilarating sight in the world than Colonel Fauconberg in the uniform of the Northern Horse.'

'So be it.'

As Lambert's troops mustered in their ranks on the manicured lawns of Red House, Rebecca helped Fauconberg into his scarlet jacket lined with gold braid. He pulled on his knee-length black boots that gleamed in the light through the window. Rebecca rubbed the brass buttons of his jacket with a silk handkerchief and brushed away pieces of lint. Fauconberg stood up and looped the belt of his sword over his shoulder. Rebecca fussed with Fauconberg's sandy hair before placing his hat on his head. Finally, she stood back as if to admire her handiwork.

'There never was such a picture of vigour and elegance than the man who stands before me now,' she said. 'If there be any justice in the world, then General Lambert will leave us in peace.' She stepped forward, stood on her tiptoes and kissed him on the cheek.

'He shall not break me, my lady. That is my promise to you.'

Fauconberg bowed to Rebecca and marched out of the library. He walked down the long red passage towards the grand entrance and opened the large wooden front door of Red House. As Fauconberg stood at the front of the house with his back straight, he stared in astonishment at the sight of an entire army setting up camp on the grounds of the property. Seven large bronze Drake cannons, each towed by a team of four horses, were churning up the manicured lawns, while hundreds of cavalry men were dismounting and leading their horses towards the paddock. At least twelve hundred musketeers and pikemen were unfurling tents in the deer park, while teams of officers were directing the army's massive baggage train into Mary's Field.

Fauconberg had spent most of the year restoring the hundred and twenty acres of grounds and gardens of Red House, and Lambert's army was turning it into a quagmire of mud in front of his eyes. In the distance, Fauconberg spotted the mayoral coach of the City of York making slow progress along the long Red House driveway.

Major General Lambert was sitting astride his horse on the front lawn, barking instructions to a clutch of junior cavalry officers. Since the retirement of Sir Thomas Fairfax, the death of Oliver Cromwell and the collapse of Richard Cromwell's second Protectorate, Britain had descended into a network of competing military dictatorships, with Lambert controlling the largest force from his base in Yorkshire. Lambert had just returned from a campaign in nearby Cheshire to crush a revolt led by the royalist George Booth. England was teetering on the cusp of anarchy, and Lambert was keen to head off any signs of trouble nearer to home.

The door opened behind Fauconberg, and Rebecca took her place next to him. She had changed into a flowing pale-blue gown she had brought with her from the exiled royal court. Fauconberg gasped at her beauty. The neckline of her bodice was low, revealing her slender shoulders. It was narrow at the waist, but the silk skirt billowed in folds to her feet. Fauconberg grasped her hand as much from his own desire, as to protect her from the lascivious glances of the two thousand soldiers who stared at her. The camp quietened and then stilled as the soldiers became aware of their presence. Lambert turned to face the pair then urged his horse into a trot to join them. He halted his horse on the gravel pathway, five yards from the door, and dismounted. An aide-de-camp took the reins of the major general's horse as Lambert bowed low to Rebecca and kissed her hand.

'My Lady Slingsby, you are indeed more beautiful in person than I had dared to believe. I am honoured to meet you.' Lambert was a forty-year-old Yorkshireman with a boyish face. But his looks were deceiving. He was a ruthless soldier and a veteran of more than a dozen battles. He turned to Fauconberg.

'Ah! Colonel Fauconberg of the Northern Horse. The man I chased for nigh on four years in the Civil War, without success. Your vicious band of rogues inflicted more damage on my regiment than any other. You will surrender that dangerous-looking sword to me forthwith.'

'I think not, Major General. This sword is very precious to me. I have taken my oaths; therefore, I am free to bear arms.' The two men eyed each other warily.

'As you wish, Colonel. It matters little to me.'

'May I ask why you camped your army here at Red House? We have not the provisions for such a large body of men.'

'That will become clear presently. In the meantime, certain rumours have been reported to me about your presence in Cheshire.'

'You should not listen to such ill-founded gossip.'

'The rumours suggest you were complicit in George Booth's rebellion.'

'I'm flattered you needed the protection of two thousand soldiers to put these scandalous accusations to my face, but I can assure you the rumours are false.'

'False? Can you prove these rumours are so?'

'It is not up to me to prove or disprove such wild rumours, since that is all they are. But since you ask, had I taken part in Booth's rebellion, your army would have been defeated, you would be lying face down in a muddy ditch at Winnington Bridge, and Prince Charles would now be king. But since none of these things happened, the rumours must be false.'

Lambert laughed. 'You were an impetuous, ill-disciplined young cavalryman in the Civil War. You only rose to fame because you confounded our armies with your recklessness and perplexing battle tactics. It was pure luck you were not routed every time you took to the field.'

'I was a mere boy at the start of the Civil War, yet the Northern Horse outwitted you at every turn. If I took to the field today, I would be more than just a thorn in your side.'

Lambert stepped closer to Fauconberg and lowered his voice so Rebecca could not hear. 'Do not try my patience, young man. You are a mere ex-colonel. I am a major general, and one who does not tolerate the stench of treachery. My soldiers might be awed by your wartime exploits, but I have learned each man has his weakness. Yours is your fondness for the woman at your side, and it is a weakness I intend to exploit.'

'Lady Rebecca has many powerful friends, and you would be wise to avoid incurring their wrath,' Fauconberg countered.

'If you are referring to Sir Thomas Fairfax, he is now an old and feeble man, and rumour has it he is nearing death. He can no longer protect your woman from judgement, nor keep you from the scaffold, where you belong.'

They were interrupted by the arrival of the gilded mayoral coach from York led by two powerful-looking Yorkshire coach horses. The coachman sprang down from driver's seat, hobbled the horses, and then pulled down the steps. A large, booted foot belonging to the recently appointed Mayor Watson emerged from the open door. The mayor gathered his black-and-gold robes around his rotund frame and stepped into the cold air. He was followed by Benedict Bourcher, the new Alderman of York; William Dowsing, the iconoclast; and John Stearne, the self-styled witch pricker. Rebecca gasped. Relations with Bourcher had become hostile since she had turned down his marriage proposal and her neighbour had devoted his energy to spreading malicious gossip about her.

'I have reason to believe that General Monck, who is presently in Scotland with his army, is scheming to commit an act of treachery against the republic,' Lambert continued in a lofty manner. 'Hence I design to intercept him here, or thus dissuade him from marching south to London.' He glared at Fauconberg. 'There are members of the royalist Sealed Knot society here in my own county of Yorkshire who may be tempted to assist Major General Monck.'

'I know of the Sealed Knot, but they are pretenders. I would not deign to join such a rabble,' Fauconberg said.

'Whilst I am here, I intend to make this house my headquarters and I do not welcome the presence of potential traitors in my midst. You must be gone by nightfall, but Lady Slingsby may remain here under my protection.' He bowed to her once more.

'You may wish me gone, Major General, but which of your men will risk losing their head trying to evict an experienced cavalry officer from his estate?' Fauconberg patted the hilt of his sword.

Lambert considered his options, then wafted his hand in a gesture of dismissal. 'Then keep out of my way, Fauconberg. I'm a busy man and do not need any further distraction from you.'

'Pray tell me, General,' Rebecca asked Lambert. 'What are those four scurrilous officials doing on my grounds? They have been forbidden to ever set foot here again.'

'All in good time, my lady. But first let us take Eucharist in your splendid chapel, after which we can discuss the details of my requisitioning Red House.'

* * *

The army chaplain closed his bible and gestured to Lambert that the long, turgid Presbyterian service was at an end. Lambert rose from his position at the back of the chapel and ambled towards the altar. The little chapel was full, and soldiers were spilling into the aisles, peering down from the gallery and crowding around the open doorway. The smell of unwashed bodies competed with the aroma of oak panelling, furniture polish and burning candles. The interior gloom gave the proceedings a sombre atmosphere.

Rebecca gripped Fauconberg's hand as they sat in one of the choir pews, away from the gaze of the mass of soldiers and the four York dignitaries. Fauconberg glanced sideways at Rebecca and noticed she had paled and had a frightened expression. Her hand was shaking, and she was breathing in sharp bursts. He squeezed her hand to convey his reassurance and tightened the grip on the hilt of his sword, the Enlightener, with his other hand.

Lambert bowed towards the altar, then turned to face the congregation. He pulled out a document from his coat pocket. 'The gentlemen of York have petitioned that they wish to bring forth proceedings against Lady Slingsby of Red House in the Parish of Moor Monkton.' The congregation murmured at the news, forcing Lambert to raise his hand to quieten them.

'The charges are as follows. Firstly, that she has committed the sin of procreation with a person or persons unknown out of marriage, resulting in the birth of two godless and fatherless children. Secondly, that Lady Slingsby deprived her neighbour Alderman Benedict Bourcher of ownership of Red House by colluding with the Committee for Compounding with Delinquents and bribing them with the sum of eleven thousand two hundred pounds. Lastly, that she has committed the sin of witchcraft against Alderman Bourcher, causing the death of seven cattle, the demonic possession of his two daughters, and invoking unnatural and ungodly feelings of lust in Mr Bourcher towards the accused.'

At the mention of witchcraft, the chapel erupted into scenes of chaos.

'What say you to the charges, Lady Slingsby?' said Lambert, looking her in the eyes.

Fauconberg put a restraining hand on Rebecca's shoulder, then rose from his pew. 'The charges are the fabrication of Alderman Bourcher, an embittered man who has failed as a father, a farmer and a suitor. Lady Slingsby is not some defenceless old hag that Stearne has the habit of tormenting, but a respected person of letters and a woman of noble birth. I have trained for three years as a lawyer at Cambridge and will defend her to my last breath.'

'Your point is well made,' replied Lambert. 'As major general of all the parliamentary forces in England and Scotland and by the powers vested in me, I hereby dismiss the two civil charges levelled against Lady Slingsby. Unfortunately, the charge of witchcraft is a church matter and beyond my jurisdiction. I therefore place Lady Slingsby into the care of Mr John Stearne, who has one week to extract a confession. Mr Fauconberg, you will remain under house arrest until Mr Stearne is done with her.'

CHAPTER 5

York Court House,
one week later

The smell of unwashed bodies crowding the York courthouse choked the air as the throng of morbid onlookers awaited the trial of Lady Rebecca Slingsby. John Stearne the witch pricker and chief prosecutor posed at his desk facing the judge's bench. He had spent the previous half-hour riling spectators into a state of righteous indignation and promising them a thrilling day of entertainment. Few had met Lady Rebecca, but Stearne assured them she was responsible for whatever misfortune had beset them in recent months. Next to Stearne was his chief witness, Alderman Bourcher, who was wearing the pained expression of a man who had succumbed to the malfeasance of Rebecca's black magic.

The judge, Justice John Holt, entered the court room. He was a young man of little experience, who had recently been promoted following the purge of royalists from the profession. Despite this, he was a man of conviction who carried few of the moral prejudices of his predecessors. Wearing long robes that reached to his ankles and a severe black coif, he rapped his gavel on the sound block and roared for the court to be silent.

Fauconberg sat at the defence attorney's desk in a state of high anxiety as he waited for Rebecca to be brought into the room. He had been denied access to her since she had been taken into Stearne's custody.

'Bring in the defendant,' Justice Holt demanded of the two soldiers at the back of the court. Moments later, onlookers began jeering and hissing as the doors opened and two men dragged the confused and bedraggled young noblewoman into the court room. Bruised, dazed and shackled, she was shoved into the chair in the defendant's dock.

Fauconberg stared in horror at the pitiful spectacle. At first, he was unable to accept the woman in the dock was Rebecca Slingsby. Her once lustrous hair had been shaved from her injured head and her shoulders were misshapen as if her arms had been dislocated from their shoulders. Her hands were mangled and her green eyes were sunken as if she had been deprived of sleep since her arrest. Outraged, Fauconberg regathered his wits and approached Justice Holt.

'My Lord,' he said with an intensity that matched his anger. He pointed straight at John Stearne. 'That man has tortured my client in the most egregious manner. Lady Slingsby is not in a fit state to stand trial and I insist she receives medical care, else she is at risk of imminent death. She is a high-born lady and has two infant children, for pity's sake. If she dies during trial, then John Stearne, Alderman Bourcher, William Dowsing, and all those who perpetrated the cruel and wicked treatment of this noble lady, should be tried for murder.'

Justice Holt glanced at Rebecca, who was slumped in her seat. 'A high-born lady did you say? I can scare believe your claims. She looks like an old crone to me.'

Fauconberg dug into his jacket pocket and retrieved Sir Henry's locket containing the miniature portrait of Rebecca. He slapped it onto Justice Holt's desk.

'No old crone, Your Honour, but the fairest and most noble woman in Yorkshire. She is cousin to thirteen of the most influential families in Yorkshire, and each one will be outraged at what this ... vile creature ...' he pointed once more at Stearne, '... has done to her. All this to appease the vanity of a wicked bully ...' he pointed at Alderman Bourcher, '...who could not accept her rejection of his marriage proposal.'

Justice Holt stared for some time at the portrait of Rebecca. As he looked towards the battered and bruised woman who was slumped semi-conscious in the dock, his expression turned to outrage.

'Guards! Remove the lady's shackles and fetch a doctor at once! And for the love of God be quick about it.' The judge pointed his finger at John Stearne.

'You, man. Approach the bench immediately.'

'Yes, at once, Your Honour.' He scuttled across the court floor to join Fauconberg at the bench.

'Have you illegally tortured this noble woman?'

'No, Your Honour.'

A weak voice rose from the dock. 'He has tortured me most grievously, Your Honour. He hung me from a hook by my arms and put weights on my feet. He has crushed my hands with the screw and pricked me with sharp needles each night to keep me awake. I am no more a witch than any other godly person in this court.'

'Rebecca! Forgive me for not preventing what this evil man has done to you,' Fauconberg cried out in despair as he gazed at the pitiable sight in the dock. 'I swear he will suffer for his cruelty.'

'Do not despair, my dear Samuel, for he has not broken me. I stayed strong for you and the honour of the Slingsby family. I have endured his cruelty so no other wretched and unfortunate woman would follow me to the gallows.'

'Stearne tortured you so that you would implicate other innocent women?' asked the judge.

'Yes, your honour. He said he would let me sleep if I delivered five other good women of York into his clutches.'

The court went silent as the physician and his handmaiden rushed into the courtroom. They waited as the soldiers removed Rebecca's shackles, and then wrapped her in a blanket. The physician and the handmaiden supported her as they led her to the court's sick bay.

'This is not seemly,' protested Stearne. 'Justice must be done. She hath the devil's mark on her left thigh!' He turned to the appalled spectators, who minutes earlier had been baying for a hanging. 'God's will must not be denied!' he screeched.

'Shame on you, witch pricker, for tormenting the womenfolk of York,' came a response from the back of the court.

'Go back to East Anglia where you belong!' cried another.

'You're not welcome here, you charlatan,' said an old lady, who minutes earlier had been calling for Rebecca's blood.

Justice Holt banged his gavel into the sound box once more. 'I will have order in the court room.' He turned to face Stearne. 'I will not have you oppress any more unfortunate wretches in England again. This case is dismissed, and you are to return to Ipswich at once.'

'Your honour, you deprive me of an honest living. Hanging witches is my job.'

'Enough! You will spend two days in the stocks in front of the Guild Hall, where the good women of York can throw foul matter at you. Guards! Take this despicable creature away!'

Justice Holt turned to face Alderman Bourcher. 'You! Yes

you, man! Approach the bench.'

Bourcher rose from his seat at the prosecutor's desk.

'Is it true you brought this vile and vexatious case against the good Lady Slingsby?'

'Your Honour, she has done me wrong. She has bewitched my cows and sent demons to torment my daughters. She has brought the pox on me, even though I slept not with any impure wench these past few weeks.'

'He beats his son and daughters each Sabbath, Your Honour. He has invoked God's wrath on himself. He is a brute who knows not how to run his farm,' said Fauconberg.

'You would have a noblewoman tortured and hanged because you lost a few cows?' asked the judge incredulously.

'It is only just and proper, Your Honour.'

'Your case is dismissed. Now, get out of my sight.'

'I will take my cause to Major General Lambert. He is the highest authority in the land and his army camps in my fields. He will mete out proper justice to these royalist traitors.'

But Justice John Holt had already moved on. 'Guards! Place this brute in the stocks next to the witch pricker till he sees reason. And clear the rabble from the court room. Now, Clerk Simms, who's next on the day's agenda?'

CHAPTER 6

Red House,
December 1659

For the first time since leaving the physician's clinic, Rebecca seemed at peace. Her expression was no longer haunted, nor did she cry out in her sleep. Outside the three-storey red-brick mansion, the wind howled as a winter storm rattled the roof tiles while broken twigs and leaves clattered against the windows.

'The laudanum will help her slumber,' said Dr Wickham. 'It is a mixture of my special herbs, sherry wine and opium. The opium comes from the Mogul Empire in India and has remarkable properties. I will leave you with a bottle but use it sparingly, for the next shipment from India will not dock in London for six months.'

'Thank you, Doctor. Will she recover from her torment?'

Dr Wickham sighed heavily. 'She will bear no more children. The witch pricker used some barbaric instruments to examine her female parts. We live in cruel times, Mr Fauconberg. I wish no ill will on anyone, but I trust John Stearne will receive his just reward in the fires of hell in due course.'

Fauconberg clenched his fists. 'His time will come sooner than he expects when I make a special trip to Ipswich.'

'It was fortunate I did not hear that last remark, Mr Fauconberg, but I will shed no tears at his parting.'

'Did you fix her shoulder?'

'I was able to reset her dislocated shoulder, though she did cry out most pitifully. And her hands will recover in time, but she may suffer stiffness in her fingers for the rest of her life.'

'My poor, dear Rebecca,' said Fauconberg, shaking his head.

'As you can see, I took the liberty of removing the skin tag from her left thigh just before you entered the room. We do not want any more witch prickers taking an interest in her for what is a most natural and benign blemish to her skin.'

'Was it not dangerous to cut it off?'

'I used the sharpest knife in my collection. I have a theory that cleanliness is next to godliness, so I soaked the knife in brandy before making the incision. My medical colleagues ridicule me for such practices, but I have yet to lose a patient to infection. Now we must balance her humours. We are most fortunate the moon is precisely positioned in the night sky for a bloodletting.'

Fauconberg watched on with interest as Dr Wickham pulled a glass jar from his bag. Swimming in the water were half-a-dozen leeches. He unscrewed the lid and pulled out a two inch-long leech with a pair of tweezers. He placed the leech in a wine glass and placed the glass over the small wound on Rebecca's left thigh. Rebecca stirred but did not wake. Within seconds, the leech had placed its sucker over the wound and was gorging on her blood.

'The leech will reduce the swelling and promote the healing process,' Dr Wickham explained. 'They are very clean animals so there is no risk of putrefaction. They are indeed one of nature's wonders.'

'I cannot thank you enough, Dr Wickham.' Fauconberg combed his fingers through Rebecca's shorn hair, which had grown a few inches since her ordeal.

'Lady Slingsby's physical injuries will heal in good time, but alas, her mind has been damaged by her ordeal. She will need all her faith in God to pull through.'

'She has faith in abundance.'

'Even so, if she descends into a dark pit of melancholy, the best cure is a good bloodletting. I will leave you with the remaining leeches.'

'Thank you, Doctor. You have been most kind,' said Fauconberg, showing Dr Wickham out.

'What of her two infants? Are they both well?' the doctor asked.

'Helen, our chambermaid, takes good care of them. They are full of cold, this being mid-winter, else they are as robust as oxen.'

Wickham delved into his leather bag. 'I have just the potion for their ague. It is a mixture of celery and parsley seeds ground into a paste with honey and a little wine. Give them two teaspoons each morning as they rise and again as they are put to bed. And move them not from a warm room to a cold bed.'

'I will discuss the measures with Helen, and with Rebecca when she awakes. Thank you, again.'

'You are welcome, young man. My servant will send you my invoice on the morrow.'

* * *

As the grey winter days gave way to a dreary puritan Christmas made bleak by the outlawing of traditional festivities, Rebecca's health steadily improved. As was customary at Red House, she delivered a basket of fresh meat, vegetables and eggs from the estate's farm to each of her employee's families. Wearied by her exertions she slumped onto the cream coloured chaise longue in the withdrawing room. Before she could close her eyes and succumb to exhaustion, Fauconberg knocked on the door and entered the room. He had an anxious look on his face as he bowed to her.

'Please excuse my intrusion my lady, but I bring worrisome tidings. General Lambert is returning from his campaign to the Scottish borders and has a warrant for my arrest. It is said he means to hang me and place you in Bourcher's custody. We must gather the infants and head for the coast.'

Rebecca sighed in the knowledge that her suffering was not yet over. 'I cannot move from here as Luke has the ague. He would not survive such an upheaval.'

'Then I will show you the priest hole in the attic where your father hid for an entire year. You can rest there while Luke recovers. I have stocked it with provisions for a fortnight. You and the boys will be safe there, but I pray Lambert does not make Red House his headquarters again.'

'You will not stay with me?' Rebecca grasped his hand as if terrified of being left alone.

'I must organise a sturdy boat and a loyal crew to take us to safety in Holland. I will return for you once it is arranged.'

'We cannot abandon Red House so easily,' Rebecca implored.

'I promised your father I would protect you from harm, but anarchy has descended on this land and the situation is dire. We can but hope the house will be returned to your family if Prince Charles returns from The Hague to claim the throne. Come, bring the candle.'

Fauconberg led Rebecca up the main spiralling staircase to the first floor of the house. They walked past what had been Sir Henry's study and along a narrow corridor. On the left was a staircase leading to the attic complex, which stretched the length of Red House. Fauconberg placed his arm around Rebecca's waist and assisted her fragile body up the steep steps. At the top were two doors. The left door opened into a neat room, which served as a guest bedroom. The right-hand door revealed a storage room containing a jumble of old furniture, chests of discarded clothes and long-abandoned possessions.

'Be not afraid, my lady. The entrance to your hiding place is in the guest bedroom.'

Fauconberg led Rebecca into the guest room on the left. 'Helen will be the channel of communication between us. She is a resourceful woman and will get any message through to me. She will leave fresh food and a pitcher of water beside the basin each morning at five of the clock, and empty it again at six. You will be safe as long as you do not leave the hidden room.'

'How will my letters reach you if you are caught and imprisoned?'

Fauconberg took her by her free hand and led her to the cushioned couch under the attic window in the guest's bedroom. As they sat down, he stroked her cheek with his hand. 'I cannot lie. Lambert is a powerful and resourceful man. His spies are everywhere, and he will pay well for news of my whereabouts. But the governor of York prison is a member of the Sealed Knot and will assist with my escape should I be taken. I shall not hang, despite General Lambert's best efforts.'

'Pray, do not risk your life for me, Samuel. It is too much to ask.'

Fauconberg gripped her hand gently, taking care not to hurt her splintered fingers 'When I return for you, it will be in the middle of the night. You must be ready to leave for the coast with Will and Luke, and such possessions you need for a long and perilous voyage to Holland.'

Rebecca's head dropped and a tear rolled from one eye. 'I fear that when I return to Holland I will be scorned by polite society. John Stearne and his three old crones tore me asunder most grievously with their wicked instruments. I will not bear a child again and my hands will forever be clawed like those of a beast of the earth.'

'The father of your children will accept you for who you are unless he has a heart of stone. Stearne could not destroy your beauty nor your spirit, and your hands will heal in time.'

Rebecca shook her head. 'You do not understand. The man

who sired my children is not like you. He cannot acknowledge as his consort any woman with such impairments as I have sustained, nor one who has stood trial for witchcraft.'

'If you introduce me to this man, I will reason with him.'

'I cannot, for there are matters of state that transcend my own happiness. I have taken a vow of silence as profound as any that my father took to his grave.'

Fauconberg rose and helped Rebecca to her feet. Then he strode to the bookcase adjacent to the large four-poster bed and slid his hand behind it to reveal a hidden latch. He swung the bookcase on its hinges, being careful not to disturb any of the books. Behind the bookcase was a small doorway leading to a long, narrow passage. Fauconberg beckoned Rebecca, who gathered her candle and joined him at the entrance to the passageway.

'I built this passage with Sir Henry ten years ago, when he was hiding from the Roundheads. Even Helen did not know of its existence till yesterday. Follow me and close the bookshelf behind you.'

Fauconberg crawled through the doorway, then turned and took Rebecca's candle, placing it on the floor while he helped her through. He stood once he was in the passageway. It was narrow and he had to bow his head to avoid hitting it on the sloping roofline. The passage had been lined with thin layers of wood panelling and had been swept clean. A layer of matting on the floor deadened the sound of his footsteps. He picked up a spare candle from a nook that had been built close to the passage entrance and lit its wick using the flame from Rebecca's candle.

'This passageway runs the length of the roofline of Red House,' said Fauconberg. 'Come, follow me.' He gently took her hand. They walked for fifty feet until they came to a small, bare room containing a single bed and a wooden table.

'My father hid in this room for an entire year?' said Rebecca in disbelief. 'Even the most zealous hermit would lose his mind in such wretched solitude.'

'Indeed, he would have done had this been his chamber, but it was no more than a ruse to confound the Roundheads had they discovered the passageway.' Fauconberg walked towards a brick column at the far end of the room that looked like it was part of a chimney. He sat on his haunches and tapped a layer of bricks near the base of the chimney. The tapping sounded hollow. 'The lower level has been replaced by a wooden panel on which has been plastered a layer of thin bricks, so it looks like part of the chimney. But see, if you push the brick that is eighth from the floor and the fifth from the edge like so, it releases a latch on the other side.'

The brick-veneer panel moved inwards towards the false chimney and Fauconberg ducked low to enter the small cavity. He turned to his left and then to his right, where another narrow entrance led to a larger, more opulent bedroom.

'Where have you gone?' Rebecca cried out in alarm as she entered the false chimney.

Fauconberg laughed and beckoned her with his candle to join him in the hidden bedroom. 'So now you see how Sir Henry was able to hide from Cromwell's troops for a year, despite them searching high and low.'

'The bedroom looks so fresh and new,' Rebecca said in wonder.

'I have cleaned it up for you and there is a pair of shutters that can be opened for fresh air. But you must close it at night lest the light from your candles be seen from outside. Your bed is comfortable and there are cots for Will and Joe. I have stocked the shelves with books, and if you wish to paint, I will bring your paints, brushes, and a selection of canvases. The larder is stocked with biscuits and dried fruit. Helen will deliver milk, bread, ham and fresh vegetables from the garden to the guest bedroom whenever she can.'

'This is indeed a wondrous hidden room. I shall want for naught.'

'It will not be for long. A week at the most.'

'Is there a way out of this chamber other than the false chimney?'

'Indeed there is, but it is treacherous.' Fauconberg led her to the shutters at the far side of the room and opened them inwards. The shutters were clad with the same brick-veneer as the panel on the chimney, so they blended perfectly with the outside wall. Daylight flooded into the hidden room. A stiff breeze blew into their faces and the room was filled with the wintry smells of the Yorkshire countryside.

'If you look amongst the ivy,' he said, 'you can see I have

affixed a series of iron rungs to the wall adjacent to Sir Henry's study below, and then onwards to the rose bed. The window in Sir Henry's study is always unlocked and can be opened from outside. But it is a perilous step to the study and if you were to fall in the attempt, it would result in certain death.'

As Fauconberg was on the point of closing the shutters he noticed movement beyond Mary's Field at the extremity of the estate. Twenty horsemen were galloping towards Red House, raising a cloud of dust behind them.

Fauconberg sighed. 'Lambert's troops have stolen a march on us. I fear my lodgings tonight will not be on the east coast of England but in York gaol.'

CHAPTER 7

York Gaol,
Walmgate Bar, York,
31st December 1659

Fauconberg peered through the exterior bars of his cell at York Gaol and watched as the workmen hammered the final nails into the crossbeam of the gallows. It had taken three days to complete the structure, during which the sawing and hammering had taken a toll on his nerves. The smell of sawn wood mixed with the stench of filth from the streets below wafted to his cell. Despite the early hour and the freezing chill, a small crowd had gathered in the snow-filled streets in anticipation of Fauconberg's execution. It was not every day a royalist sympathiser was executed, and front-row seats were selling at a premium.

There had been no letter from Rebecca and no visit from the Sealed Knot society during his week-long incarceration. He was still wearing the clothes in which he was arrested, although he had been given water and soap to clean himself. The jailers arrived daily to provide him with stale bread, two ounces of cheese, an apple and a half-pint of ale. Every second day they would change his ablutions bucket.

Fauconberg heard the lock of his cell door open, and two sturdy soldiers entered.

'Are you ready for the scaffold, mate?' asked the first soldier.

'What, today?' Fauconberg asked in alarm. 'I have not yet appeared before a judge.'

'General Lambert wants you dead before eleven of the clock, pal,' replied the second soldier. 'General Monck is marching south from Scotland with a large army and Lambert don't want you anywhere near it.'

'I don't have my fresh shirt or breeches,' Fauconberg said, looking for excuses to delay his trip to the scaffold, 'and I demand to see a priest.'

'Your clobber arrived this morning, mate,' replied the first soldier, 'and the priest is waiting for you in the antechamber.' He looked at Fauconberg. 'Look, if you don't give us no trouble, I can slip you half a bottle of brandy while you change into your hanging garb. It'll numb the pain and ease your passage to the great beyond. Now, get a move on. We're changing shift in twenty minutes.'

With a rising sense of panic, Fauconberg looked for a way out, but both soldiers were hardy veterans, and he knew the prison would be crawling with guards. His mind wrestled with the competing desires to escape his inevitable fate, or die with dignity in the manner of Sir Henry. Yet Slingsby had had months to prepare himself for death, whereas Fauconberg had expected to be whisked from the gaol by the secretive royalist Sealed Knot society. But such assistance had not been forthcoming and now Fauconberg found himself being escorted down the prison steps towards the gallows antechamber, to prepare himself for his hanging. Fear and doubt hit him like the stormy waves of a North Sea tempest.

On the first floor of the gaol, the two soldiers led Fauconberg along a gloomy corridor towards the antechamber, where they stopped before a heavy wooden door.

'Good luck, mate,' said the first soldier as he slipped a half-consumed bottle of brandy into Fauconberg's jacket pocket. He said the words in the manner of a man wishing his friend well on a first date. 'Swig it down fast. It won't be so bad if you're half-pickled before the drop.'

'Thank you.'

The second soldier rapped on the oak door with the hilt of his pistol. 'Prisoner Fauconberg here for his last dance,' he yelled. Then he turned to Fauconberg. 'I fought you at Preston. You and your Northern Horse regiment scared the living bejesus out me. You almost carried the day with your charge at General Lambert's command centre. It caught him by surprise and he ain't forgiven you since.' He allowed himself a small chuckle. 'It don't seem right to be hanging a war hero. Even one from the other side.'

At that moment, the door opened and a shawled priest appeared in the doorway.

'He's all yours, brother,' the first soldier told the priest. He peered into the room to check the replacement guards were present. Two armed men at the far end of the room saluted in acknowledgement of the handover.

The antechamber was a well-illuminated room that connected

to the gallows via a set of ornate French windows and a balcony. A simple altar, a wooden cross and kneeler had been constructed in a screened-off section of the room, to allow the condemned to make peace with God and receive a blessing from the priest. Next to the kneeler was Fauconberg's trunk containing his execution garments, which had been delivered from Red House.

The two guards kept to themselves in the far corner, as if embarrassed to interrupt the condemned's final moments of quiet contemplation before his death. Beside the two guards, a drunkard dressed in cavalier-style clothing was manacled to his chair. Fauconberg assumed he would have company on the gallows, and he found the thought strangely reassuring.

The hooded priest gestured to the kneeler, as if encouraging him to utter one last prayer prior to his execution. Fauconberg ignored the priest and eyeballed the two guards. They looked familiar and did not have a military bearing. He considered the prospects of overpowering the two guards, but the priest took a firm grasp of his sleeve and once more pointed at the kneeler. Fauconberg sighed as he faced the reality of his situation. Both guards carried loaded muskets. He was never going to get out alive and he did not wish to give the morbid onlookers the satisfaction of an undignified death. Reconciling himself to his fate, Fauconberg knelt in front of the priest and clasped his hands together in prayer. As he began to recite the Lord's Prayer, the priest pulled out a note from the sleeve of his robes, on which was written the twenty-third psalm. Fauconberg read aloud from the note:

'The Lord is my shepherd; I shall not want. He maketh me to lie down—'

The priest snatched the note back from Fauconberg before turning it around and placing it once more in his hands. To Fauconberg's surprise, on the reverse of the psalm was a letter from Rebecca. His heart leapt and he drank in the contents of the missive:

My dearest Samuel, loyal Steward of Red House and noble Colonel of the Northern Horse.

I send sombre tidings that necessitate your speedy return to Red House.

Fauconberg sighed at the impracticality of the request before continuing to read the letter:

Our neighbour Benedict Bourcher, being emboldened by the nearby presence of twelve thousand of General Lambert's soldiers, has returned to Red House to falsely claim it as his own. To curry favour with General Lambert, he has sent all two hundred of our thoroughbred horses to the general as a gift, and in return Lambert has signed a document recognising Bourcher as the rightful owner of Red House.

It is said that within days there will be a mighty battle between the two great generals, Lambert and Monck, at Marston Moor. People say that if Monck prevails, then it will herald the return of Prince Charles to the throne and the restoration of the monarchy. But I trust not General Monck, for he is as ambitious as all the other generals who compete for the title of Lord Protector.

My dearest Samuel, I write of still worse tidings. For not perceiving of any recovery in the health of my infant son Luke, and desirous of a cure for his ague, it did beget me to leave the hidden bedroom to seek out the help of our physician, Dr Wickham. But I was seized by Benedict Bourcher in my own scullery before I was able to make good my escape from Red House. Now Bourcher is threatening to burn me as a witch if I do not consent to marry him by the end of New Year's Day and countersign the title deeds of Red House as his dowry.

So now my two infant sons, one being most grievously ill, are trapped in the secret bedroom, and Bourcher has me at his mercy. He has threatened to murder the children if he finds them. I implore you to return to me as you did promise, lest Bourcher carry out his threats. I have instructed Helen to care for the infants as best she can and deliver this note to your hand and to no-one else. I am distraught that the prison governor has not freed you from York Gaol, but if he has been indisposed, I have sent my gardener, Mr Jones; Robert the stable lad; and our blacksmith, Mr Connolly, to assist your escape.

I pray God delivers you home to me before it is too late, my beloved Samuel.

Your ever-devoted Lady Rebecca Slingsby

Fauconberg looked up at the priest and watched in astonishment as she removed her hooded cowl, revealing herself to be Rebecca's pretty maid, Helen. She put her finger to her lips, then whispered frantically, 'Off your knees, my lord. Your clothes are in the trunk. Mr Jones is keeping watch and Joe the stable lad has your weapons.' She pointed to the two fake guards at the far side of the antechamber. 'The prison governor is of the Sealed Knot and has given us ten minutes to flee the gaol before he raises the alarm. Make haste, Master Samuel.'

Fauconberg sprang up from the kneeler and rushed to the trunk. Feelings of profound relief almost overwhelmed him, although he resisted the urge to embrace Helen. Within one minute he had donned his colonel's uniform and pulled on his heavy cavalry boots.

'I laundered your uniform for you only yesterday,' Helen said as Joe the stable lad handed him his sword, dagger and pistols. Fauconberg pointed towards the semi-comatose man who was shackled to the chair. 'Who's the drunkard?' he asked in a whisper.

'Timothy Lester,' answered Helen. 'The crowd expect a hanging and he is of a similar build and complexion to you.'

'You're not going to hang him, are you?' asked Fauconberg, appalled at the prospect of an innocent man taking the drop in his place.

'Of course not. That's the hangman's job. Timothy Lester is a notorious rapist, thief and a drunk. He has long flirted with the hangman's noose; we're just bringing forward his destiny.'

Jones the gardener picked up the discarded monk's cowl and gave it to Fauconberg. 'You must slip this cowl over your colonel's uniform and head downstairs towards the rear exit. There you will meet Jim Connolly the blacksmith, who has charge of your horse. Her ladyship implores you to make all haste for Red House, but take care to avoid General Lambert's army, which prepares for battle on the fields of Marston Moor.'

'But what about you? How will you escape?' Fauconberg asked.

'Once we have escorted the unfortunate Mr Lester to the scaffold, we will meld with the crowd and make our own way out of York. But fret not. Most of the soldiers of York are away with Lambert, or else have deserted him to join General Monck. There is much confusion in our city, as the two great armies of England are set to clash not ten miles hence. But now you must go, Master Fauconberg. The crowd outside are restless for a hanging and if they discover Mr Lester is not who they think he is, they will raise the alarm. You must be well clear of the gaol by then.'

They were interrupted by the hangman, who was banging on the French doors from the outside. 'Bring forth the prisoner,' he said in his broad Yorkshire accent, pointing at Lester through the windows. 'Ah'm a busy man tha' knows; I ain't got all day.'

CHAPTER 8

In the street outside York Gaol, Fauconberg discarded his priest's cowl and gave it to his blacksmith. In return, Jim Connolly handed him his broad cavalier hat with its right-hand brim pinned to the crown.

'Your stallion, Monty, has been fed, watered and rested,' Connolly said, handing him the reins. The chestnut stallion's warm breath clouded in the freezing air and the blacksmith patted its flanks. 'He will carry you to Red House in two hours at an easy pace. But mind you avoid Lambert's scouts. They are combing the lanes searching for Monck's vanguard, although the general is not expected to arrive till after New Year's Day.'

As Connolly helped Fauconberg mount his charger, a cacophony of angry voices erupted at the front of the building where the gallows were located. It was followed by the clanging of bells and a call to arms.

'It seems the hangman has discovered the imposter on his scaffold,' Fauconberg remarked. 'Timothy Lester will live to rape and pillage another day.'

'Then you should tarry not,' replied Connolly. 'The mob will go a-hunting and the sheriff will send news of your escape to General Lambert. They will set traps for you betwixt here and Red House. You could outwit them by detouring around Marston Moor from the south, and then approaching Red House from the west. It will add two or three hours to your journey, yet it will keep you safe from Lambert's men.'

'Thank you, Mr Connolly. I am much obliged,' Fauconberg said. He touched the brim of his hat, then spurred Monty southwards. He had not galloped twenty yards along the snow-filled street when a mob of thirty men rounded a corner to block his way.

'There he is!' yelled a rotund man in a green coat. 'Drag him back to the gallows.'

Fauconberg drew his sword, spurred Monty into a full gallop and charged at the centre of the mob. He roared the Northern Horse Regimental battle cry, causing the throng to scatter in all directions. The sound of his charger's hooves clattered on the slippery, cobbled street and echoed from the closely packed buildings.

'Lower the gates!' a man in military uniform shouted as Fauconberg headed towards the narrow, barbican-shaped structure known as Walmgate Bar, which guarded the southeastern extremity of York's formidable walls. The rusty portcullis was in poor repair and had not been lowered since the siege of 1644. As the guard struggled with the crankshaft, Fauconberg ducked under the descending spiked portcullis and out into Barbican Road, which ran parallel with the city walls.

Fauconberg galloped alongside the southern walls of the city for half a mile, hoping he would reach the Fishergate Bar and the road south before the garrison's soldiers streamed from the castle. A company of guards on the city walls raised their heads above the parapet twenty yards to his right and fired their muskets in his direction, but their musket balls flew high and wide. The massive bulk of the castle loomed over the ancient Roman walls like a stone colossus, and he could see dozens of men scrambling for their weapons and bellowing for their horses.

To his relief, he reached the junction of Barbican Road and Fishergate before the mounted men could block his path and he headed south, away from the hubbub of the city. But still he was not safe. Shopkeepers and curious onlookers ran out of their houses into the slushy, sewer-lined, cobbled street to investigate the source of the commotion. A few tried to block his path while others threw shovels, rakes and buckets at him to knock him off his horse, but their aim was erratic. Then he was clear of the urban streets and into the countryside beyond.

Fauconberg was two miles from the city when he heard the thundering of hooves behind him. He looked over his shoulder and saw fifty mounted horsemen stream over the Fosse River bridge and gallop down Tower Street like excited hunters on the trail of a fox. With his route to Red House blocked by Lambert's army and an entire troop of horsemen on his trail, Fauconberg realised he only had one chance of survival.

* * *

The imposing edifice of Nun Appleton Hall, home of the retired Sir Thomas Fairfax, emerged from the fog-filled countryside.

Fauconberg spurred on his tired horse, but it was blown after the long gallop from York. The horsemen on his trail had chased him in relays, preserving the strength of their own horses. Fauconberg entered Nun Appleton Hall's deer park, with its towering oaks and manicured grass. The house was topped by a magnificent cupola and its two wings jutted from the main building. He was only half a mile from the sanctuary of Lord Fairfax's home, yet the soldiers of York had overhauled him and capture was inevitable.

'Colonel Fauconberg! You led us a merry chase. Captain Haywood of the Yorkshire Horse at your service.' The soldier from the chasing troop removed his hat and bowed in his saddle.

'Nathan Haywood!' said Fauconberg in astonishment. 'My goodness, it must have been ten years since we last rode together. I thought you had been killed at Preston.'

'I was indeed as good as dead,' replied Haywood. 'I lost half my scalp and my wits with it, yet by the grace of God and the skills of the surgeons I lived to tell the tale. After two years of convalescence I recovered in full, but it was five long years before I could ride again.'

Both men dismounted and embraced by the low fence that enclosed the flower garden, with its ranks of tulips and roses. Then, feeling self-conscious under the gaze of the hardy Yorkshire troopers, they moved apart but continued to smile and shake hands.

'Why did you not call on me at Red House?' Fauconberg asked of the man who had been his loyal deputy throughout the Civil War.

'I needed employment to feed my wife and four children. God forgive me but since your father was imprisoned for treason, I could not be both a paid soldier and a friend to the Slingsby family.'

'You are here to take me back to York for my hanging?'

Haywood laughed. 'We are members of the Sealed Knot and we have declared for General Monck. It was our intention to spring you from the gallows and ride with you to the Scottish border, where Monck's troops are gathered. But instead, we discovered a drunken rogue had taken your place on the scaffold. We were much confused until we saw you ride like the devil from Walmgate Bar. You will be safe with us till we reach Monck's army.'

'Is Monck for the restoration of Prince Charles to the throne?'

'Who knows? He is a warlord like the other major generals. At least he has not declared against the restoration.'

'I would relish the opportunity to fight one last battle with you, my friend, but first I must return to Red House to free Lady Slingsby from the clutches of Benedict Bourcher. He has threatened to burn her at the stake if she does not agree to his marriage terms by the end of New Year's Day. That is one day hence.'

Haywood shook his head sadly. 'I was much smitten by Rebecca when I saw her last, but I fear she is lost. Twelve thousand of General Lambert's troops stand betwixt Nun Appleton and Red House, and his scouts are everywhere. Even with fifty men, it would be foolhardy to risk an encounter with them.'

'Hence why I came to call on the good grace of Lord Fairfax of Cameron. He was commander-in-chief of the Commonwealth of England until his retirement. He might escort me through Lambert's army to Red House. I might yet save her from the clutches of Benedict Bourcher.'

Captain Haywood stroked his beard. 'I would not be so sure. You almost killed Lord Fairfax at Selby. He might rather hang you than give you safe passage to Red House.'

'That is a risk I'm prepared to take. Rebecca was his favourite niece when she was a child.'

Captain Haywood considered the situation. 'My troops are at your service, Colonel. I wish nothing more than to see you lead one last cavalry charge against Lambert's army.'

Fauconberg smiled and shook hands with Captain Haywood. 'Thank you, my friend. With such fine men at my side, I have no doubt we could break clean through Lambert's ranks should it be necessary. We will finish the job we started at Preston.'

* * *

The Great Hall of Nun Appleton was located beneath the imposing cupola in the central structure of the building. The walls of the hall were adorned with portraits of Sir Thomas's illustrious ancestors. A blazing fire surrounded by an ornate chimneypiece took the edge off the winter's chill. Fauconberg waited for news of his arrival to reach Sir Thomas and spent the time examining the crests of the great northern families the Fairfax family had married into. His eyes were drawn to a seated lion holding a shield bearing the images of two leopard's head *argent* and a horn. It was the Slingsby coat of arms.

Fauconberg heard the door open and the swish of silk skirts behind him as a young woman entered the room. 'I'm afraid Sir Thomas sends his regrets, but he is unable to see you today. He is discussing urgent matters of state and cannot be disturbed. But perhaps I can ask the kitchen to prepare a hot meal for you before you continue your journey?'

Fauconberg studied the poised young woman who had given him the unfortunate news. She looked familiar, regal rather than pretty, and had a strong Fairfax nose similar to his own.

'Moll?' he said. 'Little Moll?' He realised he was looking at his half-sister, Mary Fairfax, who had married the Duke of Buckingham the previous year. She was ten years Fauconberg's junior and he recalled the little girl whom he had once bounced on his knee before the outbreak of the Civil War.

'Sam? My brother Sam? Is that really you?' She clasped her hand to her mouth.

'Sir Thomas told you about me?'

'I have known you were my brother for many years, although my father forbade me to contact you because of the scandal it might bring to the family. I thought Lambert had sent you to the scaffold this morning. I was most distressed at the news and have been praying for your soul ever since.'

The woman who had become the Duchess of Buckingham rushed forward to embrace him. After a while she released him, then stepped back to examine him closely. 'My, how you have changed. I remember you as a shy teenager and yet as I look at you now, I have never seen a man so handsome. God has bestowed so many favours on you.'

'And you are every inch the perfect duchess. George Villiers, the Duke of Buckingham, could not have found himself a more beautiful wife.'

Mary Fairfax took his hand. 'Come with me. I will insist my father takes a minute from his deliberations to greet his prodigal son.'

***

'Colonel Fauconberg,' said Fairfax as Fauconberg entered the smoke-filled drawing room. 'Have you come to finish me off? You spent eight years chasing me around Yorkshire with your damned pistol and broadsword.' The old commander-in-chief rubbed at his arm where fifteen years before, Fauconberg's musket ball had come within an inch of ending his life. He wore an exasperated expression at the unexpected intrusion. 'Forgive me if I don't get up. My war wounds have taken their toll, and I am not as sprightly as I once was.'

Fauconberg scanned the hostile faces in the room. Fauconberg recognised the three colonels: Bethell, Smithson and Rossiter. Standing on his own by the fireplace, warming his back, was General Sir Thomas Morgan. Morgan was General Monck's second in command and he was in deep conversation with Fairfax's men. Mary Fairfax's husband, the royalist Duke of Buckingham, sat next to his father-in-law, and next to him was Sir Henry Arthington, Fairfax's brother-in-law. Two men were smoking by an open window: Brian Fairfax, cousin to Lord Thomas Fairfax; and Edward Bowles, the family chaplain. It was rumoured Bowles and General Morgan had been the go-betweens in secret negotiations between Monck and Fairfax to restore the former parliament. As one they stared at Fauconberg with a mixture of curiosity and suspicion.

Fauconberg bowed to the assembled gentry. 'My deepest apologies for the intrusion, gentlemen. I understand your meeting is of considerable importance.'

'Pray tell me, Colonel Fauconberg, are you for Monck or Lambert?' asked Brian Fairfax.

'Lambert tried to hang me this morning, so I suppose I must be for Monck.'

'That would decide any man's loyalty, for sure,' Bowles said. He could not hide the smile that spread on his thin lips.

'Yet still, I trust not Monck,' Fauconberg continued. 'Like the other major generals, he schemes to sit on Cromwell's vacant seat as the new Lord Protector.'

Sir Thomas shifted in his chair. His many war wounds were causing him considerable discomfort. Yet he was still an imposing man with jet-black, shoulder-length hair, dark eyes and a neat black chin beard and moustache. His face was angular, accentuated by his long, aristocratic nose. Sir Thomas had been nicknamed 'Black Tom' during the Civil War for his swarthy appearance.

'I sent a message to George Monck on the twenty-first of December,' Fairfax said. 'I told Monck that if he desires the restoration of the former representative parliament, I will support him. According to our guest General Morgan, Monck and I are as one.'

Morgan inclined his head in confirmation.

'Does that mean the return of Prince Charles Stuart from exile?' Fauconberg asked.

Sir Thomas considered the question that had remained unspoken until then. Fairfax had been the man most responsible for the defeat of the royalists in the Civil War. Unlike Cromwell, he was known as a man of great integrity, who had been generous to his defeated enemies and modest in his political ambitions. He had objected to the beheading of King Charles in 1648 and refused to take part in the invasion of Scotland in 1650, resigning his position of commander-in-chief of the armed forces in protest.

'Such talk is treasonous,' he said softly. 'But nonetheless, it requires an answer. It could mean Charles Stuart's return if parliament so desires and if the prince agrees to strict constitutional conditions,' he said at last. 'Especially if it avoids yet another bloody civil war.'

'Then I am for Monck, but principally I am for you, my Lord Fairfax,' Fauconberg announced.

'Gentleman,' Fairfax announced as he struggled to his feet. 'May I introduce you to my firstborn, Samuel Fauconberg. It was his misfortune to be born illegitimate due to my ... youthful indiscretions, yet he is my son nonetheless, and the best cavalry officer I ever faced in battle. Despite his numerous attempts to kill me, he would be a considerable asset to our cause.'

'He served our forces with great distinction for one so young,' said the Duke of Buckingham, 'although he was a notorious hot head.'

'My Lord Fairfax,' said Fauconberg. 'When I shot you in the arm, I did not know you were my natural father. Sir Henry did not reveal that secret to me till the morning of his death. Even then, he was most circumspect.'

'Sir Henry was ever a man of honour, and his wife, Barbara, was my cousin. You were most fortunate to be taken into his household. You should know I tried to intercede on his behalf prior to his execution, but Cromwell would have none of it.'

'Thank you, my lord. But I am here to beg a favour from you.'

'I thought as much. Few people come here for any other reason.'

'The Lady Rebecca Slingsby is a prisoner in her own house, held captive by our neighbour Benedict Bourcher.'

Fairfax frowned. 'I know of Benedict Bourcher. He is a grasping, treacherous man.'

'He has threatened to burn Rebecca at the stake on New Year's Day if she does not agree to marry him – against her will, of course.'

'He cannot do that! He would be tried for murder.'

'He accused her of witchcraft some months ago, although the judge threw out the case. Bourcher means to use the confusion of the forthcoming war with Lambert to execute his plan.'

'I was always fond of Rebecca,' said Fairfax. 'She was a charming child. Yet I do not see what I can do. Lambert's troops are at Marston Moor and block our path to Red House.'

'You do not have to fight him, my lord. Just persuade him to let me pass through his ranks unmolested.'

'Ah, but I do have to fight him, Colonel Fauconberg. I have promised General Morgan I will attack Lambert's rear on the morrow, so Monck can threaten his vanguard despite his inferiority in cavalry. I take it you will join us, Colonel?'

'I would be honoured.'

'And how many men do you have?'

'Only fifty, my lord. But they are hardy veterans of Preston and Worcester.'

'Fifty? Splendid! That is more than the rest of us combined.'

'You intend to attack Lambert with less than one hundred men?' said Fauconberg, incredulous.

'We are hoping to attract at least five hundred Yorkshire gentlemen to our cause on the way to Marston Moor.'

'But still. Five hundred against twelve thousand?' Fauconberg looked at Fairfax in astonishment. 'It will be a slaughter.'

Fairfax laughed. 'Do not forget we will be at the head of five hundred of Yorkshire's *finest* gentlemen, fifty of which will be veterans of your Northern Horse. That will even things up.'

'But surely ...'

'Come now, Colonel. We do not have to defeat Lambert, merely threaten him from the rear till Monck comes to our aid. Such odds never concerned you when you were tormenting my New Model Army. Have you become timid and indolent since you last rode into battle?'

'Of course not.'

'Then it is settled. In the morning, we ride to Marston Moor, and should you be so disposed, you may have the honour of leading the charge with your fifty horsemen. If you survive that encounter, you may continue onwards to Red House to rescue Lady Slingsby.'

CHAPTER 9

1st January 1660

It was the first day of the new decade, but few in Fairfax's mounted column felt like celebrating as it snaked its way through the heart of the frosty Yorkshire countryside. Steam billowed from the sweating horses and the sound of chomping bits and heavy hooves echoed on the frozen ground near Oglethorpe Hall.

The upright posture of the one hundred gentlemen of Yorkshire who sat astride their magnificent chargers reflected the conviction of men who had moral certainty on their side, but faced unsurmountable odds. At the head of the column, Fairfax and Fauconberg rode side by side and the two ex-soldiers swapped stories of past military exploits. Fairfax probed his son's views on politics, religion and family affairs, and listened to his answers without judgement.

'Do you know why your sword is called Enlightener?' Fairfax asked.

Fauconberg stared in astonishment at Fairfax. It seemed little escaped the veteran general's attention. 'I know not, my lord. It was always thus. Perhaps my sword enlightens God's enemies to their sins at the moment of death.'

Fairfax laughed. 'Not so, Samuel. Engraved on the hilt of your sword is the Fairfax family motto: *De audacia venit illustratio*. From courage comes forth enlightenment. I always thought your actions during the Civil War embodied the spirit of the Fairfax motto.'

'Are you saying the Enlightener was once yours?' Fauconberg said with a mixture of pride and bewilderment.

'Indeed. It was the most precious thing I owned and has been passed down from Fairfax father to son for centuries. It was the least I could do for my only son, whom I could not raise as my own. It would make me proud if you would consider the Fairfax family motto as your own.'

'I would be honoured, my lord ...'

Fauconberg stopped his horse and pointed towards the crest of a distant hill, where a large body of mounted men had gathered. They had been shadowing Fairfax's column for the past twenty minutes and outnumbered their small party almost two to one. A group of riders had detached themselves from the main body and cantered down the hill towards them.

'Are they Lambert's scouts?' Fairfax asked, his eyes squinting towards the crest of the hill. 'My eyesight is not what it was.'

'I think not,' replied Fauconberg. 'They are dressed as cavaliers.'

'Then we should pick five men of our own and ride out to meet them,' Fairfax said. He turned to his son-in-law, the Duke of Buckingham; his cousin Brian Fairfax; and his trusted aide Sir Henry Cholmley. 'Would you be so kind as to accompany Colonel Fauconberg and me to meet the incoming horsemen?'

'Surely,' replied Cholmley. 'Are they ours?' he asked Fauconberg as he rode alongside him.

'Who knows? They are dressed as royalists, but their uniforms are tattered, and their weapons are in sore need of repair. They could be brigands seeking easy pickings,' Fauconberg suggested. 'It is best we keep our wits about us.'

They cantered towards an ice-covered stream known as Firgreen Beck, then waited on its east bank. The stream would offer them some protection from an unexpected assault.

'Greetings, gentlemen.' Fairfax lifted his hat to the approaching party. 'May I enquire about your loyalties and intentions?'

The captain of the cavalier troop was unshaven and had a wild look in his eyes. It appeared the rogue horsemen had been on the road for several months.

'General Fairfax?' the astonished captain said as he recognised his opposite number.

'Indeed. But you have me at a disadvantage. Your name if you please, Captain?'

The captain fingered his pistol but remained silent. He cast an eye over the motley Yorkshire gentry as if calculating the odds of a quick victory.

'His name is Captain James Stapylton,' said Fauconberg. 'He served with me at Naseby. He was a brave horseman, but he was unseated when he continued the charge long after I had sounded the cavalry's return to our lines.'

Stapylton stared at Fauconberg, and then at Fairfax. 'Colonel Fauconberg. Why are you riding with this man? He was once your mortal enemy.'

'Enemies no more,' replied Fauconberg. 'We are riding to take the field against Lambert.'

Stapylton laughed. 'There have been many rebellions since Cromwell's death and yet Lambert has crushed them all. Why do you suppose you will prevail while all others have failed?'

'Because this time it is not we who are the rebels. With Lord Fairfax at our helm, we are the true authority in the land. It is now incumbent on General Lambert to explain why he would take up arms against his old commander-in-chief, Lord Fairfax.'

The Duke of Buckingham pushed his horse forward and addressed Stapylton. 'You dress like a royalist, yet you live off the land as an outlaw. Why is this so?'

Stapylton sat straight on his horse and pushed his chest out a little further. 'We are royalists, and hardy veterans at that, but times are hard, and we must live off our wits. Our property has been confiscated and we are fined by Lambert's cronies every time we try to earn an honest living.'

'Then this is your chance to restore that which you have lost. If you have honour in your veins, you will join Colonel Fauconberg's Northern Horse, for this is as much a royalist cause as a parliamentarian one,' said Fairfax.

'And if you fail?'

'We will not fail, for our task is not to defeat Lambert, but to hold him at bay until General Monck arrives from Scotland. We will be the stone in his shoe and the lead weight around his neck,' said Fauconberg.

Stapylton considered the situation. 'If Colonel Fauconberg believes your cause is just, then it must be so. My men will ride with you to Marston Moor for one last charge of the Northern Horse.'

* * *

As the small army continued in a broad northwest sweep towards Marston Moor, word spread among the towns and villages that the gentlemen of Yorkshire and the Northern Horse were on the march to take on the tyrant John Lambert. Young children ran out of their homes into the freezing fog to wave them on their way. Curious women in their aprons and bonnets stood at their doorways and uttered words such as 'Bless you, Lord Fairfax', while others pointed at Fauconberg and blew kisses in his direction. Eager young men and Civil War veterans alike grabbed their old military jackets, muskets and swords to join their swelling ranks and form a rudimentary company of foot soldiers.

Fairfax called a temporary halt to the march on the outskirts of Wetherby to feed the men and water the horses. Five of Fauconberg's soldiers were posted as sentries to guard against a surprise attack. As the cavalry officers lit their campfires against the chill and prepared a simple broth, dozens of well-wishers and curious onlookers surrounded the camp. Thirty more horsemen and seventy-five foot soldiers joined the ranks of the little army, until its numbers swelled to almost five hundred.

As General Fairfax called for a resumption of the march, a breathless rider dressed in the uniform of Lambert's Irish Brigade rode into the camp. Steam rose in clouds from his beige mount. Suspicious infantrymen fingered their muskets and some shouted insults at the horseman. The rider eyed the soldiers around him, then spotted Fauconberg on his horse and rode towards him. Fauconberg gripped his sword hilt at the unexpected intrusion, but relaxed as he recognised the interloper.

'Major John Devizes.' Fauconberg saluted the dashing cavalry officer. They had shared a study at Cambridge University five years before. In normal circumstances he would have embraced his old friend, but five hundred pairs of suspicious eyes glared at the intruder.

Devizes returned Fauconberg's salute. He forced a smile, but it was clear he felt intimidated by the presence of so many enemy troops. 'Colonel Fauconberg. It has been too long since our days at Cambridge. Pardon the intrusion, but I have in my possession a letter from my commanding officer, Colonel Redman of the Irish Brigade.' He reached into the breast pocket of his red coat and pulled out an envelope bearing the wax seal of Colonel Redman. 'It is to be opened by none other than General Fairfax.'

'And you wish me to escort you to the general?'

'Indeed. I would be most obliged if you would vouch for my character.'

'It would be an honour.' Fauconberg turned to Captain

Haywood, who had ridden to join them. 'Would you be so kind as to organise a mug of ale and a slice of pie for our guest? When he is refreshed, we will escort the Major to the general's tent.'

'It would be my pleasure, sir.'

* * *

General Fairfax broke the seal on the letter and scanned the contents. 'So General Lambert is aware of our approach?' he said. A look of concern crossed his dark features.

'Yes, my lord,' replied Major Devizes. 'He is preparing his army for battle as we speak.'

'Then why is Colonel Redman giving me this information?'

'Because his troops will not fight you and wish to switch their allegiance. Many of our officers served under you at Naseby. And of those who did not, many fought with Colonel Fauconberg. The alternative is desertion, and they will not suffer the shame of such action. Far better to die with a clear conscience under the Fairfax banner.'

'What of Colonel Redman?'

'He is of the same mind as his men. He is offering you his services and that of the entire Irish Brigade should you deem them worthy of your command.'

'There are no finer soldiers in Europe than the Irish Brigade. How many men can he take to the field?'

'Twelve hundred, my lord.'

'And what of the size of General Lambert's army?'

'Just over twelve thousand.'

'Good grief. And their quality?'

'The best, sir. They are all veterans of many battles. They cannot be beaten by a force as small as yours. Even one comprised of so many fine Yorkshire gentlemen.'

'We'll see about that. But thank you, Major Devizes. I am most grateful to you. Will you ride with all haste to advise Colonel Redman we will be most grateful for his support?'

'Indeed, my lord.' The major bowed low, then turned to leave Fairfax's makeshift shelter.

* * *

'It's a trap' said the Duke of Buckingham. 'It would be madness to lead an army as small as ours into the teeth of the enemy without the element of surprise.' The duke rubbed his hands together to warm them against the freezing air. A flurry of snowflakes dropped from the grey, overcast sky.

'I'm inclined to agree,' replied Fairfax. 'We risk everything on the word of a young major and the validity of his colonel's letter. The prudent course of action would be to bypass Lambert's army, take our forces to my estate at Denton and await the arrival of General Monck from there.'

The three parliamentarian colonels – Bethell, Smithson and Rossiter – all nodded their heads. 'Even if the Irish switch sides, we would have less than two thousand troops against more than ten thousand. It would be a slaughter,' said Colonel Smithson.

'It is no trap,' Fauconberg replied. 'Major Devizes would have no part in any act of treachery. If proof be needed, he warned us against a direct assault against Lambert's veterans.'

'Then we should avoid a direct confrontation, just as General Fairfax suggested,' said Colonel Smithson.

'I said such a course of action would be prudent, but no war was ever won through excess of caution. What would the Northern Horse do in such a situation?' General Fairfax said, looking at Fauconberg.

'I would put my faith in Colonel Redman of the Irish Brigade. If they join our ranks, Lambert's battle order may crumble into disarray. I suspect it's not just the Irish Brigade who have not the stomach for a fight against their former allies.'

Fauconberg was taken aback by the babble of disapproval that greeted his advice. Fairfax raised a hand to silence his advisers. 'Colonel Fauconberg, are you willing to lead one last charge of the Northern Horse against Lambert's centre? It would be a marvel to behold.'

'I am, but it may not be necessary, my lord. I was once reckless and vain in battle, but no more. Victory may be possible by turning Lambert's vanity to our advantage.'

'You intend to taunt Lambert into making an error of judgement?'

'Not Lambert's judgement, my lord, but that of his soldiers. My intention is to compel each man at Marston Moor to search his soul. Then he must decide whether he is on the side of anarchy and puritanism as represented by Lambert or for peace, prosperity and a kinder, more tolerant society.'

'The Northern Horse was once a force to be feared,' replied Fairfax, 'for none was braver. But with age, its commander has acquired the cunning of a fox and Lambert must worry for his future. We will ride with all haste to Marston Moor.'

CHAPTER 10

Marston Moor

An icy wind howled across the moor as if the collective ghosts of four thousand slain warriors from the first battle of Marston Moor were protesting at their intrusion. The original battle in 1644 had been a decisive victory for the parliamentarian forces, resulting in the loss of King Charles I's northern stronghold. The royalist cause had never recovered from the disaster and once again, the dismal moor was preparing for a slaughter.

General Lambert's army of twelve thousand veteran soldiers stood in battle formation across the plain of Marston Moor. Lambert had been Fairfax's brilliant young protégé during the Civil War, but he lacked his mentor's charisma. He positioned his forces on the crest of the hill facing the River Nidd, just as Fairfax had done sixteen years before. His soldiers were impregnable and majestic, but they were war weary, and most had not received their meagre pay for over three months. It was only their famed discipline that stopped them from melting back to their homes. They had just returned from a long and fruitless march to the Scottish borders in an unsuccessful attempt to draw General Monck's inferior forces into a decisive battle that would determine the future of the realm. Yet Monck had slipped their net and Lambert had withdrawn his forces south to Marston Moor to intercept the old warrior should he attempt to march on London.

Lambert's soldiers shivered. Their position atop the hill exposed them to the icy gusts. Their once magnificent uniforms were tattered, and their boots were falling apart in the harsh Yorkshire winter. Gnawing away at the army's collective spirit was the knowledge the political structure of the Commonwealth had collapsed, and anarchy was spreading across the nation like a plague. At least five separate major generals were posturing for the position of Lord Protector.

'Who are these vagabonds approaching us from the woods?' Charles Fleetwood enquired of General Lambert. Fleetwood, who had married Oliver Cromwell's daughter Bridget, had once been the supreme commander-in-chief of the armed forces until the spiteful Rump Parliament had removed him from office. In retaliation, Fleetwood had dissolved parliament, thrown in his lot with Lambert and appointed himself as acting head of the country. However, Fleetwood was as impotent as every other aspirant to the highest office in the country.

'My spies tell me it is none other than General Fairfax at the head of five hundred so-called Yorkshire gentlemen,' replied Lambert.

'Fairfax? By God! I thought he was dead. We can't possibly incorporate these ... northern louts into our army. General Monck would make mincemeat of them. But if Fairfax is coming to lend his support to our cause, then I suppose it is no bad thing.'

'Um, Fairfax does not come to support us, but to challenge us.'

'Nonsense,' replied Fleetwood. 'Fairfax retired ten years ago. He is crippled by his wounds.'

'Colonel Fauconberg of the Northern Horse is at his side. If his cavalry joins with Monck's army, then our superiority over the enemy in numbers and quality of horse will be nullified.'

'What?' Fleetwood's cheeks turned scarlet with anger. Fleetwood's infantry had been routed by Fauconberg's Northern Horse at Carlisle in 1648. 'I thought you had hanged him?'

'The meddlesome traitor has cheated the hangman's noose.'

'No matter, he will be dancing a merry jig at the end of a rope before the day is done. Give them a taste of iron with a round from the artillery. That will teach them for their impertinence.'

'My dear Fleetwood, we cannot fire on General Fairfax. Half of my men served under him during the Civil War.'

'Would you rather be insulted by five hundred brazen Yorkshiremen? If we do not show sufficient resolve, there will be rebellions up and down the length of Britain.'

Lambert sighed. 'I will order a single salvo across his front. Let us hope the old fool has not completely taken leave of his senses.'

* * *

Lance Bombardier Ingles of Lambert's Artillery brigade watched the arrival of Fairfax's five hundred Yorkshire gentlemen with astonishment. The gunner held a length of lighted cord soaked in saltpetre, known as a slow-lit match, close to the touch-hole of his bronze eight-foot Drake cannon, and awaited orders from his commanding officer. His gun battery was positioned between a regiment of pikemen to his right and Colonel Redman's Irish Brigade to his left. Confusion reigned throughout Lambert's army as they recognised the banner of their former commander-in-chief approaching their front.

Ingles watched General Fairfax dismount stiffly from his charger. Fairfax took his war standard from his sergeant and planted it in the frosty ground in an act of provocation to Lambert. There was no longer any doubt his intentions were hostile. Ingles stared north over the horizon to see if Fairfax's challenge had signalled the arrival of General Monck's ten thousand troops from Scotland, but there was no sign of his army.

Ingles' heart rate quickened at the prospect of action. Yet he struggled with his conscience as he followed the movements of General Fairfax, whom he had revered for two decades. He recalled the fear, smoke, noise and stench of battles past under the banner of Black Tom. Fairfax had always put the safety of his soldiers ahead of personal glory and in return, the soldiers had developed a personal bond with their former general that had stood the test of time. The familiar figure still possessed a formidable battlefield presence despite his advancing years and the debilitating effects of his multiple war wounds.

Ingles watched as Fairfax remounted his horse and spoke to the senior cavalry officer at his side. The two men rode towards Lambert's intimidating army as if they were inspecting their own troops at a military parade. They were at the foot of the hill and within easy cannon shot of Lambert's artillery. Ingles willed Fairfax to retreat beyond the range of his cannons lest he provoke Lambert into firing a salvo at the old warrior.

'My God, that's Samuel Fauconberg riding with General Fairfax,' said Gunner Harris, who had been in the royalist artillery at the battle of Worcester in 1651. 'I never thought I would see the day when the two of them rode side by side in battle.'

'Prepare canister!' yelled Battery Commander Brigstock. 'We can finish this sorry business right now with a well-aimed shot at Black Tom and Colonel Fauconberg.'

The battery commander was a zealot who was as ruthless in battle as he was intolerant of religious dissent in civil life. The canister was designed to rip open upon detonation and would spread its lethal contents in a conical formation, causing a wide swathe of destruction. From a range of eight hundred yards, even a poorly aimed shot would be sufficient to maim the two men at the bottom of the hill, and Harris was the best gunner in England.

Lance Bombardier Ingles and Gunner Harris sprang to action. Despite their reservations they were well trained and disciplined artillery men. In their peripheral vision they saw the three other teams of gunners in their section were also preparing to replace shot with canister. Harris placed a piece of lead plate over the touch-hole to prevent any stray sparks that might cause an accidental discharge. Then with extreme caution, Ingles inserted a long pole up the barrel. The pole was tipped with two intertwining pieces of metal shaped like a giant corkscrew, designed to pull out the pieces of wadding surrounding the cannon ball. It was a dangerous task; a premature detonation of the gunpowder in the barrel would kill the gunners instantly and send their dismembered bodies flying across the battlefield. With a sigh of relief, Ingles withdrew the long-handled wad-screw complete with remnants of old cloth from the gun barrel, and then depressed the barrel downwards so it was pointing towards the frozen ground. The five-pound iron ball refused to leave its nest of gunpowder and dried grass near the base of the bore. With the help of six other men, they heaved and shook the rear of the cannon until the ball rolled harmlessly from the cannon's muzzle and landed on the grass with a thud.

After Harris had swabbed the bore with a sponge attached to the rammer, to clear out any remaining debris, Ingles inserted the cylindrical canister made of tin, packed with nails, iron fragments, glass shards, sand and sawdust into the barrel. As Ingles manoeuvred the canister towards the wadding in the breech of the cannon using his long-handled rammer, Harris adjusted the height of the barrel and swung it two inches to the left. General Fairfax and Colonel Fauconberg were sitting ducks and Gunner Harris willed them to ride back towards the relative safety of their tiny army.

'Aim!' shouted Battery Commander Brigstock.

The two Civil War commanders stared into the bore of Harris's cannon and chatted together as if discussing the impact of the impending salvo. Fairfax raised his hat towards his enemies in acknowledgement of their professional bearing, then turned his horse back towards his little army. Fauconberg did the same and the two commanders set off at a gentle trot back towards their lines.

'Fire!' bellowed Brigstock. His voice echoed across the battlefield, but no-one moved a muscle. Ingles held the slow-lit match close to the touch-hole but was unable to bring himself to ignite the pan of gunpowder that would result in the obliteration of Fairfax and Fauconberg. The three other cannons in the battery also remained silent.

'Fire!' repeated Brigstock.

Only the sound of the wind and the screeching of a distant eagle disturbed the silence of the moor.

'If I have to repeat my order a third time there will be a court martial,' warned Brigstock.

Still the cannons did not fire as Fairfax and Fauconberg continued their sedate journey back towards their awaiting troops. Battery Commander Brigstock barged his way towards Ingles and tried to seize the forked *botefeux* that held the slow match from him. There was a short tussle, but Ingles ended the dispute by dousing the match into the sponge bucket.

'Arrest this man!' screamed Brigstock, pointing at Ingles.

Before anyone could move, there was a commotion to their left among Colonel Redman's Irish Brigade. An order was bellowed to shoulder arms and twelve hundred of Lambert's finest troops slung their muskets across their shoulders.

* * *

'By the left, quick march!' yelled Colonel Redman and the entire brigade stepped out of their ranks and marched in the direction of General Fairfax's tiny army.

'Who the hell ordered the Irish Brigade to attack?' General Lambert yelled from his command post at the crown of the hill.

'At least Colonel Redman is showing some initiative,' replied Fleetwood. 'Even on its own the Irish Brigade outnumbers Fairfax three to one.'

'Perhaps you are right, but he has made himself vulnerable to a counter charge from Colonel Fauconberg's horse.' He turned towards his adjutant. 'It appears the battle has begun. Please ask Major Kenworthy of the Light Horse to make ready to support the Irish.'

'At once, sir,' replied Colonel Jackson the adjutant.

'Why are the Irish not presenting arms?' Lambert said to Fleetwood. 'Have they forgotten their most basic training?'

'One must admire their discipline. They are marching into battle in perfect parade ground formation,' replied Fleetwood.

Lambert and Fleetwood watched with mounting concern as the Irish Brigade reached the bottom of the hill. Still, they had not unshouldered their rifles.

'Redman is leaving it a bit late,' said Lambert. 'They will shortly be within musket range of Fairfax's infantry.'

'Should I order the Light Horse to charge, sir?' said Lambert's aide-de camp, Colonel Jackson.

'Yes, that would be wise, Colonel. It will give Fairfax something to think about while he faces the Irish Brigade. But for the love of God, tell Major Kenworthy to keep a wary eye on Fauconberg.' A shiver ran down his spine as he remembered the many occasions on which his troops had been mauled by Fauconberg's Northern Horse.

'Fairfax's Yorkshiremen are cheering,' muttered Fleetwood. 'One must admire their spirit even as they are at the point of being overrun by the Irish.'

'Something is not right,' replied General Lambert. 'Fairfax's muskets should have opened up by now.'

'Fauconberg's cavalry has taken to the field,' said Fleetwood. His voice shook with trepidation. 'And still Colonel Redman does not present arms. He has left it too late! My God, it will be a slaughter!'

Lambert put his field glass to his eyes and sighed with relief. 'The rebel army is surrendering without firing a shot! Fairfax is doffing his cap to Colonel Redman. I had expected better of him.'

'He does not look like he has surrendered to me. His troops are not throwing down their muskets,' said Fleetwood.

'That's strange. The Irish Brigade is taking position on Fairfax's left. Why on earth would they do that?'

A red-faced Colonel Jackson came rushing back to Lambert.

'Major Kenworthy and his Light Horse are refusing to charge, sir. He said his men will not fight General Fairfax.'

'For the love of God,' said Lambert, ashen-faced. 'The Irish Brigade has deserted to the enemy, and the cavalry is refusing to obey orders.'

'We still outnumber the rascals five to one,' replied Fleetwood. 'Time to teach them a good lesson, I say. Send in the guard. That will sort out these scoundrels.'

'We cannot send in the guard without the support of Kenworthy's cavalry,' Lambert countered. 'They are our finest men and Fauconberg would slaughter them.'

Lambert considered his options. The desertion of the Irish Brigade had rocked him to the core. They were doughty fighters, and his remaining men would not relish a fight against a brigade who minutes earlier had been their brothers in arms. Even if he defeated the combined forces of Fairfax's army of 'Yorkshire gentlemen' and his disciplined Irish Brigade, the humiliation of losing the Irish to Fairfax might be sufficient to ruin his political ambitions.

He cursed his old mentor Fairfax, just as he heard a popular ale house drinking song carry on the wind from the enemy troops. It was a version of 'A health to all good fellows' that had once been popular among the parliamentarian troops during the Civil War. At the height of Fairfax's popularity, the words had been changed to 'A health to good Tom Fairfax'. The song was still sung in those taverns brave enough to defy the Puritans. The tune, which had once been a comfort to Lambert during the hardships of the Civil War, now mocked him. Yet despite himself, he found his left foot tapping in time to the catchy melody.

'Enough of this tomfoolery!' he said to his aide-de-camp. 'It's time to throw down the gauntlet. No army on earth could withstand such overwhelming odds, even with Fairfax and Fauconberg at their head. We shall open with a ten-minute artillery barrage. Shoot any man who refuses to do his duty. When they are softened up, send in a brigade of light infantry to attack the Yorkshiremen directly. We shall isolate the Irish Brigade against the woods to their rear using a detachment of Major Whitehead's dragoons.'

'May I suggest sending in the Staffordshire pikemen and musketeers to outflank their right wing, General?' said Colonel

Jackson. 'That way we can cut off their line of retreat. There will be a hefty butcher's bill for Fairfax to pay tonight.'

'Excellent suggestion, Colonel. And have the guards on standby ready to mop up. Threaten to hang any man who refuses to charge. But for God's sake make sure no harm comes to General Fairfax. I don't want a full-scale mutiny on my hands.'

'Yes, sir. I will pass the word around that he is to be captured alive.'

'Excellent. We will send him back to Nun Appleton where we can keep a close eye on him. With luck, we can keep the old man's involvement in this debacle a secret from the public.'

Charles Fleetwood stared at the small army at the opposite side of the battlefield, then broke into a grin. 'Belay that order, Colonel Jackson. The enemy is asking for quarter, after all. Colonel Fauconberg himself is riding towards us with a white flag in hand.'

CHAPTER 11

Red House

Benedict Bourcher sat on the cream-coloured chaise longue in Rebecca's withdrawing room, propped his mud-caked boots on the satin-cushioned footrest and belched loudly.

'There's too much French frippery in this house,' he complained to the iconoclast William Dowsing. 'How is one supposed to get comfortable on this contraption?' Bourcher abandoned any attempt at decorum and smeared the clods of dirt and horse manure from the vegetable garden onto the expensive satin fabric. 'I would ask Rebecca's maid to clean up this mess, but no matter how often I beat the silly woman, she refuses to obey even the simplest of commands.'

'My bill for cleansing the estate of idolatry is one noble,' said Dowsing. He had just finished destroying all signs of popery, both real and imagined, from the buildings. 'If you would be so kind as to pay in sterling silver coin, I'll be on my way.'

'One noble!' thundered Bourcher. He was shocked at being charged a third of a pound.

'Ah, but the chapel was full of idolatry and needed a thorough cleansing. It was unfitting for a fine Puritan like yourself to worship in a den of superstition.'

Dowsing had wanted to destroy Slingsby's magnificent stained-glass window, but even Bourcher had objected to such wanton vandalism. As it was, Dowsing had destroyed two images of the Virgin Mary and a wooden cross.

'One must admit that substituting the Latin words of Slingsby's motto for English ones on the four wooden plaques was worth the cost,' admitted Bourcher.

'Indeed. Appropriating the Slingsby family motto as your own will give the Bourcher family great prestige.'

Bourcher puffed out his chest at the perceived compliment. 'Yes, although it was necessary to remove the word "kindness" in Slingsby's motto and replace it with the more manly "discipline". You can collect the money from my wife on your way out.'

'You are married already?' Dowsing asked. 'I thought Lady Slingsby was still considering your offer.'

'Not as such. But the time is close. The wedding will take place tonight. Hence why I asked you to cleanse the chapel of idolatry.'

'Then my congratulations are in order. I bet half a crown with Alderman Watson that she would refuse you. You must be a persuasive man, for Lady Slingsby is a wilful child.'

'I built a pyre in the stable yard and told her I would burn her at the stake should she refuse.'

Dowsing laughed and slapped his thigh in merriment. 'And she believed you?'

'I do not make idle threats. She has rejected me twice already. Once she has paid your fee, she will spend the rest of the day chained to the stake on top of the pyre. If she rejects me thrice, they will be her last words before she burns.'

'Very wise. It is remarkable how quickly a woman will come to her senses when handled with a little firmness.'

'It was necessary, for no amount of kindness would get through to her. I had to remind her the witch pricker has destroyed her womanhood and left her with two clawed hands. Despite these repulsive afflictions, I graciously offered her my hand in marriage. Yet still she refused me.'

'The mysteries of women are beyond comprehension.'

'She said Samuel Fauconberg would take my head from my shoulders if I ever laid a finger on her. I told her that would be impossible as he was swinging from the end of a rope in York Gaol.'

'Fauconberg did not hang. It was reported he escaped the noose yesterday morning.'

'Dear God! How could that be?' Bourcher turned pale and involuntarily touched his neck.

Dowsing laughed at Bourcher's discomfort. 'Relax. Your wedding can proceed as planned. My spies tell me he was captured on the battlefield of Marston Moor, and he will face the firing squad at sundown.'

* * *

Marston Moor

'My terms of surrender are harsh but fair,' Lambert said to Fauconberg. 'Colonel Redman of the Irish Brigade will be tried for treason and shot at dusk. He will be at your side when you face the firing squad. General Fairfax will be placed under house arrest at Nun Appleton, where he will remain for the rest of his life. The rest of your so-called Yorkshire gentlemen will be marched to London in chains. Now, dismount and hand yourself over to Colonel Jackson.'

'You misunderstand the reason for my presence here, General,' replied Fauconberg. He threw the white flag into the hard ground at Lambert's feet. 'I come not to surrender, but to parley. I request speedy passage through your army so I can make haste to Red House without harassment.'

'Permission denied! You are hereby placed under arrest. Do not think you can escape your fate a second time,' replied Charles Fleetwood. He turned to General Lambert. 'The impertinence of this man is beyond comprehension. Guards! Take him away!'

Fauconberg drew his sword from his scabbard and scowled at the men who had approached his horse with their muskets drawn. 'Did you think I would venture into this den of wolves unless the leader of the pack had been neutered?' he said, pointing at Lambert. 'His army no longer has the stomach for a fight.'

'The Irish Battalion will pay for their treachery,' replied Lambert. 'But we still outnumber Fairfax by five to one. This battle will be over within the hour.'

Fauconberg replaced his sword in its scabbard and leaned over in his saddle. 'Listen to your pike men on the right wing of your army. They are singing "A health to good Tom Fairfax". On your left wing, your musketeers are melting away towards the inns of Long Marston. Your artillery is limbering their cannons in readiness to join the Irish Battalion. Your army is disintegrating as we speak.'

There was an awkward silence as the five men from Lambert's elite guard hesitated to arrest Fauconberg. They stood transfixed at the sight of large swathes of their army laying down their weapons. Individual squads of men were rushing down the hill towards Fairfax's army, who in turn cheered every man who joined their ranks. Lambert gasped as a whole brigade of six hundred light cavalry detached themselves from his battle formation and rode down the hill to join Fairfax. Their guidons and colours were flying high, but their sabres and pistols were sheathed. The Yorkshire gentlemen were protected by two of

General Lambert's finest units and they were growing stronger by the minute as the defections continued apace.

'This means nothing,' Lambert said to Fauconberg as he drew his pistol and aimed it at Fauconberg's chest. 'My guards number almost five thousand and they are the best in Europe. They at least will remain loyal to me till the last. They have stood by my side for thirteen years and our bonds are forged in blood and iron. I admit the battle will be bloodier than I had anticipated, but they will be more than a match for your rabble, with or without the Irish Brigade and my Light Horse.'

Fauconberg sighed, then turned away from Lambert and addressed the guards directly. 'Who among you would fire upon Lord Fairfax of Cameron, the man who led you to victory in the Civil War? Who would harm the man who protected you during your darkest days and who now, in return, seeks your support? Over yonder ...' he pointed towards the opposing army, '... is a man of principle who seeks a just peace and an end to the anarchy and bloodshed.' He looked at Lambert and Fleetwood. 'Do you not see that General Lambert courts the office of the Lord Protector? Under his dictatorship he would offer you nothing but further bloodshed, the continued suppression of theatres, alehouses, sports, and the continuation of harsh Puritan rule. Is that what you seek to inflict on the good people of England, after all that they have suffered?'

A tall, elegant officer of the guards yelled out, 'General Fairfax wants a return to the monarchy! I will not tolerate that.'

'General Fairfax seeks only an end to the chaotic rule of the major generals and a return of traditional parliament,' replied Fauconberg. 'It will then be the duty of parliament to elect the ruler of the country, not Fairfax.'

The officer could find no flaw in Fauconberg's logic. He hesitated a while, then addressed his troops. 'Then I am with General Fairfax.'

'And I,' replied a young subaltern. 'I am tired of fighting my fellow countrymen.'

There was a murmur of assent among the elite guardsmen surrounding Fauconberg.

'I will not mutiny against General Lambert,' said Colonel Jackson. 'I have fought with him too many times to betray him now.'

'Who was it who promoted you from captain to colonel for your bravery at Naseby?' replied Fauconberg. 'Was it this man ...' he pointed at Lambert 'or General Fairfax?'

Jackson looked down at the ground in confusion as feelings of mixed loyalty swirled through him. 'Indeed, it was Sir Thomas Fairfax,' he admitted.

'Do not wait for General Monck to ride down from Scotland to claim victory. Make it clear to Monck that it is to Fairfax you owe your allegiance, and that you will countenance no other political settlement than a return to full parliamentary democracy. We have been divided for too long. In God's name, if you do but one thing for your unfortunate, war-ravaged country, then do that.'

All those in earshot cheered Fauconberg. A rendition of 'A health to good Tom Fairfax' broke out among the Guard. As they did so, Lambert's remaining army began to fragment. Some started walking from the battlefield towards the Long Marston ale houses, while the bulk of the army ambled down the hill towards Fairfax's ragtag army of Yorkshire gentlemen.

'It appears you have lost both your army and your dignity,' said Fauconberg. 'Not a shot has been fired today, unless you wish to commit cold-blooded murder by shooting me with your pistol. Make your choice wisely, General Lambert, for history is waiting to pass judgement on you.'

Lambert held his pistol level with Fauconberg's heart, and his finger trembled on the trigger. Then, as if the weight of responsibility was too much to bear, he lowered his pistol arm and let the weapon drop to the ground. He gazed at his disintegrating army, dropped to his knees, and buried his head in his hands.

Fauconberg reached into his coat pocket and extracted a document scribbled on a piece of white parchment. He leaned down from his horse and handed it to Lambert.

'What is this?' Lambert said, raising his head and squinting at the document.

'My bill for the two hundred horses you stole from Red House. They are the finest horses in all England and are worth one hundred and fifty pounds each. You will see Lord Fairfax has agreed with my estimate and believes my bill is most reasonable. Now if you would excuse me, I have urgent business to attend to.'

As thick clouds darkened in the sky above, Fauconberg spurred on his horse and galloped in the direction of Red House.

CHAPTER 12

The storm hit just as Fauconberg galloped onto the grounds of Red House. The row of sycamores planted by Slingsby's gardener swayed like drunkards in the wind. Their boughs bent and twisted as the vicious, biting wind threatened to strip them bare. Thunder echoed around the fields like the booming of heavy artillery. Fauconberg gripped his hat and bent his head against the squall. Sheeting rain poured down his collar and froze him to the bone. His horse became skittish as bolts of lightning flashed in every direction and illuminated the barns and surrounding fields of the estate.

In the distance he could see the dim, flickering lights of the chapel and prayed he had not arrived too late to prevent the wedding. He slowed his tiring horse to a canter and soon he arrived at a gravel path that led to the imposing front door of Red House.

Fauconberg continued past the house and on towards the chapel. The heavy oak chapel door was shut but he could hear the tortured sound of Slingsby's chamber organ, which had been built by Thomas Dallan twenty years before. The sound was diabolical, as several of the keys were broken and the organist lacked the skill to compensate. The congregation droned tunelessly in accompaniment to both the broken organ and, it seemed, the howling of the wind.

Fauconberg unsheathed his sword and lifted the latch of the chapel door with its tip. The door swung open on its creaking hinges and without dismounting, he guided his horse through the chapel doorway, ducking low as he went.

In his sombre Puritan attire, Benedict Bourcher stood at the altar waiting for his bride. He was drunk on cheap whisky, and he swayed on the arm of his best man, Alderman Watson. The alderman toyed with a pair of cheap wedding rings as he made a tone-deaf attempt to sing the words to the psalm. Half-a-dozen of Bourcher's inebriated cronies lounged in the pews at the back of the chapel. The heavy atmosphere within the chapel reeked of incense, furniture polish, and alcohol.

The reluctant, veiled bride was being manhandled down the aisle by William Dowsing. Her tattered, dirty wedding dress was ill-fitting, and her whimpers were drowned by the cacophony from the organ and the jeering of the lecherous men in their pews. Fauconberg shivered, but not from the cold, for the scene resembled a black mass rather than a wedding.

Fauconberg pulled his two flintlock pistols from his waterproof saddlebag and checked the priming pans to see if the powder was still dry. Then he cocked the hammers with his thumb and aimed his first pistol at Dowsing. Too late, the iconoclast turned to see Fauconberg still mounted on his horse. A pitiful moan escaped his lips and his eyes pleaded with Fauconberg for mercy. Fauconberg pulled the trigger and the hammer's flint struck the iron frizzen, causing a spark to ignite the gunpowder in the pan. The lead ball exploded from the pistol into Dowsing's right kneecap, shattering it into fragments. Dowsing dropped to the floor of the chapel and howled in disbelief and pain as his blood pumped onto the chequered black and white tiles.

'You will live, Dowsing,' said Fauconberg as he pocketed his used pistol and transferred his second pistol to his right hand. 'But if you desecrate this chapel with your presence again, the next ball will go through your dark heart.' Fauconberg turned to the bride, whose dress was splattered with Dowsing's blood and bone fragments. He reeled in confusion as the unwilling bride to be removed her veil. The entire congregation gasped in astonishment as Rebecca's maid, Helen, revealed herself.

'Helen? What is the meaning of this knavery?' Fauconberg said. 'Where is Rebecca and why are you in her place?'

But it was Bourcher who answered. 'Lady Slingsby stands before the gates of hell, where she is to be joined in matrimony by her master, Satan.' He had a triumphant expression on his face. 'You are too late to save her. I left her burning at the stake, for she refused my hand for a third time. What further proof is needed that she prefers the company of demons to that of mortal men?'

'Then why proceed with this ridiculous charade of a wedding?'

'The aldermen of York demanded a wedding if I am to claim Slingsby's dowry, and a wedding they shall have. One bride doth look like any another behind the veil.'

Fauconberg raised his pistol and pointed it at Bourcher. 'Is it true this man has murdered Rebecca?' he said, directing his question to Helen.

'I know not, sir. He chained Mistress Slingsby to a stake in the stable yard. Mr Bourcher lit the straw at the base of the pyre, but the storm may have dowsed the fire.'

'So, she could yet be alive?' A resurgence of hope flared within him.

'Mr Bourcher added lamp oil, a keg of gunpowder and fresh straw to the base of the pyre in the stable yard, but I have not heard an explosion.'

'Then we must fly like the wind to the stable yard before it is too late.'

'Yes, Master Fauconberg,' said Helen. She clutched her white skirts and ran from the chapel.

Fauconberg turned the horse around in the narrow confines of the chapel aisle and ducked once more under the chapel doorway. Once outside in the driving rain, he galloped the short distance to the stable yard. Every few seconds, thunder crashed and lightning illuminated the stonework of the nearby buildings.

Fauconberg entered the stable yard and to his relief saw the pyre, some five feet high, was still intact. But thick black smoke billowed from its base and the occasional flame licked at Rebecca's feet. Rebecca was shackled to a large wooden post, slumped semi-conscious against the restraining chains at the apex of the bonfire. Her tattered white dress was scorched from the heat. Her face was stained with soot and the tracks of her tears were etched into the grime that plastered her cheeks. Fauconberg was alarmed to see her torso and legs were covered in burns. Fauconberg leapt from his horse and climbed up the smoking bonfire towards Rebecca.

'Please save her, Master Fauconberg!' cried Helen as she arrived at the yard, out of breath and her voice cracking with emotion.

Fauconberg's eyes watered and his lungs heaved as the smoke from the smouldering wood assaulted his senses. Some of the logs at the base were glowing red and they hissed in the rain. Occasionally a branch flared up, only to be doused by the downpour. To his horror Fauconberg saw a small, blackened gunpowder keg had been placed in the heart of the pyre. It was nestled on top of pile of glowing embers.

'Dear God,' said Fauconberg as he unsheathed his sword. He covered his mouth with a handkerchief and swung Enlightener at the heavy chain that pinioned Rebecca to the stake. The sword shuddered on impact and yet the chain remained intact.

Rebecca stirred, and then opened her eyes. She looked delirious from the pain and close to death, yet she still managed to look proud and majestic. 'My dear Samuel, what have I done to deserve such cruelty at the hands of these wicked men?' she asked. Her voice was weak, and she seemed past the point of sufferance.

'I cannot cut through the chains, my love,' Fauconberg said in despair. The smouldering embers had become too hot for him to bear, and the smoke was suffocating. 'I will try to dismantle the pyre and let the tempest douse the fire.'

Rebecca shook her head. 'You must leave the stable yard. The gunpowder will soon explode.'

'I can't leave you, Rebecca. I would rather die with you.'

'No, my love, you must go straight to the hidden room to rescue my sons and take them to Holland, for there are many who wish them dead.'

Fauconberg climbed down from the pyre as the heat became intolerable. 'What would you wish of me, my beloved Rebecca?' He held out his pistol, indicating he could end her suffering with one merciful shot.

Again, she shook her head. 'This place must be cleansed of its evil before I can rest in peace.'

'I don't understand?' said Fauconberg. Tears were streaming down his cheeks, but not from the smoke. The anguish he was feeling for Rebecca threatened to rip his soul from his body. 'Are you asking me to kill Bourcher for what he has done to you?'

'No, my love. Go now while I gather what strength I have left. And be it God's will we meet again in heaven.'

Rebecca fell silent and her expression became focused. She mouthed a few words that sounded like an incantation, then looked towards the heavens as if summoning the forces of nature. The thunder intensified and lightning flashed around them. Fauconberg could bear Rebecca's suffering no more. He considered putting an end to her pain with his pistol, but he could not bring himself to fire the shot. Instead, he mounted his horse and rode out of the stable yard, beckoning Helen to follow him. He took one last anguished look at Rebecca and turned towards Red House.

As he arrived at the rear door to Red House, an explosion rocked the stable yard and flying masonry forced him to duck low in his saddle. The keg had exploded and with it, Rebecca's suffering had ended. Simultaneously a crash of thunder, much louder than the sound of the exploding gunpowder, caused him to look up to the rain-filled sky. A ball of lightning exploded from the sky and smashed into the chapel entrance fifty yards away, causing more destruction than any cannonball he had seen on the battlefield. A foul, sulphurous odour and dark, thick smoke filled the air.

Fauconberg stared in disbelief as injured and disfigured men staggered from the shattered doorway of the chapel. He watched the tall, powerful shape of Benedict Bourcher crawl from the chapel's threshold. His left leg had been crushed by falling masonry and half the flesh had been torn from his face. His right eye was missing, leaving a bloodied eye socket, yet he stared straight at Fauconberg with his remaining eye. As he crawled towards Fauconberg, he laughed dementedly.

'Look no further for proof that Lady Slingsby was betrothed to the devil. The wicked hag struck me down even as she departed this life. But her malice was in vain, for the aldermen of York, in their infinite wisdom, have pronounced Rebecca and I man and wife, and granted me Red House.'

Fauconberg dismounted and walked towards Bourcher till he loomed over him. 'She did not marry you. You murdered her in the stable yard in the cruellest way possible.'

'The gunpowder will leave no trace of her remains and the aldermen are willing to swear the lightning ball that hit the chapel obliterated her moments after she said her vows.'

'Then you shall not live to enjoy the fruits of your deception,' replied Fauconberg as he unsheathed Enlightener from its scabbard.

'Go ahead, Fauconberg, it matters naught to me, for I have already taken the two most precious things in life from you and my heirs will have the pleasure of seeing you walk the scaffold. I have decreed unto them that this place must forevermore be a seat of learning. Those who attend this place will be taught the strictures of puritanism as decreed by our blessed Lord Protector Oliver Cromwell. They will restore his godly Commonwealth and bring forth everlasting glory to England.'

Fauconberg slashed down his sword. Bourcher's head separated from his shoulders and rolled like a bloodied bowling ball into the drainage ditch leading to the cesspits of Red House.

PART TWO

*"The secret of freedom lies in educating people,
whereas the secret of tyranny is in keeping them ignorant."*

— **Maximilien Robespierre**

CHAPTER 13

Red House School,
Cromwell dormitory,
February 1988

Sam Faulkner crammed the pockets of his dressing gown with three chocolate bars, two packets of fruit gums and a can of Coke. He crept over to the adjoining bed and roused the thirteen-year-old occupant who was asleep under his sheets and blankets, curled in the foetal position to ward off the brutal cold of the Yorkshire winter.

'Sullivan, wake up. It's midnight and time for the feast.'

Sullivan stirred and pulled his blankets back over his head. 'It's too cold,' he muttered. Faulkner grabbed hold of Sullivan's blankets and like a matador, stripped them from his bed with a flourish.

'Bastard,' muttered Sullivan.

'Get up and wake the others,' Faulkner insisted. He was already at the next bed and had stripped the covers from Cedric Humphries' bed. 'Humphries. Out of your sweaty pit! The midnight feast is on,' he said.

Five minutes later, twelve shivering boarders from the senior Cromwell dormitory had donned their dressing gowns and slippers, and were gathering their stash of sugary snack foods from hidden locations under and around their beds. Three of the boys held torches to guide their colleagues around the darkened dorm. Cromwell was the largest of Red House School's seven dormitories. It spanned half the length of the top-floor attic and had a bird's-eye view of the chapel roof from its eastern window.

'Keep the noise down and follow me,' Faulkner said as he walked towards the large chest of drawers that concealed the entrance to the secret passage. 'Delaney, give me a hand moving this chest of drawers,' he said to the largest of the boys. 'And move it quietly. We don't want to wake Bourcher,' he said, referring to the headmaster, whose living quarters was below their dormitory. The headmaster was a strict disciplinarian whose fondness for the cane bordered on brutality.

'I don't feel well,' said Humphries. He was a delicate child and his nerves were getting the better of him. 'I think I should go back to bed.'

'Don't be so wet,' replied Moody, a stocky Australian boy who had a taste for adventure and a nose for trouble. He had already felt the sting of Bourcher's cane three times that term.

Delaney and Faulkner eased the chest of drawers away from the wall to reveal a small, white-painted door about three feet high. The door was locked, but Moody had managed to pick the rudimentary lock several days before and had left it ajar.

'Last chance for anyone who wants to chicken out,' Faulkner said, daring his prep school colleagues to return to their beds.

Faulkner opened the door, which creaked on its rusty hinges. The smell of stale, fusty air hit them like a life force and several of the boys inched away from the fetid interior. He scanned the long, dusty passageway with his torch. At the far end of the passage was a small chamber. It was littered with the debris of generations of wayward schoolboys. Discarded sweet wrappers, fizzy drink bottles, old copies of *Beano* and a scattering of *Commando* war comics were strewn across the floor. Faulkner had never seen such an uninviting place in which to hold a midnight feast and a return to his bed appeared a more attractive proposition.

'What's it like?' said Moody, straining to see over Faulkner's shoulder.

'It's brilliant,' Faulkner lied. 'Follow me, everyone.' With a feeling of dread gripping his soul, he climbed through the narrow doorway and into the passage.

'This is bloody amazing,' Moody said in his Australian accent. 'Come on, guys,' he urged the hesitant thirteen-year-olds behind him.

Faulkner brushed away the layers of cobwebs that stuck to his sandy hair as he made his way forward into the gloom. He had to force himself to continue towards the cold, bare and uninviting chamber at the end of the passageway. Once there he settled himself on the grubby floor with his back to a brick column that he assumed was the chimney. His position gave him a view back along the corridor from which he had just come. He reached into his dressing-gown pocket and pulled out a Mars bar. Moody chose a spot on the opposite side of the chamber and slumped down with his back to the plastered wall. He kicked at the decades of detritus to clear a space for his feet and pulled a can of Coke from his pocket. 'Bloody bonza, hey?' he said between sips of Coke, and then burped to show his appreciation.

'Where are the others?' Faulkner said.

'They're coming,' said Moody. 'At least some of them anyway.'

'Here's Sullivan, Hodgson and Elliott. The rest must have chickened out,' said Faulkner.

'It's a bit spooky in here,' said Sullivan as he found a spot under the sloping roof. He tore open a packet of McVities Chocolate Digestive biscuits as he sought a hygienic place for his feet. He kicked away a 1960's copy of *Beano* with his slippered foot. 'And it smells of piss,' said Hodgson in his home counties accent. 'Whose idea was this anyway?'

'Stop your whingeing and sit down, Hodgson,' said Moody. 'And where are the others?'

'Humphries, Walters and the others have gone back to bed. They reckoned you'd made too much noise, and Bourcher was bound to hear.'

'Bourcher gives me the creeps,' said Moody.

There was a general nodding of assent as the boys tucked into their snacks.

'He's a complete psycho, if you ask me,' Moody continued. 'He gave Anderson six with the cane yesterday for talking after lights out.'

'Anderson told me Bourcher used a horse crop,' said Hodgson. 'I saw his bare backside in the changing room this afternoon as he was putting on his rugby shorts and it was covered in welts.'

'He shouldn't have been talking after lights out. It's against the rules,' said Elliott.

'Makes no difference,' said Moody. 'He'd find a reason to use the cane even if no-one had broken the rules.'

'I'm on three red initials,' said Sullivan, referring to the disciplinary system Bourcher had instigated. A list of the names of every boy in the school was displayed on a large clipboard in the terracotta tiled corridor known as the 'red passage'. A teacher or prefect could sign their initials in red ink against the name of any boy who had broken the rules during the term. In theory it was possible to get a blue initial for good behaviour, but such occurrences were rare. 'I've got a trip to the headmaster's study tomorrow.'

The boys chewed on their chocolate bars in silence and muttered their condolences to Sullivan.

'What did you get the red initials for?' asked Faulkner.

'Being late for chapel and not handing in my prep work on time.'

'Fair enough. And the third?'

'Insolence.'

'Who gave you that one?'

'Nigel Pride. Head prefect. He said I looked at him in an insubordinate manner, but I told him that's my natural expression.'

'Leave him to me. I'll teach him the meaning of insubordination,' said Faulkner.

'What're you going to do?'

'Crash-tackle him on the rugby field. He'll be limping for weeks.'

All the boys chuckled except Sullivan, who was shrouded in self-pity.

Faulkner's prowess on the rugby field was legendary. Pride, on the other hand, was more suited to academic and artistic pursuits than sporting endeavours. Pride's father, Sir Monty, was the Conservative Member of Parliament for Greater York and reputed to be one of the richest men in Britain. Pride Senior had donated money to the restoration of the school roof and funded a new gymnasium. Six months prior he had refurbished the riding stables to the extent that the school's horses were accommodated in greater comfort than the boys.

'Does three red initials always mean the cane?' Sullivan continued.

'Yeah,' said Moody. 'I've got the stripes on my arse to prove it.'

'Did it hurt?' probed Sullivan.

'I can't stop myself from larking around, so I'm an afficionado on the subject. Bourcher's got the chest and biceps of a boxing kangaroo on steroids. It was the worst pain I've ever experienced. I almost blacked out.'

'Did you deserve it?'

'If you count forgetting the date of the Battle of Bannockburn, then yeah. The history teacher, Captain McTavish, is obsessed with the battle for some reason and gave me three red initials on the spot.'

'I've often had three red initials, but Bourcher's never beaten me,' said Faulkner.

'Yeah, but you're the captain of the Rugby team,' said Hodgson.

'And you're on a low-income scholarship,' added Elliott.

'That's got nothing to do with it!' said Faulkner defensively.

'How did you get away with it then?' asked Sullivan.

'Has anyone got any Coke left?' Moody asked, belching softly.

'I've got some Fanta,' replied Elliott.

'That'll have to do.'

'I'll trade you for your Mars bar.'

'Done,' Moody replied, throwing his Mars bar to Elliott, who fumbled it in the dark. Elliott rolled the can of Fanta across the grubby floor to Moody.

'Bourcher will hear that, for Chrissakes,' said Hodgson.

'When I went to his study,' said Faulkner, continuing his story, 'he was flexing his cane, and he gave me the usual speech where he says "This is going to hurt me more than it will hurt you",' he said, trying to imitate the headmaster's overbearing voice. 'I stared straight into Bourcher's eyes and right into his deep, dark soul. Then for some reason he backed away.'

'You're so full of shit,' replied Moody as he swigged the rest of the Fanta and crushed the empty aluminium can in his hand. 'Bourcher doesn't have a soul. Come on, let's get out of here.'

'Too right,' said Hodgson. 'This place stinks like a cesspit.'

'K.V.' Faulkner said urgently, using the universal schoolboy warning code. It was derived from the Latin word *cave*, meaning beware.

'Someone's trying to get into the passageway. Torches out,' whispered Moody.

The boys held their breath in the pitch blackness and tried to make themselves invisible against the nooks and crannies of the hidden chamber. The creaking sound of rusting hinges at the end of the passageway filled the confined space.

'It's Bourcher!' Faulkner said urgently. 'He's coming up the passageway.' As if in confirmation, the light of a high-powered torch beam swept up the length of the passageway. Faulkner dropped to his left to avoid being caught in its beam. His head hit the lower section of the chimney, but instead of experiencing the harsh pain of the brickwork, he felt the much softer material of brick-veneer panelling. He heard the soft click of an ancient latch and then felt the motion of a hidden doorway within the chimney swinging inwards.

'Stay where you are!' commanded Bourcher. He was struggling to make headway through the narrow corridor. His broad shoulders made fast movement difficult, and the cobwebs were tangling in his thick black hair.

The boys scrambled in vain for cover. The chamber was bare except for discarded debris. Faulkner almost fell into the recess in the false chimney just as Bourcher entered the chamber where the boys were cowering. Bourcher swung his torch around the little room and picked out the miscreant boys like a prison guard from Colditz Castle. From within the cavity in the false chimney, Faulkner gathered his wits and eased the doorway closed behind him, making sure he did not activate the latch. The bright light of Bourcher's torch played over the chimney and specs of light flooded into Faulkner's cramped hollow.

'Where's Faulkner?' bellowed Bourcher. His voice boomed in the confines of the secret chamber.

'He didn't come in here with us,' Moody lied.

'He's not in his bed, so where is he?'

'I think he went to the toilets downstairs, sir,' said Hodgson.

'Before or after you boys decided to enter this forbidden and dangerous location?'

'He didn't come in here with us,' Moody repeated defiantly. He was as mystified as the others at Faulkner's sudden disappearance.

Bourcher continued to shine his torch into every recess of the chamber before accepting it would have been impossible for anyone to have escaped his notice. He turned towards the remaining boys and a leer spread across his face.

'Moody, Elliott, Hodgson and Sullivan. You've committed an act of reckless disobedience. You're going to learn a lesson you'll never forget. You're to report to my study in ten minutes where you'll each receive six strokes of the cane.'

Bourcher led the boys out of the narrow passageway and back to Cromwell dorm. He pointed to Humphries, who was cowering in his bed. 'You, boy! Humphries! When Faulkner gets back from the toilet, tell him to report to me at once. But if he's not back within ten minutes, you are to report to my study with the rest of the dormitory. Is that clear?"

'Yes, sir.'

Bourcher took a key from his pocket and locked the little door to the secret passage. For good measure he added a thick padlock he had brought with him from his study and clicked the lock into place. After surveying his handiwork, he manhandled the heavy chest of drawers so it blocked the door. Assured that no boy could get back in or out of the secret passageway, he focused on the prospect of meting out the impending punishment to the four terrified offenders. Not even the busybodies on the school's Board of Governors could object to the extreme retribution he had planned for them.

CHAPTER 14

Faulkner considered giving himself up. He had planned the midnight feast with Sean Moody and his sense of honour dictated he should share in the collective punishment, brutal as it would be. But his friends would consider it a small victory if he could outwit Bourcher. It would be a cat-and-mouse game. He knew the headmaster would use every means at his disposal to bring him to justice, even if it meant terrorising his friends into revealing his whereabouts.

When he was certain Bourcher had left the scene, Faulkner switched on his torch and scrambled out of the recess in the false chimney. He marvelled at the ingenuity of the seventeenth-century builders who had created such an ingenious hiding spot. He had heard about the priest holes from his history teacher, Captain McTavish, and imagined the false chimney was such a refuge.

Faulkner retraced his steps until he came to the small door that led to his dormitory. He pushed the door, but it would not move. With a rising sense of panic, he realised it had been locked from the outside. He tapped on the door, to alert the boys in the dormitory, but there was no response. Bourcher must have sent them all to his study to witness the humiliation of Moody, Sullivan, Hodgson and Elliott. Faulkner felt the confines of the dusty passageway press in on him like the coils of a python and he forced himself to think clearly. Whoever had designed this network of passages must have planned an alternative escape route.

Faulkner took several deep breaths, then headed back along the corridor to the false chimney and once more he scrambled into its recess. He shone his flickering torch around the confined cavity and let out a long sigh of relief when he discovered a double bend in the brickwork that led to a substantial bedroom. The room reminded him of an exhibit from the York Museum. The floor was covered in an inch of dust that billowed at his feet and cobwebs hung in clouds from the corners of the room. Rising emotions of curiosity and fear gripped his soul, but when his torch flickered and dimmed there was no doubt which emotion had the ascendancy. He slapped and shook the torch until a bright light shone from its beam once more.

He swung the torch around the room and hunted for a way out. As he did so he heard the muffled voice of Bernard Bourcher resonate through the thin floorboards in the room below. He was directly above the headmaster's study. He heard his own name mentioned followed by a prolonged silence.

'Loyalty is a noble thing,' Bourcher was saying. 'But I will ask you again: Where is Faulkner?'

Faulkner tiptoed to the middle of the room, trying not to disturb the dust. He stepped onto a loose floorboard, which creaked under his foot. To his hyper-sensitive brain, it resonated like a kettle drum in the Royal Albert Hall. He froze and waited for Bourcher's booming voice to shout out a challenge from the study below.

'Very well,' Bourcher said. 'If you insist on maintaining your silence, you can expect no leniency from me. Moody! Step forward.'

Faulkner continued searching the room for an exit. A wooden four-poster bed dominated the wall adjacent to the attic storage room. Decaying linen sheets and blankets were still in place, but centuries of dust, cobwebs and detritus made Faulkner shudder. A selection of mildewed books sat on a small bookshelf on the opposite wall, and two matching cots were nestled at the foot of the bed. He noticed a large wooden trunk positioned against the exterior wall below a pair of heavy wooden shutters. Despite his predicament, curiosity got the better of him and he headed towards the chest with the light-footed dexterity of a tightrope walker. He noticed neat copperplate writing etched on the lid, half-hidden by the dust. He wiped off the dust with his dressing-gown sleeve and read the name: *Lady Rebecca Slingsby.* Faulkner opened the creaking latches that held down the trunk's lid and shone his torch into the interior. He pulled his head away as the smell of mildew and rotting fabric assailed his senses. Scraps of silk from a seventeenth-century gown filled the trunk. Next to the gown were a pair of women's delicate leather shoes that were coming apart at the stitching. He pushed the clothing aside and pulled out a red velvet purse containing more than a dozen pieces of jewellery inlaid with precious and semi-precious stones. He threw the purse back in the trunk and leafed through sheafs of legal and personal documents before closing the lid in disappointment. He had been hoping to discover Civil War memorabilia, such as Colonel Fauconberg's legendary sword, Enlightener, which was rumoured to be a lost treasure of Red House.

Once more he heard Bourcher's booming but muffled voice resonate from the study down below. 'Bend over the desk, boy. This is going to hurt me far more than it will hurt you.'

'Yeah, right!' Faulkner said derisively. His eye was drawn to the two cribs at the foot of the bed. As he approached the first crib, the unmistakable sound of the swish of a cane rasped from beneath the floorboards at his feet. It was followed by a meaty 'thwack' as it landed on Moody's bare buttocks.

'One!' boomed Bourcher.

Faulkner headed towards the nearest crib and stared inside. It was empty and he moved to the second.

'Two.'

Faulkner gagged and covered his mouth as he stared at the centuries-old skeletal remains of a small child wrapped in a moth-eaten blanket. Its tiny teeth were set in a mocking grin and its empty eye sockets held Faulkner in an iron stare from which he could not tear his gaze.

'Three ... Four ... Five ...'

The wind blew hard and rattled the shutters on the far wall. Faulkner experienced a moment of terror and tried to keep his rising sense of panic under control. He imagined himself trapped in this sinister chamber with no food or light. He had to find an escape route before his torch gave out. He tore his gaze away from the second crib and walked back to the trunk under the shutters. He stood on the trunk and searched for a latch on the shutters.

'Six!'

Faulkner sighed with relief that Moody's torment had at last ended. He spotted the latch and grunted in satisfaction.

'Seven.'

'Bastard,' Faulkner muttered. Every child at Red House knew six strokes of the cane was the maximum permitted by the school governors. Then he frowned as he realised the latch had rusted through. Try as he might, he could not shift it.

'Eight.'

Faulkner decided he would use the metal butt of his torch to hammer the latch free. But timing was everything. Bourcher was nothing if not metronomic with his strokes, allowing six seconds in between each to allow the pain to build to a crescendo.

'Nine.' Faulkner crashed the end of his torch against the latch just as the ninth blow landed, but the latch would not budge.

'Ten ... Eleven.' The latch moved a fraction of an inch as Faulkner timed his blows of the torch to match Bourcher's strokes of the cane.

'Twelve.' The latch sprang open, and Faulkner pulled the old shutters inwards, revealing a small, windowless frame, just big enough for an adult to crawl through. The torch flickered and he realised the batteries would not last much longer.

'Let that be a lesson to you, Moody.'

'Yes, sir,' Moody replied in a tone that dripped with defiance.

'It is customary to thank me for your punishment, boy,' Bourcher said.

A gust of wind seeped into the bedroom, creating a minor dust storm. The opening was blocked by a thick layer of ivy that covered most of the façade of the southern wall. Faulkner separated the thick strands of ivy so he could climb through.

'Well?' Bourcher boomed. Faulkner could hear Bourcher's voice from his study window below.

'I don't believe that's appropriate, sir, seeing as you've given me double the number of strokes permitted by the governors,' Faulkner heard Moody respond to Bourcher. Faulkner felt pride that his friend could maintain such dignity in the face of Bourcher's brutality.

'Sullivan! Step forward and bend over the desk.' Sullivan was not cut from the same hard granite as Moody, and he could hear Bourcher's next victim whimpering in fear. Faulkner climbed onto the ledge of the window and surveyed his surroundings. His heart sank; there was a sheer drop of almost forty feet to a rose garden below. The wind was buffeting him as if trying to pull him to his death from the ledge. He shone his torch beneath the ledge and noticed a rusty iron rung protruding beneath the tangle of ivy. Before he could get a proper look, the light on his torch dimmed and faded to black. There was no way he could navigate the labyrinth of passageways and secret rooms in the dark so he would have to climb through the open window. He swung a leg into the inky blackness below. After several seconds of frantic scrambling, his foot touched the reassuring sturdiness of the iron rung. He reached up and pulled the brick-veneered shutters closed so as not to leave any evidence of his escape. The rusty latch clicked back into place, and he was committed to the perilous climb.

The wind plucked at his bulky dressing gown as he searched for a second rung. He breathed a sigh of relief as his slippered foot found it and he worked his way down the ladder. Mercifully, the sound of the caning in Bourcher's study was obscured by the howling wind. He reached a rung that had rotted through, but he managed to bypass the perished step. When his eyeline was parallel with Bourcher's study window, he leaned across and peered through the glass. The window had fogged up as all eleven boys from Cromwell dorm watched the humiliating spectacle. They had their backs to the window and Bourcher had worked himself up into a righteous fervour as he applied himself to his work, oblivious to those around him.

Bourcher had finished with Sullivan and was sweating profusely. He stripped off his jacket and stared at the window. Faulkner ducked his head back and flattened himself against the ladder. The ivy was thick, and he buried himself deep into its foliage.

'Open the window, Humphries,' Bourcher boomed. 'It stinks in here.' Bourcher was a fresh air freak and would prowl the dormitories after midnight, throwing open windows even in the dead of winter.

Humphries slid open the sash window. Seconds later, Bourcher's head appeared at the opening and he leaned out. He was less than two feet from where Faulkner was clinging to the rusty iron rungs. Bourcher breathed in the icy Yorkshire air while Faulkner stared down at the headmaster's bull-like head. Bourcher was indeed a powerful man. He wore thick, black-rimmed spectacles and his neck muscles bulged as he drank in the air. Bourcher filled his lungs once more, then marched back into the bowels of his study. 'Elliott, step forward!' he commanded.

Faulkner waited until Bourcher reached the third strike, then peered once more through the open window. The boys all had their backs to the window and were mesmerised by the brutal spectacle taking place in front of them. Bourcher's huge biceps rippled as he leaned into each stroke like a lumberjack felling an oak. Sweat poured from his brow as he battered his victim.

Faulkner took his chance. He swung his body to the right and placed both feet on Bourcher's windowsill. He was still more than twenty feet above the gravelled driveway and a slip would result in severe injury or even death. He let go of the ladder and grasped the underside of the open sash window, levering himself inwards towards the study. With the nimbleness of a cat, he landed lightly on his feet in the study behind the row of boys just as Bourcher landed his last stroke on Elliott's buttocks. Having completed his work, Bourcher stared into the distance with the rapt expression of a zealot experiencing a divine revelation.

'Let that be a lesson to you, boys. I will not tolerate disobedience. The school rules are sacrosanct and are there for your own protection.' He closed his eyes and put his hands together as if in prayer. 'Some boys took their punishment like men,' he said softly. 'That is to be commended. Physical punishment is character building, and the pain will bring you closer to God. Enduring this trial will guide you in your path towards wisdom and leadership. But there were those who did not express gratitude for their punishment, or snivelled like infants.' He looked at Moody and Sullivan. 'There will be no place in this school for those who lack moral fortitude.'

Faulkner composed himself and tried to meld with the boys. His heart was still racing from his perilous escape from the floor above. He shuffled next to Delaney, the stocky boy who had helped him move the chest of drawers covering the doorway to the secret passage. Delaney looked startled to see Faulkner standing next to him, but then smiled conspiratorially. He plucked a loose strand of ivy from Faulkner's hair and tossed the offending foliage out of the open window.

'Has anyone found Faulkner yet?' growled Bourcher menacingly. 'I want him in my study in the next five minutes. Mark my words, he will experience my wrath for his disobedience.'

'I'm here, sir,' said Faulkner.

Bourcher looked confused. 'How did you get here?'

'What do you mean, sir? I've been here all along.'

'But you weren't in your bed, and I didn't see you come into the study.'

Faulkner shrugged his shoulders as if he was not responsible for Bourcher's lack of awareness.

Bourcher glared at the boys, urging them to betray Faulkner, but the room remained silent.

'Oh, never mind,' Bourcher said. 'Cromwell dormitory, you are dismissed and let that be a lesson to you all.'

CHAPTER 15

Board of Governor's meeting, Red House School

'We've received an anonymous complaint, Bourcher. It simply won't do. We have our reputation to think of,' said Chairman of the Board of Governors, Sir Monty Pride.

'It must've come from that snivelling new matron, Agnes Gates,' replied Bourcher. 'I'll fire her first thing in the morning.'

The chairman sighed loudly. 'You can't just fire her on a whim. She will demand compensation, just like the last one. And we run the risk of her squealing to the press.'

'Perhaps we might address the cause of the complaint rather than shooting the messenger?' suggested the Reverend Kitchen. 'You know, the one about the frequency and savagery of the headmaster's beatings? Are they strictly necessary?'

'Indeed, they are,' responded Bourcher. 'The bible supports my position on this matter.' Bourcher put on his best Lawrence Olivier voice: '"Do not hold back discipline from the child. Although ye strike him with the rod, he will not die." Proverbs 23, verse 13. I'm trying to bring up a generation of young men who will follow in the footsteps of the Victorian Empire builders. You can't do that without giving them a damned good thrashing every now and then.'

'I see you're well versed on bible quotes relating to corporal punishment, Mr Bourcher. But I'm not convinced by a verse that's only redeeming feature is that we are stopping short of murdering the unfortunate children in your care.'

'The headmaster does have a point though,' countered Sir Monty. 'It's in our articles of association that we follow the moral strictures of Oliver Cromwell. Red House has won the Yorkshire prep schools seven-a-side rugby competition two years in a row. Our first fifteen has not lost a game since 1986, including the '87 tour of South Africa, Australia and New Zealand. Cromwell would've been proud of our achievements.'

'And we've gained a reputation for administrative excellence since Mr Bourcher replaced his father as headmaster five years ago,' chipped in John Green, the school's bursar. 'Our finances have improved by fifteen per cent year on year. I feel we must allow the headmaster some latitude with his disciplinary techniques if they continue to produce such excellent results.'

'Sean Moody has third-degree lacerations to his behind,' persisted the reverend. 'We can't ignore such brutality.'

'Has Moody complained?' asked Bourcher.

'Well, no, but ...'

Bourcher smiled. 'Then the only question is what do we do about the matron? I can't abide disloyalty.'

'We'll pay her off like we did with all the others,' sighed the exasperated chairman. 'But if I read any more "anonymous letters" about your overexuberant disciplinary techniques, then I will be accepting your offer of resignation. Do I make myself clear, Headmaster?'

'I would like it minuted that Sean Moody provoked me with his defiant attitude. That was why I was forced to give him *twelve* of the best.'

'Excuse me! Did I just hear you say twelve of the best?' said Professor Trindall, the academic standards officer, peering over his half-rimmed spectacles. 'Dear Lord! I thought we agreed six was to be the maximum?'

'Six for the original offence and another six for his back chat,' countered Bourcher.

'Can we please move on?' said Sir Monty.

'Where are we going to get another matron from?' said the Reverend Kitchen. 'The agency is refusing to send any more of their staff here. They find the atmosphere at Red House too oppressive.'

'Do we really need a matron?' said Bourcher. 'In my opinion, they're a bad influence on the boys. They distract them from their studies and make them soft.'

'For goodness' sake, Headmaster,' said the reverend. 'We're trying to produce the next generation of leaders, not stormtroopers for a future invasion of Poland. We need a matron to look after the boys' medical wellbeing and to ensure their pastoral care, especially the junior boys. The only other female on the staff is Miss Sharp, the piano teacher, and she's over eighty.'

'Pastoral care? What nonsense! Next, you'll be demanding hockey and netball is introduced into the sports curriculum,' thundered Bourcher. 'The boys are soft enough as it is.'

'With all due respect, some of these boys are as young as seven and won't see their mothers for ten months of the year, particularly those from the Commonwealth countries. Without the nurturing instinct of a matron, half these boys will develop deep-rooted psychological issues,' the reverend pressed.

'Perhaps I can offer a suggestion?' said the bursar. 'My goddaughter has just finished her A Levels and wants to study paediatric medicine at Cambridge University. She's been advised to take a gap year so she can get practical experience caring for children in an institutional environment.'

'She sounds perfect,' said the reverend.

'The boys would eat her for breakfast,' said Sir Monty.

'She's made of stern stuff,' replied the bursar, 'so she won't be intimidated by the boys. She's from an illustrious family and exudes a natural authority. Quite a looker too, by all accounts.'

'All the more reason to keep her away from the boys,' the headmaster scoffed.

'Eighteen is a bit young,' challenged Sir Monty. 'She should at least have a modicum of nursing experience.'

'Nonsense,' said Professor Trindall. 'We've hired at least four male gap-year students in the last ten years. The boys looked up to them because they could relate to them.'

'And the gap-year students don't torment the boys like the more senior members of staff,' said the reverend, glaring at Bourcher.

'What qualifications does she have?' asked the chairman.

'Straight A's in Biology, Physics and French. Her mother is chief surgeon at Guys Hospital in London and her father owns a pharmaceutical company. I think she cuts the mustard.'

'I don't see we have much choice. She starts on the first day of the Lent term,' said the chairman.

* * *

'Faulkner, what was the date of the Battle of Bannockburn?' said Captain McTavish, rolling the 'r' in 'Bannockburn' like a connoisseur savouring the finest Highland malt. He was a proud veteran of the Second World War, although his war record was never discussed.

'Sir, it was 1314.'

'Aye, correct, laddie. It was a day when the rivers ran red with English blood and the flower of Scotland, led by Robert the Bruce, avenged the misdeeds of Edward Longshanks.' McTavish gazed out of the window as if he were trying to re-imagine Scotland's golden age.

'I heard Robert the Bruce was a Yorkshireman,' Faulkner retaliated.

'Nonsense!' McTavish thundered back. 'Although I do admit he was descended from an Anglo-Norman family who had significant land holdings in Yorkshire.'

'Are you a royalist or a parliamentarian, sir?' Faulkner asked, trying to steer the history teacher away from the gory details of Scotland's most famous battle.

'We're all parliamentarians here,' McTavish said. 'It's in our charter.'

'But wasn't Red House built by the famous royalist cavalier Sir Henry Slingsby.'

'Aye it was. I shouldn't be telling you this, but Sir Henry was an honourable man who was executed for his principles. In some ways that made him a better man than Cromwell. That's why every pupil who leaves this place is referred to as an Old Cavalier.'

'Did Red House produce any great soldiers?'

'Aye. The best cavalry commander in the Civil War was Slingsby's steward, Colonel Samuel Fauconberg. He was the owner of the famous Enlightener sword, which was said to have separated over one hundred Puritan heads from their shoulders.'

'What happened to Fauconberg?'

'Fauconberg was tried for the murder of Benedict Bourcher during the chaos that preceded the restoration of King Charles the Second in 1660. He would have ended up on the gallows.'

'I thought he was a man of principle, like Slingsby?' said Faulkner. He felt devastated that one of his heroes from history was not as noble as he had once believed.

'He may have been a great soldier, but it's rumoured he went to his death a broken man for failing to repay his debt of honour to the Slingsby family.'

'Does the school have any other connections with the Civil War?' asked Moody.

'There are two boys in this school whose ancestors played decisive roles in the Civil War. One of them is sitting right here in this classroom.'

The boys looked around at each other. Nigel Pride, the head boy, grinned at his classmates.

'Indeed, our head boy, Mr Pride, is one of those.'

'What did Pride's ancestor do?' asked Faulkner.

'He was the instigator of Pride's Purge, the most infamous assault on democracy in British history. After Charles the First had been defeated and captured, most parliamentarians wanted to negotiate with the king to impose a just settlement, but Thomas Pride wasn't having it. On 6th December 1648, Pride and his militia prevented one hundred and forty moderate members of parliament from entering the debating chamber. The remaining eighty radical MPs voted to put the king on trial for treason. Two months later, King Charles was beheaded and so began eleven years of authoritarian rule.'

'Who's the other boy with a famous ancestor?' asked Elliott.

'None other than wee Jimmy Stuart,' replied McTavish. 'He's a new boy and an indirect descendant of the Stuart dynasty.'

'Could he be king one day?' asked Hodgson.

McTavish laughed. 'The last remaining Stuart monarch, Queen Anne, died childless in 1714. The royal Stuart line, including Bonnie Prince Charlie, died out a century later. But many believed their distant cousins had a much stronger claim to the throne than George of Hanover, who succeeded her. All fifty-six Stuart claimants were excluded from the line of succession because of their catholic beliefs. Jimmy Stuart may have more royal blood in his veins than our current monarch.'

'What did Mr Bourcher's ancestors do in the Civil War?' said Moody.

'Nothing of importance, although the elder Bourcher was one of the regicides who signed Charles the First's death warrant. The records state the younger Bourcher married Lady Rebecca Slingsby in 1660 and so his heirs inherited Red House. There was a long and bitter legal dispute surrounding the title deeds to the house. The Bourcher family claimed Rebecca Slingsby had signed the deeds over to them as a dowry. Rebecca's brothers stated the document was a forgery and the marriage never took place.'

'Surely Lady Slingsby herself could have settled the matter?' said Faulkner.

'That's what makes the whole mystery so interesting. There was a great storm over Red House on the night of the wedding and the chapel was hit by a lightning ball. Half of the congregation was killed, and Lady Rebecca's body was never found. The surviving witnesses were all pre-eminent councillors of York, and they vouched for Benedict Bourcher's version of events.'

'What about the rumours Rebecca Slingsby wasn't killed in the chapel but was burned as a witch in the stable yard?' asked Elliott.

'Those allegations were made by Colonel Fauconberg during his trial, but the councillors of York dismissed them as the ravings of a deranged and distraught mind.'

CHAPTER 16

The two first-year pupils knocked on the study door of head prefect, Nigel Pride, and his deputy, Michael Lambert. Despite the freezing Yorkshire weather, the new boys were wearing the light-blue corduroy shorts and long grey socks as prescribed by the school's uniform policy. As a nod to the three inches of snow that blanketed the school and its grounds, they were permitted a long-sleeved grey shirt, and a grey pullover with black-and-white piping around the neckline.

Their crime had been to skip the compulsory early morning cold shower designed to toughen up the boys. Long queues of shivering boys were compelled to snake their way under the row of six icy-cold showers at a slow walking pace. Any boy who rushed through would be required to suffer a second cold shower.

Like most new boys, known by their fellow students as 'ticks', they came from well-to-do families. But at Red House they found themselves at the bottom of the social hierarchy and thrown into a spartan regime of cold showers, prison-style food and a disciplinary system reminiscent of the nineteenth-century British Army.

'Yes? What is it?' came the muffled reply from inside the head prefect's study known as the 'captain's cabin'.

'It's Mattingly and Stuart. You asked us to report to your study.' Mattingly's timid voice was barely audible. He was eight years old but looked much younger.

'What? Oh, the two ticks. Give me a minute.' Strange rumbling sounds emanated from within the study before the door opened. 'Well, don't just stand there. Come in,' came the exasperated voice of the head prefect.

Mattingly and Stuart walked into the study with trepidation. Two beds on opposite sides of the room were unmade and soiled clothing littered every corner of the room. Unwashed plates and dishes lay scattered throughout the study, some of which were growing strange fungal life forms. The smell in the study was palpable and had a pungency rivalled only by the riding stables.

Lambert sneered at the two terrified new boys. He had entered puberty at twelve years of age and was the only boy in the school who could boast a five o'clock shadow. He had a voice like the singer Barry White and a domineering presence on the rugby field. His lack of intellect was countered by his intense loyalty to Nigel Pride.

Pride matched Lambert for height but his physique was as delicate as a ballet dancer, earning him the sobriquet 'Giraffe Pride'. He had a long beak of a nose on which was perched a pair of wire-rimmed spectacles.

'What did you say your names were, ticks?' asked Pride.

'Mattingly,' said the red-haired boy.

'Stuart,' squeaked the smaller of the two youngsters. He had long, blond, curly hair that had somehow missed the attentions of the school barber. His doe-like eyes had misted over and he sniffled miserably. He longed for the comforts of home, the warm embrace of his mother and the attentions of his doting but annoying younger sister.

'Ah, yes. The two boys who skipped their cold showers. It simply won't do. We must maintain the highest possible standards. How do you expect to become high achievers if you don't take your cold showers?'

'Don't know,' admitted Mattingly.

'How many red initials are you on, Mattingly?' said Lambert, cutting to the chase.

Mattingly looked downcast. 'Two.' He was caught like a rat in a trap. Bourcher did not discriminate between delicate eight-year-olds and hardened senior boys like Moody when it came to matters of discipline.

'And you?' he said, staring at Stuart.

'None,' whispered Stuart, quaking.

'Then consider it your lucky day, because we're not going to give you a red initial or send you to Bourcher's study,' said Pride.

'Thank you,' said Stuart, his eyes brimming with gratitude. Mattingly looked suspiciously at Pride and Lambert.

'But we cannot let this act of defiance go unpunished,' continued Pride. 'You need to learn the values Mr Bourcher believes are necessary for Red House pupils. Those values include respect for your elders and betters, piety, hard work and orderliness. You can start by cleaning up our study during the lunch break.' Pride picked up one of Lambert's stiff, muddied rugby socks lying in the middle of the floor and tossed it into the pile of discarded clothing in the corner. 'You can take this pile of dirty clothing to the laundry basket, wash the dishes and take them back to the refectory. When you've finished that you can make the beds and clean the stains on our desks with a cloth and some disinfectant. We expect this study to be spotless when we return from rugby practice.'

Mattingly looked horrified at the prospect of being treated like a domestic servant. His father was a high court judge. He jutted out his chin and stared defiantly at the head prefect. 'The new matron, Miss Vavasour, says the juniors shouldn't have to do chores for the prefects. She said it's demeaning.'

'Does she really?' replied Pride. 'And does she know my father is Chairman of the Board of Governors and that I could have her sacked with a simple phone call?'

'Don't know,' mumbled Mattingly, looking down at the floor.

'We'll soon set her straight on that matter. We can't have the matrons running around telling ticks like you what the head prefect can and cannot do. It's absurd.'

'Matron says cold showers in the middle of winter will make us all sick,' continued Mattingly.

'Ah, so it was the new matron who encouraged you to skip your cold shower, was it? Mr Bourcher will be interested to hear that the new matron is undermining discipline among the ticks.'

'No, it wasn't!' Mattingly shook his head vigorously.

'Let me teach you some simple facts of life. The matron has one job to do and that's to hand out cough mixture to the boys in the surgery after prep. She has no say on school matters. She does not teach, coach rugby or run any school activities. And if you go back to matron to complain, then we'll know you're a sneak. And because she is a woman, with no power, no-one is going to listen to her anyway. Now, be sensible and do as you're told.'

Mattingly remained silent.

'Then, you give me no choice. As head prefect I'll be giving you a red initial, which means you'll be reporting to Mr Bourcher's study to explain your behaviour. You know what that means?'

Mattingly nodded his head but refused to show remorse.

'You, boy,' he pointed towards Stuart. 'You can clean our study during the lunch break.'

'On my own?' Stuart looked aghast at the magnitude of the task. 'I don't want to touch those filthy socks.'

'Well, they're not going to pick themselves up, are they?' Pride looked across at Lambert and shook his head sadly. 'What's the world coming to? The ticks have lost all respect for their superiors and need to be taught the natural order of things.'

* * *

There was a record turnout at Rebecca Vavasour's evening surgery. Word had spread that the new matron was young, pretty, and had taken a keen interested in the boy's welfare.

Faulkner joined the long queue and waited in line as dozens of boys presented her with an array of ailments both real and imaginary. Most complained of a sore throat, which necessitated the administration of a teaspoon of cough mixture, while others proudly showed her their rugby bruises and sprains like medals of honour.

Faulkner arrived at the front of the queue and showed his right hand to Rebecca Vavasour. The joint of his thumb was swollen and bruised after a mistimed tackle during the afternoon's victory over their fierce rivals, Aysgarth School.

'Ah, the gallant captain of our First XV rugby team has suffered a battle injury,' said Rebecca, taking his hand and examining it closely. It's Sam Faulkner, isn't it?'

'Yes, Miss Vavasour.' He was flattered she knew his name after only one week at the school. 'I messed up a tackle. Their number eight caught me with a fend and I couldn't use my shoulder to bring him down properly. Then he trod on my hand as he fell.'

'Yes, I watched the game. It was extraordinary. You danced through the opposition almost at will and scored three tries. I believe you could go all the way to the top with the right encouragement.'

'Thank you, Miss Vavasour.' Faulkner blushed at her compliment.

'We need to bring out that bruise,' she said, happy to have a genuine injury to treat. 'I'm going to apply *Arnica montana* cream to your thumb to reduce the bruising, then bind it up to give it support. The bindings will need to be changed daily, so you'll have to return to surgery for the next three days. Is that okay?'

'Yes, ma'am,' Faulkner said, scarcely believing his luck.

'I was checking out the sports facilities. I've convinced the sports master, Mr Fox, to form a school hockey team. He wasn't happy to start with, but he eventually agreed.'

'Good grief. Foxy is a rugby man through and through. How did you manage that?'

'I told him I would coach the team. I was captain of the Yorkshire girls' under-eighteen side.'

Faulkner gazed into her emerald-green eyes with newfound respect. She had finished rubbing ointment onto the bruise and was applying strips of gauze around his thumb. Her hands felt soft and warm, and her touch induced a strange tingling sensation throughout his entire body that he had never experienced before. 'What position did you play?' he asked.

'Centre half. Yorkshire won the national championships twice while I was in the team.'

'That's so cool.' Faulkner felt a tribalistic bond with Rebecca, and pride that she had won two trophies for his beloved Yorkshire. 'I've never played hockey but I'd like to give it a try.' Then he had to correct himself. 'After the Yorkshire schoolboys seven-a-side rugby tournament has finished, of course.'

'You'd be most welcome. The trials start after half-term.' Rebecca cut off the surplus gauze with scissors and tied a knot in the end. 'Is that too tight?'

'No, it feels good. What other sports do you play, ma'am?'

'I competed at national level in show jumping but I didn't win any medals.' She reached for the roll of sticking plaster and pulled off a long length, which she cut into four separate strips. 'Mrs Green, the bursar's wife, wants me to take over the riding classes for the junior boys.'

'I enjoy riding,' Faulkner said a little too quickly. He had given up riding the previous year to focus on rugby, but now he felt a renewed wave of enthusiasm for the activity. 'Why are your classes only for the juniors?'

Rebecca smiled. A ringlet of chestnut-coloured hair escaped from her chignon, and she pushed it back into place using a feminine gesture that played havoc with Faulkner's senses. He became aware of her intoxicating scent and noticed for the first time the delicious curves of her body and her long, slender legs. Faulkner found himself blushing once more at her smile, but she seemed not to notice.

'I've noticed the junior boys seem to be carrying the weight of the world on their shoulders, when they should be carefree and enjoying this stage of their lives. Some of them look scared out of their wits. I can talk to them during their riding lessons.' Rebecca wound the first strip of the sticky tape around his thumb and picked up another strip.

'They'll be fine,' said Faulkner. 'It didn't do me or my friends any harm.'

'You may feel that way now, but who knows what psychological harm your classmates may experience in later life?' she said as she weaved an artistic pattern of tape around his thumb. She smoothed the resulting masterpiece down with her slim fingers.

'I don't understand. Mr Bourcher says strict discipline will make us better leaders.'

'It'll make you resilient – and that's a fine quality in a young man. But there are other leadership qualities you should learn, such as compassion, empathy and even humility. Without those virtues you could become overbearing and self-obsessed. If you want to be a successful rugby captain, then your teammates need to know you care about their accomplishments more than you care about your own.'

'So, the seniors won't be able to ride with you?'

Rebecca laughed. 'I might need one or two of the seniors to help me out. Perhaps you could organise a roster for me?'

'Of course,' Faulkner said. He would ensure his own name would be top of the list.

CHAPTER 17

'How am I expected to play in boots as filthy as these?' Lambert said, holding out his size eleven Adidas boots to Stuart. He loomed over the terrified youngster to emphasise the enormous discrepancy in their height and weight. 'It'll put the school to shame, and it'll be your fault.'

'But I've got to finish my Latin comprehension. Mr Grimshaw wants it by five o'clock and I'm only halfway through.'

'Don't be so wet, Stuart,' piped in Pride. He was sitting at his desk building an Airfix model of the German battleship *Bismarck*. 'I've heard you're a swot, so you'll finish it in plenty of time.'

'But I've already cleaned your room and made your beds.'

They were interrupted by a knock at the door. 'Oh, what is it now?' Pride yelled at the door. 'We're busy. Go away!'

A more insistent, louder knock suggested the visitor would not be dissuaded.

'Bloody ticks won't leave us alone,' Pride muttered to Lambert. 'Come in then, if you must,' he said to the unwelcome visitor.

The door handle turned and Rebecca Vavasour entered the study. Her nose wrinkled at the stench in the room. She marched across to the window and levered it open. A blast of chilly air streamed into the study.

'Um, women are not allowed in the boys' bedrooms,' Pride said nonchalantly. He glued a scaled-down, fifteen-inch gun to the turret of the *Bismarck* and placed it to one side.

'Your study does not classify as a bedroom during daylight hours, and I have reason to believe you've been cajoling Mr Stuart here into carrying out demeaning domestic duties for you. Mr Bourcher banned this abhorrent practice at my insistence last week.'

'That's simply not true. Stuart's not doing any domestic duties for us,' Pride retorted.

'Then why is he holding a pair of muddy rugby boots twice his size?'

'There are traditions at this school that do not concern matrons,' Pride replied. He picked up the plastic gun turret and placed it securely onto the foredeck of the *Bismarck.*

Rebecca reached across and took the Airfix model from Pride's hands. 'It's either Miss Vavasour or ma'am to you, young man. It's time you learned a bit of respect. Is it not customary in this school for boys to stand up when an adult enters the room?'

'Yes, but you're just a—'

'Then stand up.'

Pride sighed but clambered to his feet.

'You too, Mr Lambert.'

Lambert stood and, as was his custom, used his considerable bulk to overshadow his visitor.

'Mr Lambert, you're in obvious need of a shower. You can stand next to Mr Pride.'

'Yes, ma'am.' He sniffed at his own armpits to check the veracity of her statement.

'Were you or were you not intimidating Mr Stuart into carrying out domestic duties for you?'

'No, Miss Vavasour. Stuart asked to clean my boots because he enjoys it,' Lambert lied.

'Is that true?' Rebecca said, looking at the new boy.

Stuart looked at Lambert and Pride, then at Rebecca to assess which way the balance of power was tilting. 'No, ma'am,' he said eventually. 'Lambert made me do it.'

'You little sneak!' Pride glared at the new boy.

'I'm giving you both a red initial and you're banned from having any boys under the age of eleven in your study. Is that clear?' said Rebecca.

'Yes, ma'am,' said Lambert.

'You can't give me a red initial,' said Pride, horrified. 'I'm the head prefect and—'

'... your father is the MP for Greater York and the Chairman of the Board of Governors,' Rebecca completed Pride's sentence for him. 'I've heard it all before and it cuts no ice with me. This school does not operate in isolation from society. There are school inspectors, courts of law or even newspapers that have a say in how our schools are run.'

'But if you give me a red initial, my father will kill me,' pleaded Pride.

'I doubt it,' replied Rebecca. 'But I'm willing to give you boys a choice. You can accept a red initial, or you can complete a duty roster with the rest of the boys.'

'Really?' Pride said, not believing his luck. 'What do we have to do?'

'The two of you can muck out the stables tomorrow with the fourth formers during your lunch break. They haven't had a good scrub in weeks.' Rebecca scanned the room and wrinkled her nose. 'But by the state of your study, you will be quite at home among the filth and squalor.'

'Mucking out the stables? I'm not doing that! That's a job for the ticks, not the head prefect.'

'Suit yourself,' said Rebecca, walking out of the study.

* * *

'Why on earth did you volunteer to babysit a dozen ticks on a horse ride?' said Moody as he wrestled to keep his stallion, Black Star, under control. Black Star was evil-tempered and prone to bolting back to the stables at the first sign of weakness from his rider. Moody was an accomplished rider, but even he was struggling with the wayward horse.

Faulkner nodded in the direction of Rebecca Vavasour, who was guiding a terrified eight-year-old on a leading rein.

'You dirty old man,' quipped Moody. 'The boys in the first-fifteen rugby team reckon you're going soft. Next thing you'll be trialling out for her hockey team.'

'As a matter of fact, I will be. But not until the Yorkshire seven-a-sides are over.'

Moody laughed. 'Don't get too carried away. She may not be here much longer. I've heard Bourcher can't stand her. He thinks she's undermining discipline and corrupting the values of Red House.'

'Where did you hear that?'

'You really have had your head in the clouds, haven't you, Faulkner? Apparently, Pride complained to Bourcher that she entered the head prefect's study without permission.'

'So, it's okay for Pride to treat the ticks like slaves, but when he gets caught out, he goes squealing to Bourcher?'

'That's the system. If anything upsets the local MP's son, just stand back and watch the fireworks go off.'

Faulkner turned right into the hundred-acre wood that was

part of the Red House Estate and waited while Moody wrestled with Black Star.

'You don't notice because you're part of the system. The captain of the First XV has privileged status,' said Moody once he had Black Star under control. Black Star stopped in his tracks and decided to feast on the lush grass by the gate. 'Come on, you brute,' Moody yelled as he pulled Star's head up and cajoled him into the woods.

'That's not true,' replied Faulkner. 'I'm a rebel, like you.'

'Then why have you never seen the inside of Bourcher's cane cupboard? I get that privilege every month and my backside looks like something you'd find in an abattoir.'

'I told you. I can stare him down... and I don't get caught.'

'I hate to break it to you, Faulkner, but Bourcher has picked you out as a leader of his fourth Reich or whatever system he imagines will make Britain great again. As the captain of the First XV, which hasn't lost a game in three years, you validate his brutal methods.'

They rode in silence for twenty minutes through the woods before they reached a wide trail that ran between the tall pine trees. It was arrow-straight and continued for a mile. It was the perfect place for a gallop. Rebecca was fifty yards ahead and struggling to control the twelve hyperactive ticks on their ponies. Two had meandered away from the group and were heading towards a dense and foreboding clump of pine trees, like lemmings to a cliff edge. Rebecca signalled to Faulkner and Moody to catch up with the pack.

'Faulkner and Moody. I brought you along so you could help me control the juniors. Will you please do so?'

'Sorry, Miss Vavasour,' Faulkner replied. He yelled at the two giggling ticks who had meandered into the woods and were riding towards a peat bog. It took him just two minutes to round up the strays. 'Have some respect for your riding instructor,' he told them, then winked to show them he was not chastising them.

'Which one of you boys would like to race me to the end of the trail and back?' said Rebecca.

Faulkner looked at Moody. Black Star had just tried to nip one of the first-year boy's legs with his vicious yellow incisors. 'I'll buy you a Mars bar if you let me race Miss Vavasour,' he pleaded with Moody.

Moody sighed loudly. 'Go on, then, but if she wins you must take on my kitchen duty roster for a week.'

'It's a deal.'

Faulkner swung his horse around so it was level with Rebecca's chestnut mare. Her horse, Juniper, was a fine-looking Holsteiner with a white flash on her withers. Rebecca had owned the horse since childhood and brought it with her to Red House. Faulkner realised Rebecca's superior horsemanship would give her an advantage, although Juniper was a show jumper rather than a racer and was getting on in years. Faulkner's stallion, Bullet, was a reddish-brown American quarter horse in its prime, and known for its explosive turn of speed over short distances. Faulkner knew he would have little control of Bullet once his horse reached a full gallop. His racing strategy would be to hang on for dear life and wrestle the horse around for the return run.

Moody raised his arm. 'On your marks!'

Faulkner felt a quiver of anticipation run through his mount and he sensed the raw power of the American quarter horse beneath him. He glanced across at Rebecca, who was wearing an expression of studied concentration. Her lustrous hair spilled from under her riding hat and her eyes were set straight ahead. Adrenaline surged through his body, and it was not in anticipation of the race.

'Get set,' Moody continued.

'Pay attention,' Rebecca rebuked Faulkner, 'or you'll fall off.'

Faulkner nodded, embarrassed that Rebecca had caught him staring at her. He tried to focus on the task at hand.

'Go!'

Rebecca took an immediate lead as Faulkner dithered in the saddle. Realising his pride was on the line, he kicked Bullet a little too hard in the ribs. Bullet accelerated from a standing start like a hot rod in a drag race, causing Faulkner to lurch backwards in the saddle. He swayed like a drunkard and his left foot slipped from the stirrup. His centre of balance listed to the right as Bullet chased down Juniper like a guided missile. Bullet veered right to overtake Juniper, catapulting Faulkner to the left and almost throwing him from the saddle.

The end of the track loomed into view and Faulkner hauled at the reins to stop his horse from crashing into the dense wood beyond. But he was too late, and he found himself whipped by low-hanging branches from the pine trees. The track had transformed into a muddy bridle path and Bullet was slipping on the treacherous surface. Faulkner managed to regain control and located his left foot back into the stirrup. As he manoeuvred Bullet around, Rebecca reached the end of the trail, executed a graceful turn on Juniper and began her home run. It took Faulkner ten precious seconds to emerge from the wood and regain the trail. Rebecca appeared to have gained an insurmountable lead.

Faulkner spurred Bullet into a gallop and this time he was ready for the horse's sudden acceleration. 'Let's go, Bullet,' he whispered as he crouched low in the saddle. Rebecca was already halfway to the finishing line and the ticks were cheering like banshees. Moody was attempting to clear them away from the path of the oncoming horses like a sheepdog rounding up a troublesome flock.

Bullet's hooves danced over the trail in a blur as he reached top speed and Faulkner felt the exhilaration of the wind in his face and the raw power of the horse beneath him. Juniper was tiring as the finish line approached and Faulkner still had a fighting chance of catching Rebecca. He urged Bullet on and heard the squeals of excitement from the first-year boys as he closed the gap. He drew level just as Moody dropped his arm to signal the race was over.

'Who won? Who won?' clamoured the ticks as Rebecca and Faulkner slowed down their horses, and then turned back around to join the throng at the finishing line.

'Um ... it was very close,' Moody said, unable to split the two riders.

Faulkner suspected Rebecca had won by the finest of margins but waited for confirmation from his friend.

'Um ...'

'It was Faulkner by a nostril hair,' Rebecca exclaimed to the excited boys. A few of the ticks, who were star-struck by their new matron, booed in a light-hearted manner while others cheered for Faulkner.

'I think Miss Vavasour may have ...' Faulkner said, attempting to be gallant.

'Nonsense,' replied Rebecca firmly. 'Although, how you

managed to cling onto Bullet on the outward leg will remain one of life's great mysteries. We'll have to brush up on your horsemanship, Mr Faulkner.'

'Yes, ma'am,' Faulkner replied. The prospect of additional horse riding lessons with Rebecca was a delicious proposition.

'You do realise that was the closest Bullet has ever come to losing a race?' Moody said to Faulkner.

The early spring sunshine peeked from behind the clouds, and they rode past a clutch of snowdrops on the side of the bridle path leading back to the entrance to the woods. Black Star kicked at a Shetland pony on which was perched a tiny new boy, who burst into tears. Rebecca calmed the tearful child, and then rode to Faulkner's side.

'Keep your back straight, Sam, and hold your reins close to the saddle. You're not auditioning for a Hollywood cowboy movie.'

'Yes, ma'am,' Faulkner said as he adjusted his posture. It was the first time a member of staff had used his Christian name in five years and his chest swelled with pride. He noticed Bullet responded to his upright posture by changing his gait.

'That's much better. The two of you make a handsome pair. A horse responds to a confident tone and an authoritative posture. The horse will also respond well to kindness and the knowledge that the two of you are part of a team. They're no different from humans in that regard.'

'Did I really win the race?' Faulkner asked.

'Maybe. But that wasn't the point.'

'What do you mean?'

'Did you feel the exhilaration of testing yourself to the limit? Did you realise winning is not about bulldozing your way to victory, but having a strategy?'

Faulkner nodded. 'Bullet should have won by a mile and yet Juniper lead for most of the race.'

'Exactly. And what is your strategy for winning the Yorkshire schools seven-a-side rugby competition?'

'We've worked on a few moves and practised our tackling.'

'Those are tactics and skills. You need a strategy. When I captained the Yorkshire girls' hockey team, we had a strategy for each team we played and for winning the overall competition.'

Faulkner was intrigued. 'What was your strategy?'

'We were the smallest and most inexperienced team in the competition, but we used our superior fitness levels and speed to our advantage. Our forwards pressed the opposition defenders into making mistakes so our strong midfield could play most of the game in the opposition's half. That nullified our own weaknesses in defence.'

They arrived at the gate to the woods and guided the ticks onto the lane leading to Red House. Moody had taken to his role as sheepdog with passion and was mustering the stragglers.

'Why did you decide to spend a year at Red House?' Faulkner asked the matron.

'My family has strong connections with Red House, going back to the days of Sir Henry Slingsby. I wanted to absorb the atmosphere and do some research into my heritage.'

'What do you think of the school?'

Rebecca frowned at the question as if something was on her mind, but then smiled at Faulkner. 'I think you are a fine cohort of young men, and you live on a beautiful estate.'

'But something is troubling you?'

Rebecca was silent for a while, and then she sighed. 'Never lose your free spirit, Sam, or your independence of thought.'

'Are you saying we can't think for ourselves?'

'The school is training you to be the leaders of the future, but in a very draconian way. I fear some of you will emerge overly entitled and too obedient to authority.'

Faulkner bristled at her words. 'But the boys are proud of what we've achieved here. For such a small school we have one of the best sporting and academic records in Yorkshire.'

'You have every right to be proud, Sam. But the values you're being taught are from a bygone age. The British Empire has gone and it's not coming back, despite what Bernard Bourcher may wish. The leaders of the future will be respectful of others and will be comfortable with all segments of society. They will encourage those who are less fortunate than themselves but still love their country and its democratic values. If you don't understand that, you'll stand out like a museum relic.'

'Bernard Bourcher tells us the unemployed are lazy wastrels and the sick are a drain on society. Only hard work, discipline and piety will save the country.'

'Do you really believe that, Sam?' Rebecca studied her protégé as she awaited his answer.

Faulkner shook his head. 'I think Bourcher's a psycho. I can't take anything he says seriously.'

'But others do. And some will be indoctrinated by his values. The boys look up to you, Sam, much more than they do Pride and Lambert. That's why I'm asking you to stay true to your values – for their sakes.' She pointed to the swarm of ticks behind her who had lost all semblance of control and were reenacting Custer's Last Stand on their ponies. 'Do you understand?'

'I think so,' Faulkner answered uncertainly. They rounded a corner in the road and the imposing sight of Red House came into view. Moody spurred Black Star into a trot and caught up with Faulkner and Rebecca. The road was narrow, and the three horses bunched together. Faulkner's leg pressed against one of Rebecca's black leather riding boots and delicious jolt of energy ran through him. He struggled to make sense of this strange physical longing for the elegant woman on her chestnut mare. He felt himself blushing and steered Bullet to the right, to end the physical contact that had caused his bewildering feelings, but then he felt empty and disappointed when they were gone.

'Are you okay? You look a bit hot and bothered,' Moody said to Faulkner.

'It must be the after-effects of the race.'

'Well, I hope it's not the flu,' Moody said. 'The seven-a-side tournament starts in two weeks.'

'Thank you, boys, for looking after the juniors,' Rebecca said as they approached the stables.

'If the ride had lasted any longer, I would've needed psychotherapy,' Moody replied with a grin.

They rode past the rear of the main school building and the grassy oval on which the children relaxed during their breaks. A concrete strip had been embedded in the middle so that a cricket net could be erected during the summer months. To the left of the oval was the school's stable yard, which housed the science lab and a row of cottages, as well as the stable block. They rode under the imposing archway on which was displayed the school clock, and then dismounted from their horses in the stable courtyard.

'You two can take your horses into the stables while I look after the young ones,' Rebecca said. 'When you're done, please return here and help me unsaddle their ponies.'

Faulkner felt his cheeks flush with heat once more, but this time the heat source seemed to emanate from the far corner of the stable yard. The heat felt like a physical fire and threatened to singe his skin. He swayed with sudden delirium, and he experienced an overwhelming sense of déjà vu. His emotions seemed wracked with utter despondency and the world seemed to turn black around him. His lungs choked with the smell of acrid smoke and his skin felt drenched with rain, even though his rational mind knew it was a fine spring day. A distant, pitiful female voice filled his head. He struggled to make sense of her words, but they were indistinct and archaic. Then the inexplicable sensations vanished as suddenly as they had arrived, leaving him feeling distraught and frightened, but craving to hear the soft, beguiling voice once more.

CHAPTER 18

Moody knocked on the door of the sick bay, located upstairs next to the headmaster's living quarters.

'Come in,' replied Rebecca. She was wearing a surgical face mask and was seated on the edge of Faulkner's bed. She dipped a damp flannel in a bowl of water and mopped her patient's brow.

'I've brought him some trash mags to read and some biscuits,' said Moody. 'How's he doing?'

Rebecca indicated Moody should put on a face mask from the shelf of surgical supplies.

'He's caught Romanian flu from somewhere,' Rebecca said. 'One of the symptoms is a high temperature, which may have caused his hallucinations. It's lucky you managed to steady him before he fell onto the cobbles in the stable yard.'

'Do you think he'll be fit for the rugby sevens?' Moody said, with a concerned look. Moody was the team's scrum half and had developed an almost telepathic understanding with his captain and fly half.

'It's possible. He's a fit young man, but he caught a severe dose of the flu, and won't have much time to recover.'

'Have any other boys caught the flu?'

'No, it's strange. Usually in a boarding school, when one boy catches it, then it spreads like wildfire. It's lucky we managed to isolate him before he became infectious. Ah, he's waking up now.'

Faulkner opened his eyes and scanned the sick bay as if trying to recall where he was. His throat was still sore, and his mouth and nostrils felt as if he had been smoking cigars. He recognised Moody and Rebecca, and smiled.

'Can I leave now?' he asked Rebecca. 'I feel much better.'

Rebecca put her hand on his forehead. 'You still have a temperature. We'll keep you here overnight, and then see how you feel in the morning. Sean has brought you some Hobnobs.'

Faulkner ignored the biscuits but grabbed one of the three war comics that lay on the table next to his bed and read the title: '*Panzer onslaught*. Cool,' he said.

Rebecca frowned. 'Those trash mags will rot your brain. I think I should replace them with classical literature. How about

Charles Dickens, or something by the Bronte sisters?'

Faulkner pulled a face and Rebecca laughed. 'I can see you're getting much better. We should have you out of here in a day or two.'

* * *

Bernard Bourcher stalked the corridors like a leopard in search of prey. The juniors were in their dormitories, while the senior boys were completing their prep or engaging in small talk in the library. Two fifth formers were engrossed in a game of chess; others were writing letters to their parents, who were based in various corners of Britain and the Commonwealth. A small knot of boys leafed through their stamp albums and bartered with each other.

Bourcher stood in the doorway of the library, his presence dark and threatening. The boys stiffened like impalas, sensing the presence of an unwelcome predator. The smell of stale whisky hung heavily on Bourcher's breath and the fifth formers knew from bitter experience this presaged the threat of imminent violence. Bourcher swayed as he scanned the library for evidence of a misdemeanour. A minute passed by and only the ticking of the library clock could be heard.

'Carry on, boys,' Bourcher muttered at last.

'Goodnight, Mr Bourcher,' the fifth formers sang out in unison. Their relief was palpable.

Bourcher turned and staggered down the terracotta tiled passage until he reached the display shelf. Dominating the centre of the shelf was the initial board. He reached for the board, but it slipped from his grasp and clattered onto the red tiles just as Moody rounded the corner. Moody considered backtracking to the relative safety of the main staircase before Bourcher could make eye contact, but he was half-a-second too late.

'Well don't just stand there, boy. Pick it up.'

'Yes, sir.' Moody approached the swaying headmaster and picked up the board, which bore half-a-dozen blue initials and a plethora of red ones.

'The winds of change are blowing, Moody. The winds of change are a-blowing.'

'Yes, sir,' Moody repeated. He gagged at the noxious

combination of sweat, cheap cologne and stale whisky that hung over the headmaster like a cloud of gnats. Moody trod carefully through the metaphorical eggshells that symbolised the headmaster's volatile state of mind.

'A powerful force is sweeping the land. The feeble-minded and the insidious do-gooders tremble before its might. A new Jerusalem is being built right here in the Vale of York, Moody.'

Moody had heard the drunken monologue many times before and it usually presaged a vicious beating for some unfortunate child. His brain scrambled to work out an exit strategy. 'Yes, sir. I was just heading to the library to finish my prep. It's due first thing in the morning.'

'Check the initial board, boy. Has anyone received three red initials?'

'No, sir.' Moody sensed Bourcher's disappointment at his answer.

'How many initials do you have, Moody?' Bourcher was not averse to lowering his threshold from three to two red initials when he was in a predatory mood.

'Two, sir.'

'Two! That simply won't do. Would you care to explain yourself, boy?' The leopard had selected its prey.

'They're both blue. One was for full marks in maths and the second was for looking after the ticks during riding lessons.' Moody tried not to look too smug. His recent good disciplinary record owed more to good fortune than any change in his attitude.

'Oh!' Bourcher sounded deflated. 'Well done, Moody. Is there anyone on two *red* initials?'

'No, sir.' Both Sullivan and a new boy called Nixon had received two red initials, but Moody was counting on Bourcher's inability to read close up without his reading glasses.

'That's impossible. Check again.'

Moody scanned the list again, hoping Bourcher would not snatch the board from his grasp and take it to his study. He needed to distract Bourcher and noted with satisfaction that Pride and Lambert had both received a red initial. 'There's been no new red initials since yesterday, sir, unless you count the ones given to Pride and Lambert.'

'What? Who gave my head boys those initials?'

'Don't know, sir. The initials against their names are new. I've not seen them before.'

'Give me the board.' Bourcher grabbed the board from Moody's hands and, holding it at arm's length, squinted at the offending handiwork: '*R... J... V,*' he muttered. His whisky-addled brain struggled to recall the owner of the initials. Finally, it dawned on him. 'Rebecca Vavasour!' he roared. 'She's a matron, not a teacher. She doesn't even have the authority to give initials.'

'She's standing in for Monsieur Moreau, the French teacher, for the rest of the term. And she's also chairing the teacher's common room meetings till half-term. That qualifies her to give initials, sir.'

'Ridiculous! She's just an eighteen-year-old girl, for heaven's sake. Tell me, Moody, what possible justification could she have for giving red initials to my head boys unless it's to spite me?'

'Perhaps you should ask *her*, Mr Bourcher. Miss Vavasour's in the sick bay looking after Sam Faulkner. He's come down with Romanian flu.'

'Romanian flu, did you say?'

'Yes sir. It's highly infectious. It gives you a sore throat, high temperature and hallucinations.'

'Oh! Then I won't bother Miss Vavasour just yet. I'll discuss the matter with Pride and Lambert directly. Carry on, Moody.'

* * *

Bourcher barged into the head boys' study like a bull at a gate. Pride scrambled to hide the half-eaten packet of chocolate biscuits he had confiscated from one of the junior boys, while Lambert tucked his trash mag under his duvet. Both boys sprang to their feet.

'Good evening, Mr Bourcher,' they chorused.

'What's this about you boys getting an initial from the matron?'

Pride turned pale. It was evident Bourcher was in a dangerous and unpredictable mood. 'I can explain, sir. It was a misunderstanding. We thought we were still allowed to get the ticks to clean—'

'I won't have teenage girls disciplining my head prefects. It's unnatural,' thundered Bourcher. 'Next thing you know, women will be running the school, and then where would we be, Pride?'

Pride almost collapsed with relief that he was not the focus of Bourcher's anger. 'We tried to explain to Miss Vavasour that the ticks need to learn their place. But she thinks they're more important than the seniors.'

'My God, what's that terrible smell? Open the window, Lambert, before we all suffocate.'

'Yes, sir.'

'I'd fire the girl, but my hands are tied. Weak and feeble minds have decided the school needs a woman's touch to provide medical and pastoral care. Such mumbo jumbo will not bring back the Empire, Pride! The boys don't need linctus and a kiss before bedtime, Lambert, they need the three R's: rugby, religion and the rod. On such foundations, great nations are forged.'

'Yes, sir,' Lambert said as he raised the sash window. A force eight gale blasted through the gap.

Bourcher gripped the doorway for balance as the whisky took a firm hold of his senses. 'So, as captain and vice-captain, I expect you boys to find a solution to our little conundrum. Do I make myself clear?'

Pride and Lambert looked at each other in confusion before answering in unison. 'Yes, sir.'

'Have either of you ever wielded the cane?'

'No, sir,' they both uttered, unsure where the conversation was heading.

'You're never too young to learn. The cane is a necessary tool by which the righteous instil morality on the sinful. The future of the realm depends upon women knowing who gives the punishments and who receives them. Can I leave this matter in your capable hands?'

'Yes, sir.'

'Splendid. Carry on, Pride and Lambert.'

CHAPTER 19

For the second time that night, Faulkner woke in a state of high anxiety. His throat burned and the taste of acrid smoke in his mouth was stronger than ever. A ring of sweat had formed on his pillow where his neck and thick mop of hair had lain. He willed himself to fall back to sleep and yet he dreaded the return of the nightmares that had plagued him since he had been confined to the sick bay. He checked his watch and sighed in exasperation. It was one a.m.

He was on the point of drifting back to sleep when dread filled the pit of his stomach like the rising tide of a fast-flowing estuary. The strange sensation was both terrifying and alluring. He was being summoned by the same soft, beguiling voice he had heard in the stable yard. Faulkner pulled the blankets closer around his body and tried to fight the urge to rush to the spot where he knew a young woman had once been burned at the stake many centuries before. The wind rattled against the tiny window of the sick bay, and he knew it would be bitterly cold outside. It made no sense to rush to the place where the woman had died, despite his irrational desire to do so.

The frantic urgings of the woman could no longer be ignored, and Faulkner sat upright in his bed. Her pitiful voice was imploring him to retrieve the gifts she had hidden for her true love in the hours before she had been so cruelly murdered.

'I know not the location of which you speak, my lady,' he cried out in despair. He was shocked by his sudden outburst and assumed his fever had brought on another hallucination.

'*I will guide thee, my child.*' The voice was so weak it could have been a product of his fevered imagination, or a trick of the wind that was howling against the sick bay window. Nevertheless, it sent a chill down his spine.

'The weather is foul and I have a fever. It's not safe for me to leave this place, for Bourcher still stalks the corridors.' He listened for a response, but none came. He could only hear the wind rattling against the window and the creaking of loose floorboards as a bitter, drunken man prowled the dormitories adjacent to the sick bay.

The sensation of dread in his stomach transformed into

one of urgency. He knew the fever that had him in its grip was weakening and the hallucinations, or whatever was causing the ethereal presence that surrounded him, would soon disappear if he did not act. He wondered if the strange physical sensations he had experienced when riding with Miss Vavasour were also contributing to his confusion. Sighing deeply, he pulled back the covers and reached for his dressing gown and slippers.

* * *

Faulkner eased the door of the sick bay open and froze as he heard the floorboards creak in the headmaster's study. Bourcher was still awake, and Faulkner had to admire the man's stamina if not his mental stability. He took a deep breath and padded past the dormitories towards the back stairs. He tested the first step, which he knew would squeal like a stuck pig if he planted his foot in its centre. Step by step he worked his way down the staircase. He froze once again when he heard a door open and shut, but continued when he realised it was a fourth former making his way to the bathroom. He reached the bottom of the stairs and passed the bellroom, where the duty boy would chime ten peels of the bell at six-thirty each morning to summon the reluctant boys to the cold showers. He walked through the boot room, where eighty pairs of muddy rugby boots of all shapes and sizes were stacked in their lockers, and headed towards the grandiose back door.

The wind howled against the door and the draft cooled his ankles as he slid open the bolt and unlatched the chain. He opened the door and was struck by the force of the wind. Broken twigs and debris from the grass oval flew into the boot room and he had to use all his strength to pull the door closed after him.

He walked across the oval and headed towards the stable yard. He moved in a dream-like stance, his legs buffeted by the wind, until he came to the large arch that proclaimed the entrance to the stable complex. He risked a backwards look at the huge edifice that was Red House and thought he saw a curtain twitch in the headmaster's study. Faulkner wondered if it was his fevered imagination playing tricks, or whether Bourcher's uncanny nose for trouble had scented blood.

Faulkner hurried into the stable yard and glanced across

to the corner of the yard where the pyre had been lit centuries before. He expected to feel the heat of the fire and smell the smoke once again, but the life force he had experienced three days before had vanished. He felt both relief and a profound sense of abandonment. The possible glimpse of Bourcher at the window of his study had broken the spell. A gust of wind blew like a vortex around the stable yard and its pitch had a human quality to it, like the soft whisper of a woman's voice.

'Make for the stables! The Puritan cometh.'

Faulkner hurried into the stables where the horses were resting. It was inky black. Only the reflected light of a tepid half-moon and a handful of stars leached through the rafters and reflected from the dusty windows. He had to feel his way along the familiar stalls where he had spent hundreds of hours with a shovel and broom. The musty smell of horse manure and straw enveloped him like a familiar old blanket. He was drawn to the last stall, where Bullet was chomping on strands of hay from the manger. Underneath the manger was a small wooden trapdoor that Faulkner knew led to a cramped, uninviting service pit. Faulkner had explored the pit as a curious third former but had lost interest when he discovered it led only to the school's drainage system. Bullet turned his head on noticing Faulkner before resuming to feed.

'You, boy! Come out of the stables this instant.' It was Bourcher yelling from the stable yard and Faulkner's heart thundered against his ribcage. He would be in dire trouble if he was caught. The headmaster had not addressed him by name, and it gave him hope he had not been recognised.

Faulkner moved quickly. He opened the gate and scrambled into Bullet's stall. The horse was docile and half asleep. He worked his way around the powerful horse until he reached the hay manger. He stroked the beautiful American quarter horse on the nose to reassure him he meant no harm, then bent down to feel for the iron ring of the trapdoor. Light exploded in the stables as Bourcher found the light switch.

'If you come out now, boy, it'll make things easier for you,' Bourcher said. His voice lacked its usual authority and Faulkner realised the headmaster must be uncomfortable among the horses and did not relish the prospect of a long search of the stable on a cold night.

Faulkner grasped the ring and pulled open the trapdoor. He descended into the service pit using the iron rungs bolted to the side of the dark, dank enclosure. Closing the trapdoor behind him he found himself in near blackness. But still he was not safe. If Bourcher opened the trapdoor and shone his torch into the pit, he would be exposed immediately. As his sharp eyes adjusted to the blackness, he made out vague shapes as the stable lights leached through the tiny gaps surrounding the trapdoor. He could hear the horses above him becoming agitated at the unwelcome intrusion. They were snorting and moving around their stalls as Bourcher shone his powerful torch into every corner of the stable. Bullet was pacing around above his head, and whinnied loudly. Bourcher had entered Bullet's stall and was heading towards the trap door.

'Ouch! Don't you bite me, you vicious nag!' Bourcher called out. Then Faulkner heard the whooshing sound of a cane followed by the crack of birch on horse flesh. There was a short silence, then pandemonium as Bullet lashed out with his hooves.

Faulkner searched the confines of the service pit for a recess in which to hide. Bourcher would be in a murderous mood when he opened the trapdoor. Faulkner found the wooden door that led to the school's drainage system, but he knew it would be locked. He continued to move his hands along the brickwork until he reached the side opposite the drainage door. There was no recess in which to hide and he experienced a mild sense of panic, thinking Bourcher would not be daunted by the flailing horse for long. Then his hands touched a part of the wall that felt similar to brick-veneer panelling he had discovered in Cromwell dormitory's secret passageway. He pushed at the panelling until he heard the soft click of a concealed latch and felt the motion of a hidden door opening inwards. Faulkner stepped inside and closed the door behind him. Moments later the trap door opened, and light streamed into the service pit. For what seemed like minutes Faulkner held his breath as Bourcher climbed into the service pit and shone his torch into every nook and cranny of the dark hole. Cracks of light seeped into the priest hole in which Faulkner stood, allowing him to observe his surroundings. There was a long, narrow tunnel he knew must head in the direction of the River Ouse one hundred yards away: another of Sir Henry Slingsby's escape routes from the vengeful

Roundheads, he thought. A decrepit stool lay abandoned in one corner and several misshapen lumps of wax were stacked on a rotting side table next to the stool. Next to the lumps of wax was a package wrapped in a lanolin-coated material the size of a shoe box. Faulkner grasped the package just as the torch beam was extinguished and Bourcher climbed out of the service pit.

Faulkner waited in absolute darkness for several minutes, to ensure Bourcher had left the stables. Bourcher was not a patient man, and he wouldn't waste any more time in the draughty, malodorous stables. As Faulkner's adrenaline levels settled, he began to feel weak and wretched from the fever that had gripped him for the last three days. Still clutching the parcel, he scrambled out of the priest hole, climbed the iron rungs of the service pit and pushed against the trap door. For a sickening moment, the trap door did not budge, and he thought Bourcher may have manoeuvred a heavy object over his only means of escape. He pushed harder and felt the rush of cold air on his face as the trap door opened. Bullet had been standing on the hatch and studied him as he emerged from the stinking pit.

Faulkner knew he had to return to the sick bay before Bourcher discovered his absence. Bourcher was certain to check every bed in each dormitory to identify who was missing. He decided to opt for speed rather than stealth. He closed the trap door behind him and rushed towards the gate of the stall, pausing only to run his hands along Bullet's flank where Bourcher had struck the horse with a vicious blow. He could feel the welt where the cane had landed.

'Bourcher will pay for that one day,' he promised the horse. Faulkner opened the gate a fraction and peered to his right to check his route to the stable exit was clear. He slipped out of the stall and slid the bolt home. Just as he was about to turn and run for the exit, he felt a firm hand clamp down on his shoulder.

CHAPTER 20

'Sam! What on earth are you doing in the stables at this time of night? You're supposed to be resting in the sick bay. You'll have a relapse in this cold weather,' Rebecca whispered to him. She was wearing a dressing gown over her night clothes. On her feet she wore a pair of mud-splattered wellington boots. She was about three inches taller than Faulkner and looked into his eyes with concern.

'Are you going to report me to Bourcher?' Faulkner asked. His voice was hoarse and his temperature had returned with a vengeance. He felt weak and knew his situation was hopeless.

Rebecca put her index finger to her lips to quieten him down. 'Bourcher is waiting behind the stable yard arch for you. We need to climb out of the stables through the rear window, and then you can wait in my cottage until he returns to the main building.'

'But I need to get back to the sick bay before Bourcher finds I'm missing.'

Rebecca put her hand on Faulkner's forehead. 'You're burning up, Sam. You must've had another hallucination. I can't think of any other reason why you would've walked into the stables at one o'clock in the morning.'

'She spoke to me again.'

'Who spoke to you?'

'The witch.'

'She wasn't a witch, Sam. She was murdered by an evil man who stole her inheritance – and I'm going to prove it.' She glanced at the parcel Faulkner was holding. 'What do you have there?'

'She asked me to fetch it.'

'You poor dear. You must have a blazing fever. Come on, let's get you to my cottage.'

Rebecca led Faulkner to the stable's rear window and slid it open. She hauled herself up with the stealth of a cat and swung herself through the open window into the yard beyond. She turned around and held out her hand to Faulkner, who pulled himself through and dropped onto the soft grass beside Rebecca.

'My cottage is just around the corner. We'll need to stay in the shadows and enter through the side door. Don't make a sound and stay close. Bourcher will be just the other side of the courtyard wall.'

Rebecca took his hand and they scampered around the walls of the stable till they reached a gate leading to a stretch of open courtyard opposite her cottage. They went through the gate and dashed towards the cottage. Rebecca opened the cottage door, switched on a dim side lamp and bade Faulkner to sit on the couch.

'I must get back to the sick bay,' Faulkner insisted.

'When it's safe. Did Bourcher recognise you?'

'I don't think so.'

'Good. He won't go into the sick bay as he's terrified of catching Romanian flu. You should rest now till I give you the all clear. I'll fetch you a blanket. Try and get some sleep.'

Rebecca went to her bedroom and returned with a blanket. Faulkner had removed his slippers and was stretched out on the sofa.

Rebecca spread the blanket over Faulkner and tucked him in. 'Do you mind if I take a look at the parcel?' she asked.

'Sure. It smells like something greasy from the kitchens.' He held the parcel out to Rebecca.

'That'll be the lanolin. It was used to protect valuable items from damp. May I open it?'

'Of course.'

Rebecca fetched a pair of scissors from the kitchen and cut the lanolin-coated material surrounding the package. Inside was a wooden box wrapped in high-quality rag paper.

'There's writing on the package,' Rebecca said, 'but it's almost faded away.' She brought the parcel closer to the lamp and read the message aloud:

'*My dearest Samuel. I have always loved and cherished you despite my matrimonial duties to the court in exile. Grieve not for me, my darling despite the terrible death I am about to endure. For once this final trial is over, I will be yours in Paradise; not as I have become, but as the free spirit you once adored. Rebecca S.*'

Rebecca gazed into the distance as if absorbing the magnitude of what she had read. 'Then it's true. Lady Slingsby was married to the man she met in The Hague in Holland.' Then with trembling fingers, she untied the knot in the package. Inside the rag paper wrapping was a royal-blue silk shawl. It looked in immaculate condition and Rebecca held it to her face and took a deep breath as if trying to catch the scent of the woman who had worn it three-and-a-half centuries before, in the hours leading to her death. Beside the shawl was a well-used prayer book, which Rebecca thumbed through like a researcher on the point of a historic discovery.

Finally, at the bottom of the parcel was an intricate gold locket that would have been worn on a chain around a woman's neck. Rebecca fiddled with the clasp mechanism for a while until it sprang open, revealing two miniature portraits: one of a man and the other a woman. She stared at the portraits in confusion before she threw it on the coffee table. She glared at Faulkner. 'Has this evening's stunt been some kind of elaborate practical joke at my expense?' she accused. 'If so, it's in very bad taste.'

'I-I don't know what you mean,' Faulkner stammered.

'The portrait of Fauconberg. Did you get it painted?'

'I've never seen the locket before, Miss Vavasour. I swear it.'

Rebecca looked into Faulkner's eyes and, seeing no evidence of deception, she placed a soft hand on his fevered brow. 'Sam, this is important. It's clear that you have a deep connection with this place. It's as if the voices of the past have been trying to reach out to you. Is there anything else you've seen or found since you've been at Red House?'

'Like what?'

'Old valuables similar to this piece of jewellery, or documents that could prove this place was stolen from my ancestor, Rebecca Slingsby.'

Faulkner's mind raced back to the night he had discovered the secret chamber above the headmaster's study. He recalled his fear of entrapment, the suffocating darkness and the haunting images within the room. In the months that had since passed, the constant nightmares had made it impossible for him to separate the reality of what he had seen from the imagined. He felt that to revisit the events of that night would be deeply traumatic and would elicit a savage retribution from Bourcher if he were to find out. To Faulkner, it was an event best forgotten.

'No,' he said quietly, but he was unable to look Rebecca in the eyes.

Faulkner felt the weight of Rebecca's judgement crush him

like a stab in the heart. He cast his blanket aside and stood up from the couch, walked to the coffee table and picked up the locket. On the right-hand side was an elaborately painted portrait of Rebecca Slingsby. She bore a striking resemblance to Miss Vavasour. On the left was a young man with long, sandy hair and striking blue eyes. On his head was a wide-brimmed cavalier-style hat. Despite the differences in age and attire, it was clear he was looking at a portrait of himself in almost every detail.

CHAPTER 21

For the first time in three years, Red House was losing a game of rugby at half time. The boys had been lethargic in the final of the prestigious Yorkshire Preparatory Schools seven-a-side competition and their opponents, Malsis School, were having the game of their lives. The coach of Red House, John Fox, decided to give his charges a motivational pep talk.

'What the hell is up with you boys? If you don't win this bloody game, I'll lose my job. You're playing like a bunch of girl guides on a Sunday afternoon picnic. It's only Malsis School you're playing, not the bloody All Blacks.' Fox slapped his forehead with his palm in frustration. 'Faulkner, if you don't pick up your game, I'll hook you from the field. And Lambert, your knees aren't even dirty! What've you been doing all game? Picking daisies?'

He glared at Nigel Pride, who had not touched the ball during the entire tournament. Despite his instincts he understood that Pride, being the son of Sir Monty, was above criticism, so he let matters be.

'Faulkner, you're supposed to be the bloody captain; what've you got to say?' demanded Fox.

Faulkner looked at his despondent teammates and took a deep breath. It was true he had not had a good game. He was still labouring from the after-effects of Romanian flu, his legs felt like lead and he was struggling for breath.

'We're playing without a strategy, boys. We think we can beat them just by turning up and passing the ball to Lambert. But Malsis are closing him down before he can get into his stride and they're nullifying his hand-off by tackling low.' Lambert was nicknamed 'Iron Mike' because of the similarity of his straight arm fend to a Mike Tyson punch in the jaw.

'Just nobble their fly half while the ref isn't looking,' Fox cut in. 'He's the one doing the damage.'

'That's a tactic, not a strategy,' Faulkner said. 'Now listen, boys. They've two players always shadowing Lambert. We can take those boys out of play by moving Lambert out wide. We're good enough to beat Malsis without Lambert's pile-driver runs and it'll open a gap in the centre that Moody and I can exploit.'

'But how do we stop their fly half? He's lightning-fast and scores each time he gets the ball,' asked Moody.

'We stop him from getting the ball in attacking positions by putting Malsis on the defensive. We'll have an extra man in the middle of the field, so we need to exploit that by quick plays and darting runs from the scrum. But this will only work if we increase our tempo and find an extra yard of pace. We're only two tries behind, so let's give this a real shot.'

The boys gave a little cheer and took their positions on the field to receive kick off.

* * *

The referee glanced at his watch and noted there were less than thirty seconds of the match remaining. Red House had pulled one converted try back but were still trailing Malsis by five points. After conceding the try early in the second half, Malsis School had thwarted Faulkner's strategy by leaving Lambert isolated on the wing and were packing the midfield in a desperate attempt to hold off their fast-finishing opponents in the dying seconds of the game. The Malsis students and teachers on the side line sensed an upset victory. As the seconds ticked away, coach John Fox yelled abuse at the referee, while Bourcher stalked the touch line pointing accusatory fingers at his players.

Faulkner signalled to Lambert to return to his normal position in the centre and for Nigel Pride to take his usual place on the wing. The two boys swapped places and Faulkner noticed the look of consternation on the faces of the Malsis boys at the return of Lambert's hulking presence.

Moody fed the scrum and Sullivan hooked the ball, allowing Moody to dart round the back and regather the ball. He delivered a pass onto Faulkner's chest, who took the ball forward ten yards. Lambert loomed to his right but three Malsis boys readied themselves to gang-tackle their most feared opponent. Faulkner ignored Lambert and passed back inside to Moody, who kicked into space behind the Malsis pack. Faulkner had anticipated Moody's kick and pounced on the loose ball. He avoided the flying tackle of the large Malsis centre by swerving inside and catching his opponent off balance. Faulkner then side-stepped around the despairing Malsis scrum half's attempted tackle and accelerated into the gap. Suddenly he was in the clear and had a thirty-yard sprint to the try line.

But with fifteen yards to go, his legs turned to jelly, allowing the lightning-fast Malsis fly half to make up the ground between them. Faulkner willed himself to run faster but with the try line looming, he knew he was in trouble. Out of the corner of his eye he saw Nigel Pride loping along the wing seemingly uninterested in the play. Faulkner threw a long-range pass towards Pride a fraction of a second before the Malsis fly half crash-tackled Faulkner from behind.

Pride was unmarked and Faulkner's pass was inch perfect. Pride only needed to catch the ball and place it over the try line. But Pride snatched at the ball instead of allowing it to land on his chest. The ball spiralled from his flailing hands but somehow, he managed to regather it. Pride fell in a clumsy heap over the try line and planted the ball down.

Faulkner lined up the conversion from the touch line and kicked the ball between the posts. The referee put the whistle to his lips and blew for full time. The Red House juniors squealed with delight while the older boys clapped and cheered. Red House had won the Yorkshire prep schools seven-a-side tournament for a record three times in a row. John Fox accepted the handshakes and congratulations of his fellow teachers and acknowledged the applause of the parents on the touch line. Bourcher congratulated the chairman of the governors, Sir Monty Pride, on his son's winning try and reminded him that once again, the school's strict disciplinary methods had been validated on the field of battle.

* * *

Jimmy Stuart stood on his tiptoes and rang the doorbell of the matron's cottage in the stable yard. The eight-year-old pushed back a lock of curly blond hair from his eyes and waited for Rebecca Vavasour to emerge.

'Jimmy, what are you doing here?' she asked as she crouched down to look the diminutive first former in the eyes. 'It's almost eight-thirty. You should be in bed.'

Stuart seemed apprehensive and looked around to see if he had been followed.

'It's okay, you can tell me. What's wrong? Are Pride and Lambert bullying you again?'

'No, Miss Vavasour. Pride says he's sick with Romanian flu and you should tend to him in the head prefect's study at once.'

Rebecca felt a stab of concern that the flu had once more made an unwelcome return to the school. But something did not ring true. 'Why did Pride send *you* to fetch me, Jimmy?'

'Don't know, ma'am.'

Rebecca's maternal instincts went into overdrive as she looked into Stuart's blue eyes. She was aware he suffered from homesickness, and he would cry himself to sleep each night, much to the annoyance of the other boys in his dormitory. He was short in stature and androgynous in appearance, making him a natural target for the bullies, in both schoolboy and adult form.

'Did Pride put you up to this?'

'I don't know what you mean, Miss Vavasour.'

Rebecca sighed at the boy's innocence. 'What did Pride look like? Was he pale or red in the face? Was he sweating or shaking with fever?'

'He coughed and said he had a sore throat.'

Rebecca stood up. She would have to investigate, but she needed a male teacher to accompany her to the head prefect's study. Entering the prefect's study in the middle of the day was one thing, but after dark was a different matter. 'Okay, I'll get my things. Would you ask Captain McTavish to meet me in the sick bay, and then we'll check on Pride.'

'Captain McTavish is drunk. He's fallen asleep in the library and is snoring like a pig.'

Rebecca rolled her eyes. She knew Colin Grimshaw, the Latin teacher, was the master on duty, but he had attempted to grope her in the red passage the week before and she didn't want to give him a second opportunity.

'Oh, for goodness' sake. Is John Fox in his study?'

'I think so, ma'am.'

'Well, would you please fetch him and ask him to meet me in the sick bay? I need to collect my thermometer, stethoscope, gloves and mask. I'll wait for him there.'

'Yes, ma'am.'

'And Jimmy, if anyone picks on you again, or you just need

to chat, you should come straight to me. Do you understand?'

'Yes, Miss Vavasour.'

'Now run along. I'll be in the sick bay in five minutes.'

* * *

Rebecca had been waiting for over half an hour before Jimmy Stuart poked his shock of blond curls around the corner.

'Is Mr Fox with you?' she asked.

'Um, no. I couldn't find him.'

'Have you tried to find another teacher? Mr Strathfield, Phil Kennedy?'

'No, but I woke Captain McTavish.'

'What did he say?'

'That if I didn't leave him alone, he'd give me a red initial.'

'Right. I'll have to get Mr Bourcher.'

'He has a line of boys outside his study. I could hear Sullivan yelling out as he was getting six of the best again.'

'Okay. Then fetch Mr Grimshaw, the master on duty. Tell him to meet me outside the prefect's study.'

'Yes, ma'am.'

Rebecca gathered a selection of clinical supplies from the shelves in the sick bay and walked down the corridor connecting the dormitories and main bathroom. As she did so, she drank in the atmosphere of the stately old house that had been stolen from her family centuries before. She experienced a strange mixture of emotions as she walked past the rickety back stairs and turned a corner towards the dormitories known as Montrose and Fairfax. Just beyond those dormitories was the head prefect's study. The walls, doorways and the uneven, creaking floorboards oozed character. She imagined the whispers of her ancestors calling to her as she glided past the dormitories.

She had visited the York Museum the previous week and the curator had confirmed the locket was a genuine item of seventeenth-century jewellery. Furthermore, he had identified the miniature portraits as being those of Lady Rebecca Slingsby, and Samuel Fauconberg, the Colonel of the Northern Horse. He had even commented on the striking likeness between the woman in the portrait and herself.

Rebecca reached the door of the head prefect's study and was greeted once more by Jimmy Stuart.

'Mr Grimshaw won't come,' said Stuart.

'Why on earth not?'

Stuart looked embarrassed. 'He said he wouldn't throw you a life belt even if you were drowning at sea.'

'What a strange man. What else did he say?'

'That he had once tried to be nice to you, but you were too high and mighty to accept his offer of friendship.'

Rebecca recalled Grimshaw's drunken advances and groping hands in the red passage two weeks before. Her thoughts were interrupted by a loud groan coming from the study.

'That's Nigel Pride. He says he's really sick,' insisted Stuart.

'Okay. Thank you, Jimmy. You can leave now. You should go straight back to your bed.'

'Yes, ma'am. Goodnight.'

'Goodnight, Jimmy.'

Rebecca turned around and knocked on the study door. She was suspicious of Pride and Lambert's intentions and hesitant to enter the boys' study after dark, but the risk of a Romanian flu outbreak spreading through Red House was too serious to ignore. As the matron, it was her primary responsibility to ensure the medical wellbeing of those in her care.

'Come in,' came the weak-sounding voice of Pride. He coughed for effect.

'Are you dressed?' Rebecca asked.

'Yes, matron.'

Rebecca opened the door and walked in. Pride sat at his desk with his long, gangly legs crossed and a sly smirk on his face. 'Don't You Want Me' by the Human League was playing on his stereo. Rebecca didn't need a thermometer or stethoscope to diagnose that Pride did not have the Romanian flu or any other illness. Behind her, Lambert moved to his right to block the door.

'What's the meaning of this?' Rebecca said angrily.

'It is against school rules for females to enter the boys' dormitories or the head prefect's study unaccompanied after dark,' Pride said, smirking. 'Lambert and I feel violated. We demand an apology and retribution.' Pride clasped his hands behind his head and leaned back in his chair.

'Is that so? If you are so offended by my presence, then perhaps Mr Lambert can move away from the door, and we can sort this out in Mr Bourcher's study?'

'Mr Bourcher is busy. And he's delegated his disciplinary authority to Lambert and me.' Pride stretched to his left and picked up a vicious-looking birch from his bed.

Rebecca turned around to face Lambert. He was six inches taller than her and had the broad physique of a full-grown man. 'Move away from the door this instant,' she growled, staring him in the eyes.

Lambert did not move but brought his arms out from behind his back. In his right hand was a horse crop, which he tapped several times into the palm of his left hand. His eyes fixed on Rebecca's breasts, and he licked his lips like a starving wolf on the point of devouring a lamb. For the first time, Rebecca felt panic rise from the pit of her stomach, and she turned back to face Nigel Pride.

'Think very carefully about what you're about to do, Mr Pride. You're a young man with the world at your feet. But if you strike me with that cane, it will be an act of common assault. Not even your father's connections will be able to protect you from the consequences of your actions.'

'Oh, I won't strike you, Miss Vavasour,' Pride said, 'although Iron Mike here has developed a taste for wielding the cane ever since Mr Bourcher delegated his disciplinary powers to us.'

'You've been striking the boys?' Rebecca accused Pride. Her eyes were blazing with anger.

'As I said, that's not to my taste. Striking little boys with a cane is barbaric and should be made illegal.'

'Then what's the point of this elaborate charade?'

'There will be a beating, one way or another. Lessons need to be learned and people need to know their place. This beating will be severe and painful, but fair. It'll also be humiliating, but that's all part of the disciplinary process, don't you think Miss Vavasour?'

'I demand to be let out of this room, Mr Pride. Don't think you'll be any less guilty by making Lambert do your dirty work.'

'You misunderstand me, Miss Vavasour,' said Pride, undoing his belt and lowering his trousers. 'It will be you who will be administering the cane and I who will receive the strokes.' He offered Rebecca the cane. 'For the last six years I have watched other boys being caned by the headmaster. When I first joined the school, I thought it was cruel. I cried for the poor boys who were injured and humiliated by Bourcher. Then something changed inside me when I became a prefect and I yearned to take their place. I longed to hear the sweet music of the swish of the cane and feel the pleasure of its vicious sting on my backside. But I knew it was just a pipe dream, because my father is Chairman of the Board of Governors and chief benefactor to the school. Bourcher would never dare touch me. So, you have a choice. Either Mike Lambert gets his pleasure by beating you, or I get mine. I suggest you take the cane and swing hard, Miss Vavasour.'

Rebecca looked at Pride's scrawny, acne-spotted backside with disgust. 'Then you'll have to get your sordid pleasure elsewhere, Mr Pride. I refuse to indulge in your childish fantasies.'

'What a pity,' said Pride. 'I'm not sure I could stop Mr Lambert from bloodying your pretty rump, even if I tried.' He turned up the volume of his stereo, now playing 'West End Girls' by the Pet Shop Boys. He nodded to Lambert, who grasped Rebecca by the arm and slung her over the end of his bed.

* * *

Josh Mattingly poked his head around the door of the library and spotted Sam Faulkner, who was frowning at a battered copy of A.J. Glover's *Text Book of Comprehension, Precis Composition and Other Exercises*. Next to him, Moody was solving a series of differential equation exercises set by his maths teacher, with obvious ease. Mattingly was dressed in his pyjamas, dressing gown and slippers, and nervously entered the library. His red hair and freckles were unmistakable and two sixth formers threw their cushions at him as he sidled up to Faulkner.

'What's that tick doing in here after lights out?' said Elliott.

'I need to speak to Faulkner,' Mattingly said nervously.

Faulkner looked up from his English comprehension book. Mattingly looked like he was carrying the weight of the world on his shoulders. 'Ignore them, Josh. They forget they were new boys once. What's up?'

'Sorry to bother you, but I'm worried about Jimmy Stuart. He's been acting a bit weird tonight.'

'Stuart? He's always acting weird. I wouldn't worry about it.'

'No, something's different. He's crying, but not in his usual homesick way. He seems scared.'

'Has someone been bullying him?'

Mattingly shrugged. 'Maybe. I asked him what was wrong. He said Pride and Lambert had asked him to fetch the matron, which he did. But then he wouldn't say any more.'

'What was he doing with Pride and Lambert? They were told to leave him alone.'

'Don't know.'

'He's being a sneak,' Delaney said accusingly.

Faulkner shot Delaney a withering look.

'Why would they need the matron at this hour?' quizzed Moody.

'I think they might have Romanian flu. At least, that's what Stuart said,' replied Mattingly.

'I saw Lambert about an hour ago,' said Moody. 'He seemed cocky about something; not like someone who had the flu.'

Faulkner felt a wave of anxiety crash through his body. 'Thanks, Mattingly. I'm going upstairs to check what they're up to.'

'I'm coming with you,' said Moody.

* * *

Moody was about to knock on the door when he heard a struggle coming from within the head prefect's study.

'We'll go straight in,' Faulkner said, 'and if there's trouble, we both crash-tackle Lambert.'

Moody nodded and they barged into the study. He saw the broad back of Mike Lambert, who was holding a horse crop in his hand. Pride was attempting to pin down Rebecca, who was struggling to free herself from his grip.

Lambert turned and swung the crop at Faulkner's head. Faulkner turned his head sideways to protect his eyes but took the full force of the blow across his cheek. The searing pain almost blinded him, but he allowed his momentum to crash into Lambert's stocky frame. Lambert barely registered the impact. He was at least two stone heavier than Faulkner, but he could not avoid Moody's swinging fist that connected flush on his chin.

Lambert rocked back but did not fall. Anger blazed in Lambert's eyes, and he swung the crop in the general direction of Moody and Faulkner. Faulkner ducked under the crop and landed his fist into Lambert's midriff.

Rebecca had managed to struggle free from Pride's limpet-like grip and tried to take charge of the situation.

'Boys! Stop your fighting. Now!' she yelled.

Moody landed a second blow onto the side of Lambert's head, which sent him reeling to the floor. At that moment, Bernard Bourcher stepped into the study and surveyed the scene of destruction before him. A curious, almost triumphant expression crossed his swarthy features.

'Pack your bags, Miss Vavasour. Your services are no longer required at Red House,' Bourcher said, his voice dripping with disdain. 'I won't have you undermining discipline in my school, and I'll be notifying the police you have been ... interfering ... with my boys during the course of your duties.' He stared at Faulkner and Moody. 'You boys. Make your way to my study. You'll feel the sting of my cane and the wrath of my judgement in no uncertain manner. Lambert, pick yourself up off the floor. You can follow Faulkner and Moody into my study.'

Bourcher looked at Pride, who had slunk back to his desk unnoticed. He was flicking through the pages of *Tingay's Latin Grammar* as if oblivious to the mayhem surrounding him. 'At least there's one person in the school I can rely on to exhibit the standards of behaviour expected at Red House School. Pride, after these ... vagabonds have gone to my study, I want a full explanation.'

Rebecca tried to interject. 'Headmaster, I can give you the explanation. A serious incident has—'

Bourcher rounded on Rebecca. 'Why are you still here, woman? I told you to pack your bags. If you're not gone within half an hour, I'll escort you to the police myself.'

'Mr Bourcher, you need to hear me out. I—'

But Rebecca was unable to finish her sentence. Bourcher swung his fist and hit Rebecca with such force that her head rocked and she staggered backwards. She toppled over the edge of Pride's bed, hitting her head against the bedframe. Her vision blurred and she slumped to the floor.

Faulkner stared at Bourcher with a look of horror and

loathing on his face. 'You've killed her. You evil bastard, you've killed her!'

PART THREE

"Experience hath shewn, that even under the best forms of government those entrusted with power have, in time, and by slow operations, perverted it into tyranny."

— Thomas Jefferson

CHAPTER 22

Cavalier Tours head office,
York, United Kingdom,
May 2024

Sam Faulkner was staring bankruptcy in the face. His string of thirty travel agencies was bleeding money, and he had overcapitalised just before high interest rates and inflation had hit hard. He had known for some time he was going to have to sell most of his agencies and let go over one hundred loyal staff.

Faulkner looked around his office, which had been the centre of his life since he had hung up his rugby boots. He took a long swallow of tea to calm the nagging anxiety that had become his constant bedfellow. Following his retirement from professional rugby, he had turned his passion for exotic African travel into a thriving business. Life had been almost perfect until the COVID-19 pandemic had ravaged the travel industry. He had taken out a recovery loan from the government, but then a string of cancellations from his most valuable clients had put his business on the brink. The stress had proved too much for his former long-term lover and business partner, Eloise Hawkins. She had cashed out her shareholding at the worst possible time and compounded his financial, social and mental woes.

He turned on his laptop and scanned through his calendar. He had a meeting with a woman called Rebecca Talbot at ten a.m. and a meeting with the Yorkshire Bank at two p.m., for which he was woefully unprepared. He wondered if he could fob off the potential client to his office manager, Trudy Stanhope, while he finalised the business restructuring plan his bank manager had demanded as a condition for extending his loan.

He heard a knock at the door and Trudy Stanhope poked her head around the corner. 'Ms Talbot is early. She apologises for the intrusion but was hoping you could see her anyway?'

Faulkner sighed. 'Trudy, would you look after her for me? It's going to take most of the morning to complete my business plan.'

'I really think you should see her, Mr Faulkner. She says she wants to take a party of twenty on a luxury trip to Zambia,

Namibia and Botswana.'

Faulkner returned to his spreadsheet and stared once more at the sea of red representing his cash flow projection for the next six months. 'A party of twenty, did you say?'

'She's prepared to pay top dollar in advance if you lead the tour.'

'I haven't done that for years.'

'Then it's time you gave it another go. You've not been the same since you broke up with Eloise. If I may say so, Mr Faulkner, the business was built around your charisma, but you've recently lost your verve. If you can regain that sparkle, the cashflow will look after itself.'

Faulkner was touched by his office manager's candid concern. Trudy was an ex-British Airways flight attendant, who had been let go from her role during the pandemic. 'Nothing would give me greater pleasure than a trip to the Okavango Delta and Victoria Falls, Trudy, but unfortunately, I must focus on the business restructure. Jim can lead the tour.'

'Okay, I'll tell her. But it's a shame to miss out on the half-a-million pounds she mentioned ...'

'Half-a-million?' Faulkner looked once more at his spreadsheet. Half-a-million pounds would cover the staff wages for the next few months and mean he could kick the business restructure down the road a little longer. 'Perhaps I could make a little time for Ms Talbot,' he said, closing his laptop. 'Would you please show her in?'

Faulkner used the intervening time to tidy his desk. He ran a comb through his sandy-coloured hair and popped a mint in his mouth to mask the smell of tea. He had just donned his jacket when he heard a knock at the door.

'Come in,' he said. He walked around to the front of his desk in readiness to greet his wealthy client.

Trudy opened the door and stood aside for Rebecca Talbot. 'I'll bring your tea along in a few minutes, Ms Talbot,' Trudy said as she backed out of the office.

Faulkner's guest studied him with a level of intensity he found unnerving. Then, she caught her breath. Her gaze shifted from his face and travelled the length and breadth of his body. Finally, she scanned his small but comfortable office and nodded approvingly.

Something about the woman seemed familiar. She looked the same age as himself, although due to a woman's ability to mask her age, she may have been a year or two older, he guessed. She had a shock of shoulder-length hair that partially obscured a pearl necklace, and her emerald-green eyes enhanced her radiant smile. She was dressed in a classic knee-length dress, showing off her slender figure. She held out a well-manicured hand for Faulkner to shake. Her grasp was firm but warm and she held onto Faulkner's hand a little longer than was necessary.

'Goodness gracious, Sam Faulkner! You've blossomed into the perfect gentleman I always hoped you would be.' Rebecca Talbot stepped forward and kissed him on the cheek.

The lilt of her voice and the familiar scent of her perfume transported him back thirty-six years to his boarding school. He had last seen Rebecca Vavasour when she had been rushed, unconscious, in an ambulance to York General Hospital. The school governors had sacked Bourcher for the assault but then hushed up the incident, allowing the former headmaster to ply his brutal trade elsewhere. Rebecca Vavasour had not been reinstated by the governors, even though Faulkner had railed against their callousness and lack of regard for natural justice. But Faulkner had been a thirteen-year-old schoolboy and was powerless to intervene against a bureaucracy that had stonewalled him at every turn.

As time passed, his outrage morphed into guilt, and then shame that his former school had persecuted then abandoned the former matron. As he stood holding her hand, a swirl of conflicting emotions played havoc with his senses. He had no wish to revisit what had been a traumatic period of his life, but he could not deny he still felt drawn to this mysterious and beautiful woman.

He released her hand just as Trudy re-entered the office bearing a cup of tea. 'I see you're getting on splendidly with our guest,' Trudy said. Sam detected the faintest hint of jealousy in her voice.

'Um, yes. We're old colleagues. We were reminiscing about our time at Red House. Miss Vavasour – I mean Ms Talbot – was a member of staff,' Faulkner replied as he beckoned Rebecca to the chair opposite his desk.

'Ms Talbot is an important client now and deserves your full attention,' Trudy reminded him as she made her way out of the office.

'Of course.' He took his seat and pulled out a file from his desk drawer containing Rebecca's details and proposed dates of travel. 'May I ask the occasion for your trip to Africa?' Faulkner asked.

'I'm retiring from the family business in September,' Rebecca replied. 'I thought I would take my daughters, their partners and some close friends on a trip of a lifetime before they take over responsibility for the firm. Charlotte, my eldest, is already in her early thirties. Goodness knows, they'll get few opportunities for adventure once they're running the business.'

'Very wise. We can tailor an experience you'll remember for the rest of your lives.'

'There's one condition: I want you to be our guide.'

Faulkner felt himself being drawn into her web and he knew it would be hard to free himself if he did not keep his wits about him. 'Cavalier Tours has some excellent guides, Ms Talbot. Most are more knowledgeable and, dare I say it, sprightlier than I.' Faulkner paused. 'Will Mr Talbot be joining the tour?'

'John and I divorced last year. I'll be reverting to my maiden name once I've left the family firm.'

'I'm so sorry to hear about your marriage, Miss Vavasour.'

'Please call me Rebecca, Sam. I think you've earned that privilege.'

'Nothing would give me greater pleasure than to be your tour guide, but I've critical business to attend to here in York. My staff are depending on me to renegotiate our business loan.'

'I won't take no for an answer, Sam. I met your office manager, Trudy Stanhope, and I'm confident she can manage your affairs while you're away. I'm prepared to guarantee your loans while you work for me.'

'Work for you? I thought this was just a holiday to Africa?'

'Hear me out, Sam. I'm retiring for a reason. I've unfinished business and I can't do it without you.'

'Let me guess,' Faulkner said, exasperated. 'You still believe Red House was stolen from your family three-and-a-half centuries ago and you want it back? With all due respect, I suggest it's time to let it go, Rebecca.'

'That's what my father said thirty-six years ago when I

threatened to take Bourcher to court. And my grandfather said the same thing ten years before that. Twelve generations of the Bourcher family have profited from Rebecca Slingsby's murder because we were told "it's time to let it go".'

'I'm sorry. I didn't mean to offend you.'

Rebecca smiled and leaned over the desk to touch his arm, as if to reassure him that she was not offended. 'My family created Vavasour Pharmaceuticals as a distraction from the injustice that gnaws at our souls like a cancer. I won't let this curse afflict my daughters, Sam, and it's for that reason I came here to request your help to return Red House to its rightful owners.'

'I understand your passion, Rebecca, but I don't understand how I can help you. Why not hire a lawyer or a forensic historian?'

'Because I believe you're a direct descendant of Colonel Samuel Fauconberg, the Slingsby family steward at Red House in the 1640s.'

'The Colonel of the Northern Horse during the English Civil War?' said Faulkner, recalling his history lessons with Captain McTavish. 'That's not possible. He was executed in 1660 for the murder of Benedict Bourcher.'

'I've being doing a bit of research. A Major Fauconberg was sent to Tangiers in 1661 to set up a garrison in the new English colony. That might have been him. Then one of his descendants may have anglicised the family name to Faulkner. That happened all the time.'

'That seems like a long bow you've drawn, Rebecca, but if you're suggesting I have some spiritual connection with Red House that might give you the answers you're looking for, then I'm sorry, but I don't buy it.'

'Something led you to the package you discovered beneath the stables.'

'But if the annotated evidence in the prayer book I uncovered wasn't enough to convince a judge that Red House was stolen from the Slingsby family, then surely the matter is settled?'

'You lived in that house as a schoolboy for over five years, Sam. You were a curious child, and you explored every nook and cranny of that building like no other. There may have been other clues you discovered, even if they meant nothing to you at the time.'

Faulkner remembered the dreadful scene in the hidden room

in the attic. It had haunted him for decades, despite his attempts to put it out of his mind. He resented Rebecca's intrusion into his private guilt and tried to close her down.

'I'm sorry, Rebecca. Nothing would make me happier than to see Red House taken away from the Bourcher family, but I've a business of my own to run. I don't believe in ghost stories, and I don't want to waste any of your valuable time or money on a wild goose chase.'

Rebecca sighed at Faulkner's response. 'There's another and more vital reason I need your help.'

'As long as it doesn't involve ghost hunting, I'm happy to hear you out.'

'I'm thinking of challenging Nigel Pride for the seat of Greater York at the next election.'

'The Pride family has held that seat for over one hundred years. I wish you good luck with that.'

'The Vavasour family has a longer history in York than the Prides ever had. That's why I'm reverting to my maiden name. He can be beaten by the right candidate.'

'But you're one of Britain's most successful businesswomen. Why would you get into politics when you have nothing left to prove?'

'Because Pride is a dangerous man. He's a hardline religious puritan and a political extremist. He's just become chairman of the Freedom League.'

'The Freedom League? I've never heard of them, but freedom sounds like a good thing to me.'

'Sam. You need to wake up! The world is changing around you. They've hijacked a feel-good word like *freedom*, but these people believe in strict control. They're Nazis dressed in Savile Row suits. The only thing they're missing is a credible führer.'

'Are you sure you're not pursing a personal vendetta? I wouldn't blame you if you were, but this is an extraordinary way to get even.'

Rebecca looked as if she was about to get up from her chair and walk out of the office, but instead she took a deep breath. 'Sam, this is serious. He's a clear and present threat to democracy.'

'You don't need to beat him in an election. For some strange reason he still holds me in high regard. He's chairman of the

Old Cavaliers club and still sends me their newsletters. I'll have a quiet word in his ear and tell him to pull his head in, just like I used to at Red House.'

Rebecca sighed in exasperation. 'Since I left Red House, the Pride family has been conducting a personal vendetta against *me*. They've been making vile insinuations I was a sexual predator during my three months there. At first it seemed like a sick joke, but now it's impacting my family and my business.'

Faulkner looked appalled at Rebecca's revelation. 'I'm sorry to hear that, Rebecca. I knew Pride was a rogue, but I didn't think he would be so vindictive.'

'You have no idea, Sam. It's been remorseless. Nigel Pride has become more insidious in the last few months. He's using conspiracy theory message boards to launch his attacks against my company. Our share price has dropped twenty per cent since he started this.'

Faulkner studied the woman opposite him and felt the vestiges of his schoolboy crush resurface. 'You were the only member of staff at Red House who ever cared for my emotional and mental wellbeing, and I'll be forever grateful to you. On that basis I'm happy to vouch for you in public if Pride tries to slander you again.'

'I was hoping for a little more than that, Sam.'

'What *were* you hoping for, Rebecca?'

'That you would be by my side during the next election. You have the business skills to manage my campaign, and your high profile as an ex-rugby international would give me the credibility I need to launch my political career.'

'I'm flattered, but I'm no Richard Branson and no-one cares anymore that I once played for England.'

'That's why I thought we could be useful to each other. I could help with your ... short-term cashflow crisis, and you could be my shield against the misogynists and trolls who will try to disrupt my election campaign. As for your England career, my eldest daughter, Charlotte, once had posters of you on her wall. She begged me to see you. What do you say?'

'I don't even know your political views. You could be a communist, for all I know.'

'I run a billion-pound pharmaceutical company. Do you think that's likely?'

'Let me guess. Based on the values you taught me at Red House, you're a Liberal Democrat?'

'Close, but I'll be running as an independent. I have left-of-centre social views and right-of-centre views on the economy. I'm proud of my country and its democratic heritage. That's why I want to strangle Nigel Pride's neo-fascist crusade at birth.'

'I need time to think, Rebecca. I like to hold my cards close to my chest when it comes to politics.'

'That's why I'd like you to be my guide on our safari to Africa. We can get to know each other again and you can interrogate me about my politics. If you don't like what you see, then we can part on good terms.' Rebecca dipped into her handbag and pulled out a Coutts Silk Credit Card. 'Would half-a-million pounds paid in advance be enough for a two-month safari?'

CHAPTER 23

The River Thames, London

Faulkner sipped the cruise boat's complimentary glass of Pimm's and lemonade and grimaced at the taste. He excused himself from the throng of senior government politicians and worked his way towards the side of the boat. He looked over his shoulder to see if he was being observed, then tipped the red mixture into the Thames, making sure the slices of orange, cucumber and mint stayed in the glass.

He was unsure why he had accepted the gold-embossed invitation from Nigel Pride to join the politically themed 'Pimm's and Magna Carta' river cruise. It had arrived the same day as his meeting with Rebecca Vavasour which had piqued his curiosity. He wanted to find out for himself if there was any substance to Rebecca Vavasour's allegations that his old school colleague was a dangerous man, or whether she was just paranoid. Normally, an invitation to join a horde of self-obsessed politicians would have filled him with horror, but he reassured himself that at the very least he might pick up a new client or two for his struggling business.

The weather was perfect: a balmy thirty degrees and a cloudless blue sky; the movement of the boat created a cooling breeze that played at his hair. He donned his sunglasses and watched the Houses of Parliament slide by on the starboard side of the long, narrow cruise boat. He knew he should mingle with the guests, but didn't want to disturb the feeling of inner peace that cosseted him while he watched the procession of famous old buildings as the boat floated upriver.

An attractive woman in a blue-printed Laura Ashley dress disturbed his reverie. She had a mane of thick blonde hair cascading over her shoulders.

'Would you fetch me another Pimm's, young man?' she asked in a tone suggesting a lifetime of privilege.

Faulkner gazed at the woman through his Wayfarer sunglasses. It had been at least ten years since anyone had referred to him as 'young man', but he had kept himself in good physical condition and had been fortunate enough to retain most of his youthful good looks. The woman was in her early forties and would have once been considered striking, he thought. She had high Nordic cheekbones and Cupid's bow lips, reminding him of the singer Debbie Harry. But years of high living and alcohol had left their mark. She had an athletic physique, but it was apparent she was fighting a battle to stay in shape. Her heavy makeup could not disguise the encroaching lines around her mouth, nor the effects of hard partying on the clarity of her eyes. He had seen her on television several times and recalled she was a junior government minister with Thatcherite leanings.

'The waiter is over there,' he said, pointing out a black-suited man carrying a silver tray full of fast-disappearing alcoholic beverages.

'Oh! I do apologise. You look too fresh-faced and innocent to be a member of the Freedom League.'

Faulkner caught the eye of the waiter and beckoned him over. The junior minister selected a Pimm's from the tray, and then as an afterthought took a beer, which she handed to Faulkner.

She winked at him. 'I saw you tip your Pimm's overboard just now and figured you must be a "real ale" man.'

'Very perceptive,' Faulkner replied as he took a sip from his beer.

'Don't tell me you're a Labour backbencher?' she said. 'We do get a few of those on our cruises. They like the thrill of stepping into the shoes of their political opponents. A bit like sneaking into their better half's closet to try on a fresh look.' She fingered the name badge pinned to his lapel, then smoothed down the fabric of his suit jacket with her fingertips. 'If you ever feel the need to experiment a little ... Samuel ... do look me up.'

'I can assure you, Miss Oakton, I'm not a Labour backbencher. Nor do I feel the need to step into anyone's closet other than my own.'

'A pity.' She stared at him over her glass of Pimm's with hungry eyes. 'Then may I ask what *did* tempt you to join our cruise?'

'He came as my honoured guest,' said Nigel Pride, who had marched across the deck to join them. He kissed the junior minister on both cheeks then coiled his free arm around her waist like a malnourished python preparing to constrict its prey. 'Please excuse Penelope, Faulkner. She can be such a tease.'

Faulkner nodded at Pride and the two men appraised each other for the first time in three decades. Pride had grown even taller but still looked like a newborn giraffe taking its first steps. His jet-black hair was oiled against his scalp and thick spectacles were balanced precariously on his long nose.

'You're looking good, Nigel,' Faulkner lied. His old school colleague looked pasty and in need of a good feed.

'Are you still playing rugger, Sam?' Pride said, staring at Faulkner's toned physique with a touch of envy. It was the first time Pride had ever used Faulkner's Christian name. He turned towards Penny Oakton. 'Sam captained England for a few years, you know.'

'I still play every now and then to keep fit, but the injuries take a little longer to heal nowadays,' Faulkner admitted.

'So, if you're not a politician, then what are you? A banker, a lawyer? A captain of industry, perhaps?' asked Oakton.

'A travel agent.'

'Oh!' Oakton gazed over Faulkner's shoulder as if she thought she should catch the attention of someone of greater social standing. 'Never mind. You can upgrade me to first class on my next trip to St Moritz.'

Pride withdrew his arm from around her waist then smacked her impishly on her behind. 'Now run along, Penny. Sam and I were best friends at Red House, and we have so much to catch up on.'

'Red House? Not *the* Samuel Faulkner everyone talked about? One of Bourcher's boys? Then you must have heard all about me. I was Red House's first female head prefect, but it would have been ten years after you left.'

'To be honest, I didn't even know Red House had admitted girls to the school until I heard it had closed down,' Faulkner confessed.

'Surely you did?' Oakton sounded offended. 'We "Old Cavaliers" have always been a close-knit bunch and must stick together.'

'Penny was a legend during her time at Red House, I'm led to believe,' said Pride.

'I took no nonsense from the boys, I can tell you.' She winked at Faulkner once again. 'Red House was a more civilised institution under my head prefecture. We focused on moral and religious fortitude, and our academic results surpassed those of the Bourcher era. The cane was only used for severe breaches of our code of honour, such as disloyalty to one's own.' Oakton winked at Faulkner and brushed an imaginary piece of fluff from his lapel. 'Well, well, well, the legendary Samuel Faulkner. Unfortunately, I must mingle with the other guests, but you know where to come, especially if harsh discipline is still your thing.' Penny Oakton smiled at Faulkner, then tottered towards a knot of politicians near the stern of the boat.

Pride extended his free hand towards Faulkner, who shook it without enthusiasm. He still blamed Pride for the savage beating he had received at the hands of Bernard Bourcher and the shameful treatment Rebecca Vavasour had received from the school governors.

'Thank you for the invitation,' Faulkner conceded. 'I must say, it was something of a surprise to receive it.'

'And I was even more surprised you accepted. You've never attended any Red House reunions before. There are at least a dozen Old Cavaliers on this cruise, including Delaney, Stuart and Walters. I'll introduce you to them later.'

'They're all MPs?'

'Some of them. But most are here because our association is based on the values we held so dear at Red House. You do still believe in those values, don't you, Sam?'

'Some of them.'

'Splendid! You see, despite our minor differences, the values we learned at Red House will bind us together and make us stronger as a nation, just as the Board of Governors intended. The Freedom League is the vehicle to make that dream a reality and we want you on our side.'

'I heard you're a bunch of crazy neo-Nazis.'

Pride laughed. 'Being proud of one's country does not make one a Nazi. Far from it. We're libertarians who believe in small government, lower taxes, and personal freedoms. We value the English way of life. If you work hard and contribute to the betterment of your country, the colour of your skin, your gender, or even your religious background doesn't matter. But of course, it helps if you went to the right sort of school.'

They paused as the cruise boat went under Chelsea Bridge. Battersea Power Station loomed to the port side of the boat, while the Chelsea Flower Show gardens slid by on the starboard side. The talk of the English way of life conjured up images of country pubs, lush parklands, Twickenham, strawberries and cream, and grandiose buildings like Red House. Faulkner found himself beguiled by the pictures in his mind.

'It's time for you to take your rightful place among the leaders of our great nation, Sam. The Freedom League will be sponsoring candidates in winnable seats across the nation at the next election. Of course, we'll do this under the guise of the Conservative Party, but we're planning to take full control of the party once we're elected.'

'You've infiltrated the Conservative Party?' said Sam in disbelief.

'Keep your voice down, Sam. Not everyone on this boat is aligned with our vision. But to answer your question, we have affiliates in every party in Britain, including Plaid Cymru and the Scottish Nationalists. We even have half-a-dozen in the Labour Party.'

'Why me? I don't fit the bill of a privileged reactionary.'

'I must admit we haven't always seen eye to eye, and there were times when I resented your popularity at Red House. But with age comes maturity and I came to understand your lack of inherited wealth and your Yorkshire grit gave you a certain drive that might prove useful to the cause.'

'You mean as a party political attack dog? That's not my style, Nigel.'

'Hear me out. Your business may be failing and your personal life a disaster, but there's one thing that will remain with you for the rest of your life, and that's your Red House education. My father, the Board of Governors and Bernard Bourcher may have seemed harsh at times, but they instilled in you a love of country, an addiction to hard work and leadership qualities that would have made you an empire builder had you been born a hundred years earlier. And let's face it, Sam, you were the one everybody looked up to at Red House. I may have been head prefect, but I always walked in your shadow.'

'Bourcher called me a rebel of the worst kind and you agreed with him.'

'Bourcher is history, and I was an impressionable teenager. But his assessment of you was correct. You're a rebel, and a rebel is what we need to shake this country out of its torpor. I've convinced the executive of the Freedom League that you're the man to help us achieve it. Cometh the hour, cometh the man and all that.'

'I'm flattered, Nigel, I really am. But I don't even care about politics.'

'But you care about the state of our country?'

'Of course.'

'Then it's your patriotic duty to do the right thing. We'll sign you up to the Conservative Party this weekend.'

'Can't I be a Liberal Democrat?'

'Um, no. That's the one party where we don't have any influence and you'll have no chance of getting elected if you join them. We'll get you preselected as the candidate for Elmet and Rothwell, which is a safe Conservative seat and a twenty-minute commute from where you live. Then it's just a matter of ensuring you're briefed on local affairs and national politics in time for the election later in the year. What do you say?'

'I need to think about it. I have a business to run and responsibilities to take care of. Can I get back to you next week?'

'Of course you can. But the party will take care of all that nonsense for you. We'll bring in a host of bright young consultants to run your business and ensure it remains solvent while you're serving king and country. Look, we could get you a junior ministry in Trade and Industry. Or would you prefer the Foreign Office? You were always good at French and your knowledge of history was encyclopaedic.'

A pigeon landed on the deck of the motor cruiser and pecked at the crumbs of a cucumber sandwich dropped by a young woman in a tight skirt. The distraction gave Faulkner the opportunity to consider Pride's proposition in silence.

'I should mingle, Sam. The ball's in your court,' said Pride. 'But before I do, I need to warn you about a mutual acquaintance. I heard Rebecca Vavasour paid you a visit last week.'

'Yes. She wants to book an African holiday for her family.'

'Don't you think it's a bit of a coincidence you received a visit from her just as my invitation arrived?'

'I'm a travel agent and she wants to book an expensive holiday. I'd call it fortuitous.'

'She didn't mention anything about challenging me for the

seat of Greater York?'

'If she did, it must have slipped my mind. I've other issues to worry about.'

Pride looked thoughtful for a moment. 'I don't know how to put this politely, Sam. She's an obsessive conspiracy theorist with paranoid delusions. She believes the patriarchy is a real thing, intent on creating a totalitarian state. And she still thinks Bernard Bourcher is alive and well and plotting the overthrow of the monarchy.'

'Is Bernard Bourcher still alive?'

Pride rolled his eyes. 'He died over twenty years ago, Sam. Some say it was because Rebecca Vavasour hounded him to an early grave.'

'How did he die?'

'Suicide. He went swimming one day and never came back. Admittedly, it took the coroner ten years to sign the death certificate because there was no body, but they found his clothing on a beach in Skegness.'

'She seems well adjusted to me.'

'That's just the point. On the surface she comes across as a successful and attractive businesswoman. The press loves her. She could do my campaign real damage. But underneath she's a seething mass of feminist anger looking for a target. She's dangerous, Sam, and she may try to recruit you again.'

'What do you mean "again"?' Faulkner bristled at the suggestion he had ever been recruited.

'It was well known she tried to subvert the culture at Red House. She saw the school as the patriarchy in action and tried to undermine it from within. I'm not blaming you for falling for her charms, Sam. She was ... still is ... a beautiful woman, with a touch of class. I nearly fell into her trap myself. All I'm asking is that you be on your guard and be wary if she approaches you again.'

'She was an eighteen-year-old girl on work experience for her degree at Cambridge.'

'It's time to choose which side you're on, Sam.' Pride patted Faulkner on the shoulder. 'In the meantime, let me introduce you to Jimmy Stuart. You remember him from Red House, don't you?' He pointed to a small, fat, balding man who was swilling champagne on the opposite side of the boat. 'He used to be something of a looker at Red House, but time has not been kind to him. Nevertheless, he runs a successful IT gaming business and is loyal to the cause. We can catch up at Runnymede after I've given my speech.'

* * *

'Samuel Faulkner? Well, I never!' said Jimmy Stuart as he marched towards Faulkner. He intercepted the waiter on the way and scooped up another flute of champagne. 'Do you remember me from Red House? I must say I was in awe of you when I was a tick, but I've grown up a bit since those days.' He patted his ample belly to emphasise the point. 'How the devil are you, man?'

Faulkner shook Stuart's hand and looked in vain to see if he could escape the unwelcome intrusion.

'I hear you're something in IT?' Faulkner said. He took a step backwards to re-establish the personal space between them.

'Yes. Most of my misspent youth was in front of a laptop. I ended up buying a small software company specialising in the "Dungeons and Dragons" genre and the rest is history. I'm worth a tidy packet now.'

'Pleased to hear it.'

'How much are you worth, Faulkner? I bet you've done well for yourself.'

'Enough to get by.'

'You were always a modest one. So, you're thinking of joining the FL?'

'The FL?'

'The Freedom League.'

'Oh! I'm just curious, really. I'm not sure why I was invited.'

'Isn't it obvious? Pride wants to pack the House of Commons with Old Cavaliers so we can fulfil the destiny Bernard Bourcher and the Board of Governors had planned for us. You know, putting the "Great" back into Britain and all that.'

'It sounds rather fanciful to me.'

'Not at all. If we can get enough FL sympathisers elected, we'll purge the government of moderates and demand loyalty from the rest. The Red House Old Cavaliers will get all the top jobs, and then we can start bringing Britain back where it belongs.'

'And where does it belong? The Empire is never coming back, Jimmy.'

'Maybe not. But we can dismantle the unions, get rid of red tape, build up the navy, cut immigration, reduce the welfare state, bring back conscription and introduce the death penalty. Then, Bob's your uncle.'

'Who's going to do all that?' Faulkner asked.

'We were rather hoping you would, actually.'

'I think you've got the wrong man, Jimmy. I despise politicians.'

'That's why you're perfect for the job. Our movement needs leaders with a love of country and a sense of duty, not snout-in-the-trough politicians. And I have to say, you have the necessary charisma to charm the public. You were the best rugby captain that England ever had.'

As Stuart glanced over Faulkner's shoulder and stared at Windsor Castle, which loomed on the starboard side of the cruise boat, a dark shadow crossed his face.

Faulkner noticed his gaze. 'The royal flag is flying, which means the king is in attendance,' he said.

'Ah yes, the Windsor interlopers who stole the throne from my ancestors,' Stuart replied.

'Do you really believe that nonsense? Captain McTavish only said it to wind you up. He knew you were a descendant of the Stuart dynasty.'

'The fact remains that in 1714, my ancestor James Stuart had a far greater claim to the throne than the German George of Hanover. By rights, it should be yours truly on the throne.' Stuart belched and patted his ample stomach.

'Then we can say the nation dodged a bullet in 1714.'

Stuart scrutinised Faulkner's face, unable to tell if his ex-school colleague was engaging in friendly banter or being serious. 'The movement sees the current king as an impediment to its aims, so don't get too sentimental about the Windsor dynasty,' he said in a fit of pique.

'Really? The king seems quite sensible to me.'

'On the contrary. His views are too sanctimonious, verging on woke. And he's more predisposed to political interference than is good for the country. We suspect he'll veto some of our more radical legislation, and the Freedom League has decided he's got to go.'

Faulkner glanced at a long, sleek cruise boat heading down the Thames in the opposite direction. Its trailing wash caused their boat to rock in the gentle turbulence.

'You'll have to excuse me for a moment,' Faulkner said. 'I think I'm going to throw up.'

CHAPTER 24

Edelman Becker Investment Bank, London, October 2024

Vance Messervy sat at his desk at the international investment bank Edelman Becker and opened his leather briefcase. As was his habit, he was the first trader into the opulent London office.

He pulled out his laptop and loaded the spreadsheets he had been working on the previous evening. Rummaging deeper into his briefcase he extracted a small Ziploc bag containing a gram of cocaine and a shaving mirror. He tipped one third of the cocaine onto the mirror, then pulverised the coke with his Amex card until the crystals turned into white powder. When he was satisfied with his handiwork, he divided the pile into four straight lines, and hoovered them up his nose with a rolled-up twenty-pound note. He sat back in his chair to let the drug take effect.

Minutes later the chemicals hit his brain. The doubts and dark thoughts that had recently plagued his life were swept away as the cocaine high stimulated his dopamine pathways. Once more he felt like the bright young thing who had earned hundreds of millions of pounds in non-fungible token (NFT) profits for his employer, Edelman Becker.

In the euphoric fug that enveloped his brain, he replayed his moment of glory, which had astounded the risk-averse partners who ran one of the world's most respectable investment banks. They had given him six months to prove his idea that a fortune could be made selling digital artwork stored on the Blockchain. Messervy had contacted his old art school colleagues and asked them to create a series of outlandish cartoon images of dope-smoking pot plants wearing baseball caps and wraparound sunglasses. He had 'minted' them on Ethereum as NFTs, and contacted his old base metal futures clients, promising to turn them into overnight millionaires.

Messervy's collection of five hundred *Pot Plants with Attitude* had sold for five hundred pounds per image. Edelman Becker had made a quarter of a million pounds in sales overnight. But that had only been the beginning. Messervy went to work reselling their client's digital images to Hollywood actors, sporting superstars and reality TV celebrities, for millions of dollars each, bringing a glamorous cohort of new customers to the firm and taking a commission of five per cent on each sale.

Within a year, Messervy's NFT scheme had made more money than the rest of Edelman Becker's trading desks combined. He had become an instant celebrity in London society and his crowning moment had come when he had attracted the attention of the beautiful Charlotte Talbot, heiress to the billion-pound Vavasour Pharmaceutical empire. They had commenced a two-year romantic relationship, despite the hostility of Charlotte's overbearing and judgemental mother, Rebecca Talbot.

The romantic match had been the perfect counterbalance to his London 'wide boy' image and had given him serious credibility with the city toffs. Charlotte was descended from landed gentry, even if that land happened to be in the heart of grubby Yorkshire, very far from London.

That had been before the disastrous holiday Rebecca Talbot had organised in Africa for her extended family and friends. Messervy had protested to Charlotte that two months away from his trading desk without wi fi or the ability to watch his beloved Arsenal football club play would be too much to endure, but his fiancée would have none of it.

Messervy put such thoughts aside and looked at his trade positions. They painted an alarming picture. The NFT market had declined in value by over fifty per cent since his return from Africa and his clients were desperate to unload their digital artwork before the retreat became a rout. The biggest problem for Messervy was that the senior partner of the London affiliate, Jonas Becker, had privately bought two *Pot Plants with Attitude* for over five million pounds each during the peak of the market and was having to sell his Chelsea flat to cover his losses.

Messervy found himself coming down from his cocaine high. The four lines had lasted twenty minutes, and he was tempted to snort two more. For the first time he admitted to himself that he was a coke addict and his nose hurt like hell from overuse. The inevitable crash that came from his cocaine high felt like a multiple pile-up on the M1 motorway. The self-pity of his broken relationship with Charlotte washed over him like the pounding waves of a stormy beach. He blamed Charlotte's mother and Sam Faulkner in equal measure for his tumultuous break-up.

His dark thoughts now fixated on Faulkner and that confounded safari to Africa. The man was pushing fifty, thirteen years older than himself, and yet he looked like he was in his physical prime. He exuded such capability and masculinity that Messervy had felt inadequate by comparison. Faulkner had been attentive and respectful to the Talbot women, but also knowledgeable and witty. His exploits as an ex-England international had been an ever-present backdrop, yet Faulkner had been modest about his career to the point of awkwardness. Messervy had been consumed by jealousy, but his put-downs aimed at Faulkner's lack of wealth and ambition had been like water off a duck's back and made Messervy seem petty in the eyes of the women he had been so desperate to impress. Charlotte, who seemed under Faulkner's spell for the entire trip, had told Messervy to 'grow up' when they were partying on the deck of their houseboat on the shores of the beautiful Lake Kariba.

Messervy had responded to his fiancée's admonishment by hitting the drugs and alcohol hard. He had been paralytically drunk the night he had fallen overboard from the houseboat into the crocodile-infested lake, but he had sobered up when he saw the glinting yellow eyes of the monstrous reptiles gliding silently towards him. He had screamed louder than Charlotte had during their viewing of the new *Exorcist* movie at the Odeon the previous summer.

The dreadful experience had been compounded by the humiliation he had felt at being rescued by Faulkner. By contrast, Faulkner had acted like he had swum a couple of training laps at the local swimming pool and had waved away any fuss from the Talbot women. Instead, he had made them a round of coffee with a flawless love heart etched in the froth. Then he had excused himself before retiring alone to his cabin for the night. Charlotte had dumped Messervy the very next day.

Messervy had no intention of playing the helpless victim. Since his return from Africa, he had immersed himself in the darknet. His computer was loaded with software packages such as 'The Onion Router', which guaranteed anonymity while he was making secretive transactions on the dark web. The software allowed him to trade NFTs and cryptocurrency under various aliases, thereby avoiding the inconvenience of paying taxes on his trades. More recently, the dark web had become a safe and reliable source of supply for his cocaine habit.

Since his return from Zambia, he had developed a fascination for neo-fascist internet forums that had matched his sombre mood. He had flirted with sites run by the National Rifle Association, 'Stop the Steal' message boards and even an anti-vax forum. But he found them shallow and predictable.

By pure luck he had stumbled upon a forum on the dark web calling itself the Protectorate. Its members were intelligent, urbane and rational – unlike the crazies infesting many of the sites he had previously frequented. The Protectorate was an ideas forum, whose stated aim was to bring back the values and policies that had once made Great Britain the undisputed powerhouse of the world. Its main contributor was a character called 'Purge', who Messervy suspected was a senior politician within the government.

Purge's views were hardline without being puerile or nonsensical. Purge advocated for lower taxes, personal responsibility and hard work. He wanted to bring back national service and rebuild the navy to something like its former glory. Messervy found Purge's arguments for the re-industrialisation of Great Britain compelling, and the picture Purge painted of a prosperous, confident, pub-loving Britain was silky-smooth and beguiling.

There was a secondary contributor called 'Iron Mike', who was appealing for online recruits who would turn Purge's vision into reality. His recruits would become the twenty-first-century version of Oswald Mosley's infamous 1930s 'Blackshirts', but instead of wielding clubs and fists, they would use their IT and gaming skills to troll their political opponents into subservience.

In the next few minutes, Vance Messervy signed up as a fully-fledged 'Darkshirt', pledging his loyalty to Purge, Iron Mike, and the ideals of the Protectorate online forum.

* * *

Clifford Street, York, UK

Rebecca Vavasour's election office buzzed with energy. A dozen young volunteers rushed from desk, to desk, to desk, to organise photo opportunities and favourable media publicity for their candidate. A woman wearing a University of York sweater ordered promotional material in readiness for election day in two weeks' time.

The eastern wall of the plush office was covered by a bank of monitors, which broadcasted a dozen different news channels to the campaign staff. At the far end of the office near the window, Rebecca had created a miniature TV studio, which doubled as an informal meeting area. A leather sofa and two matching easy chairs surrounded a smoked-glass coffee table, on which were placed a selection of upmarket lifestyle magazines. Opposite the studio, a serviceable kitchenette offered the campaign staff and guests the opportunity to relax and enjoy coffee and biscuits. The broad window behind the sofa offered glimpses of medieval York, including Clifford's Tower, a medieval fortress perched atop an imposing grass mound.

Rebecca sat down on one of the leather chairs, smoothed down her skirt, then beckoned Faulkner to the chair next to her. She crossed her legs and waited as her assistant made some last-minute adjustments to her hair and makeup.

'My apologies, Sam. Austin Chambers from *Look North* is coming to interview me in ten minutes. He's a friend of Nigel Pride and may give me a grilling.'

'He may look intimidating, but he's fair. He enjoys the cut and thrust of a challenging interview and appreciates intelligent responses. I think you'll get on well with him.'

'So, have you thought about my offer?'

'To be your campaign manager?'

'Of course.'

'It's a hard decision for me. I feel conflicted.'

'In what way?'

'Despite my dislike for Bourcher and the school governors, I'm proud of what we achieved at Red House. Many of my former classmates have attained high political office, which is astonishing for such a small school, and there are another thirty or so old boys who are standing as candidates in this election.'

'You should be proud, Sam. You were a natural leader at Red House. That's why I was so keen to teach you compassion and respect for those less fortunate than yourself. I know you'll be a credit to the community, whereas Nigel Pride will create a government in Bernard Bourcher's image.'

'Nigel Pride isn't the monster you think he is, Rebecca.'

'You need to think this through, Sam. Pride epitomises the worst Red House had to offer. He's a danger to democracy and if you let him, he'll use every dirty trick in the book to discredit me.'

The activity in the office went up a notch as Rebecca's office manager ushered in Austin Chambers and his entourage.

'Let's continue this conversation after the interview. Perhaps I can convince you then,' Rebecca said as she rose from her chair.

'Of course. If you can convince Austin Chambers you're a worthy opponent to Nigel Pride, then you'll have a pretty good chance of convincing me too.'

* * *

Austin Chambers had a reputation for eviscerating politicians who were vague with their answers and loose with the truth. He could reach the nub of an issue in the first few minutes of an interview and probe for any character weaknesses using his soft, beguiling Yorkshire accent. Many a political career had crashed and burned following their encounter with Chambers.

Faulkner watched from the wings of the makeshift TV studio as Chambers warmed up with a few easy questions. He asked if she was surprised by the recent Gallup poll that showed her running neck and neck with Pride, despite her status as an unknown independent candidate. Rebecca suggested she was offering the voters a moderate and sensible alternative to Pride's hardline views. Her record as a successful businesswoman and one of the largest employers in the area was important to voters, and her two hard-working daughters were an asset to her campaign.

After his initial barrage of questions had been answered with openness and considerable charm, Austin Chambers asked Rebecca a series of more probing questions. He queried the authenticity of her campaign platform, her focus on family values and her desire to combat social division. He questioned her political inexperience, but appeared impressed when Rebecca lambasted her opponent's more contentious hardline policies. When Chambers complimented her on her refreshing approach and firm grasp of the issues, Rebecca smiled into the camera as if she were sharing a moment of private intimacy with the audience. Faulkner realised she would steal the hearts of three quarters of a million *Look North* viewers and that Nigel Pride's political ambitions had been holed below the waterline.

It was not just the viewers' hearts she had stolen. Long-dormant feelings welled up inside Faulkner and he chided himself for his previously aloof behaviour towards Rebecca. He knew he had only one course of action to take, and he must do it immediately.

CHAPTER 25

Like all good conspiracies, the explosive allegations Vance Messervy was about to post onto the Protectorate forum contained a grain of truth. He had discovered Rebecca Vavasour had worked as a matron in an all-boys boarding school for three months as part of a work-experience programme. There had been some kind of scandal at the school that had been hushed up during her tenure. The details were vague and no actual witnesses could be traced, but the furtive imaginations of the site members would do the rest.

Iron Mike had boasted he had recruited over two hundred of Britain's best online gamers and social media trolls to act as a virtual army for the Freedom League. Their mission was to spread conspiracy theories and disinformation like honey to the judgemental social media readers and sensationalist press. Their goal was to create a false sense of crisis within the country and generate the narrative that only the FL could solve the contrived problems they had sown into the minds of the gullible. The Darkshirts were to be the Freedom League's shock troopers and the social media 'pile on' was to be their weapon of choice.

Messervy had expected Rebecca Vavasour and her family to be a prime target for a Darkshirt pile on. After all, she was a moderate candidate running against the de-facto leader of the FL, Nigel Pride in the constituency of Greater York. But the call had not come and Messervy had run out of patience. He would light the fuse in the most vicious way possible whether Iron Mike was ready or not.

It served the bitch right. He had been unable to concentrate at work as his craving for cocaine increased. He had lost his appetite and developed involuntary muscle spasms in his face. He suffered regular nose bleeds and sniffled continuously, much to the irritation of his former boss Jonas Becker. Becker had summoned him to his top-floor office and complained that Messervy's irate NFT clients were threatening to sue the firm for their huge losses sustained on his worthless digital art. Messervy had laughed at Becker's naivety and suggested the NFT market would rebound to record highs. But the market had continued to tank, and in any case Messervy was too busy surfing the dark web for up to eight hours a day to care about Edelman Becker's pampered clients. He had lost his job, and blamed Rebecca Vavasour, Sam Faulkner and their damned African jaunt for his spectacular fall from grace.

He had not heard a single word from Charlotte, even though he had sent a huge bunch of roses, several emails and dozens of texts begging her for another chance. The stuck-up bitch had unfriended and blocked him on Facebook, and then ghosted him on all social media platforms. He had once considered shielding her from the attention of the Protectorate's Darkshirts when the shit hit the fan, but now the gloves were off.

At last, the file he been waiting for arrived with a 'ping' on his laptop. It had been sent by a graphic artist he had met on the dark web called Shagmeister. He opened it up and smiled at the subtle transformation Shagmeister had made to Rebecca's campaign photograph. The original photo had been a still from her *Look North* interview, but instead of looking coquettish when she had glanced sideways at the camera through her fringe of silky hair, Shagmeister had made her look conniving and cruel. Her eyes had been narrowed into a squint and he had added a hint of red to the whites of her eyes. Rebecca's smile had been turned into a snarl and her nose had been given a slight twist to make it look crooked. Shagmeister had accentuated the lines in her face to age her by ten years and had given her a jowly appearance. The resulting image could not have looked more demonic had it come with a pointy black hat and a flying broomstick. To the casual reader it was the same image that had taken the country by storm, but the subtle changes would give his article a sinister twist. He smiled as he crafted the title of his article, 'Lust for power or lust for Britain's innocent children? The shameful secrets of Big Pharma's political predator.'

* * *

'Hey boss, how's the campaign going?' Charlotte said as she walked into Faulkner's glass office at Rebecca's campaign headquarters. She had her mother's stunning looks, combined with an easy-going nature and a self-depreciating sense of humour.

Each afternoon at four o'clock she would take time off from

her role as chief executive officer of Britain's fastest growing pharmaceutical company, to check in on her mother's campaign. She called him so often that Faulkner now knew her mobile number by heart.

Charlotte was holding two takeaway coffees from the Castle Tea Rooms and handed one to Faulkner. She perched on the near corner of his desk and propped an elegantly shoed foot on a cardboard box full of election posters. Faulkner sighed in mock disapproval at her casual demeanour but then smiled at her like an indulgent older brother. She had taken her break-up with Vance Messervy badly, but Faulkner had assured her that she was far better off without his controlling behaviour and casual use of party drugs.

Faulkner tore his gaze away from Charlotte's long legs and punched a series of keys on his laptop. 'Your mother is a phenomenon. According to the latest Ipsos MORI poll, Rebecca has a seventeen per cent lead over Pride, with ten days to go. With a lead that big, she should be working on her acceptance speech.'

'But you still have doubts?'

'Nigel Pride is one of the most experienced and conniving politicians in Britain. There's a reason his family has held Greater York for almost a century.'

'But what could he do at this late stage? You said yourself, Mum has all the momentum and because she's an independent, she presents a small target.'

'There was the incident at Red House that Pride might try to exploit.'

'But you said Pride wouldn't bring it up because it would be more damaging for him than it would be for us.'

'Pride is so far behind in the polls he might just take the nuclear option.'

Charlotte stood up and paced the office. She had the demeanour of a young lioness defending her territory. 'I won't allow that sleazy, pompous man to destroy my mother's reputation for a second time.'

'Leave that to me. After all, that's why she hired me. And don't forget you have an appearance with your mother and sister on Saturday at the York Barbican. It's being televised and could be worth ten thousand votes.'

Faulkner's phone trilled and he pulled it from his pocket. 'Excuse me, Charlotte. I'd better take this. It could be *The Telegraph* replying to my request for an interview.'

'Sure, I'll check on the team and see if they need any help.'

Faulkner smiled as Charlotte left the office and answered the phone. 'Good afternoon. Sam Faulkner speaking.'

There were three seconds of silence before a gravelly voice came online. 'Sam, it's Cedric Humphries from the *Yorkshire Herald*. Umm, I'm not sure if you remember me. We were at Red House together?'

'Ah, yes. Humphries! What a surprise. How are you doing these days?' Faulkner remembered Humphries as an awkward, delicate child who was often on the wrong end of Bernard Bourcher's beatings, even though he took care to avoid the schoolboy shenanigans.

'Umm, I'm well. And what about you? Are you still playing rugby for the Saracens?'

'I gave up ten years ago. I only play to keep fit now.'

'We always knew you would end up playing for England. But … umm … I'm afraid I'm the bearer of some rather awkward news and I wanted to reach out to you before we go to press.'

'Really?' Faulkner replied.

Humphries sounded apprehensive, as if he were not relishing the conversation that was to follow.

'I understand you're running Ms Vavasour's election campaign for the seat of Greater York?'

'Correct.'

'We wanted to give you the right to comment on our exclusive story before we publish.'

Faulkner's stomach began to churn. He gripped the phone harder and leaned forward in his seat. 'What exclusive news would that be, Cedric?'

'There's been an allegation that Rebecca Vavasour sexually violated eight boys at Red House.'

'Cedric, that's malicious nonsense and you know it. Who on earth gave you that slanderous story?'

'I'm afraid I'm unable to divulge my sources.'

'You don't need to. I know it was Nigel Pride.'

'Umm … no, it wasn't him actually.'

'Cedric, you of all people can't print this. You were there, for goodness' sake and would know there's no truth to the allegations. It's going to end up in a nasty, drawn-out legal case, and the *Yorkshire Herald* will get sued for millions.'

'Our legal team has cleared the story, Sam. There are eight reliable complainants.'

'Including Pride?'

'No, he's staying quiet.'

'Who're the others? Let me talk some sense into them.'

'They're protected witnesses, Sam. The police won't allow anyone to talk to them.'

'The police? For fuck's sake, Cedric, what have you done?' Faulkner put the phone down on the desk and ran his fingertips through his hair before snatching it up again. 'Listen, Cedric, you need to examine your conscience. You're hanging an innocent woman out to dry because Nigel Pride wants to play dirty politics.'

'The *Yorkshire Herald* felt it was its civic duty to report these serious allegations to the police. After all, we're talking paedophilia here.'

'How can you have fallen for this cheap trick, Cedric? Even *The Sun* wouldn't touch this story. Think, man. You signed the petition asking for Rebecca's return after the Board of Governors sacked her. If I remember correctly, you cried like a baby for weeks when they refused to reinstate her.'

'There's no need to make this personal, Sam. I can't remember any petition but of course, if you can produce this petition by six o'clock tonight, we can include it as part of our story.'

'At least give me twenty-four hours to sort this out. You owe Rebecca that, at least.'

'No can do. If we don't run with it, our source will go to the *Daily Mail*.'

'I'm warning you, Cedric, when this is over, I'll be coming for you.'

'Then I'll take that as your comment on the story. We're publishing first thing in the morning.'

CHAPTER 26

Austin Chambers scented blood. 'There are eight allegations of sexual misconduct, Ms Vavasour. Surely you can't deny them all?'

'Seven, actually. One of the so-called incidents involved my campaign manager, Sam Faulkner, who was present at the time, and he's denied any of these allegations took place. The rest are vague insinuations. This has all the hallmarks of a dirty tricks campaign and only a fool would take them seriously.'

'So, you're branding the electorate of Greater York as fools?'

'You made that inference, Mr Chambers, not me. What I'm saying is the voters of Greater York are far too smart to fall for such an obvious stunt.'

'Let's look at these allegations. Three suggest you groped boys during your evening surgery, one accused you of prowling through their dormitories at night and a further two suggested you hugged them without their consent. These are serious charges, Ms Vavasour.'

'I was a matron in charge of the boys' medical and pastoral welfare. Two thirds of the boys had at least one serious rugby injury during their time at the school. Tending to their injuries was my job in the same way a doctor or a nurse must tend to the physical needs of their patients. Similarly, comforting homesick eight-year-olds who have received six strokes of the cane is not child abuse in any normal person's mind. Rather, I was discharging my responsibilities for pastoral care to those who had no access to their mothers.'

'What about the charge you examined a child's naked bottom in the boy's bathroom?'

'I was summoned to the bathroom by the Reverend Kitchen to examine several deep lacerations to a boy's gluteus muscles and welts to his lower back caused by the administration of *twelve* strokes of a horse crop by the headmaster. At no point was I alone with the boy.'

Chambers leaned towards the cameras as if he were going in for the kill. 'I understand the Reverend Kitchen died twenty years ago, so it's just your word against the complainant's. How can the voters of Greater York trust you when such serious charges have been levelled against you, Ms Vavasour?'

'Because there was only one boy who ever received twelve strokes of the cane during my tenure as matron. That boy's name is Sean Moody, and he has sent me an email from Sydney in Australia, saying he's not made any allegations against me, and he recalls the Reverend Kitchen was present at all times. He suggests someone is trying to sabotage my election campaign and he's looking forward to suing the *Yorkshire Herald* for weaponising a personal matter that caused him considerable trauma.'

'But that still leaves six complainants. You cannot dismiss them all as hearsay.'

'Those six remaining complainants have two things in common. They're all standing for election, and they're all members of the Freedom League. Do I have to join the dots for you, Austin? I thought you were smarter than that.'

Chambers leaned back in his seat and raised his arms in capitulation. 'I see. It does appear as if the accusations are flimsy at best. You must understand, we believed it was in the public interest to raise these issues on live television and you've answered the allegations most eloquently. I thank you for your time and wish you best of luck in the election.'

'I have one more point to make,' said Rebecca. 'Since this story was leaked by the *Yorkshire Herald*, my lead in the polls has slipped from seventeen points to just five. It's a sad day for democracy when lies and half-truths can be published without regard for the consequences of those actions. It shouldn't be the candidate with the dirtiest bag of tricks who wins the day.

'Well said, Ms Vavasour. I think we can all agree on that.'

* * *

'You were amazing,' Charlotte said as she hugged her mother. 'I think we're back in business.'

The strain of the previous days was starting to show on Rebecca's face. Her eyes, which usually sparkled with life, had a haunted look to them. She slumped into the soft leather chair and accepted the glass of wine Faulkner offered her. She tried to relax and gazed at the hive of activity in her campaign office.

'Six days to go! It feels like the campaign has been going on forever,' Rebecca said as she sipped her wine.

'I've issued a writ for libel against Cedric Humphries at the *Yorkshire Herald*. I don't think we'll be hearing from him again,' said Faulkner.

'Do you think that's wise?' Rebecca asked. 'We don't want to get the press offside.'

'It shows we're serious. There may be other attempts to discredit you.'

'How are the polls looking after the latest *Look North* Interview?' Charlotte asked.

'There's been a small jump. We have an eight per cent lead. The main thing is we've stopped the rot for now,' Faulkner replied. 'However, I'm not convinced we've dodged the bullet.'

'How can that be?' said Rebecca. 'Even Pride's most vocal supporters are suggesting the *Yorkshire Herald* took their article too far.'

'Our social media analysts are picking up a surge in activity designed to discredit you. You've become the target of a concerted campaign by a rag bag of extremists, misogynists and trolls. I'll monitor the situation over the next few days, but if this trend continues it'll do considerable damage to your campaign.'

* * *

Vance Messervy topped his glass to the brim with vodka and slammed it down his throat in one motion. He savoured the burning sensation as it ran down his throat. It was his fifth shot since midnight, but it was doing little to ease his mood. Iron Mike was not happy about his unsanctioned and amateurish attempt to discredit Rebecca Vavasour, claiming it had been clumsy and easily foiled. Although her lead in the polls had slipped from seventeen points to eight, it was still a winning lead. Iron Mike called for greater discipline and threatened to expel any Darkshirt who stepped out of line. The best conspiracies he said, were more obscure, more cryptic. He quoted the example of the legendary 'Q', whose Nostradamus-style posts had sent his conspiracy-obsessed followers into a lather.

Messervy staggered his way through the detritus on the floor of his living room and opened the laptop he used solely for surfing the dark web. He signed on using his dark web identity,

'Plague', and activated his VPN address, which he knew would keep his browsing activities secure. Once in the darknet, he joined the legions of drug dealers, information leakers, arms dealers, pornographers and hackers who were trading their illicit material for cryptocurrency. Also on the web were myriad law enforcement agencies posing as criminals, attempting to entrap the unwary.

In a rare moment of lucidity, Messervy had flushed his remaining three ounces of cocaine down the toilet in a futile attempt to kick the habit. His nasal passages had almost worn through, and he was finding it difficult to function. But his need for a cocaine rush was all consuming. He typed in the web address of the drugs marketplace 'DrDoper' and waited for it to open. It offered him a bewildering choice of Peruvian flake, premium uncut, pure fish scale, Norwegian high-quality, and German uncut. Feeling like a Sainsbury's customer faced with an aisle full of shampoo brands, he dithered until he selected ten ounces of 'premium uncut II'. He transferred one thousand pounds from his Bitcoin wallet into DrDoper's Bitcoin account, using a fake email address and a package locker service. On a whim he placed a second order for two ounces of Peruvian flake on behalf of a thirty-four-year-old woman from York, whose name happened to be Charlotte Talbot.

He smirked as he typed in Charlotte's real contact details. Charlotte's inbox would soon be inundated with spam for unsavoury products, scams and phishing emails.

Messervy typed in a second URL, and the familiar Protectorate message board greeted him. He cracked his knuckles in anticipation of a long night on the keyboard. He knew he was mixing with serious political heavyweights but due to the anonymity rules of the site, it would be impossible to tell whether he would be corresponding with the Prime Minister of Great Britain, a party staffer or a random extremist. One former contributor known as 'Six' had convinced Protectorate members he was a senior MI6 operative, until he had been exposed as a thirteen-year-old schoolboy with a fondness for John Le Carré spy novels. Despite Six's fall from grace, he had left an indelible impression on Messervy. Six's heady mixture of espionage, politics and conspiracy had set the board alight during the teenager's brief period of celebrity.

Messervy intended his posts to be equally mysterious and, if anything, even more cryptic. He briefly considered Iron Mike's call for restraint and discipline from his Darkshirts, but then dismissed those warnings. Messervy was going for broke, and it would be up to the Protectorate to keep pace.

He opened a new thread entitled 'The Gordievsky Tapes'. Oleg Gordievsky had been a colonel in the Russian KGB, but for ten years he had been in the pay of MI6. Code-named 'NOCTON', he had delivered a treasure trove of invaluable information to his British handlers. Messervy swallowed his sixth vodka and began to type what he hoped would be the start of a major new conspiracy:

NOCTON told MI6 about an explosive allegation, but then three crucial hours of debriefing tapes went missing. How do I know? I was NOCTON's interrogator in '85.

They watch me 24/7 but have not yet compromised the Protectorate site so I'm safe here for the moment.

Putin had a secret British daughter in 1968. Let's call her Jezebel. Putin's blood money keeps her rich and powerful. The coming election is the trigger to rouse her from her slumber. Her mission? To devastate this green and pleasant land with sulphur and fire, pillars of salt, and woke politics (Ez16, 48–50).

Beware the Cavalier attack dog who guards Jezebel.

Follow the breadcrumbs, Great Britons, or face the consequences.

– Plague.

Messervy rested his alcohol-befuddled head on his forearms but avoided the temptation to fall asleep. He tried to re-read what he had written but the words danced in front of his eyes. After six vodkas, his utterings no longer made any sense to him anyway, so he hit send. Iron Mike would be as mad as a cut snake, but Messervy no longer cared.

* * *

The Conspiracy Today podcast, Live on YouTube

'Welcome to another edition of *Conspiracy Today*. I have the pleasure of welcoming to our studios our regular expert on Cold

War-era conspiracies, Professor Colin Teale. Tell me, Professor, what do you make of this intriguing snippet sent to us by one of our subscribers this morning?'

'Well, Jennifer. Thank you for the invitation to your show.'

'You're most welcome, Professor.'

'As you know, I'm someone with deep connections to MI6, and happen to be Britain's foremost expert on coded messages of this type.'

'Do you believe it's a hoax, as one of our listeners has suggested?'

'We must never discount that possibility, but it's clear the author has access to sensitive classified information on our most famous Russian spy, Igor Gordievsky.'

'Such as?'

'The reference to NOCTON.'

'What's so special about that?'

'My understanding is NOCTON was the codename given to Gordievsky by MI6. The fact it's capitalised, as was the practice at the time by MI6, lends authenticity to the author's claim.'

'What do you suppose was in the missing tapes the author who refers to himself as "Plague" was warning us about?'

'Now we're coming to the crux of the problem. The information was deemed too sensitive even for those higher up in government, such as Margaret Thatcher. The author is suggesting Putin had an illegitimate daughter when he was sixteen years old, and she has been living in England ever since as a Russian sleeper.'

'Could Putin have had a secret daughter?'

'Indeed! Vladimir Putin has two legitimate daughters and many illegitimate ones, if rumours are to be believed.'

'What kind of threat is Plague warning us about?'

'We're dealing with some kind of moral threat rather than a terrorist event.'

'How did you arrive at that conclusion?'

'Ah! I did some research. The reference to EZ16 is from the *Old Testament*. Let me quote you from Ezekiel, Chapter 16: "Now this was the sin of your sister Sodom: She and her daughters were arrogant, overfed and unconcerned. They were haughty and did detestable things before me. Therefore, I did away with them as you have seen". The ancient City of Sodom is mentioned, which leads me to believe some kind of vile ritual is about to take place on Tuesday following the election.'

'But Gordievsky predicted this in 1988! Why has it taken so long for Agent Plague to reveal the secret to us now?'

The Professor sighed in exasperation at the naivety of the question. 'He's under the close eye of the Cabal's security forces. Perhaps this was his first opportunity?'

'Do you have any clues to the identity of Putin's secret daughter?'

'None as yet. The breadcrumbs left by Plague are obscure. Especially the reference to the Cavalier attack dog who guards Jezebel. I'll leave that task to your subscribers.'

'Thank you for your insights into this intriguing mystery, Professor.'

'You're most welcome, Jennifer.'

CHAPTER 27

Barnsley, Yorkshire

Joel Skinner removed his thick glasses and wiped their smudged lenses with a tissue. After twelve hours of continuous activity on his laptop, a migraine pulsed through his brain like the beating black heart of a cobra. He popped four paracetamol capsules from the silver foil and washed them down his throat with a can of Red Bull.

Skinner's 'Emo' appearance, lack of sporting prowess and stutter had always made him a target for the cool kids, except when they needed help with their homework. He had graduated from grammar school in Barnsley with straight A's in Maths, Physics and Chemistry, but two unsuccessful interviews for a job as a software engineer at the local glassworks factory had left him with a profound sense of persecution and a grudge against society. He had withdrawn to the safety of his bedroom and turned to competitive gaming on the internet under the pseudonym 'Hades Helltrooper', where he had made enough cryptocurrency from his gaming addiction to afford the latest tech, a second-hand Mini Cooper and a wardrobe dominated by black clothing.

He activated his VPN, logged onto a specialist forum dedicated to decoding the sensational claims of a British intelligence insider known as Plague, and began a new thread. He called it 'Plague's prophesies deciphered' and began typing:

After twenty-four hours of research, I have cracked Plague's prophesy ... He downed the remnants of his Red Bull and tossed the empty can into his overflowing bin. He sensed a delicious surge of adrenaline in the pit of his stomach as he typed. There were two dozen regulars active on the message board, and he craved their 'thumbs ups':

Plague is warning us about a woman from the elite called Rebecca Vavasour. His breadcrumbs are leading us to the article in last week's Yorkshire Herald about her history of child molestation. "Beware the Cavalier attack dog" kept me guessing half the night, but then it hit me. Rebecca Vavasour's campaign manager and accomplice, Sam Faulkner, has a travel agency named Cavalier Tours. Plague is warning us the Cavalier is an agent for the Cabal, and Cavalier Tours is nothing more than their northern headquarters.

Skinner pressed send and felt a quiver of anticipation as his post hit the forum's website. He could imagine the kudos he would get from his fellow conspiracy theorists for cracking Plague's obscure message.

Skinner smiled in delight as he received his first 'thumbs up'. It was from 'Krypt Kreeper', a regular board participant, but not the sharpest tool in the box. His computer pinged and a new post popped onto the screen:

How does this NOCTON character know all this stuff? Krypt Kreeper wrote.

Gordievsky was a colonel in the KGB. He knows everything, Skinner replied.

Why was Plague quoting weird religious texts from the bible? Krypt Kreeper persisted.

A second thumbs up hit his thread. It was from the ultra-militant 'Ballsov Titanium': *That bible reference freaked me out too.*

Rebecca Vavasour has two daughters, Charlotte and Athena. That's how I worked out the identity of Jezebel, wrote Skinner. *Plague is suggesting they're fat, lazy, arrogant bitches.*

Five more thumbs up had appeared on Skinner's thread, and he felt an adrenaline rush every bit as powerful as five Red Bulls.

You've got to admit, Putin's secret daughter, woke politics and a bible reference all seems a bit far-fetched, even for this forum, wrote 'Shagmeister', the board's graphic artist.

Maybe Plague was stoned when he wrote it, suggested Ballsov Titanium.

Skinner felt the shadows of self-doubt creep into his mind and his deep-rooted insecurities return. He needed the forum's affirmation like an astronaut needs oxygen. Three more posters joined the conversation, including the shadowy 'Recusant'. Skinner beamed with pleasure at his keyboard. The Recusant was known as the 'big dog' and possible founder of the forum.

Congratulations on deciphering Plague's prophesy, the Recusant wrote. *The question is, what are we going to do with this information? We can't let Putin's daughter turn our beloved England, this land fit for heroes, into a new Sodom and*

Gomorrah.

We should dox the entire Vavasour family before they inflict their woke politics on us, suggested Ballsov Titanium. *How do we get hold of their personal details?*

I saw Charlotte Talbot had bought two ounces of cocaine on the dark web using her legit email address and mobile number, wrote Skinner, his self-confidence returning.

Then the silly bitch deserves what's coming. I'll post her address to my gamer buddies, wrote Krypt Kreeper. *They'll love screwing with her head.*

I'll share her number with my 3000 Telegram Messenger contacts, wrote Shagmeister.

So, we're agreed, wrote the Recusant. *Jezebel and her daughters must be silenced.*

* * *

Faulkner drove his Land Rover down the narrow roads of Marston Moor and past the memorial to the famous Civil War battle that had taken place three hundred and eighty years before. He recalled Captain McTavish had once taken him and a group of history students on a field trip to the battleground, to watch a re-enactment of the battle by members of the Sealed Knot society.

He turned left towards the village of Moor Monkton, then crossed the busy York Road onto the two-mile driveway leading to Red House Estate. The old school crest was still displayed on a prominent white sign, even though the school itself had closed several years before. Declining enrolments, strict government legislation and changing social trends had meant the small, isolated boarding school could no longer pay its way.

Faulkner allowed his memory to feast on the once familiar but largely forgotten twists and turns of the narrow country road. As the Red House woods loomed to his left, he recalled the numerous rides he had taken there on his American quarter horse, with Sean Moody and other school colleagues. He had reconnected with Moody on LinkedIn and was happy to learn his former friend ran a successful software company in Sydney.

Faulkner spied the imposing red-brick building in the distance that had once been the centre of his world. It was smaller than he remembered, but no less imposing. It still dominated the landscape and emanated an aura of immutability. It was a building that had paid host to Civil War soldiers, Victorian era gentry, and generations of high-pitched schoolchildren.

As he parked his Land Rover in the visitor car park, he pulled out the strange invitation he had received from his bitter old school rival Michael Lambert. The ex-vice school captain was now a retired brigadier. Faulkner had learned on the 'Pimm's and Magna Carta' river cruise that Lambert was a practising arms dealer with clients in several despotic African, Middle Eastern and South-East Asian regimes. What had intrigued Faulkner was that Lambert was renting Red House Estate as the headquarters of his arms-dealing business.

Brigadier Lambert was standing ramrod straight at the grand entrance to Red House as he waited to greet him. Lambert was wearing battle fatigues, even though he had retired from the British Army five years earlier. He still presented an imposing physique, but his olive-green Gurkha jumper could not disguise the beginnings of a paunch, nor could his maroon beret cover the flecks of iron grey in his hair. His jaw was still set firm as if in defiance of his acne-scarred complexion. Attached to his belt was a vicious-looking recurved Gurkha *khukuri* knife, glinting in the weak autumn sunlight.

Despite their often fractious relationship at Red House, Faulkner smiled as he shook Lambert's hand. He was pleased to note he stood two inches taller than the brigadier and he was able to match the other man's grip with ease. At Red House, Lambert had towered above him, but almost forty years on he could tell the ex-soldier was daunted by his presence.

'At ease, Brigadier,' Faulkner said in jest.

To Faulkner's surprise, Lambert took the military 'at ease' stance and placed his hands behind his back. An awkward silence ensued before Faulkner issued the command to 'carry on'.

'Are you still playing rugby, sir?' Lambert said, to disguise the awkwardness of the situation.

'Please call me Sam. Only socially. It takes me too long to recover from the knocks and bumps nowadays. Yourself?'

'I'm ashamed to say I gave up rugby after leaving Gordonstoun School. I stopped growing after I left Red House. But I always knew you'd end up playing for England. I followed your career when you started playing for the Saracens. You could dance your way through a crowded opposition midfield like Rudolf Nureyev.'

'I believe I still have the imprints of your famous hand-off etched into the side of my head,' replied Faulkner with a wry smile.

Lambert laughed at the memory. 'Yes, I caught you a good one, but you made up for it with your ferocious tackling in every training session thereafter. You were the only one who could tackle me.' He stared into the distance as if trying to capture the good times in his mind's eye. 'I told my wife, Jasmine, that the proudest moment of my life ... apart from marrying her and the birth of our twins ... was winning the Yorkshire prep schools seven-a-side rugby competition for the third consecutive year.'

'It was indeed a proud moment ... I understand you're renting Red House?' Faulkner enquired, changing the subject.

'It suits my purpose and the rent was cheap. I'm afraid it's not in the best state of repair. The roof leaks like a sieve and the heating bills are a nightmare.'

'What is your purpose, if you don't mind me asking?'

'We'll get round to that later, but I'm sure you're itching for a tour of the old school and its surrounding buildings. It hasn't changed much, although I've had to board up a few of the rooms. A few places are out of bounds, even for an eminent Old Cavalier like yourself.'

Faulkner was surprised at Lambert's cordial, even reverential tone. They had been bitter foes at Red House and Lambert had been Pride's most loyal wingman.

'Thank you, Brigadier. I'd appreciate a trip down Memory Lane.'

* * *

'I'll leave you two boys to reminisce about the good old days,' said Jasmine Lambert in her clipped Cheltenham Ladies' College accent. She was tall and thin, and the perfect spouse for a British Army brigadier. Like Lambert, her hair was turning slate grey and was tucked into a neat bun behind her head. She picked up her glass of pinot grigio and marched out of the study at the double.

Faulkner had enjoyed his tour of the old school and its grounds. Lambert had shown him the infamous row of cold showers, the classroom block, and the stable yard, where a local stable lad had been grooming four horses. The familiar sights, sounds and smells brought memories flooding back. Lambert showed him the refurbished dormitories, where rows of neatly made beds lay as if waiting for the ghosts of schoolboys past to return. On an impulse, Faulkner had asked if they could head to the attic to see *Cromwell* dormitory, but he had been disappointed when Lambert said it had been boarded up due to the dangerous state of the floorboards. Finally, they had visited Sir Henry Slingsby's chapel, where the smell of furniture polish, the sight of empty wooden pews and the magnificent stained-glass window had transported him back to his childhood as effectively as any time machine could have done.

'I imagine you're wondering why I invited you here,' said Lambert. He put down his mug of tea and turned to face Faulkner.

'The thought had crossed my mind,' replied Faulkner.

'Nigel Pride told me you attended his Pimm's and Magna Carta river cruise during the summer.'

'That's correct.'

'Yet, you still chose to become Rebecca Vavasour's campaign manager?'

Faulkner shrugged. 'I was never a fan of politics. My presence as her campaign manager is to ensure a fair contest. I owe her that at least, after all we put her through.'

'As do I, Sam. The incident in the head prefect's study in 1988 has weighed on my conscience for too long. I suffer a profound sense of shame each time I think about it. I would like to assuage my guilt.'

'That's very noble of you, Brigadier, but I fear you may be too late. I've reason to believe she'll be subjected to an abusive social media onslaught in the lead up to polling day that will be impossible to counter. I suspect most of it will come from members of FL's so-called Darkshirts.'

Lambert sat back in his chair and steepled his fingers under his square-set chin as if in deep thought. 'You see, I was very much under the influence of Nigel Pride at Red House. He helped me with my studies, and I watched his back. The incident with

Rebecca Vavasour was out of character for me. I was besotted by her at Red House and yet Pride persuaded me to go along with his little stunt. I don't know what would have happened if you hadn't come into the study when you did. I shudder every time I think about it. In a way, I'm grateful to you and Moody for knocking me senseless.'

'Will you repeat that in court if Rebecca is forced to defend her reputation?'

'You misunderstand me. I'm a fully paid-up member of the Freedom League. I still hold dear the values of Red House and my loyalty to Pride remains firm.' He pointed towards the rows of old school photographs adorning the far wall of the library. Generations of Old Cavaliers in cricket whites and rugby jerseys stared back at them. 'Behold some of the most gifted young men England has ever produced. Men such as these made Britain the powerhouse nation it once was, and they could do so again. You're in at least a dozen of those photos, Sam, and in each one you were the captain of our all-conquering rugby team. At your feet are three Yorkshire schools seven-a-side championship trophies, one All-England school gala trophy, and a shield commemorating an eight-match unbeaten tour of South Africa, Australia and New Zealand. You were the most outstanding pupil to have ever walked the famous red passage. You should be leading the movement to remake Britain, not wasting your time running a second-rate travel agency.'

'I happen to enjoy running a "second-rate" travel agency.'

Lambert sighed. 'You had the ability to skip through an entire opposing first-fifteen rugby team without them laying a finger on you for the whole match. The boys looked up to you, Sam, in a way they did not look up to Nigel Pride or me. You're still their natural born leader and should be leading the Freedom League to glory. Will you not, even at this late hour, join our campaign?'

Faulkner took a sip of his tea. 'I'm not a politician, Brigadier. And like you, I feel that we, the Old Cavaliers, owe Rebecca a debt for the scandalous treatment she received at Red House. This is my way of repaying that debt.'

'She was asked to leave Red House because her values did not align with those of the school.'

'Then why did you bring me here?'

Lambert looked out of the French windows as if he were

wrestling with his conscience. Then he looked Faulkner in the eyes. 'If you ever repeat in public what I'm about to say, the consequences for you will be dire.'

'I understand. It will not be repeated.'

'I do not wish to compound my personal feelings of guilt towards Rebecca by taking part in the social media witch hunt that is about to take place.'

'So, what are you proposing?'

'A quid pro quo. You scratch my back and I'll scratch yours.'

'I'm listening.'

'The coming social media pile on against Rebecca Vavasour has not been sanctioned by me or anyone in the Freedom League. The Darkshirts' fascination for the scandal in the head prefect's study could be as damaging for Pride and me as it would be for Rebecca. I can give you the IP addresses of those renegades who have planned this.'

'The damage may already have been done. My analysts are picking up large volumes of hostile online chatter aimed at damaging her reputation.'

Brigadier Lambert laughed. 'You have no idea, do you? Once they unleash their firestorm of disinformation on the gullible, the angry, and the disaffected voters of Greater York, Rebecca's reputation will be destroyed. She wouldn't even get a job packing shelves at Tesco's.'

'And you're concerned Rebecca might reveal details about Pride's unusual sexual tastes?'

'Pride would deny it, of course, but you know what the press are like once they have the bit between their teeth.'

'How do I stop them? I need more than their IP addresses; I need names and contact details.'

'How you stop them is up to you. Even I don't have those details, just their online personas and their IP addresses.' Lambert handed Faulkner a cheap plastic USB.

'What else is going on here at Red House, Brigadier?'

'I'm telling you this as one Old Cavalier to another and on the assumption you'll join our movement once your infatuation with Rebecca is over.'

'I'm not infatuated with Rebecca, but do go on.'

'Oh. Pride must have been mistaken then. But I wouldn't blame you even if you were. I'm forming a mercenary army of one hundred elite troops. We already have thirty fully trained soldiers based here at Red House in the areas that are out of bounds to the uninitiated.'

'They're billeted in *Cromwell* dorm?' Faulkner suggested.

'The officers are in Cromwell and the non-commissioned ranks are billeted in Montrose and Belasyse dormitories. Eventually we'll open the other dormitories. The old refectory will become the mess and the playing fields will become our parade ground. It'll be just like the old days,' Lambert said with a nostalgic glint to his eye.

Faulkner ran the risk of probing too far, but discretion had never been one of Lambert's attributes. He decided to press on. 'May I ask the purpose of this mercenary army, Brigadier?'

Lambert hesitated but Faulkner held Lambert's gaze like a severe-looking general.

'The FL does not believe Britain's return to greatness will be achieved without eliminating a rag bag of violent radicals who may oppose our agenda.'

'You're recreating Oswald Mosley's Blackshirt movement from the 1930s?' said Faulkner. He almost choked on his tea. 'Or Hitler's SS?'

'I find that comment insulting,' replied Lambert. His back stiffened and his chin jutted aggressively. 'The fine young men joining my force are intelligent ex-SAS soldiers, whereas Mosley's Blackshirts were common thugs.'

'Well, that's reassuring,' said Faulkner in a sarcastic manner.

'Exactly. The problem is some of my recruits are a tad ring-rusty and that's the other reason I invited you to Red House Barracks.'

'Red House *Barracks*?'

'Yes, sir. Red House will become the nerve centre the most elite and ruthless paramilitary force on earth. I'm sure Sir Henry Slingsby would have been proud to see his former home used for such purposes.'

Faulkner doubted it, but he kept his opinion to himself. 'You do realise I've had no military training whatsoever. I don't see how I can help.'

Lambert laughed. 'I don't expect you to lead the brigade into battle! Good Lord! No, I want you to arrange a trip for them to Namibia. They're going to take down the rebel Caprivi

Liberation Army on behalf of the Namibian government. A nice little earner, and the brigade needs a bit of live action to brush away the cobwebs.'

Faulkner was appalled. 'I take *tourists* on safaris, not mercenaries.'

'Your choice, sir. I can get someone else. But that's the deal. You get my soldiers into Namibia posing as tourists on a hunting trip, and I'll give you the IP addresses of our Darkshirt renegades.'

Faulkner blew out his cheeks and considered his options. Sometimes it was necessary to deal with the devil to achieve a greater good. He stuck out his hand towards Lambert. 'I think we can shake on it, Brigadier.'

CHAPTER 28

Barnsley, Yorkshire

Joel Skinner took off his glasses and breathed on their lenses. He wiped them clean with the bottom of his black T-shirt and replaced them on his nose.

It was the day before the Recusant had decided the digital harassment of Rebecca Vavasour should begin. The timing of the attack was designed to commence at seven p.m. on the eve of the election, when most people would be watching the TV news or scanning their social media pages. The renegade faction of the Darkshirts had been tasked with trolling every influential media outlet in the country. Skinner would start with the Yorkshire Herald, then spread his insinuations about Vavasour to his entire contact list and every social media outlet he had access to.

Skinner had worked himself into a fury of righteous indignation. He had spent the previous days surfing the comforting echo chambers of dozens of radical conspiracy theory websites. By constant repetition and reaffirmation of Agent Plague's conspiracies, he believed with absolute certainty Rebecca Vavasour was on the cusp of destabilising the morals of Great Britain. Her company, Vavasour Pharmaceuticals, was producing drugs that were turning the working class into woke-minded sheeple controlled by the global elite of the World Economic Forum. Well, now she would pay the price for betraying her country.

* * *

Yorkshire Herald headquarters, Leeds, UK

Cedric Humphries completed the draft version of his editorial column that was to be published on election day. The *Yorkshire Herald* had decided to throw its substantial weight behind Nigel Pride, despite claiming to be a politically neutral newspaper. Many staff had expressed their displeasure at the *Herald's* blatant political partisanship. However, Humphries had reminded them the paper had traditionally been a Conservative broadsheet and the members of the Pride family had been on the *Herald's* board for over a hundred years. Humphries neglected to mention to the staff both he and Pride were Old Cavaliers, classmates, and fellow members of the FL.

Humphries altered a few words of his editorial to make it more emphatic, amended a typo, then leaned back in his chair in satisfaction. The editorial acknowledged the paper's previous allegations about Rebecca Vavasour's past at Red House had been discredited, but insisted there was no smoke without fire. He flirted at the very edges of the UK's Defamation Act 2013, but there was no mistaking the 'malice aforethought' in his column.

He questioned Vavasour's motives for running for parliament by suggesting she was seeking to take Britain to a dark age of loose morals, military appeasement and economic weakness. By contrast, Pride would rebuild Britain's navy and save the great British pub. The editorial concluded by suggesting it was the duty of every responsible voter in Greater York to re-elect Pride to the seat that was *his by right*.

* * *

Heathrow Airport Terminal 3, Regus meeting room

Faulkner checked his watch for the fifth time in as many minutes as he waited for Sean Moody to meet him. The plush Heathrow Airport executive meeting room in which he sat had all the comforts of a first-class airport lounge but was furnished with an array of practical but comfortable office furniture and the very latest business technology.

It was eight p.m. and his old friend would be boarding Qantas flight QF2 to Sydney in twenty minutes' time. It would be the first time Faulkner would reunite with him in person since they'd left Red House in 1988. He had discovered on LinkedIn that Moody ran the largest artificial intelligence company in Australia specialising in combating cybercrime and deepfake software. With a USB containing Brigadier Lambert's time-sensitive information burning a hole in his pocket and not knowing where else to turn, he had requested an urgent online Zoom meeting with Moody. Moody had replied within seconds, saying he was mid-Atlantic on an Airbus A380 flying from New York to Sydney, but had a two-hour stopover in London and a business meeting in Singapore. He suggested the two of them meet at Heathrow in the executive meeting room.

Faulkner drained the remaining contents of his beer and decided to grab another from the self-serve bar at the far end of meeting room. It was obvious his old school friend had been delayed and would be texting his apologies shortly. He helped himself to a bottle of Cotleigh 'Barn Owl' Premium Ale and poured it into a glass.

'Hey! Where's my beer, you old pommy bastard?' yelled a tall, thickset man with a hipster beard, from the entrance to the lounge. The Australian accent was unmistakable, and his shabby chic image suited him perfectly. A dozen executives in tailored suits tut-tutted their disapproval at his noisy arrival.

'Sean? Sean Moody?' said Faulkner. He grabbed a second beer from the minibar and levered the cap from the bottle. Before he was able to hand it to his old friend, he was enveloped in a suffocating bear hug.

'Mate, you've aged well,' said Moody, looking Faulkner up and down. 'Are you still playing rugby?'

'Now and then. But what about you? I believe you're on the Forbes Rich List?'

'Yeah. I'm just about holding my shit together. But...' he patted his modest paunch '... jetsetting the world isn't doing my exercise regimen any favours.' He looked at Faulkner and grinned like the thirteen-year-old Aussie larrikin Faulkner remembered so fondly.

'Are you sure you've got time to talk? Your plane boards in fifteen minutes.'

'I've phoned my team in Sydney. They've persuaded Qantas to develop a technical fault that will delay QF2 for half an hour. It's cost me a grand or two, but if your list of IP addresses turns out to be half as valuable as I think it is, then it'll be money well spent.'

Faulkner double-checked he still had the USB in his pocket and felt the reassuring shape of hard plastic against his hip. He steered Moody towards his table at the far corner of the meeting room.

Moody drained half of the beer from his bottle with one

swallow then burped softly. 'Bloody Pommy beer. Tastes like it's been strained through an old sock.' He downed the rest of his beer in three seconds and waved to the lounge staff to fetch him another. 'Look Sam, we've got to get you to Sydney to meet the missus and the kids before we turn into a pair of geriatrics. But in the meantime, you'd better tell me where you got that data file from.'

Faulkner pulled out the USB from his pocket and slid it across the table towards Moody. 'Two dozen aliases and their IP addresses. That's all I've got.'

'Who are these guys?'

'Keyboard warriors. Renegades from Brigadier Michael Lambert's so-called Darkshirt digital brigade.'

'What, *our* Mike Lambert? The vice-captain of Red House?'

'The very same.'

'I didn't think he was smart enough to be an IT specialist.'

'He's not. He's Nigel Pride's head of security and has a team of geeks and gamers at his disposal. He runs the twenty-first century version of Oswald Mosley's Blackshirt thugs, both digital and physical.

'Well, well, well. Pride and Lambert are still as thick as thieves and up to their usual shenanigans. Who's the target of the intended troll attack you mentioned in your email?'

'Umm … Rebecca Vavasour. She's running against Pride in the General Election, which is in two days' time. According to Lambert, the attack starts tomorrow at seven p.m. It's timed to have maximum impact on the outcome of the election.'

'Rebecca Vavasour, the old Red House matron?' Moody gave a big belly laugh and lightly punched Faulkner's shoulder. 'You dirty dog! I should've known.'

Faulkner looked pained. 'I'm trying to prevent Pride from undermining British democracy. The fact that Rebecca happens to be the object of his coordinated cyber-attack is coincidental.'

Moody winked at Faulkner. 'Of course it is. Is she married?'

'Divorced.'

Moody shook his head in mock exasperation, then picked up the USB and examined it closely. He reached into his jacket pocket and pulled out a microcomputer, which he placed on the table. Moody switched on the device and inserted the USB. He ran a quick anti-virus scan on the USB and opened the file. He scrolled through the data, then whistled.

'What is it?' asked Faulkner, intrigued.

'Lambert is playing with some seriously bad dudes. I recognise at least half of the pseudonyms on the list. Some are known associates of a character named the Recusant. We've been chasing him for over twelve months. Each time we thought we had him, he's given us the slip.'

'Who's the Recusant, for goodness' sake?'

'He runs a dark web marketplace called *Battlefield Z*. Originally it traded in military antiques and war memorabilia, but in the last two years it's gone seriously badass.'

'What do you mean?'

'Two years ago, the Recusant was approached by a Russian cybercriminal gang, whose own dark web marketplace called *Z Stalker* had been taken down by the FBI. The Americans had strongarmed Putin into arresting the ringleaders, but within a year the main culprits had been released and started up again, using the Recusant's UK-based marketplace as a front. It provides all the usual dark web services.'

'Such as?'

'Despite its respectable "war relics" shop window, it deals in drugs, credit card fraud, ransomware-as-a-service and cryptocurrency laundering. It turns over billions of pounds a year.'

'And this guy, the Recusant, is the ringleader?'

'In name only. The Russians keep the serious money, but the Recusant will get his cut for sure. Enough to make him a very wealthy man.'

'How wealthy?'

'Tens of millions of pounds a year. Maybe more. Certainly enough to give him serious influence in his chosen field.'

'Extremist politics?'

'We think so.'

'So, why is the data on the USB so important?'

'By giving us the IP addresses of the main actors, we can put a trace on their transactions and bypass their VPNs and multiple layers of encryption. Our friend Lambert thinks we're going to shut them down, but we won't. Once we know enough about their digital footprint, we'll steal their identities and infiltrate the *Battlefield Z* syndicate. Lambert has just handed us the keys to the front door of the biggest criminal gang since the Mafia first ate pasta, and he's too thick to know it.'

'So, this information may lead you to the Recusant?'

'Exactly. We can lay a sting that might just catch the Recusant and his honchos in the act. We can withdraw his funds, disable his servers and get the feds on his case before he knows what day it is. This could be the biggest cybercrime bust in history.'

'When you say "catch him in the act", you do mean *before* the act, don't you? In less than twenty-four hours, these guys are going to launch a vicious trolling campaign on Rebecca. It'll destroy her, and I can't allow that to happen.'

'It doesn't work like that, Sam. Without a trail of digital transactions to follow, we'll have no trigger event and no evidence. It could take months, maybe years of patient detective work to make the connection. The feds won't act unless we gift wrap them the smoking gun, place it on a silver platter and lay it at their feet.'

'If Rebecca is trolled, Pride wins the election. If you can stop the trolls in their tracks, Rebecca wins. It's that simple. Rebecca doesn't deserve to get screwed over by Pride a second time. Even that low-life Lambert thinks it's a step too far.'

'I can hack into the computers of these Darkshirt renegades and create a bit of digital mischief. But once I do that, the Recusant will know we're onto him and he'll go underground.'

'That's the deal.'

'You're asking me to let the biggest cybercriminal gang on the planet walk free to protect the reputation of your girlfriend? These guys are turning our kids into coke addicts, Sam.'

'She's not my girlfriend, but ... yeah.'

Moody looked at his laptop and grimaced. 'The airline has put a call out for me. They're closing the gate in five minutes.' Moody snapped his laptop shut and downed the rest of his beer. 'I've gotta rush, Sam.' He stood up and gave a brief man-hug to his old friend. As he strolled towards the exit he paused and looked over his shoulder. 'Can you trust Lambert's data, Sam? I'll be taking a massive gamble by messing with their servers without the proper evidence.'

'I think so. Lambert doesn't have the intelligence to send us on a wild goose chase.'

'That's good enough for me. Look, the office in Sydney opens in a couple of hours. I'll email the file across to the team and we'll see what we can do.'

'I owe you one, Sean.'

* * *

Barnsley, South Yorkshire

As soon as Joel Skinner clicked on the URL that had been sent by the Recusant, he knew something was wrong with his trusty laptop. The operating system was running at a snail's pace, the screen's colours were pallid, and the keys were unresponsive. His home page flickered and turned blue. A string of code flashed across his screen as the system performed a bug-check analysis. This was replaced with the words 'DRIVER POWER STATE FAILURE (9f). A DRIVER HAS FAILED TO COMPLETE A POWER IRP WITHIN A SPECIFIED TIME.' Worse was to follow. The wording 'SEARCHING FOR USER GENERATED CRYPTO CURRENCY USING PROTOCOL 486' flashed on his screen before more random code appeared at the bottom.

'No. This can't be happening,' Skinner muttered. He hit the power button with his index finger to switch off the laptop, but the code continued its relentless march across his screen: 'SEARCHING EXTERNAL DRIVES IN 5... 4... 3... 2... 1...'

The screen turned black, and the image of a smiling 'V for Vendetta' Guy Fawkes mask ghosted onto the centre of his monitor, its sightless eye sockets mocking him. It was a sure sign he had been hacked by cybercriminals. Skinner watched in horror as his seven separate cryptocurrency exchange accounts appeared at the bottom of the screen. The accounts contained all the Bitcoin, Ethereum, Litecoin and Ripple he had earned in three years of gaming, equivalent to forty-three thousand pounds. A giant cursor controlled by an unseen hand hovered over the first account and clicked the 'Transfer Bitcoin' button. He watched in despair as his computer monitor displayed the words: 'TRANSFERRING THE CONTENTS OF COINBASE ACCOUNT 556.22.6678 to ACCOUNT [ANON R367G2NVBg51] in 5... 4... 3... 2... 1... COMPLETE. THE BATTERED WIVES' SOCIETY OF SKEGNESS THANKS YOU FOR YOUR GENEROUS DONATION. TRANSFERRING THE CONTENTS OF BINANCE ACCOUNT...'

Skinner scrambled across his room and yanked the plug from the router, but whatever malware was controlling his computer continued to drain the contents of his crypto accounts. In desperation he flung his precious laptop to the ground and smashed it into fragments with the thick soles of his emo-style boots.

* * *

Yorkshire Herald headquarters, Leeds, UK

Cedric Humphries hovered his mouse over the 'Transmit' button and prepared to send his explosive editorial to the production team. Before he was able to do so, an email pinged in his inbox, and he huffed in annoyance. He noticed the email was from the *Yorkshire Herald's* hard-nosed proprietor, Sir Eric Hardcastle, scion of the Yorkshire landed gentry. The title of the email was characteristic of Sir Eric's blunt language: *'Read this now!'* Sir Eric had already torn several strips off Humphries for his earlier article on Rebecca Vavasour, and he did not fancy a repeat performance. With a rising sense of trepidation, he opened the email.

It was blank except for a single file in an .exe format. It was typical of Sir Eric to use an obscure programme to deliver his message, but there was no mistaking his intention. The title of the file was 'C Humphries termination package'.

With trembling hands and wide, disbelieving eyes, Humphries clicked on the strange file. Instantly his screen turned blue, and a string of meaningless code spread across his screen. A moment later, the screen turned as black as Hades and the animated mask of one of the most famous Yorkshiremen in history, Guy Fawkes, materialised onto the screen. Its sightless eyes mocked Humphries for his crass stupidity in activating the malware-ridden payload sent by a nameless foreign hacker.

Humphries knew what was coming next, as the *Yorkshire Herald* was meticulous in training every employee on the menace of cyber-attack threats. Sure enough, the words he was dreading appeared in large, blood-red script at the bottom of his screen:

Oops! All very important file encrypted and no longer

possible to access. Nobody and never will be able to decrypt and restore so many critical Yorkshire Herald file. But not to despair. To unlock so many file, send eight million pounds in BTC to Bitcoin address ...

CHAPTER 29

High Petergate, York, election day

Faulkner guided Rebecca to her breakfast table at Bennett's Cafe in the Centre of York. He had selected a table with a view of the magnificent gothic York Minster cathedral, which dominated the city. Faulkner pulled out her chair, and then pushed it forward as she sat down. It had been raining, but an unexpected burst of winter sunshine lit up the city, causing the pavements of High Petergate to shine like marble. A colourful rainbow arched over the Minster, causing Rebecca to catch her breath.

'A lucky omen?' she said to Faulkner as he took his seat. 'But, for whom?'

Faulkner considered his reply before responding. He had checked the polls half an hour before, and they had indicated Rebecca would win comfortably. Even accounting for a significant margin for error, it was evident she had unseated Nigel Pride, and she would be the first ever independent MP for Greater York. He had called Sean Moody at first light, who had confirmed their sting on the FL's renegade Darkshirts had succeeded beyond their wildest expectations. Their servers had been temporarily disabled, the threatened pile on had not occurred, and no wild conspiracies theories had been published in the newspapers.

He glanced at Rebecca and caught his breath. She had prepared well for her inevitable interviews with the press later in the day. Her smart, tailored outfit, elegant black boots and tasteful jewellery made her look the model of a professional businesswoman at the height of her power. She had engaged a professional makeup artist, who had accentuated her high cheekbones, sparkling green eyes and soft, feminine lips. She was fidgeting with her napkin as her nerves threatened to overwhelm her. Her expression changed from a nervous smile to trepidation as she considered how the outcome of the election would impact her life and the future of the country. Faulkner marvelled that she was still as beautiful and idealistic as the blossoming young woman he had first met at Red House. But the intervening years had given her a level of sophistication that only added to her allure.

He reached across the small table and grasped her hand. It was the first time he had ever done so. He felt the delicious rush of adrenaline at the contact of her hand, but also apprehension she might withdraw it.

'Rebecca, look at the Minster for me. Do you see how it personifies all that is majestic about this city? It's welcomed the great and the good to York for over eight hundred years. Today, it will be the setting for a famous election victory speech. Nigel Pride doesn't have the numbers, and that speech will be delivered by you.'

Rebecca looked Faulkner in the eyes and smiled like a child. Only the faintest crinkle at the corners of her eyes betrayed her age. She squeezed his hand, then bent her head to kiss the tips of his fingers. 'Sam Faulkner, you of all people cannot be certain of that. Yesterday you were hinting our campaign would be derailed by a vile social media campaign.'

'It's been dealt with.'

'See? I told you that you worry too much.' She leaned across and cupped his chin in her free hand.

'It's my job as your campaign manager to worry about you.'

'I'll not forget the favour you've done for me by taking charge of my campaign ... I know you had divided loyalties.'

Faulkner squeezed her hand a little tighter, then held it against his cheek. 'My loyalties have never been divided. The minute you walked into my travel agency, I knew I had no choice. Your values have guided my life like a pole star for almost forty years.'

Rebecca blushed modestly. 'If I've only been able to influence one person in my life for the better, then it makes me proud it was you.'

'After the election, you'll influence the lives of millions. That's why I chose to help you.'

'Are you sure it was just my moral guidance that attracted you to me, Sam?' She smiled and Faulkner's heart fluttered at her words.

'When I first set eyes on you all those years ago, it was as if a ray of warm summer sunshine had transcended the bleak winter that was crushing my soul. Even during the intervening years, you've been in my dreams. I've never felt so much love as when

I'm with you, Rebecca.'

'I'm five years older than you, Sam. Doesn't that bother you?'

'Why should it? You don't look a day older than the young woman I adored at Red House.'

Rebecca leaned in once more and kissed Faulkner on the lips. Faulkner savoured their taste for the first time.

'Could I take your order please, sir and madam?' said the young waitress as she hovered with a clipboard. They separated like guilty teenagers and scrambled to pick up their menus.

'Umm ... Yorkshire tea and raisin toast, please,' Faulkner said.

Rebecca chuckled at Faulkner's embarrassment. 'I'll have a macchiato and one of your delightful blueberry muffins. Thank you,' she said, handing the menu back to the waitress.

The waitress covered her mouth in surprise. 'Oh, miss, aren't you that politician Rebecca Vavasour?'

'Yes, I am, Linda,' Rebecca said, reading the girl's name badge. 'I hope you'll be voting for me in the election?'

'Of course. Even my dad, who's only ever voted for Nigel Pride, said it's time for a change. My brother, Liam, said there were a few funny rumours about you going around on the internet, but I told him they were all rubbish. Everyone can see you're a lovely lady.'

'Well, thank you, Linda.'

Linda did a clumsy half-curtsy, and then rushed into the kitchen. 'Look who's just walked into ...' Her voice faded away as the kitchen door closed behind her.

'Now where were we?' Rebecca said with a coy smile on her face. 'Oh yes, I remember!' She leaned across the table and placed her hand around the back of Faulkner's head and pulled him closer before kissing him for a second time.

* * *

Sam placed a twenty-pound note on the table, then helped Rebecca with her coat. She took his hand, and he was surprised at how pleasurable that small but intimate gesture of affirmation felt. Although Rebecca maintained her natural composure as they walked on to High Petergate together, Faulkner noticed she had an extra spring in her step. Her hand clasped his firmly, the pulses of their wrists touching and racing together as one. The tips of her fingers caressed the back of his hand, as if hinting of more intimacy to come. Faulkner stole a glance at Rebecca as they ambled towards the car park where his car was located, three hundred yards away. She looked confident and happy. She noticed his gaze and flashed a lover's smile at him. Faulkner's heart skipped a beat, realising they had just made a silent commitment to each other. He returned her smile and gave her hand a tender squeeze in return.

As they approached his Land Rover, he fished in his pocket for his keys but could only feel his wallet and mobile phone. With an apologetic look he released Rebecca's hand and checked his other pockets.

'Rebecca, I'm so sorry, I must have left the car keys in the cafe. I can't believe it. I must have left my brains in there as well.'

Rebecca smiled and gave Faulkner a knowing look. 'I think I can understand why,' she replied. 'Don't worry, I'll wait by the car for you.'

'Will you be okay while I run back?'

'How much trouble do you think I can get into in two minutes?' said Rebecca in mock admonishment.

* * *

Joel Skinner dipped his head low and retreated into the shadows of a doorway as Faulkner jogged past him. He had been stalking Jezebel since five a.m., but she had been guarded by the man he recognised as the Cavalier. But now she was on her own and he intended to confront her about her plans to corrupt British society. He pulled his hoodie over his head and loped towards the green Land Rover parked fifty yards away.

'Oi, you! Are you Rebecca Vavasour?' he shouted at her as he approached.

In his conspiracy-addled mind she displayed all the mannerisms of a demonic being. She turned to face him, and her wicked green eyes scoured his soul. She displayed no fear or hostility as he closed the distance between them. She should have been cowering in fear as he approached, but her evil powers had fortified her. The Jezebel was a year or two older than his own mother and yet he found himself physically drawn to her.

He had to remind himself she was playing a trick on his mind, intended to take away his righteous fury.

'Good morning, young man. Will you be voting today?' she said in a soft, cultured Yorkshire accent.

Skinner felt his rage evaporating as he stood transfixed by her beguiling presence. He needed to act quickly before he fell under her spell and the Cavalier returned.

'This election is bullshit,' he managed to utter. 'It's been rigged so Nigel Pride can't win.'

But Vavasour just smiled as if indulging the fantasy of a small child. He found his rage returning. 'You're a paedophile, a witch and a whore,' he continued.

'Those are just silly, vicious rumours people made up on the internet. No-one ever takes them seriously. The best thing you can do is read about each candidate's policies and make up your mind for yourself.'

'What're you going to do about replacing my laptop and my stolen Bitcoin, you bitch?'

'I don't know what you mean. What's happened?' For the first time Rebecca realised her life was in imminent danger and she looked around for Faulkner. At that same moment, Skinner pulled a nine-inch kitchen knife from his coat sleeve.

* * *

Faulkner found his Land Rover keys on the restaurant table and smiled sheepishly at the waitress before dashing back into the street. He jogged the short distance to the carpark, then stopped as he saw the threatening scene ahead. A gawky youth in a hoodie was wielding a vicious-looking knife in an erratic manner, as if he was on methamphetamines or some other drug. Rebecca glanced over her assailant's shoulder and spotted Faulkner. Her eyes expressed relief, but also extreme anxiety.

'Put the knife down, mate,' Faulkner shouted in a clear, authoritative manner. He ambled towards the youth so as not to agitate him further. 'I know you don't mean any harm, but I need you to settle down before someone gets hurt.' Faulkner closed the gap to twenty yards.

'Back off, fuckwit, or I'll slit the bitch's throat from ear to ear.' The attacker moved behind Rebecca and looped a long, skinny forearm around her neck, using her as a shield. He pulled her backwards, so Faulkner's Land Rover was behind him. 'Throw me the keys!' he demanded.

'I can't do that,' Faulkner said in a reasonable manner. 'She needs to come with me. Just walk away now, and I promise we can forget this ever happened.' Faulkner took a few steps closer.

'I can't let her go. She must die. She's Putin's daughter and a paedophile.'

'She's just an innocent woman hoping to make the world a better place.'

'She's a Russian sleeper sent to corrupt England. You want proof? Last night she destroyed the computers of every Darkshirt in my group. Only the Elite has the power to do that.'

Faulkner realised he was dealing with a mind so entrenched in conspiracies that rational argument was futile.

'Your computer's crashed? Look, I'll give you the money to buy a new one, but you need to put the knife down.' He took another step forward.

'Don't come any closer. I mean it.'

Faulkner raised his hands in mock surrender. 'Look, I'm on your side, mate. What's your name?'

'Joel.'

'Okay, Joel, you can take the car. Just let Rebecca go. Let me give you the keys.'

'If you try anything, she gets it.'

Faulkner made a big show of searching his pockets, and then pulled out his keys. 'Here, take them,' he said throwing them in a wide, looping arc towards the man.

The assailant reached out to catch the keys. As he did so, Faulkner sprinted forward and used his full momentum to crash into Skinner, pushing him off balance and forcing him to release his grip on Rebecca. Skinner's knife blade slashed viciously where Rebecca had been moments before. The knife sliced through Faulkner's heavy jacket and tore deep into the flesh of his arm. Pain seared through his body as his blood dripped onto the pavement below. Faulkner swayed to avoid the next thrust, which was aimed at his stomach, and swung his fist into the side of the Skinner's head. He connected cleanly and felt bone breaking. Skinner's spectacles smashed onto the pavement as he slumped across the bonnet of the Land Rover and collapsed in a heap on the ground. Faulkner kicked the knife under the Land Rover, then pulled Rebecca clear of the danger and held her tightly.

'It's okay, you're safe now, my darling,' he whispered in her ear. The attacker was lying motionless on the ground ten yards away.

Rebecca was shaking with shock and tears welled in her eyes. 'Just hold me, Sam. I'll be fine in a few minutes.'

Faulkner kissed her forehead and rested his cheek against her shock of chestnut coloured hair. He felt a surge of anger towards Skinner. He turned his head to glare at the man whose mind had been destabilised by wild conspiracies and Freedom League propaganda. Skinner was struggling to get back on his feet. He looked dazed and he clutched the side of his face with his left hand, as if nursing a broken bone. Faulkner made a move towards him, but Rebecca tugged at his sleeve.

'Let him be, Sam,' she said. 'Let this be a day for celebration, not vengeance.'

'Get out of here, now!' Faulkner yelled at the assailant, pointing to the car park exit.

The youth took two steps towards the exit then hesitated. He turned back around, and his face contorted into a mask of fury as if something had tripped inside his brain. He pulled a grey-looking object from his pocket

'It's a gun! Get down, Rebecca!' Faulkner yelled as he sprinted towards the assailant.

There was a loud explosion as Skinner fired a wild shot in Faulkner's direction, then turned and raced towards the exit.

Rebecca clutched her chest, where blood was oozing from a deep wound. Her face registered disbelief anyone would want to harm her in such a violent manner. She swayed on her feet as her strength ebbed and her legs buckled underneath her. Faulkner rushed forward and caught her in his arms before she hit the ground. He eased her down using his body as a pillow to make her as comfortable as possible. Then he cradled her head against his chest. He knew with dread the wound was fatal, and Rebecca had moments to live. Nevertheless, his instinct was to staunch the blood flow and keep her alive long enough to call an ambulance.

Rebecca opened her eyes and tried to smile at him, but she

coughed as a fleck of blood trickled from the corner of her mouth. Pain racked her body, but she regathered her composure.

'Samuel, what have I done to deserve such cruelty?' she asked. Her voice was weak and accented with a strange, archaic dialect.

'He's gone now. He can't harm you anymore. Stay with me, Rebecca. I'm going to call an ambulance.' He reached for his phone and dialled 999. He spoke to the operator, provided their location and prayed they would arrive in time.

'Samuel, I ask one thing of you before I depart this life.' Her voice was so weak he had to lean in closer to catch her words.

'What is it, my love?'

'That you watch over my girls. They are still so young and there are many who wish them harm.'

'Of course, Rebecca. But who would wish them harm?'

'Bourcher.'

'Bourcher is dead. He can't harm your family anymore.'

'Promise me, Samuel, before it's too late.' She held his hand tighter as if she were gripped by panic.

'I swear it.'

Rebecca managed a weak smile, then gasped in pain once more.

'I'm burning, Samuel. The flames are too intense. I am done for. Be it God's will we meet again in heaven.'

Faulkner was shocked at what she had said. She sounded like a woman from a different age. 'I'm here for you always,' he managed to reply.

Faulkner heard the ambulance sirens in the distance and willed them to hurry. Rebecca twisted her head and looked towards the sky. She uttered a string of strange-sounding words that made no sense to Faulkner, and then fell silent.

Faulkner didn't notice the ambulance that arrived two minutes later. A young female ambulance officer checked Rebecca's pulse and shook her head at her colleague.

'She's gone, sir,' she said to Faulkner. 'You can leave her with us now.' She frowned as she noticed the deep cut to his jacket and the blood seeping down his arm. 'You need to jump into the ambulance with us, sir, before that approaching thunderstorm hits us. Your wound looks nasty and it's going to need medical attention.'

CHAPTER 30

Vavasour Hall, Bishop Monkton

'If I could have your attention, please,' Faulkner said.

It was the first time the senior members of the Vavasour family had gathered at Vavasour Hall since Rebecca's funeral six months before. Faulkner had found the close presence of Rebecca's family reassuring after enduring months of private grief.

He was seated at one end of a large dining table in the Vavasour ancestral home. He unfurled a plan of the hall and its grounds, and spread it across the gnarled table. It highlighted the elaborate security features he was proposing to install. At the far end, Athena and her husband, Steve, were spoon-feeding their fifteen-month-old child, Sebastian, while Charlotte, who was on Faulkner's left, was staring at the evening news on the wall-mounted TV.

'My God, the new prime minister is such a sleaze bag,' Charlotte said as she watched the latest parliamentary scandal unfold. 'He's got seven million pounds in an undeclared bank account in the Cayman Islands, and he hasn't paid a penny in tax for three years.'

'Allegedly,' Faulkner corrected her. 'This seems more like a political stitch-up than a genuine case of tax evasion. Look, could we get back to the new security arrangements for Vavasour Hall?'

'Sam, we appreciate your concern about our safety,' said Steve. He was a successful accountant roughly the same age as Faulkner, but had greyed prematurely and was fighting a losing battle against middle-aged spread. 'But we're all capable of looking after ourselves. Athena is six months' pregnant and the last thing she needs is to be frightened by this nonsense you're talking about a fictitious Darkshirt Brigade.'

'I made a promise to Rebecca that I would protect Charlotte and Athena from harm. It was her dying wish and it's a promise I intend to keep. The minimum I can do is upgrade the security systems in your homes.'

'We all understand you were very fond of Rebecca, Mr

Faulkner. Perhaps a little too fond, if truth be told.' Steve grasped Athena's hand protectively. 'And, if you weren't able to protect Rebecca from a half-stoned kid, how do you expect to protect my family from serious criminals?'

'I think we should hear Mr Faulkner out, darling,' Athena said. 'And there is no need to be so vindictive. Mummy thought the world of him.'

'Enough to clear his million-pound debt, I heard. I'd be interested to know what kind of relationship Mr Faulkner had with her.'

Charlotte, who had been preoccupied by the unfolding government crisis on the BBC news channel, turned to face her brother-in-law. She laid a protective hand on Faulkner's arm.

'While Sam is a guest at Vavasour Hall, he will be treated with respect,' she said in a reasonable manner. But there was no doubting the fire in her eyes. 'Do we all understand this?'

'Yes, of course,' Steve muttered. 'My apologies, Mr Faulkner. It's just that I'm not happy about being dragged halfway across Yorkshire to Vavasour Hall with my pregnant wife to talk about security. And frankly, it wasn't *my family* that was bequeathed the Vavasour family estate in Rebecca's will, so I don't know what its security arrangements have to do with us.'

'Steve, don't be so vulgar,' Athena admonished her husband.

'I was happy in my old flat in York, as it happens, but as the senior member of the Vavasour family, the responsibility for its maintenance and upkeep now falls on me,' Charlotte replied.

'No apology is required, Steve,' Sam responded, stepping in to deflect a family squabble. 'The security arrangements also involve Vavasour Pharmaceuticals, where Athena is working as the chief operating officer, so her presence here is vital. We can run through the security arrangements I've made for your Aysgarth home another time.'

'I think Steve's earlier insinuation about your relationship with our mother is the reason he should apologise,' said Athena. 'Neither Charlotte nor I had ever known Mum to have been so happy as when she reached out to you last year.'

'Yes, I was very fond of Rebecca,' admitted Faulkner. 'I regret it took us thirty-five years to acknowledge our feelings for each other.' He paused to regain control of his emotions. He noticed Athena was dabbing a tissue to her eyes, while Charlotte rubbed his shoulder in a display of compassion. 'But what I regret most was that I failed to protect her from the bullet of a crazed conspiracy theorist while she was in my care. It's something I will have to live with for the rest of my life.'

Charlotte nodded. 'Mum told Athena and I after her marriage to my father had ended that she had always followed your career and achievements with such pride.'

Faulkner looked up with surprise. 'Why didn't she come to me earlier?'

Athena dabbed at her eyes once more. 'Because she was traumatised by her experience at Red House and by the vicious allegations about her relationship with the boys.'

'The boys worshipped her,' Sam said his voice betraying his emotions. 'She cared for the younger boys like a mother and for the seniors like an elder sister. She knew we were being mistreated and she wanted to protect us. There was nothing more to it than that, Athena. Don't let anyone tell you otherwise.'

'We've always known it, Sam,' said Charlotte. 'It was me who persuaded her to visit you in your travel agency because I was in awe of the man who had captained England to victory in the Six Nations. I thought you would lay her ghosts to rest. And when you became her campaign manager, it made my heart sing.' Charlotte fixed Steve with a stare. 'And just so everyone's clear, Sam refused to accept any money whatsoever from the Vavasour estate for running Mum's campaign. I insisted the money was his, but he wouldn't take it.'

'And because our mother died on the morning of the election, Nigel Pride won the seat of Greater York by default,' said Athena. She wiped a tear from her right cheek. 'He's now the deputy prime minister and chancellor of the exchequer. It just feels so wrong that he's benefited from Mum's murder; there should've been a by-election.'

'There would've been a by-election had she been a member of a political party, but as she stood as an independent, Pride was deemed to have won the seat,' Faulkner said. 'Believe me, I spent enough time with the Electoral Commission trying to persuade them otherwise.'

'There may not need to be a by-election,' Charlotte said. Her attention had wandered back to the unfolding news. 'Three more government ministers have been implicated in the Cayman

Islands tax fraud scandal, including the foreign minister, the defence minister and the secretary of state for trade. The leader of the opposition is calling for the government to resign and for a new general election.'

'Perhaps you should run as an independent, Sam?' Athena suggested. 'I'm sure Mum would've wanted that.'

'Your mother was successful as an independent because the Vavasour family name is so respected in York. Any rival candidate to Pride would have to be affiliated to a political party. Besides, the government sits on a fifty-one-seat majority. They can ride out any political scandal, no matter how bruising.'

'There goes another cabinet minister,' said Charlotte.

'Who is it this time?' Steve asked.

'Alex St John-Phelps, the Attorney General,' replied Charlotte.

'Good Lord! I was at Oxford with his son, Brendan,' Steve replied. 'His family had a reputation for being so morally upright we nicknamed them The Saints.'

'There's no news on Pride yet, but the scandal is still unfolding,' said Charlotte.

'I smell a rat,' said Faulkner. He rolled up the security plan for Vavasour Hall and placed it on the sideboard. 'It'd be most unusual for so many unconnected politicians to have offshore accounts with the same bank in the Cayman Islands. Even the amounts in each account are similar.'

'They might all be in on the same investment scheme?' suggested Charlotte.

'They do have one thing in common. They're all members of the government's moderate wing,' said Faulkner. 'They've been keeping Pride's Freedom League faction in check for years.'

'Are you suggesting Pride is sabotaging his own government?' said Charlotte.

'It's possible. The government's majority is large enough for a spot of factional bloodletting. The prime minister and his moderate allies could be the target of a well-orchestrated internal coup. The perpetrator could be Pride, or it could be any one of the several different factions within the governing party.'

'It all seems a bit far-fetched to me Faulkner,' said Steve. 'I must say, your talk of political coups and Darkshirts is all too much for Athena. I think it's time we got going. It's an hour's drive to Aysgarth. You can send the security plans to us there.'

Athena pulled a face, as if Steve were making an unnecessary fuss.

Faulkner stood. He did not want to put Charlotte in an awkward position by being alone with her at Vavasour Hall. 'I'm afraid I must head back too. I've a busy day at the travel agency tomorrow.'

Charlotte looked disappointed. 'You don't have to leave just yet, Sam. I haven't even had the chance to look at the security plans for Vavasour Hall.' She was interrupted by the chiming of the doorbell. 'That's strange. I wasn't expecting visitors at this hour. Who could it be?'

'I think we should all head to the door together,' said Faulkner. 'I'll lead the way.'

Faulkner headed the group as they left the dining room. They walked through the library and into the grand entrance hall, where an array of family portraits and paintings of hunting scenes decorated the walls. The marble floor was a chequerboard pattern of black and white tiles, on which an antique Persian rug took pride of place in the centre. To their right, a large sweeping staircase led to the maze of upstairs bedrooms and bathrooms.

Faulkner strode towards the imposing entrance door. In an alcove next to the door, the formality of the entrance was tempered by a neat row of Charlotte's outdoor footwear, including a pair of black riding boots, muddied hiking boots and two pairs of running shoes. Faulkner switched on the porch light, unlocked the door, and opened it just sufficiently to speak to the interlopers.

Standing at the top of the steps leading to the driveway was a policeman book-ended by two men in military fatigues. An unmarked police car with its flashing blue light was parked at the top of the driveway.

'I'm looking for a Mr Samuel Faulkner,' said the police officer.

'That's me,' said Faulkner.

'What's going on?' said Charlotte as she strode forward and stood shoulder to shoulder with Faulkner.

'I have a warrant for Mr Faulkner's arrest.'

'On what charge?' Faulkner demanded.

'Accessory to the murder of Miss Rebecca Vavasour,' replied the police officer. 'The accused, Joel Skinner just named you as his accomplice.'

Faulkner could just make out Steve muttering to his wife in the hallway. '*I knew it! I just bloody knew it,*' he whispered.

The police officer did not present his warrant and the two accompanying soldiers had a slovenly, paramilitary demeanour suggesting they were not regular army officers. Faulkner considered challenging the three men on the validity of the arrest, but he did not want the situation to turn ugly in the presence of Charlotte, Athena and her family.

'This is an outrage.' Charlotte almost spat the words at the policeman. 'Mr Faulkner almost lost his own life trying to defend my mother from a conspiracy theorist crackhead.'

'It's okay, Charlotte,' Faulkner reassured her. 'I'm happy to cooperate with these gentlemen. I'll be back out on the streets soon enough.'

'I'll organise you a lawyer.'

'If you would be kind enough to accompany me to the car, sir,' suggested the police officer.

Faulkner walked with the three men to the dark-coloured BMW. One of the men in military fatigues took the driver's seat, while the other two sat either side of Faulkner in the rear passenger seat. As the car drove down the long driveway, Faulkner glanced over his shoulder and saw Charlotte was arguing with her brother-in-law. Then they were swallowed up by the inky blackness of the night.

'Would someone mind telling me what this is all about?' Faulkner asked the two men who were wedged either side of him.

There was no response from any of the men in the car. 'Fair enough,' Faulkner muttered. He shuffled in his seat, trying to get comfortable.

'If you don't stop your fidgeting, mate, we'll slap the handcuffs on you and throw you in the boot,' said the irritated policeman.

'How about one of you gets in the front passenger seat? That way, there'd be a bit more room,' replied Faulkner.

'How about you shut your fucking mouth?' said the paramilitary officer, drawing his pistol.

'Um, the Knaresborough police station is that way,' said Faulkner, pointing towards the turnoff. 'This way leads to the A1.'

'Last warning, mate,' said the soldier as he jammed the barrel of his pistol under Faulkner's chin.

An uncomfortable silence descended on the car as they drove along the Boroughbridge Road, then joined the A1. After ten minutes they turned left onto the A59 in the direction of York. It was when they turned left once more onto the familiar Red House Lane that Faulkner realised where he was being taken.

'I should've guessed,' Faulkner said as the grand old building came into view. 'My old friend Mike Lambert wants me close by while he plots his coup.'

The paramilitary soldier raised his fist to strike him, but Faulkner stared him down. 'I know for a fact Lambert wants me unharmed, but I'm more than happy to sort this out in the boxing ring at Red House, if you're up for it.'

'It won't be sorted out in the boxing ring, mate. It'll be a bullet in the back of your head when you're least expecting it.'

* * *

The unmarked car drove past the visitor's car park and around the grass oval at the back of the main building. The long concrete strip that had once served as a makeshift cricket pitch in summer and an unofficial ice rink in winter was still there. The two giant oak trees nicknamed 'Adam' and 'Eve' that had stood since Slingsby's time still dominated one corner of the grounds, and the stables, located across the oval from the main building, remained as he had remembered.

But everything else had changed. The place was thronged with paramilitary soldiers going about their business. Many carried semi-automatic rifles, and all walked with urgency. An olive-green lorry was parked at the door of what used to be the boot room, where Faulkner would unlace his muddied boots after a gruelling game on the rugby field. The lorry was unloading aluminium ammunition boxes for British Army light-support rifles. The officer supervising the delivery examined an underslung grenade launcher from a wooden box and nodded his approval.

Opposite the oval, the old school clock on the stable archway registered fifteen minutes past nine. The car drove under the archway and came to a halt in the middle of the stable courtyard.

Faulkner climbed out of the car and stretched his stiff back. It was obvious events had taken a more serious turn than he had anticipated and his relationship with Lambert would no longer guarantee his safety. As he breathed in the night air, something felt out of place and unnatural. He wanted to bask in the comfortable sounds and smells of the stable, which had been the focus of his childhood days at Red House. Instead of the earthy scents of hay, horse manure and saddlery he was expecting, the stables smelled of fear and human misery.

Faulkner's reverie was shattered by a sickening blow to the head he received from the pistol butt of the paramilitary officer he had antagonised in the car. His brain filled with bright light and he reeled from the impact, but he was determined to stay on his feet. He managed to sneer at the soldier. He wanted to say 'Is that all you've got?' but his brain was scrambled, and the words would not come. He noticed the phoney policeman and the second paramilitary officer had lit cigarettes and were blowing acrid smoke in his direction.

'He's not so cocky now,' said the policeman.

'Let's get him into the cells and call it a day,' said the second militia man.

They each took an elbow and half-dragged him into the stables. Faulkner reeled in shock at the transformation. The old stalls that had once been filled with horses and ponies had been replaced with rough concrete cells with thick doors, each with sliding bolts and imposing padlocks. They took him to the rearmost cell that had once been the domain of his favourite horse, Bullet.

They opened the wooden door and shoved him onto the thin bed of straw lining the floor of his cell. The police officer pulled a compressed air pistol from his holster and inserted a small cylindrical projectile into the chamber. He raised the weapon and aimed it at Faulkner's thigh. A muted crack reverberated through the stable as the tranquiliser dart exploded from the gun and the sharp needle embedded itself into his flesh. The barbiturate flowed from the projectile into his bloodstream. The effects made him groggy, and he battled to keep his eyes open. One minute later, he was lying unconscious on the cold bed of straw.

* * *

Faulkner was jolted awake by a bucket of freezing water that had been thrown over his prone body.

'Wakey, wakey,' said a man dressed in a khaki colonel's uniform. He had a trimmed pencil moustache and the military bearing of a regular soldier in the British Army. He was wearing his service dress uniform complete with medals, polished Sam Browne belt and glossy black parade shoes. Every crease in his uniform was perfect.

'Was that necessary?' Faulkner complained.

'I've been told there's an Old Cavalier in cell seven who's gone rogue,' replied the colonel in a clipped upper-class accent. 'I assume that's you. My job is to make you see sense.'

'And how do you intend to do that?' Faulkner tried to clear his head, but the sedatives were still making him drowsy. His neck ached from sleeping on the straw and the cold had permeated his bones. He levered himself off the floor, and then steadied himself against the whitewashed concrete wall of his cell. He scanned his surroundings without drawing attention to himself. The floor near the back of the cell where drainage had run was still original. The cells had a temporary look to them, and Faulkner guessed they were not intended for long-term prisoners.

'A bit of tough love to remind you of where your true loyalties lie. You should be used to that, being a Red House old boy.'

'Where's Brigadier Lambert?'

'In the study, waiting for you.'

Faulkner looked at his watch. It was six-thirty in the morning.

'I allowed you an extra thirty minutes of shut-eye,' the colonel said. 'Reveille is at six o'clock sharp.'

'You're most kind Colonel ...?'

'Clarke of the Yorkshire Regiment, 1st Battalion, at your service. I'm on a month's leave from my unit, so I thought I'd do my bit to help the Freedom League sort out this political shit fight. I feel it's my patriotic duty as an old boy.'

'You're an Old Cavalier?'

'Indeed. Fairfax House, 1996.'

Faulkner held out his hand. 'Pleased to meet you, Colonel Clarke. Sam Faulkner. Newcastle House, 1988.'

Colonel Clarke stopped in his tracks. 'Good Lord. *The* Sam Faulkner who captained England at rugby?' He shook his head in disbelief. I was captain of the first fifteen, but the sports master, John Fox, never let me forget I was stepping into your illustrious boots.'

'I can imagine. Fox was never a pleasant man.'

'Do you still play? It looks like you've kept up with your training.'

'Just socially. Too many injuries. Look, Colonel Clarke, if you're at my service, would you mind fetching me a towel? I'm freezing my nuts off here.'

'Corporal Hopkins! A towel for Mister Faulkner at the double,' the colonel yelled over his shoulder.

'Yessir!' came the reply from within the bowels of the stable complex. Thirty seconds later, Faulkner was drying his face and hands with the rough towel.

'You can clean up in the showers, but I must warn you, this will be your sleeping quarters until we can be certain of your allegiance.'

CHAPTER 31

Faulkner stared at the rows of black-and-white school photographs that lined the wall of the library as he waited for Brigadier Lambert to make an entrance. The civilian trousers and shirt Colonel Clarke had lent him were a size too small, but not uncomfortable.

He had been the captain of the all-conquering Red House rugby side from 1986 to 1988 and in each team photo, he was seated in the middle of the second row, holding the rugby ball, with the school year painted in white in the centre of the ball. A collection of silver trophies was placed in front of the younger boys, who sat cross-legged in the front row on the grass at Faulkner's feet. The boys stared at the camera with the arrogant confidence of young men who knew they could not be beaten. The British Empire had long gone, but these youths were born to lead, and raised to be ruthless in the pursuit of excellence.

He tried to recall the names of the serious-faced pupils in each of the photos. He recognised his friend Sean Moody instantly. Moody had managed to position himself to Faulkner's right in each photo, even though his talent at rugby was based on raw strength rather than skill. There was Sullivan in the back row next to Delaney, and the hulking form of Lambert sat to the extreme right. He recalled the orange-haired Humphries and the bandy-legged Elliott standing behind him, but the names of the others had slipped his mind.

He moved to the whole-of-school photo for the year 1988. Eighty-two students and fifteen members of staff were crammed into four rows, in a grainy black-and-white photo with the magnificent backdrop of the ivy-covered Red House School behind them. Bernard Bourcher and his wife were seated in the centre of the second row like the lord and lady of the manor. Seated either side of them were the other members of staff. Strict protocol ensured the senior staff were positioned closest to Bourcher and his wife. Six positions to the right of Bourcher's wife sat Rebecca Vavasour. She was the most junior staff member, but her movie-star looks and charismatic presence had glamourised an otherwise mundane school photograph. The seven school prefects were entitled to sit next to the staff, and Faulkner remembered how he had muscled his way into the seat next to Rebecca. The photographer had requested everyone squish together as much as possible and Faulkner had obliged so his left shoulder and hip had touched those of Rebecca. The delicious sensations of her warmth, softness and delicate perfume had almost overwhelmed him. But he was saddened as he looked at the photo. The woman he had idolised for most of his life had been snatched from him in the cruellest of circumstances and this grainy photograph was the only one in which the two of them were pictured together.

'Once a Cavalier, always a Cavalier, hey, Faulkner?' It was Brigadier Lambert, who had strutted into the library. Faulkner tore his eyes from the grainy photograph.

'If you say so,' replied Faulkner. Lambert was wearing his brigadier's dress uniform, including peaked cap and swagger stick. The stick was an antique, but it reminded Faulkner of Bernard Bourcher's favourite cane. Lambert had always been an enthusiastic supporter of corporal punishment.

'You're on probation till we can be assured of your loyalty,' Lambert said. 'Just don't push it.'

'What's with the stuffy uniforms today? Colonel Clarke was in his service dress uniform too. Are you expecting royalty?'

'Close, Faulkner. A new government, perhaps.'

'I don't recall that the old one has been dismissed yet.'

'The current government is weak and pathetic. It's become embroiled in a tax haven scandal and the country is going to the dogs. The prime minister has no vision for the country other than tax cuts for the wealthy. There's to be a new government today.'

'You're planning a coup?'

'Britain does not have coups,' said the lanky, bespectacled figure of Nigel Pride, who had entered the library. 'Our history teacher, Captain MacTavish, would be turning in his grave if he heard you say that. Coups are for grubby South American countries. No, we have *purges*, like the one carried out by my illustrious ancestor.'

'Pride's Purge', said Faulkner. 'One hundred and forty MPs were excluded from parliament in 1648, thereby giving the Puritan rump the numbers to arrest and behead King Charles the First.'

'Very good. However, my purge will be called a cabinet reshuffle,' said Pride as he turned on the Smart TV in the corner of the library. It was the only concession to modernity in the library. Everything else was as he remembered from his school days, including the ivory and ebony chess set with the missing white bishop, and the black 1970s rotary telephone from which the children were occasionally allowed to call their parents. Pride flicked the remote control until *Sky News* appeared on the TV. 'This gathering feels very nostalgic doesn't it, Faulkner? The last time we were together in the library we were watching *Dr Who* and *Jim'll Fix It*. But I think you'll find the next few hours will be much more educational.'

'Can you explain, why I'm here?' asked Faulkner. 'It appears your coup – sorry, your "cabinet reshuffle" – is proceeding quite well without me.'

'Our guest seems rather ungrateful for our hospitality,' Pride said to Lambert. 'Perhaps we should've disposed of him while he was snoring like a helpless baby in the stables last night.'

'The ungrateful bastard took advantage of my good nature when I tried to help him out with a certain social media issue. He compromised my entire digital Darkshirt Brigade for over three months, and it cost the movement over a million pounds to fix it.'

'Perhaps you should apologise, Faulkner?' Pride suggested.

'It was a member of his Darkshirt Brigade who murdered a good friend of mine. There's not a cat in hell's chance I'll apologise.'

'Ah, yes, the delightful but unfortunate Miss Rebecca Vavasour. I was saddened by the manner of her death, even though we were political rivals. You have my deepest condolences.'

Faulkner studied Pride. He was either a very good liar or genuinely upset about Rebecca's death. 'What do you want from me, Pride?'

'Should the new government elect me as the new prime minister, as seems certain now, I'll be appointing a new cabinet. You'll be pleased to know of the twenty-one members of cabinet, seventeen will be drawn from the pool of Old Cavaliers, including some who told me they'll defect from the Labour Party and the Scottish Nationalists. My new government will be known as the

"Cavalier cabinet". It has a certain charm to it, don't you think? This is our chance to run Britain as Bernard Bourcher intended. We can make this country fit for heroes once more.'

'Well, that's all very nice, but I still don't know how that involves me.'

'For goodness' sake, Faulkner. Wake up! Red House was a small, high-achieving school that punched massively above its weight. Academically we were one of the best in Yorkshire, despite being under constant threat of bankruptcy. But it was our reputation at rugby that made us famous. We posted cricket scores on our rivals for three years, and why do you think that was?'

Faulkner shrugged his shoulders. 'It wasn't down to Bourcher's excessive use of the cane.'

Pride stood and walked to the row of school photographs. 'In the 1950s, Red House won three Yorkshire rugby championships. In the '60s it won seven, including a national championship. The '70s were somewhat lean, with two Yorkshire championships. But then we come to the 1980s.' Pride stabbed at five photos from 1982 to 1988. 'We won so much silverware, the school had to build a second trophy cabinet in the refectory. From 1986, we won every bloody competition we entered, including our tour of Cape Town, Sydney and Auckland.'

'So what?'

'You were the captain, Faulkner. The boys worshipped you and believe it or not, it was your spirit that embodied what it meant to be an Old Cavalier for decades afterwards.'

'I'm no longer a schoolboy, Pride. I've moved on and I'm quite happy running my little safari business. I've no interest in politics, and I don't see how I can help you.'

'You may have no interest in politics, but politics is very interested in you. Half of the proposed Cavalier cabinet will only accept their portfolios if you endorse the new government.'

'I don't endorse it. I believe in democracy and the rule of law.'

Pride scowled at Faulkner. 'I did tell them your loyalty to the cause is questionable, but they've instructed me to do what it takes to get you to back us.'

'They can't outsource their guilty consciences to me. I'm not even a member of parliament.'

'We can fix that. The parliamentary Old Cavaliers have

recommended we make you a peer and you can sit in the House of Lords. That'll allow you to join the Cavalier cabinet and give our FL faction a working majority.'

'Nonsense. I don't have a drop of noble blood in me.'

'That's not a prerequisite these days, so we feel it's appropriate to make you a baron. How does Baron Faulkner of Marston Moor sound to you?'

'Very pretentious and unnecessary.'

'I find your ingratitude most tedious, Faulkner. Nevertheless, the Old Cavaliers have requested I put the offer of a cabinet position to you. You may even choose your portfolio.'

'It may have slipped your mind, but I ran Rebecca's campaign *against* you. Why would I then join your government? The press would have a field day.'

'We'll take care of the press. We can cite Winston Churchill as someone who changed parties twice. Most of the press hacks have been briefed about the proposed cabinet reshuffle and are prepared to support us. They're sick of Britain's rapid descent into mediocrity and are intrigued by the concept of the Cavalier cabinet. What do you say?'

'Look Pride, you have the wrong man. I happened to have a talent for chasing an egg-shaped ball around a paddock. That hardly qualifies me as a power broker.'

Pride sighed deeply. Once more he stabbed at the 1988 rugby photograph hanging on the wall. 'Just look at yourself in that photo, Faulkner. You were a bloody colossus. A rugby god. Untouchable, imperious and all-conquering, but with that annoying, self-depreciating manner that made you a natural born leader. If it had been you who ran against me at Greater York, I doubt I would have won a single vote. My God, every time I look at you in that photo, I doubt my sexuality ... and don't you dare tell Mrs Pride I said that,' he added hastily.

'I can assure you the feeling is not reciprocated,' Faulkner said, folding his arms. 'Okay. Just out of curiosity, what's your ideology? Rebecca told me you were a closet Nazi.'

Pride laughed contemptuously. 'Not even close. Britain doesn't have authoritarianism in its DNA. This will be a particularly British revolution. We're going back to the 1650s. We're going to combine the ruthlessness and organisational efficiency of Oliver Cromwell, with the dashing spirit and chaotic flamboyance of the Cavaliers, epitomised by Colonel Samuel Fauconberg of the Northern Horse. That combination of opposing styles sums up why Red House was so successful in the mid-1980s, and I intend to transplant that formula into national politics. It's the fulfilment of Bourcher's vision. Can you imagine Britain rising back up the ranks of great nations until, once again our island nation becomes unbeatable?' Once more Pride stabbed at the three rugby photos.

'And your policies?'

'Of course, we'll build up the navy. That alone will restore national pride and will be worth the investment. And the army too, but that can come later. We're going to grow Britain's industry with a series of well-targeted investments in the new renewable and technology sectors. And I want us to build sleek, sexy cars again – like the MGB and the Triumph Stag but without the oil leaks. No more outsourcing our skills and production lines to our foreign competitors for a pittance. I intend to lower unemployment to less than three per cent in the first term of parliament. Anyone left on the dole will be given a taste of national service. That'll teach the shirkers the meaning of hard work. The Cavalier cabinet is all about industriousness—'

Pride's rhetoric was interrupted by a knock on the door. Colonel Clarke entered the room, snapped to attention and saluted Brigadier Lambert.

'Sorry to interrupt you, gentlemen, but the purge is about to begin,' he said.

'Splendid,' said Pride. He rubbed his hands in anticipation of the events to come. 'Thank you, Colonel. Brigadier Lambert, you're due at your command post.' Pride turned back to Faulkner. 'Sit back and enjoy the show. We can continue our conversation later.'

CHAPTER 32

Faulkner stared in astonishment at the images on the 55-inch ultra-high-definition TV. Over three hundred paramilitary soldiers bearing rifles and small arms had ringed the Houses of Parliament on a typically overcast London morning. A group of high-ranking military officers had gathered at each of the main entrances, in apparent support of a knot of police officers from the Met. Their job, they were telling a sympathetic press, was to protect the police, who were serving arrest warrants to more than thirty members of parliament who had been accused of tax fraud. Helicopters were flying overhead, and police sirens sounded in the distance.

A large, vocal mob of placard-waving protestors, incensed at the rumours of tax evasion by their political leaders, were hurling insults at the politicians as they arrived for work. An elderly lady with a wheeled shopping bag was shaking her walking stick in the direction of Big Ben. A rotund man with a strong Liverpool accent was swearing at the befuddled MP for Bishop Stortford, who had found himself too close to the unruly crowd.

'There's no cigars and caviar in Wormwood Scrubs prison where you're headed, mate,' yelled the Liverpudlian.

'Traitor!' yelled a tattooed man wearing a Guns N' Roses T-shirt.

Faulkner watched the TV in stunned silence as the cameras focused on the home secretary. He stood on the steps of the grandiose 'Peers Entrance' to parliament and was having a blazing argument with a polite but insistent police officer, who was reading him his rights. The directional microphone picked up snippets of their conversation: 'This is an absolute outrage ... I've never even had a parking ticket never mind an arrest warrant ... My lawyer will be hearing about this scurrilous stitch-up ...'

Tina Savage, a young female presenter from *SKY TV*, was interviewing the defence minister, Geoffrey Forrester. He was staring at his arrest warrant in his trembling hands. His face glowed red with indignation and humiliation.

'Can you tell us what's going on, Minister?' asked the breathless TV reporter.

'It's a complete disgrace,' he said. 'An affront to British

democracy. Parliament has seen nothing like it in over three centuries.'

'What do you have to say about the three million pounds you've been hiding from the British public in your Cayman Islands tax shelter, Mr Forrester? Would you like to apologise?'

'You're asking me about an unpaid tax bill when there's a bloody coup d'etat going on in the most famous symbol of democracy on the planet? Why aren't you reporting on *that*?'

'I'd hardly call it a coup, Mr Forrester. More like a peaceful protest at the rampant political greed and corruption that's infested parliament. Will you be applying for bail?'

'This is an obvious plot by members of the Freedom League and the police are supporting them. My moderate faction has been holding the FL at bay for years, but with us out of the way they'll have the numbers to replace the government with a bunch of hardline ultra-nationalists.'

'You're saying the police are behind this?' asked Savage, looking incredulous. 'That's just conjecture.'

'Yes ... I mean no ... well, maybe some police ... I don't really know.'

'I can see you're very upset and confused by the turn of events, Mr Forrester. Perhaps if you and your colleagues had paid their taxes, this crisis would never have happened.'

'I have been paying my taxes! To suggest otherwise is slander.'

Savage couldn't conceal her contempt for the defence minister. 'Good luck with that line of defence, Mr Forrester. You're going to need it.' She turned back to the cameras. 'This is Tina Savage reporting from Parliament Square on a historic day for the beleaguered government.'

Faulkner turned to Pride. 'Why aren't you in parliament today if you're intending to take over as prime minister?'

'Because I want you by my side when I enter London in triumph. You might not feel ready for leadership just yet, but we can make you a figurehead until you've discarded your L-plates, so to speak. You can leave the dirty politics to me.'

'Neo-Nazis in need of a führer? Now I've heard it all.'

'Don't be so supercilious, Faulkner.'

'So, how does it play out from here?'

'Do you remember Jeremy Sedgwick from the school choir? He could play the chapel organ like a young Mozart. We used to tease him endlessly about his squeaky voice.'

Faulkner shook his head.

'No? Anyway, he's now the junior undersecretary for trade and he's going to propose a vote of no confidence in the government. With the thirty recalcitrant MPs out of parliament, the vote will be a certainty and Sedgwick will propose me as the interim prime minister.'

'And if your coup fails?'

'Then Swotty Sedgwick will become the sacrificial lamb, just like the old days.'

Once more they stared at the television. The crowd was becoming larger and more hostile.

'I need your answer now, Faulkner. The Cavalier cabinet and your country depend on you.'

'This doesn't sit well with me, Pride. I need time to think.'

'You've got ten minutes. There's no middle way. If you join us, then you and I can build the new Jerusalem right here in England's green and pleasant land.'

'If I refuse?'

'I'm sorry to say you'll never leave Red House alive. You know too much and you're too dangerous an opponent.'

'I could take my chances.'

'You should know that the same arrangement applies to Charlotte and Athena Talbot. I cannot allow anyone from that family to run against me in the seat of Greater York again. Do you understand?'

Faulkner nodded.

'Good,' said Pride. 'Now sit and think for a while. I've a few phone calls to make. When I next set foot in Westminster, I'll be the acting prime minister. Don't you feel proud that Red House will finally have a prime minister in its ranks?'

Faulkner shrugged.

'Splendid! If you need anything, Colonel Clarke will be right outside the library door.'

* * *

Faulkner considered his options. He did not agree with Pride's blatant attack on democracy, and he knew there was more to the Cavalier cabinet's agenda than Pride had let on. It would be a government that would change the way of life in Britain and one that could descend into militarism, religious intolerance and dictatorship. He would not want to be associated with such a regime and had little desire to be embroiled in a political career, even if it was as a figurehead. Yet he knew he was the one person who could moderate the extreme measures Pride would otherwise inflict on an unsuspecting nation.

He considered the ramifications of the choice he had to make. Pride had guessed correctly that Faulkner would sacrifice his own life rather than betray his principles. Pride had therefore brought Rebecca's daughters, whom he had sworn to protect, into the equation. Faulkner had come to love and respect Charlotte and Athena, and would not risk their lives. Faulkner felt like a chess player facing checkmate. Five minutes later, Pride returned to the library.

'Well?' said Pride. 'Are you with us or against us?'

'I need five minutes alone in the chapel. I must reconcile my decision in a more fitting place.'

'I never took you for a religious man, Faulkner. Perhaps you're not a lost cause after all.'

'There's a lot about me you don't know. Recent incidents have transformed my perceptions of spirituality.'

Pride looked at his watch. 'Very well. I'm expecting a call from Jeremy Sedgwick in five minutes. Our moment of destiny is approaching. You've got till then. Colonel Clarke will escort you to the chapel, then he'll bring you back the minute I get the call. I believe you've already surrendered your mobile phone?'

Faulkner nodded. 'Your goons took it from me after they pistol-whipped and tranquilised me in the stables.'

He waited while Pride summoned Colonel Clarke, then followed him out of the library. They walked along the red passage and through to the old changing rooms, where a side door led to Sir Henry Slingsby's chapel.

Faulkner pushed the weighty chapel door and it creaked on its hinges as it swung open. The familiar smells of oak panelling, furniture polish and candle wax transported him back to his school days. He stared at the magnificent stained-glass window behind the altar and glanced down at the worn black-and-white-tiled flooring, where centuries of worshippers had queued to receive the sacrament.

He glanced at the little pulpit and then at the rows of pews. Colonel Clarke appeared equally affected by the solemnity of the chapel. He placed a hand on Faulkner's shoulder, then signalled to the lone soldier who was praying in one of the pews that he should leave.

'I'll be right outside,' said the colonel. 'I know how precious these personal moments can be when you have life-changing decisions to make. Just holler out when you're done.'

'Thank you, Colonel. I appreciate it.'

'I'll try to give you as long as I can,' Clarke said as he closed the chapel door behind him.

Faulkner stared at the stained-glass window depicting the heraldic emblems of the old Yorkshire families related to Sir Henry Slingsby. He allowed his mind to absorb their collective wisdom, knowing they had experienced bloody civil conflict and the painful reconstruction of their nation in its aftermath. Then, with absolute clarity of thought, he grabbed a candle from the altar, a box of matches from the drawer, and headed towards the back of the chapel.

* * *

The last pew on the left hand side of the chapel had once been the exclusive domain of Captain McTavish. No-one had dared to sit on that hard wooden bench while he had been the History master. Images of the tough old Scotsman flashed through his mind. McTavish had a menacing, Churchillian presence that terrified the pupils, and yet he had a reputation for being fair-minded and supportive. Faulkner crouched to examine the wooden panel that lay beneath the pew which had supported McTavish's expansive backside for decades.

Faulkner tapped on the wooden panel. It appeared to be part of the fabric of the chapel building, yet it sounded hollow. He ran the tips of his fingers along the edges of the panel until he felt a metallic protrusion. There had been rumours of a short tunnel running beneath the chapel, but no-one had been game enough to find out for sure. The chapel was an intimidating place for young pupils, especially at night.

There was a polite banging at the chapel door. 'One minute, Faulkner.' It was Colonel Clarke. 'You need to wrap up your prayers and make your way out.'

'I'll be out shortly,' Faulkner yelled back.

Faulkner pushed on the edge of the panel where he had felt the metal protrusion and heard the locking mechanism click. It opened a fraction of an inch. Faulkner hooked a finger into the gap, pulled at the panel and swung it open on its rusty metal hinges.

'Mr Faulkner, Nigel Pride is insisting I bring you back to the library at once,' Clarke yelled from behind the thick wooden chapel door. 'Would you please make your way out of the chapel?'

'On my way,' Faulkner responded.

The entrance to the pit was narrow, and he reversed his six-foot frame, so he was crouched on his belly facing Captain McTavish's old wooden kneeler. He allowed his legs to drop into the blackness and his right foot touched what he assumed was the top rung of a metal ladder. He lowered himself further so only his head and shoulders remained above ground.

Faulkner heard the door to the chapel open and the footsteps of at least a dozen soldiers march up the aisle.

'He's not in 'ere,' said one of the soldiers in a broad Yorkshire accent.

'The cunning bastard,' replied Colonel Clarke. 'Check the gallery upstairs.'

'Yessir.'

Faulkner heard the clumping of military boots running up the old wooden staircase leading to the gallery. He glanced to his right and saw the polished shoes and razor-sharp creases of Colonel Clarke's military trousers in the aisle just yards from his head. He swung the panel back towards him and grimaced as the rusty hinges squealed in protest. The click of the closing latch sounded like a firecracker in the confined space of the hidden chamber beneath him. He held his breath and waited for the clatter of heavy boots to swarm to his position, to investigate the source of the noise.

Instead, Clarke bellowed out to his soldiers. 'Keep the noise down. I can't hear myself think down here.' There was a pause before Clarke talked again in a calm, measured manner. 'Mr Faulkner, I recommend you come out from your hiding place now, and we'll forget this … misunderstanding. However, if you refuse to cooperate, my orders are to put you in front of a firing squad and dispose of your body in the Red House woods. The choice is yours. My men will not leave this building until you're found, dead or alive.'

Faulkner decided to press on. His survival would depend on whether Clarke had heard the rumours about the priest hole beneath the chapel and whether there was indeed a tunnel connecting it to the grounds outside. If the priest hole was a dead end, he would be caught like a rat in a trap.

* * *

Faulkner felt his way along the dank tunnel by the dim light of his flickering candle. The tunnel smelled of raw sewerage and he had to crouch low to avoid the sagging wooden beams that were in imminent danger of collapse. A tangle of roots brushed against his hair and insects scuttled in all directions at his approach. At one location a side wall had caved in, and he had to dig through a pile of soft earth with his hands to make progress.

He cursed as yet again, a draft from an unknown source extinguished his candle. He was left in total blackness, unable to see his hand in front of his face. He felt disorientated and he imagined himself trapped in a long, narrow coffin six feet below the surface. He forced himself to calm down and reached into his pocket for the box of matches. He pulled out what he knew to be the last match and struck it against the side of the matchbox. He felt the stem of the match snap, but he managed to hold onto the flaring match stub with his fingertips. The sulphur and phosphate scorched his fingers, but he held on long enough to light the wick of the candle. He flicked away the spent match then sucked on his seared fingertips to ease the pain. He cupped his left hand around the flickering flame as if he were protecting the source of life itself and continued to inch along the tunnel. He sighed in relief as he spotted the outline of a ladder fixed to a thick slab of timber that signalled the end of his journey.

Faulkner examined the ladder. The bottom three rungs had rusted away from the timber and the seven above them looked precarious. He set the candle on the floor of the tunnel and began climbing. He eased his way to the top and pushed at the metal hatch above his head. It was stuck solid and as he pushed harder, timber and soil cascaded to the floor of the tunnel, missing his precious candle by inches. He spat soil and debris from his mouth and as he did so, he heard faint voices coming from the hidden chamber beneath the chapel.

'It's pitch black in 'ere,' one of the voices said.

'Go fetch a torch.' It was the voice of Colonel Clarke.

'It's fucking spooky,' said the soldier. 'I'm not sure Faulkner would've come down here.'

'He must have,' said the colonel. 'We've searched everywhere else.'

'Nope. He's not in here,' said the soldier. 'It's packed full of old relics and worthless clutter, but there's no sign of Faulkner.'

Faulkner transferred his attention back to the metal hatch and searched for a latch, but there were no noticeable protrusions.

'Hang on,' said the distant voice in the chamber. 'There's a tunnel entrance behind this old cupboard. Pass me down my semi-automatic and I'll check it out.'

'Here, take this,' said Clarke. 'It's the new SA80 A3 rifle. We received a consignment from the army yesterday. If we must take down Faulkner, we might as well do it in style.'

Faulkner pushed at the metal hatch once more, but it remained as immovable as bedrock. Six feet below him, the candle spluttered and dimmed before regaining its full brightness. In the moment when the shadows jumped and the light intensity increased, he saw the track of a rusty rail on which the hatch was designed to slide open and closed. Faulkner gripped the edge of the hatch and attempted to slide it forwards. It moved half an inch before his fingers slipped from the hatch. Once more dirt and debris poured in from above, showering his head and shoulders with soil and extinguishing the candle below him, but revealing a thin shaft of daylight above his head. Then the light from a powerful torch beam played along the length of the tunnel.

'This tunnel isn't safe,' said the now-familiar voice of the soldier. He sounded much closer than he had moments before. 'I can hear dirt dropping from the ceiling.' The torch beam illuminated the broken rungs of the ladder below Faulkner's feet then played along the crumbling walls of the tunnel.

'Keep going,' replied Clarke. 'We must be certain Faulkner isn't hiding in the tunnel.'

Faulkner gripped the edge of the panel once more and used

all his strength to slide it along the rusty rails. A cascade of soil, weeds and rocks drained into the tunnel and Faulkner waited until it had slowed to a trickle.

'The fucking roof's collapsing!' yelled the soldier in alarm. 'I'm getting out of here.'

Faulkner scrambled through the hatch and out into the open air. For good measure he slid the hatch closed behind him and covered it with soil from the garden bed in which he was standing. He allowed his eyes to adjust to the bright sunlight, and then scanned his surroundings. He had emerged near the visitor's car park to the side of the main building. A squad of soldiers was marching in the opposite direction around the far side of Red House but otherwise, the coast was clear. He doubled over and ran for the cover of the trees bordering the school playing fields. Then hugging the line of hedges, he jogged along Red House Lane for a mile until he reached the entrance to the woods. Just as he reached the cover of the thick trees, he heard the *thump, thump, thump* of rotor blades as a helicopter took off from the farmyard and began a systematic search of the immediate vicinity. Faulkner moved deeper into the woods, checked his watch, then settled down to wait.

At eleven a.m. on the dot, Faulkner stepped out of the woods and crouched low in the long grass. Two minutes later, a bright-red mini drove around the bend of Red House Lane and slowed to a halt opposite the bridlepath. Faulkner emerged from the grass and opened the car's passenger door.

'You cannot believe how pleased I am to see you,' Faulkner said to the driver.

'Get in!' Charlotte commanded. She pulled the blanket she used for ferrying her pet saluki to the local park from the back seat and spread it over the passenger seat. It was covered in dog hair and stank of urine.

'You stink, Sam! Where the hell have you been?' said Charlotte.

'Down the Red House sewerage system, being chased by a man with a semi-automatic assault rifle.'

'Very funny. I couldn't hear you very well on the phone when you called an hour ago. You're lucky I came. I should be attending a Vavasour Pharmaceuticals executive meeting.'

'Yeah, sorry about that. I called you on an old 1970s rotary phone in the Red House library in the two minutes I had when I was left alone. I was surprised it still worked.'

Charlotte reversed the car, then set off back the way she had come. She looked across at Faulkner and touched the bruise on the side of his head with her fingertips. 'I've been worried sick about you, Sam. The police said they had no record of your arrest.'

'It's a long story and you're going to have to trust me on this one. There's been a coup in London and I'm now public enemy number one. We need to head to Leeds Bradford Airport and take the first flight out of the country.'

'What do you mean "we"? I've got a pedicure at two o'clock this afternoon.'

'Yes, *we*. You happen to be public enemy number two.'

'My God! What about Athena, Steve and Sebastian?'

'They need to get the hell out of here too. They're also on the list.'

CHAPTER 33

Mosman, Sydney, Australia

Sean Moody opened a bottle of pinot gris and wrapped a white serviette around its base to catch the droplets of moisture. He poured a serving into Charlotte Talbot's glass like a master sommelier and hovered at her shoulder until she had raised the glass to her lips, savoured the wine and nodded approvingly. Then he moved to the opposite side of the table and repeated the process with Athena. He placed the bottle into a silver bucket of ice and returned to the bar fridge, where he extracted two bottles of Coopers Pale Ale.

'Get that down your neck,' he said to Faulkner, who was turning the butterflied prawns on the barbecue.

'Cheers,' Faulkner said as he clinked bottles with Moody.

It was a warm evening considering the Australian winter was only weeks away. On the opposite side of the harbour from Moody's expansive veranda, the distant Opera House flaunted its grandeur in a panoply of ever-changing colours as the centrepiece of Sydney's 'Vivid' light festival. The lights of the boats on the calm waters of Sydney Harbour twinkled and a double-decker train rattled southwards across the Harbour Bridge.

'Thanks for putting us up for a few days while we sort ourselves out,' Faulkner said.

'No worries. You can stay as long as you like. I must say I thought you were overreacting bringing the Talbot girls and the sprog over here with just the clothes on their backs. But Pride's new Cavalier cabinet has wasted no time in detaining hundreds of their political enemies on trumped-up charges.'

'Have you heard from Athena's husband, Steve Marshall? He refused to get on the plane with his family.'

Moody nodded. 'We've tracked him down via his digital footprint. Marshall's a serial WhatsApp user. He's just taken out platinum membership of the FL, and has been given a senior finance role within the party HQ. I haven't told Athena yet. I thought I'd leave that to you.'

'Okay, I'll tell her.'

'Those prawns are done,' Moody suggested.

Faulkner scooped up the prawns from the barbecue and loaded them onto a silver server before carrying them to the table. He sat down next to Charlotte and offered her the seafood platter.

'Put another shrimp on the barbie?' Charlotte said, attempting a Crocodile Dundee accent as she selected four butterfly prawns, three oysters and a Balmain bug.

'Dear, oh dear! Paul Hogan hails from Sydney, not Bangalore,' said Moody.

'Um, we've tracked down Steve,' Faulkner said as he offered Athena the platter.

'Oh, thank God,' she replied. 'I've been worried sick. Did he say why he hasn't called?'

'He's got a new job as the Freedom League's chief treasury officer. They must be keeping him busy.'

Athena turned pale and covered her open mouth with her hand. 'The pig! How could he do that when we're on the run from Pride and his honchos? Just wait till I see him next.' Despite her defiance, a tear rolled down her cheek.

'I'm sure there's a rational explanation,' Faulkner said, trying to mollify her.

'Please start everyone,' Moody said. 'We can't let Sam's prawns go cold.'

'I don't want to put a dampener on the proceedings, but can we have the news on in the background?' said Charlotte. 'I want to see what Pride is scheming next.'

'Has he been sworn in as prime minister yet? It's been weeks since the Cavalier cabinet took power,' said Moody as he aimed the remote at the outdoor television screen.

'Not yet,' replied Faulkner.

'Isn't that unusual?'

'Unprecedented. It usually happens within minutes of the previous prime minister's resignation, but the king's been in bed with the flu.'

'Or so they say,' said Charlotte. 'I think he's considering the legality of Pride's so-called cabinet reshuffle.'

'He's risking civil war if he doesn't swear in the new government,' replied Faulkner. 'The armed forces are backing Pride. He's promised to double the size of the army, build another six nuclear submarines, order fifty more F-35 Lightnings, eight destroyers and a new aircraft carrier.'

'Lambert's Darkshirt Brigade is generating propaganda on a scale not seen since Dr Goebbels in 1933,' said Moody. 'In the last couple of days there's been a pile-on attack against the king.'

'They're demanding he swears in the Cavalier cabinet or abdicates,' said Faulkner as he speared a giant prawn with his fork. 'Another glass of wine?' he asked Charlotte and Athena.

Charlotte shook her head, but Athena drained her glass and held it out for Faulkner to refill. 'Thank you, Sam,' she said.

'It's the news from Britain now,' Athena said, pointing to the TV screen on the wall. Moody turned up the volume as a sombre newsreader stared at the camera. Her breathless tone of voice suggested astonishment at the turn of events in the mother country.

'And in developing news in the United Kingdom, the king has confirmed he will not be swearing in the new government known as the Cavalier cabinet. A palace spokesman stated the king considers the recent cabinet reshuffle to be a coup d'état and has declared the new provisional government to be illegitimate. The king has called for fresh elections, to overcome the current political stalemate. The acting prime minister, Nigel Pride, has called the king "badly advised" and suggested he abdicate in favour of a family member who will carry out their constitutional duty.'

The newsreader turned to the channel's London correspondent. 'I have with me Simon Gormley, who is an expert on British constitutional matters. Simon, is this the greatest constitutional crisis in Britain since Edward VIII was forced to abdicate from the throne?'

'No, it's much worse than that, Jacinta,' said Gormley. 'This crisis bears similarities to 1642, when England descended into civil war. It's the Puritans, Wallis Simpson and Brexit rolled into one. Unless either the king or the acting prime minister agrees to a humiliating backdown, it will result in serious civil unrest. We're already seeing troops and armed militia clash on the streets of London.'

They were interrupted by a ping on Faulkner's mobile phone.

'I do beg your pardon,' said Faulkner as he glanced at the message on his screen.

'What is it? You look as white as a ghost,' said Charlotte.

'It's just a prank text. I'll delete it.'

'What does it say?' Charlotte insisted.

'His Royal Majesty the King requests the pleasure of the company of Samuel Faulkner and guest at Buckingham Palace at four p.m., Tuesday 3rd June.'

'It must be a prank. Why would the king want to see you?' said Moody.

'Or it's a trap by Nigel Pride to trick you into returning to London,' said Athena.

'My goodness,' said Charlotte. 'That's in three days' time. We need to get you a new suit and some decent shoes.'

'It doesn't make any sense. You're public enemy number one,' said Moody.

'Perhaps the king wants to see me *because* I'm public enemy number one. He must have realised I have influence over the Cavalier cabinet and wants me to talk some sense into Pride.'

'You can't go back, Sam. You're a marked man,' said Athena. 'Pride's security forces will take you down as soon as you set foot back in Britain.'

'I can't sit by while Britain drifts into civil war. I must do something.'

'Look, my company has a unit specialising in infiltrating cybercriminal gangs,' said Moody. 'Let me at least organise you a false passport and get you some basic training in counter-surveillance fieldcraft.'

'I'm coming with you,' said Charlotte.

'There's not a cat's chance in hell you'll be getting on that plane with me!' replied Faulkner.

Charlotte took a sip of her pinot gris and looked at Faulkner with a glint in her eyes. 'This is an invitation from Buckingham Palace we're talking about,' she replied. 'Just try and stop me.'

CHAPTER 33

Leeds Bradford Airport, Yeadon, Leeds, UK

Security at Yeadon airport was tight. A dozen policeman patrolled the terminal building and two army officers carrying semi-automatic rifles scanned the incoming passengers. The atmosphere hung heavy with menace, and travellers were whisked away by security forces almost at random.

The couple at the front of the immigration queue looked like any other British tourists returning from Corfu. The male was tall, well built and had the remnants of sunburn on his nose. He sported a lairy T-shirt and knee-length chinos. In his left hand he carried a duty-free bag containing a bottle of Metaxa brandy and a giant bar of Toblerone. The female who accompanied him was in her early thirties, self-assured and attractive. A pair of expensive sunglasses was perched on top of her thick mane of long chestnut hair, and she pulled at her mid-thigh-length skirt, drawing attention to her shapely, tanned legs.

'They're having an affair,' whispered a mature-aged woman to her husband several places behind them in the queue.

'How can you tell, Gracie?' replied the husband. He was staring at Faulkner with a mixture of jealousy and admiration.

'Well, look at them. He's having his mid-life crisis and she's the right age. About half his age plus seven.'

The immigration officer looked at Charlotte and beckoned her forward. Faulkner remained in the queue. Charlotte smiled at the officious-looking woman behind the desk, who was wearing a light-blue uniform shirt complete with important-looking epaulettes. The officer studied Charlotte's passport with the intensity of a raptor searching for carrion. 'Do you have any political affiliation with the Communist Party, Miss Grey?' she asked Charlotte.

'No,' Charlotte replied.

'Thank you. You may proceed.'

Faulkner stepped forward and handed over his passport. He smiled as Charlotte had done, but he was rewarded with an icy glare. She leafed through the pages of his passport before placing it under a scanner.

'What was the purpose of your trip to Corfu, Mr Jones?' she said, reading the name on the passport.

'I was on holiday.'

'Was the lady who was stood next to you in the queue travelling with you?'

'No,' he lied. 'We just got chatting.' The immigration officer accepted his answer and continued to study Faulkner's passport. She squinted at her computer screen once more.

'Have you had any correspondence with any member of the royal family in the last three months?'

'No.'

'Have you ever taken drugs?'

'What? No.'

'Have you ever had a criminal conviction under Sections 52 of the Sexual Offences Act 2003?' she continued in a monotone manner.

'What? Are you serious?' Faulkner said before he could stop himself.

Her demeanour changed at his tone, and she tapped away at her computer for what seemed like minutes while the members of the queue behind Faulkner huffed with impatience. A trace of satisfaction appeared on her lips before her deadpan expression returned. She looked up from her screen and nodded to a pair of police officers who had been monitoring the long queue. Then she turned her steely gaze to Faulkner.

'I'm afraid we're going to have to ask you a few more questions in the interrogation room, Mr Jones. The police will escort you there.'

'Is there a problem?' Faulkner asked. 'How long will this take?'

'You might be there a while. There are about thirty detainees ahead of you who are deemed to be a risk to public morality.'

'But that's preposterous! What's going on?'

But the immigration officer had lost interest. 'Next!' she signalled to the man of Asian appearance who had been standing behind Faulkner.

* * *

The interrogation room was dingy, airless and filled to capacity with weary, confused and semi-mutinous travellers. Faulkner woke from his sleep and scratched at the three-day old stubble that had accumulated on his jaw. He was seated on a hard red-plastic seat and he stared at his watch. It was six p.m. and every fibre in his body ached with fatigue. He had been travelling for thirty-six hours in economy and would have paid a month's earnings for a workout, a warm shower and a flat bed. The room smelled of unwashed bodies and he wondered how much of it emanated from him. A wave of anxiety hit him as he thought of Charlotte. He hoped she had had the good sense to leave the terminal building and he worried how she would fend for herself in the new authoritarian Britain in which they had arrived.

A senior police constable entered the room and almost recoiled at the stench. 'Dear God!' he said. He scanned the room, spotted Faulkner and marched up to him.

'Mr Samuel Faulkner?' he said.

Faulkner knew the Home Office would have worked out his passport was a fake within minutes and to continue the pretence would have been futile. He nodded at the officer and stood up, pleased to be able to stretch out.

'I'm arresting you for entering Britain on a counterfeit passport. That's a serious offence, which carries a penalty of up to ten years in prison. Samuel Faulkner, you do not have to say anything, but it may harm your defence if you do not mention when questioned something which you later rely on in court. Anything you do say may be given in evidence. Do you understand?'

Faulkner nodded miserably.

'If it was up to me, I'd take you straight to the Leeds nick and throw away the key, but for some strange reason you've attracted the attention of the home secretary. She wants to see you.'

'In London?'

'No, Home Secretary Oakton is at her private residence in Pocklington. But don't get any funny ideas. You'll be under guard for the duration of your visit.'

'Penny Oakton?'

The police constable nodded. 'I don't envy you, mate. She has the reputation of being like an unexploded hand grenade that's just had its pin pulled out. You don't want to be in the vicinity when she goes off. Believe me, I've come close a couple of times.'

'Penny and I met at a Freedom League function. But I didn't

realise she's the new home secretary. I've been working under cover for a while now. Look, can I at least take a shower before we set off?'

'The Freedom League? You're a member?'

'Goodness gracious, no. In my business one must be apolitical.'

'You're not with "Six" by any chance, are you?' said the officer. His hostile attitude had changed to something approaching respect.

'Six?'

'MI6. The Secret Service. Ms Oakton has a thing about James Bond types.'

'Umm, I'm not at liberty to say. My mission was classified.'

'I bloody well knew it!' replied the officer. 'That explains why you were travelling under an assumed identity. You don't look like one of those woke activists making trouble for the new prime minister.'

'My shower, officer? The boss expects her operatives to always look their best.'

'Superintendent Newbiggin, at your service. Of course, Mr Faulkner. We'll get you tidied up and presented to the home secretary in no time.'

'Excellent, Superintendent. Would you be so kind as to update me on the latest political situation once we're in the car?'

* * *

Charlotte stepped off the airport shuttle bus and set off down the Yeadon hill known as 'The Steep' towards her red mini. It was getting dark and threatening to rain. Three drunks tailed her and one shouted leery comments in her direction as she quickened her pace. She had rarely encountered such brazen behaviour and had the sensation the depraved segments of society had slipped the leash.

She was still regathering her wits after having seen Faulkner arrested at the immigration desk. She had considered staying at the airport to see if she could find a way to assist him, but a slight shake of his head had warned her to make good her escape while she could.

The airport had been a hotbed of military activity. Six army

Spartan reconnaissance vehicles were parked outside the main terminal and the short-stay car park had been commandeered by two ominous-looking Challenger 2 tanks. A company of eighty infantry soldiers protected a battery of multiple rocket-launch systems. Hundreds of khaki-clad soldiers fidgeted with their weapons while their colleagues prepared their rations on the hulls of the fighting vehicles.

The streets were empty of civilians, reminding Charlotte of the height of the COVID-19 pandemic. Every so often, Charlotte noticed shadowy figures skulking in dark alleyways, or hiding in hedges as if they belonged to a nascent resistance movement.

Charlotte was relieved her car was still in the residential street where she had left it. It was undamaged but dirty from weeks of rain. She turned the key in the ignition, but the motor wheezed like a smoker with chronic bronchitis and refused to fire. She looked over her shoulder and saw the drunks were still swaggering their way towards her. Charlotte turned the key once more. The starter motor clicked repeatedly as the last of the charge drained from the battery. She pumped the accelerator slowly three times, waited ten seconds, took a deep breath then turned the ignition key once more. To her relief the engine spluttered and fired into life. She selected first gear, eased off the clutch and sped into the darkness.

Charlotte took the A61 towards Bishop Monkton. Faulkner had warned her it would be dangerous to return to Vavasour Hall and they had booked a holiday cottage five miles further north, near the picturesque town of Ripon, as a bolt hole. The holiday letting company had told Charlotte the keys to the cottage were in the miniature wall safe next to the electricity fuse box and had provided her with the four-digit code to the safe. But as she drove past the quaint little pub called The George in the hamlet of Dove Bank, the lure of making a ten-minute diversion to Vavasour Hall exerted an irresistible pull on her. She had not collected her baggage from the airport carousel, and needed a fresh set of clothes, a spare cosmetics bag and her laptop. She could be in and out in no time but just to be sure, she would park her car well away from the house, not that she believed anyone would be watching.

She made the right turn into Moor Road and for five minutes her headlights picked up the rich arable farmland, high hedgerows and trees that joined at the top like the tall arches of a cathedral. Memories of a happy, carefree childhood complemented the natural beauty of the Yorkshire countryside.

But the air was filled with menace. The few people she picked up in the beams of her headlights had a furtive look, as if their comfortable world was disintegrating around them. She considered turning the car around and heading to Ripon as Faulkner had intended, but the lane was narrow and the corners were almost blind. Before she knew it, the imposing bulk of Vavasour Hall loomed ahead. Charlotte stopped the car one hundred metres from the main gates of the long driveway. She killed the motor and sat for a minute before exiting the vehicle.

She avoided the main gate and slipped into the grounds by climbing over the low wall, as she had done many times as a girl. She was grateful she was wearing a pair of sensible training shoes, as she darted towards the library window, ducking low as she went. The library had a set of French doors that opened out onto the rose garden. She knew the doors had a faulty latch and they could be opened by lifting the left-hand door by its handle and pulling backwards. Within minutes she was into the house and heading towards her bedroom on the first floor. She left the lights off and moved with as much stealth as she could muster. There was a curious smell coming from the bathroom, but she assumed one of the drains must have blocked during her absence from the house.

She entered the bedroom and switched on the bedside reading light. She pulled out a small suitcase from under the bed and opened it up. Then she headed towards her walk-in wardrobe and stopped dead. Her wardrobe had been ransacked. Her underwear drawer was open, its contents strewn onto the floor. Her dresses were half-hanging from their hangers and even her shoes had been removed from their tidy rack and thrown into a jumbled heap at the back of the cupboard.

She gasped at the violation of her possessions and turned around. She knew she must leave the house quickly. But as she headed back towards her bedroom door, the main light switch was flicked on, and she was dazzled.

'So, the bitch has returned,' said Vance Messervy with a sneer. Her ex was holding a razor-sharp kitchen knife and was brandishing it like a sword. 'You're so predictable, Charlotte. I knew you wouldn't be able to resist the temptation to retrieve your gaudy, upper-class chattel, and now your vanity has condemned you.'

Vance's left hand unconsciously touched his scab-covered nose. The tip was lumpy, and Charlotte could see the cartilage separating his nostrils had been eaten away through excessive cocaine use. The bridge of his nose had collapsed inwards, making it look skeletal. His mouth twisted into a smirk as he lurched a step closer to Charlotte.

'But first you owe me one last night of extreme sex before I fillet you like a trout.'

CHAPTER 35

'Superintendent Newbiggin. Why isn't this man in handcuffs?' said Home Secretary Penny Oakton. She looked at Faulkner from behind her imposing desk, like a lioness that had cornered a wounded zebra. She removed a hair clip from the back of her head and shook out her blonde locks onto her broad shoulders.

'But he ... he told me he was an agent from the Secret Service,' stammered the superintendent.

'And you believed him?' She shook her head in despair, then looked once more at Faulkner. 'Why am I surrounded by fools, Faulkner?' she asked.

Faulkner shrugged at the question. 'I must have been very convincing. Superintendent Newbiggin and I had a most interesting conversation in the car. You've done very well for yourself in the Cavalier cabinet, Ms Oakton.'

'That's the *Honourable Minister* Oakton to you, Samuel Faulkner.'

'Should I handcuff him now, Minister?' the superintendent asked sheepishly.

'Why not? It might teach him some manners. Then you can return to your duties, Superintendent.'

'Is this necessary?' Faulkner complained as his hands were shackled behind his back and the keys handed to Penny Oakton.

'Necessary? You skulk back into the country on a false passport during a time of civil unrest and ask me if it's necessary? For all I know, you could have been intending to blow up parliament.' She made a dismissive gesture with her hand to the superintendent. 'Out!' she said. 'I'll deal with you later.'

'You may sit,' she said to Faulkner, indicating the big leather chair opposite her desk without looking up from a pile of papers she was studying.

Faulkner sat on the chair and shuffled backwards to make himself more comfortable.

'God, I need a drink. It's been a long, shitty day,' Oakton said. She stood up and walked to the bar fridge. She made herself a gin and tonic, added two lumps of ice and cut a slice of lemon, which she fixed to the side of the crystal cut glass. 'If I remember correctly, you're a real ale man.' She pulled out a bottle of Cotleigh Tawny bitter and poured it into a tall glass. She placed the glass on the edge of her desk in front of Faulkner, and then collapsed into her luxurious leather chair opposite him. She stretched out like a contented Persian cat with a troublesome mouse trapped between its paws, then took a long swallow of her gin and tonic. She tilted her head back in apparent satisfaction. 'Come on Faulkner, drink up.'

'Umm... the handcuffs?'

A trace of a smile played on her lips as she leaned back in her chair. She crossed her legs and ran the tip of her tongue on the edge of her glass. 'You need to reflect a little longer on your predicament, Faulkner. You've been under my surveillance from the moment you boarded QF1 in Sydney. How does it feel to have been outsmarted by Red House's first female school captain?'

'Very impressive,' Faulkner acknowledged. He hoped Charlotte at least had slipped through Oakton's security net.

Oakton stood up and walked around her desk with the keys to the cuffs. 'You're on parole, Faulkner. I'm releasing you from the cuffs, but you'll remain in my custody.'

'How do you know I won't just walk out of that door?' Faulkner said as he rubbed at his freed wrists.

'Because of those old-fashioned values that were beaten into you at Red House. I've shown you magnanimity and as a true Yorkshire gentleman, your personal code of honour dictates you must repay me in kind. Now, enjoy your drink.'

Faulkner had to hand it to Oakton; she had described his character to a tee. He smiled and raised his glass. 'Let's drink to magnanimity.'

The beer hit the spot. He had not had a drink since leaving Sydney. He drained half of the beer from the glass before leaning back and studying the home secretary. He had to admit she was fine-looking woman, but he knew she was as cunning as a vixen, and he must keep his wits about him.

'I must confess you led me a merry dance before I was able to get my hands on you. So, what were you doing in Sydney?'

'Is this an interrogation?'

'We'll find out eventually. You might as well tell me now.'

'Fleeing from your goons. One of them chased me up a tunnel with the British Army's latest assault rifle.'

'Then why did you return?'

'To see the king. I received a personal invitation, and you're interrupting royal business.'

'Then you made a wasted journey. He's under house arrest.'

'You've arrested the king? What the hell's going on, Penny?'

Oakton placed her feet up on her desk and crossed her ankles. The red soles of her Louboutin heels stared Faulkner in the face. 'Why are you talking politics, Faulkner? Let's talk about what we can do for each other. We have so much in common.'

'Stop changing the topic. There are tanks on the streets of Leeds. People are frightened. How can the new government have ballsed it up so badly?'

Oakton removed her feet from the desk and glared at Faulkner. 'I'll grant you, our policies might have been a tad heavy-handed. But the king is acting against all constitutional precedence by refusing to swear in the Cavalier cabinet. He'll remain under house arrest until he sees sense.'

'You're risking a civil war. The country is being torn apart.'

'Just so you know, the invitation to meet the king did not come from him. It came from me.'

'What? You lured me back to Britain under false pretences?'

'You're just annoyed because I outsmarted you, Faulkner. And don't be so moralistic. You were the one who entered the country under a false identity.' Oakton kicked off her heels, then padded towards the bar where she made herself a second gin and tonic. 'Another beer?' she asked.

'The perfect hostess,' Faulkner replied sarcastically.

'Actually, the invitation was genuine,' she said, returning to her desk with the two drinks. 'I wanted you to persuade the king to cooperate with the government.'

'Why would he listen to me?'

'He knows all about you. Believe it or not, he's been a Saracens supporter all his life.'

'Really?' said Faulkner.

'He also knows you refused to accept a leading role in the Cavalier cabinet. He trusts your advice.'

'You expect me to clean up your mess?'

'Not my mess. You see, I'm actually one of the Freedom League's moderates. It was me who insisted Pride bring you into the government to counterbalance his extremist tendencies. He was too ham-fisted to succeed even in that simple task.'

'You don't like him?'

'He's a man of conviction, for sure. But he's also pompous and narcissistic. He thinks he's the next Oliver Cromwell, but a better comparison would be Ethelred the Unready. He's a liability to the cause.'

Faulkner shrugged his shoulders. 'I'm not getting involved with the Freedom League's grubby internal politics.'

'Don't give me that, Faulkner. You snuck back into the country under an assumed name for a reason. You want to get rid of Pride as much as I do.'

'I've heard that in the new Britain, talk of disloyalty is death.'

'I'm the home secretary. The rules are what I make them.'

'What are you proposing?'

'I'm proposing we bring down Nigel Pride together. He's the one leading the country towards oblivion, not me.'

'How would we do that?'

'Ah, now I have your attention. I just had to push the right buttons.' Oakton stood up once more and fixed herself a third gin and tonic. 'Do keep up, Sam. You've barely touched your second beer.'

'Let me guess. I'm to persuade the king to swear in the Cavalier cabinet. He does so on condition Nigel Pride resigns from the Cavalier cabinet. The king then asks me who should be his replacement. I tell him Penny Oakton has all the right credentials and is someone he could work with.'

'Close, but no cigar. The king has no say on who succeeds Nigel Pride. Once you've met with the king and gained his reassurance that he will legitimise his new government, you'll address the Cavalier cabinet and persuade them the price of legitimacy is Nigel Pride's head.'

'You are talking metaphorically, of course?' Faulkner said, shocked.

'For the moment, yes. But it depends on whether Pride pledges his unconditional support to me. English politics is littered with backstabbing men whose loyalty to their female leaders could not be trusted. I don't intend to make the same mistake. Do I make myself clear, Faulkner?'

'You want me to address the cabinet, tell them Pride must go, and they must appoint you in his place?'

'You're a fast learner, Samuel Faulkner.'

'That sounds like you've just handed me a poisoned chalice. Why would I do that?'

'You mean other than serving ten years in prison for illegally entering the country?'

Faulkner took a long swallow of his beer and nodded.

'Because the alternative is civil war and anarchy. You of all people know Nigel Pride is unsuitable for leadership. Under my guidance, Britain will have a kinder, gentler but steady hand on the tiller. The people won't stand for a second Cromwell, but they might unite under a female warrior. A living personification of Britannia, if you like.'

Faulkner scoffed. 'A female führer of a totalitarian Britain?'

'I resent that remark, Faulkner. But why not? The Cavalier cabinet has fixated on you because you won a rugby trophy or two at Red House. Big deal. Did you know under my head prefecture, Red House won its first Yorkshire prep school hockey championship and reached the final of the All-England netball knockout cup?'

'Umm, no.'

'Then you're a bloody sexist like the rest of them. You see, you're not the only hero from the ranks of the Old Cavaliers, but the cabinet refuses to endorse me because I'm a woman.' Oakton seethed with indignation as she downed the rest of her gin and tonic. 'Now where was I, Faulkner?'

'Your vision for Britain.'

'Ah, yes. We'll keep the Cavalier cabinet's agenda, including rearmament, national service, and investing in new economy manufacturing jobs, but dispose of the puritan ideological claptrap and state brutality. Except for those who cross me, of course. Those who serve me loyally will be rewarded with such favours as only a woman can give. That's the future I'm offering you, Sam Faulkner. You can be my trusted lieutenant and confidant.'

'What if I refuse?'

'You won't. You love your country too much to allow Nigel Pride to become a dictator and see Britain descend into chaos. I have the support of all the visionaries in the Cavalier cabinet, but they won't approve the removal of Nigel Pride unless I have your explicit endorsement.'

'A dictator with a pretty face and a smooth way with words is still a dictator,' Sam replied.

Oakton made herself another gin and tonic. 'As you've not finished your second beer, I won't offer you another,' she said with a trace of annoyance in her voice. She walked around to Faulkner's chair and perched on the edge of her desk. Faulkner could smell her heavy perfume, which clashed with the sickly sweet smell of gin on her breath.

'I'll ignore that last remark because I happen to hold you in high regard.' She propped her foot on the end of his chair in a proprietary manner. 'As home secretary I control the security apparatus of this country. You committed an offence by entering the country on a false passport, but I'm releasing you on a good behaviour bond. You won't be able to pick your nose in public without me receiving a ten-page dossier from MI5 on the matter. If you displease me, you'll go to prison for ten years. In short, your arse belongs to me. Do we understand each other, Faulkner?'

'But we both know that's not true, don't we, Penny?' Faulkner replied. He stared into Oakton's eyes. 'All the political ambitions you've nurtured since you were head prefect at Red House depend upon my character assessment of you to the Cavalier cabinet. If I can make you the prime minister, it stands to reason I can also unmake your political career. I'll admit you're an improvement on Nigel Pride, but that's not a high bar. I'm yet to be persuaded you have more intelligence than Rupert Elliott, or are as visionary as Mark Hodgson. And just so we're clear, if your goons so much as breathe on me while I'm considering my character assessment of you, then it's game over for your prime ministerial aspirations.'

CHAPTER 36

Vavasour Hall, Bishop Monkton

'Make me a drink, bitch!' Vance Messervy demanded. Sitting at the kitchen table, his voice sounded nasal, and he had difficulty enunciating his words since the bridge of his nose had collapsed.

Charlotte moved towards the fridge. 'What would you like, Vance?' She was anxious not to antagonise him while he still held the nine-inch carving knife in his hand. He was stoned and unsteady on his feet, but she knew from experience he was capable of extreme violence. She tried not to stare at the hideous remnants of his misshapen nose, but it had a hypnotising effect on her. Her once handsome, almost beautiful fiancé now resembled a monster.

'Don't even try to use your charms to save your spoilt, rotten hide from the butcher's knife.'

'Would you like me to make you a vodka mojito? It used to be your favourite.'

Messervy tried to laugh, but the sound was distorted, and the effort caused his nose to bleed. He winced at the pain and dabbed it with a tissue. 'Why not? It'll remind you of the nights we would make mad, passionate love together.'

'May I make myself a blackcurrant mojito? Just for old time's sake?'

'Are you staring at my nose, whore?'

'No, no! Honestly, I wasn't, Vance. Would you like me to see if I can take the pain away?'

'What do you know about pain? You're not a nurse. You don't have an ounce of female compassion in you. Just self-centred ambition and an over-refined sense of your own social fucking superiority. I never was good enough for you. Just your bit of rough from Suffolk to be discarded at your whim.'

'That's not true, Vance. Look, let's talk this through. I can use one of my mother's herbal cures to ease your suffering.'

'Don't mention that old witch to me again. It was her wicked tongue that poisoned you against me.'

Charlotte opened the fridge and pulled out a bottle of soda and a half-empty bottle of lime juice. Then she went to the pantry and pulled down a bottle of vodka and a bottle of simple syrup from the top shelf. 'I'm afraid I don't have any fresh mint. I haven't been home for weeks.'

'I heard you went to Sydney with that pimp of a travel agent. Are you screwing him?'

'He's fifteen years older than me, Vance, and he was my mother's boyfriend. I wouldn't do that.'

'You're lying. You've been flirting with him since Lake Kariba. But no matter, I'll get the truth out of you when I'm filleting you.'

'Vance! We can sort this out. Look, I have some dried mint in the keeping room. It'll make your drink taste just like how you used to like it and it'll calm you down.'

Messervy stood up and walked towards Charlotte waving his knife. His eyes were unfocused and bloodshot. 'Stop snivelling,' he said. 'And don't think you can make a run for it while you pretend to fetch the mint. I'll be right behind you with my knife at your back.'

Charlotte walked to an old wooden door leading to the keeping room. Inside was a second pantry, but rows of bottles and jars of various colours and sizes lined the antique-looking shelves. Each container displayed a faded label on which the name of its contents was written in Latin in a neat, feminine hand. The room had a heady, aromatic smell. Charlotte switched on the light and walked in, but Messervy hung back.

'What the hell is this place?' Vance said.

'It was my mother's collection of rare herbal remedies. I was going to clear this place out, but it has sentimental value.'

'I knew she was a fucking witch. This proves it.'

'My mother was an eminent pharmacologist. Over half of Vavasour Pharmaceutical's products started off as samples from this keeping room.' Charlotte picked up a small stepladder from the corner of the room. She climbed the ladder and selected a jar from the top shelf containing crushed green leaves. She then moved the ladder a metre to her left and picked out a jar containing what looked like blackcurrants floating in a clear liquid.

'We're done here,' she said. She climbed down the ladder and brushed past Messervy, keeping a wary eye on the knife as she headed back to the kitchen.

Charlotte mixed the drinks, then added a handful of ice

to each glass. 'Sam Faulkner knows I'm here,' she said as she handed Messervy his drink. 'He'll be expecting me to call any time now. Why don't you put the knife down?'

'Lying cow. He'd be with you if he really cared.' Messervy sniffed at the drink. 'I can't smell the mint. What have you put in it?'

Charlotte took a large sip of her blackcurrant mojito and closed her eyes in appreciation. She had not drunk anything since stepping off the plane. 'The mint is dried. It'll take a few minutes for the flavour to permeate through the drink. But you can give it to me if you don't want it.'

Messervy took a wary sip from the glass and rolled it around his mouth. He took a larger mouthful and savoured its flavour before swallowing. 'If your mother wasn't a witch, what was all that weird equipment I saw in the basement? It freaked me out.'

'It serves you right for breaking in and snooping around. You found her museum. She collected artefacts from the mid-seventeenth century.'

'It looked like a medieval torture chamber.'

'This is an old house, Vance. It was built by my family when Red House was stolen from us.'

'Your family is fucking weird. I did the right thing by dumping you.'

'My ancestor Rebecca Slingsby was accused of witchcraft in 1659 by the man who stole her property. She was proven innocent, but he burned her anyway. My mother collected items that were used by religious zealots to torture and extract confessions from the hundreds of innocent women who were accused of witchcraft in the sixteenth and seventeenth centuries. She was going to donate them to the York Museum.'

Messervy took another sip of his drink. 'Poor little rich girl! Do you want me to feel sorry for you just because one of your ancestors met an early death? Well, my ancestors had to face death every day of their lives from hunger and disease because they were oppressed by the elite. My great grandfather was the Pentonville prison hangman. He would deliberately botch the job when it came to hanging toffs, especially the female ones.'

'You're just trying to scare me.'

'I was the first Messervy to get a respectable job in the city, but thanks to your mother and her acid tongue, I was fired from my job.'

'It was nothing to do with my mother. She didn't give you a cocaine habit.'

Messervy laughed and air whistled through the collapsed bridge in his nose, causing more blood to flow. 'How can I trust any woman again? No, my satisfaction comes from the digital world. I know how it works. I could make more money on the dark web in one transaction than your pharmaceutical company makes in a year. And it's all tax free!' He grinned and his collapsed nose made him look like a *Death's Head* mask. He took a large swallow of his mojito. 'You could've shared in all this wealth and power, but instead you'll be roadkill on my highway to greatness.'

'The authorities will track you down, Vance. They always do.'

Messervy laughed once more, then winced as the pain in his nose became intolerable. 'I'm part of the new system, Charlotte. I'm the FL's link to the great British unwashed, who will win the looming civil war for the Cavalier cabinet. I feed the public disinformation via the computers and smartphones that are at the core of their shitty, boring lives. I might have a cocaine habit, but they have an addiction to conspiracy theories. They need to believe they're being controlled by a rich cabal of globalists. It's never their fault that they're lazy, stupid, or have wasted their valuable time watching endless re-runs of reality TV shows.'

'You mentioned a looming civil war. Surely that's not inevitable?'

'You're so naïve, Charlotte. I used to like that about you. The new government needs a short but bloody civil war to eliminate the old guard and make the population compliant. Only through violence can Britain rise from the ashes and become great again. They might even need a hangman in their ranks.' He leered at Charlotte. 'The government has already given me the explosive disinformation I need to light the fire. When I've finished with you, Britain will be at war with itself.'

'Don't do this, Vance, I beg you. It's too awful to contemplate.'

'It's too late. My artificial intelligence programs are already drafting the scripts and my bots will send them out to my moderators for dissemination in the morning. My software is protected by security protocols so watertight, even your IT friend Sean Moody won't be able to breach them. Yes, I know all about him and how he almost wiped out the Freedom League's Darkshirt Brigade. You see, I've modified the algorithms and this time I've memorised all the important codes, so they're immune from his electronic spyware.' He tapped the side of his head and grinned before finishing off his drink.

'You make me sick, Vance. I used to pity you, but now I just hold you in contempt.'

Messervy lurched from the kitchen table and hit Charlotte across the face with the back of his hand. Charlotte reeled from the blow but steadied herself by clutching the edge of the sink. Messervy grabbed a length of her hair and pulled her head backwards revealing her slender throat. He raised the knife and pressed its blade against her delicate skin, drawing a thin line of blood.

'Beg for mercy, harlot!'

Charlotte closed her eyes. Her breath was ragged with fear, but she managed to shake her head defiantly.

'As you wish. I'm taking you below ground to your mother's basement where your screams cannot be heard. We can use that equipment in the way it was intended.'

* * *

Messervy dragged Charlotte down the narrow stone steps of what used to be a subterranean scullery, holding the kitchen knife against her throat. The single light bulb was barely adequate to see the gruesome seventeenth-century relics that lay scattered in the dingy, cobweb-filled basement. Charlotte had stopped struggling, but he noticed she felt heavy and cumbersome in his grip. His bravado disappeared the moment he set foot in this godforsaken basement. Beads of sweat erupted on his forehead and mild panic sent palpitations running through his chest. He released Charlotte and shoved her down the last two steps so that she fell onto the rough stone floor. He resolved to finish the bitch off quickly and set light to this dreadful place, despite his desire to give her a slow, agonising death.

He loomed over Charlotte's prone body and tried to raise the knife, but it felt like a lead weight in his hand. With a growing sense of alarm, he realised he was losing control of his limbs and the knife fell from his hands and clattered onto the stone floor.

His vision blurred and he found it hard to think rationally, as if he had taken a bad batch of cocaine.

He noticed Charlotte rising from the ground, but she was no longer wearing her patterned skirt and T-shirt, but an ankle-length dress made from coarsely woven black hemp over which was a dirty woollen shawl. She wore a frayed white bonnet over her long grey hair. Her clothing smelled of mildew, and lice scuttled from every fold. Her gnarled feet were bare and unwashed, and a plethora of warts disfigured her face.

Messervy shook his head to clear the fog enveloping his mind, but he could no longer be certain of time, place or reality. The hideous creature confronting him resembled Charlotte Talbot, but also some monstrous old crone with malicious intent in her eyes. He backed away from the creature, but every step he took required a herculean effort of will. He stumbled against an old wooden chair with oversized arm boards and a high backrest. Its decaying leather seat was covered with dead insects and rodent droppings. Unable to bear his own weight any longer, he slumped into the antique chair, knowing he would not be able to rise from its embrace until the effects of whatever drug he had taken had cleared his system.

The apparition limped closer in an arthritic manner until it loomed over him and leered into his face.

'Thou darest defile the seat in which so many of my sisters were most grievously tortured?' screeched the apparition.

Messervy shook his head. He tried to plead with the vile creature, but no sound emerged from his mouth. The crone fastened his flaccid left arm to the wooden arm board of the chair with a thick leather strap, then repeated the process with his second arm. She secured his torso to the backrest using a wide brown belt and buckled it tight so that movement was impossible.

'Thou hast awakened the spirits of my dead sisters from their slumber,' said the witch-like creature. 'They are enraged that a hangman sitteth in their midst and they crave vengeance.'

Messervy felt the remaining energy drain from his body and his eyelids drooped. He wondered if unconsciousness might save him from the nightmare he knew was to follow. Then in a moment of lucidity, he understood what had happened to him. 'You've poisoned me, you bitch,' he managed to utter. 'You're screwing with my head.'

Then the moment of clarity was gone. He watched as the old crone shuffled to a bench containing an array of diabolical devices. She ran a wizened hand over half-a-dozen sharp implements, then selected what looked like a fetid old dog collar. Attached to the collar was a rusty double-ended fork with sharp prongs jutting from each end. She brought the implement towards Messervy, who recoiled at the rotten-meat smell of the collar. She slipped it around his neck so that the lower prong pricked the top of his sternum. The second prong jutted upwards under his chin, and he had to extend his neck to avoid impaling his throat on its rusty tip.

'It's a heretic's fork, much favoured by your brethren,' she said. 'If thou lookest upwards to God, thou shalt live to see in the morrow. However, shouldst thou slumber, the device will pierce thy throat and thou wilt drown in thine own blood ...'

'What do you want from me, you old hag?'

'I want the names of the evildoers thou callest thy *moderators*. I need thy secret codes, thy ciphers, and all thou knowest of this plot to restore the hated Puritans to power.'

'Never!'

The witch cackled, as if amused by Messervy's defiance. 'When the spirits of my departed sisters have finished with thee, thou shalt beg to give me the information. For no man in Christendom could survive more than one night in the chair.'

* * *

Sean Moody waited at his office in Sydney while Charlotte fiddled with the settings on her computer ten-thousand miles away. He thought she looked tired. Her fresh-faced features and charming smile had been replaced with a worried frown and there were dark rings under her eyes as if she had been awake all night.

'I'm going to share my screen with you,' Charlotte said. 'Is there anything you can do with this information?'

Moody whistled through his teeth as he stared at the screen. 'Is this for real? We've been chasing this rogue's gallery for over two years. It's the motherlode. And are those their passwords? Dear Lord, what's all that code coming through?'

'Vance said it's the Freedom League's new security algorithms for their Darkshirt website. He transferred them to me this morning.'

'With this information we can launch the biggest sting in history and round up hundreds of the biggest cybercriminals on the dark web.'

'Can you stop the flow of disinformation to Vance's moderators? He said it's going to be transferred to them in the next couple of hours.'

'If this list contains the moderator's VPN account details and the security algorithms are genuine, then the answer is *yes*, we can stop it dead in its tracks. At least until they realise their accounts have been compromised.'

'Can you validate the accuracy of the information as soon as you can? I need to make sure Vance is telling me the truth before I send him on his way.'

'Sure. But just out of interest, why did Vance give you all this stuff? It'll send him to prison for decades.'

'Let's just say he had an epiphany during the night.'

'Vance Messervy is no choir boy. It must have been one hell of an epiphany.'

'That's a pretty accurate description of what happened to him, Sean.'

CHAPTER 37

Dumfries House, Ayrshire, Scotland

'And who the bloody hell are you?' the king said without looking up as he attacked a clump of dock weeds that had encroached into the otherwise immaculate walled garden.

'I'm Samuel Faulkner, Your Majesty. You wish to see me?'

Faulkner had driven his Land Rover for four hours from Pocklington police station, escorted by three British Army Jackal armoured cars and a fleet of six police motorcycles. He was running late for his appointment because the thirsty Jackals had filled up at the Todhills Services on the M6 motorway, and again at the BP on the Ayr Road at Cumnock.

'Ah yes, the new gardener. I've been expecting you.' He passed Faulkner a hand trowel. 'These bloody dock weeds are a damned nuisance. It must be the wet weather.' The king was wearing a pair of old trousers, green wellington boots, a tweed coat with leather patches on the elbows and a flat cap. 'Well don't just stand there, man. The weeds won't pull themselves out of the soil on their own, you know.'

Faulkner knelt next to the king and attacked a weed. His pressed suit trousers were soon covered in mud. 'Actually, it wasn't the dock weeds I came to see you about, sir. I've been sent by the acting prime minister to discuss parliament's proposed Abdication Bill.'

'Good Lord!' the king said. 'Why didn't you say so? You must be that Red House chappie who used to play for the Saracens. The one whose ancestor Colonel Fauconberg commanded the famous Northern Horse cavalry brigade in the English Civil War?'

'Yes, sir. But it's most unlikely I'm related to Colonel Fauconberg.'

'Well, I'll be damned. I always thought you would captain England.'

'It was a proud moment when I put on my first captain's arm band. Is this a weed or a plant?' he asked, not wanting to uproot one of the king's prized horticultural specimens.

'You can dig that one out. It's not a weed but the plants in this garden bed need thinning.' The king looked Faulkner up and down for the first time and appeared to like what he saw. 'So that damned fool Nigel Pride has sent you to Dumfries House to persuade me to abdicate, has he? I never liked the scrawny bugger.'

'He has. He says it's the only way to avoid civil war.'

'Did you need three armoured cars and a posse of police motorcyclists to tell me that?'

'I suspect the show of force was intended to keep me under close guard rather than to intimidate you, sir. It was a long trip to Ayrshire, and I could have absconded on the way.'

'Indeed. Dumfries House is rather remote. I've been confined here for that very reason. Would you be so kind as to pass me the secateurs? This azalea needs a prune.'

Faulkner reached to his left and passed the king the clippers. 'I did notice on the way up to Scotland there were quite a few people protesting *against* Pride's provisional government. The public mood seems to have swung back in your favour in the last few days.'

'My word!' the king said. 'The government minders keep telling me the mob is calling for my head. They say it's a matter of time before they come for me with a chopper.'

Faulkner laughed. 'I can assure you that's not the case. But the military are everywhere. General Lambert has a tight grip on the armed forces.'

'So he's a general now, is he? When did he get promoted?'

'Last week.'

'Another one of your blasted Red House School chums. They call themselves the Cavalier cabinet because so many of them are from Red House, but they're behaving like a bunch of uptight puritan Roundheads.' He hacked at the azalea. 'So, go ahead, Faulkner. What's Pride proposing?'

'That you either endorse the Cavalier cabinet or abdicate the throne.'

'I won't bloody well abdicate and even if I do, none of my family will step in to support Pride's government. So, he'll have to remain illegitimate and that's my final word on the subject.'

'Just out of interest, why is this such a big issue of principle? I thought the monarchy was supposed to rubber stamp every act of parliament?'

'Because I've got one job and that's to keep the government in check. For the last three hundred years, the government and the monarchy have played by the rules, so no intervention was necessary. If I were to become a tyrant, the government would have every right to lock me up in a tower until I had come to my senses. Similarly, if a government comes to power through a coup d'état, and then proceeds to draft a raft of repressive legislation, then it's my duty to refuse them legitimacy. I feel that time has come. Do you believe I'm wrong, Faulkner?'

Faulkner thought about the king's question as he dug out another weed.

'Mind the bloody primroses, man!' the king protested.

'I do apologise, sir,' Faulkner said. 'But to answer your question, you're right to be concerned about this government's agenda. The values at Red House were based on harsh discipline and success at any cost. It was a system designed to run the British Empire. Now it's gone, the Old Cavaliers want to restore the glory days by any means necessary.'

'You're recommending I stick to my guns?'

'There are two problems, as I see it.'

'Go on,' the king said. He put the secateurs down and pointed towards a wooden bench that enjoyed a position in the sun in the middle of the five-acre walled garden. They chatted as they walked side by side towards the bench.

'Firstly, you'll need to stare down General Lambert,' Faulkner said. 'He has total command of the armed forces and is loyal to Nigel Pride.'

'That might pose a problem. Dumfries House and this walled garden are my gilded cage. I won't be able to stare down anyone unless Lambert decides to pay me a visit.'

'We'll cross that bridge when we come to it. Acting Home Secretary Penny Oakton wants Pride's job. She might succeed in ousting him, but Lambert detests her, so the army could go rogue if she becomes PM.'

'What a shambles!' exclaimed the king. 'Is she any better than Pride?'

'She's the lesser of two evils and more rational, but she still supports the Cavalier cabinet's agenda.'

'So, you're not recommending I do a deal with her?'

'No.'

'And the second problem?'

'If you refuse to provide royal assent to the new government, then they will enact legislation to have you removed.'

'They can't do that,' said the king. He sat down on the garden bench and beckoned Faulkner to sit next to him. 'I need to give my assent to any act of parliament and I won't consent to my own abdication. Who do they think I am?'

Faulkner sat down and stared at his muddy suit trousers, then tried to kick off the clumps of mud that had stuck to his shoes. The king appeared not to notice.

'Pride has unearthed a pretender to the throne,' Faulkner said. 'He's a man called Jimmy Stuart, who claims to be the most senior living descendant of James II. Pride is going to claim the "Glorious Revolution" that ousted King James II in 1688 was an illegal usurpation of the throne because it happened as the result of a foreign invasion. Hence, every royal dynasty that followed including the Georgians, the House of Saxe-Coburg and Gotha, and your own Windsor dynasty, are illegitimate. He's using your own logic against you. If you're claiming his government is illegal, then he's going to dispute your right to the throne.'

'Is this man Jimmy Stuart genuine?'

'There can be no doubt. He's had his relationship to King James II confirmed by Debrett's Peerage. He's even had a DNA test to prove it.'

The king seemed lost in thought for a while and stared at the Palladian architecture of Dumfries House. 'What do you think of the house, Faulkner?' he said.

'It reminds me of Red House, although it's more symmetrical and, of course, the colour of the brickwork is different. Both houses have a certain charm.'

'Perhaps it will be a good place to while away my retirement?'

'I'm assuming that if you were coronated, you cannot be *un*coronated, even by Nigel Pride?'

'You're correct, of course, but a modern-day monarchy depends upon the support of the public for its legitimacy. Once that bond between monarch and the public has been broken, then sixteen-hundred years of British history can be erased with the stroke of the pen. Pride is trying to break that trust and has backed me into a corner. I either give in to his totalitarian dreams or hand the crown over to the modern pretender.'

'It seems that way.'

'I suppose this Jimmy Stuart also went to Red House?'

'Yes.'

'God help us. What a nest of vipers! The damned Jacobites have finally usurped the crown of the United Kingdom. Is Jimmy ... James Stuart a good man?'

'No. He's a weasel. We used to call him Bonnie Prince Jimmy because of his regal affectations and his curly blond hair. But now he's a fat software salesman – and a failed one at that.'

'Well, let's hope he makes a good king, because I won't be the man who grants legitimacy to a neo-Nazi government.'

'He won't be. He's Pride's stooge and word has it he'll abdicate within the year in exchange for a ten-million-pound government pension and a luxury yacht. Pride will then head up the puritan republic he has craved since he left Red House.'

'Dear God.' The king placed his head in his hands before recovering his composure. 'I can't see any alternative. You can tell Nigel Pride I will be abdicating at the end of the week.'

'That may not be necessary,' Faulkner said.

'What? I don't see I have any choice.'

'What if Jimmy Stuart is *not* the most senior living descendant of the Stuart dynasty?'

'But you just said he was?'

'There's a young woman I know who I believe is a direct descendant of the eldest son of Charles II. By rights, this man should have inherited the British throne in 1685.'

'James Fitzroy, the Duke of Monmouth? But he was illegitimate and besides, he was executed for treason.'

'Not James Fitzroy, but William Vavasour, the surviving son of the marriage of Charles II and Lady Rebecca Slingsby.'

'You're drawing a long bow there,' said the king. 'Charles II had many mistresses but only one queen: Catherine of Braganza – and she was childless.'

'I spoke to the mother of the young woman in question. Before she died, she told me there was cast-iron proof a marriage had taken place in The Hague in 1646 when Charles II was sixteen. The marriage was kept secret, but it was a marriage, nonetheless. Rebecca Slingsby returned to Holland in 1658, where she conceived and gave birth to twin boys. Charles only remarried when he learned of his wife Rebecca's death in 1660.'

'Do you have that proof?'

'No. Rebecca Vavasour was never able to locate the marriage certificate, but I believe I know where it is.'

'But this doesn't help. It merely shifts the problem of succession from one Stuart to another.'

'But what if this young woman can prove she *is* the legitimate Stuart heir, but then renounces any claim to the throne in your favour? It would neuter Nigel Pride's attempts to replace you with Jimmy Stuart.'

'Even if you can find this so-called proof, that still leaves the problem of General Lambert and the armed forces. If the army doesn't stand down, there will be social division and conflict on a scale not seen since the Civil War of 1642.'

'Leave General Lambert to me.'

'Forgive me for having my doubts, Mr Faulkner, but your scheme appears to have more holes than a slice of Swiss cheese.'

'Do you have any better ideas, Your Majesty?'

'I can't say I do.' The king let out an exasperated sigh. 'When does Nigel Pride need an answer?'

'This Friday. If they don't hear from you in three days' time, parliament will vote to restore the Stuart dynasty.'

'Then you have three days to locate this so-called proof of the marriage of King Charles II to Lady Rebecca Slingsby, and persuade General Lambert to stand down his military forces. In the meantime, I'll create a right royal diversion so you can give your minders the slip to do what you must do.'

'Yes, sir.'

CHAPTER 38

River Ouse, Moor Monkton

Faulkner parked his Land Rover next to a thick clump of hedges and switched off the engine. A short distance from the car, the River Ouse reflected the light of the new moon as it meandered through the lush fields of the Vale of York on its way to the Humber estuary.

Faulkner took a moment to compose himself for what he knew would be a dangerous and difficult mission. He and Charlotte Talbot had staked out the grounds of Red House for most of the day and it was evident General Mike Lambert was preparing for a major military operation. Armoured vehicles and tanks had been arriving in a constant stream and the old playing fields resembled a parking lot for the Royal Artillery. Hundreds of soldiers were entering and leaving Red House and its surrounding buildings. He turned to look at Charlotte in the passenger seat, who, like him, was wearing black jeans and a dark, long-sleeved sweater. He watched her as she concealed her long hair underneath a black woollen hat.

'You do realise that if anything happens to you tonight, then the future of the monarchy as we know it will cease to exist?' The words tumbled from his mouth before Faulkner could stop them. Charlotte had insisted on coming to Red House with him to search for the marriage certificate and nothing he had said could dissuade her.

Charlotte smiled at him and donned a pair of black leather gloves. 'Shouldn't you be more respectful to the future queen of the United Kingdom?' she teased.

'Now don't be getting any grandiose ideas just yet,' he countered. 'I don't know if this certificate even exists.'

Charlotte reached behind her and pulled out a stubby Glock 19 pistol from her rucksack. She unclipped the magazine and checked the chamber was empty. Then she reinserted the magazine back into the handgun with a forceful strike of her palm and slipped the weapon into a concealed holster beneath her top. 'Right, let's do this,' she said.

'Hold on,' countered Faulkner. 'Where the fuck did you get

that piece?'

'I found it in Vance's bag. The one he left behind when he ran off into the sunset.'

'Do you know how to use it?'

'I was an exchange student at the University of Alabama for a year. The family I stayed with were all members of the National Rifle Association. The Glock was their weapon of choice.'

'You do realise we're about to enter Mike Lambert's military headquarters? Your peashooter won't be much use against the elite of the British Army.'

'Think of it as additional leverage if we find ourselves in a difficult situation.'

He knew further argument was pointless. 'You have aspirations to become the United Kingdom's next sovereign and yet you're prepared to blow some poor squaddie's brains out?'

'If necessary. I take it you won't be going out without protection?'

Faulkner pulled up his black jumper to reveal a leather scabbard strapped across his chest containing a Fairburn-Sykes British Army fighting knife. He unsheathed it to reveal a glistening seven-inch blade, then slid it back in its place.

Charlotte raised her eyebrows to show she was impressed. 'All for one and one for all, hey, D'Artagnan? Where's your tunnel entrance?'

'According to my research, one of Sir Henry Slingsby's escape tunnels led to a stone structure known as Red House Landing near the river.' He pointed to a stone-built jetty twenty yards away. 'If my theory is correct, we can use the escape tunnel to bypass the army barracks, their security patrols and detection cameras, and emerge from the stable block just opposite Red House.'

Faulkner jumped out of the car and sprung the boot. He grabbed two shovels and handed one to Charlotte. Then he grabbed a half-empty rucksack containing a set of burglar's tools he had bought from Toolstation in York and slipped it on his back. 'I've seen enough of Slingsby's tunnels to understand how his mind worked. If he was escaping from the parliamentarian forces, he would want to emerge on the far side of the jetty, out of sight of Red House, but with quick access to a rowing boat. I suggest we start digging a trench line four inches deep parallel to the jetty's foundations, starting from here ...' he marked the point with the toe of his boot '... and with luck we'll hit the tunnel exit. I'll start here and you can start from the other end. If we meet in the middle without striking wood, then we'll know we're digging in the wrong place.'

They dug in silence for half an hour before Charlotte called out. 'Sam, I've hit something.' Faulkner rushed over to join her and dug to clear the soil from around a small wooden trapdoor. It was in poor condition, and he shone his torch around the edges looking in vain for a latch.

'It looks like we're going to have to lever the hatch open with our shovels.'

They inserted the edge of their shovels under the lip of the wooden trapdoor, and then leaned against the handles. The rotten wood splintered into fragments. Faulkner cleared away the wood and shone his torch into the dark hole.

'At least the ladder's rungs still look solid,' Faulkner said. He eased his way into the hole, climbed down the makeshift ladder and then dropped the last three feet onto the wooden duckboard at the bottom of the tunnel. Then he looked up and signalled for Charlotte to follow. She was as nimble as a cat, but Faulkner grasped her by the waist to help her with the final drop.

'The last few rungs were looser than I thought,' Faulkner said by way of explanation. He looked awkward as he released his grip on her hips.

'Is that so, Romeo?' Charlotte said and smiled at Faulkner's reserve. 'They felt sturdy enough to me. But on the other hand, these duck boards are a bit slippery. I won't object if you feel obliged to hold my hand through the tunnel.'

'But I'm not sure if your mother would have—'

'Sam, I'm thirty-four years old and I run a multinational pharmaceutical business. I suspect my mother is smiling down on us right now.'

'I doubt it. She left me with strict instructions to protect you from harm, and yet here I am taking you into the middle of General Lambert's lair.'

'How could I not be safe when I have the heir of the great Colonel Fauconberg to protect me?'

'Actually, it's most unlikely—'

Charlotte grasped his hand and led the way down the tunnel towards the stables.

* * *

Faulkner shone his torch around the stables. The smell was familiar, but the prison cells had an unnatural and oppressive atmosphere to them. A drunken militia soldier was the sole occupant of the cells and he grumbled at the brightness of the torch as they walked past.

'We'll climb out the side window,' Faulkner said. 'The main entrance to the stables may be guarded, and I don't want to give you an excuse to use your peashooter.'

Faulkner helped her through the little window, then handed her his rucksack. He pulled himself up and wedged himself in the narrow opening.

'How did I ever get through this window all those years ago?' he said as he attempted to squirm through. Charlotte took his hand and heaved him through.

'Not bad for a man who thinks he's past it,' Charlotte said. 'We'll get you back on the rugby field in no time.'

'Keep close to the stable wall,' Faulkner said. 'We can't use our torches again until we're in the hidden bedroom. The matron's cottage is just around the corner. We'll have to break cover and cross the stable courtyard when we get there.'

They crept in the darkness, keeping to the shadows. Two sentries were sharing a cigarette just outside the stables entrance. One of them yelled at the sole prisoner to keep quiet, but otherwise their demeanour was relaxed. Faulkner and Charlotte slipped out of the shadows of the stable wall, crossed the courtyard and lingered in the little garden of the matron's cottage.

'This is where your mother lived while she was here,' Faulkner whispered.

'I can feel her watching us,' Charlotte replied. She gripped Faulkner's hand with surprising strength and looked at Faulkner with a rapt expression. 'The sensation is so strong. Sam, she's talking to us; I can hear her.'

'It may not be your mother,' Faulkner said. He turned his eyes to the spot twenty yards away in the far corner of the courtyard where the woman he knew to be Lady Rebecca Slingsby had been murdered centuries before.

Charlotte followed his gaze and her eyes widened with shock.

'I can see her, Sam.' Charlotte made a move to run to the corner of the courtyard, but Faulkner held her hand tight.

'There's no-one there, Charlotte,' he said. 'It's just a trick of the moonlight. I've been there before.'

'But she was so real. She spoke to me.'

'What did she say to you?'

'She wasn't talking to me. It was as if she was talking to someone else, but it's all slipping away like a dream.'

'Stay in the moment, Charlotte. Don't lose it. It's important.'

'Something about a four-poster bed, I think. Why are you asking me this?'

'Just humour me a little longer. What was it about the bed?'

'Something to do with the headboard, but her accent was strange and her voice was faint.'

'Did she say anything else?'

'No, but I could feel her love. It was so intense, like a living, breathing thing.'

'Your ancestor Lady Rebecca Slingsby died in that spot, Charlotte. She was telling you that she loves you.'

Charlotte's eyes filled with tears and she shook her head. 'Her love wasn't for me, Sam; it was for you. When you looked me in the eyes just now, she became me, and I was looking into the eyes of Samuel Fauconberg, Colonel of the Northern Horse.'

'And yet neither Fauconberg nor I were able to do our duty to the women we loved when it really mattered,' Faulkner said. He looked despairingly at the spot where Lady Slingsby had died.

'That doesn't matter. You both risked your lives in the attempt to save them. There can be no greater proof of your love.' Charlotte stood on her tiptoes and kissed him gently on the cheek.

Faulkner smiled. 'Let's see if we can get *you* out of here alive, and then we might continue that conversation.' He indicated the high courtyard wall they had to climb over.

* * *

Balanced on the top rung of the ladder, Faulkner removed the jemmy from his pocket and prised open the brick-veneered shutters leading to Rebecca Slingsby's hidden bedroom. The latch snapped open with a crack and he flattened himself against the thick ivy. There was a platoon of soldiers fifty yards away on the oval, inspecting their Wolfhound troop carriers by torchlight, and he was nervous the sound might have carried to them. The area around the oval was a hive of activity, even though it was well after midnight, and he suspected the soldiers were preparing for a military operation at dawn. Charlotte was hiding in the rose bed twelve yards below, waiting for his signal to scale the rusty rungs.

Faulkner pulled the ivy apart and pushed the shutters inwards. He crawled through the narrow opening and into the hidden room. He turned back around and checked there were no sentries lurking below. Satisfied he had not been spotted, he dropped two pebbles two seconds apart into the garden bed below as a signal to Charlotte to follow him up the ladder. Moments later Charlotte was standing in the room next to him, her eyes wide in wonder.

Faulkner put his fingers to his lips and pointed to the floor, to signal there may be people in the room below the chamber. He closed the shutters, and then turned on his Ledlenser torch. The beam revealed the chamber's dusty and decaying contents. The air was stale and musty, and cobwebs billowed in curtains from the rafters. Dust swirled at their feet.

Charlotte stared at the little crib containing the skeleton of her distant ancestor. It was nestled at the foot of the bed as if it were waiting for its long-lost mother to return. Faulkner had forewarned her about its gruesome contents. He pulled the stiff, matted and musty smelling blanket from the bed and laid it like a shroud over the crib, then put an arm around Charlotte's shoulders.

'Family history has it that Luke had already died of a fever, but Fauconberg was able to save his brother, William, and deliver him to Rebecca's maid, Helen, on the night of the great storm,' Charlotte said after she had recovered her composure. 'We'll return to give this child a proper burial.'

'The memory of this child has haunted me for most of my life,' Faulkner admitted. 'When I first entered this room, I was too young to comprehend what I had seen. It was like I had walked into a nightmare, and nothing seemed real. All I wanted to do was to get out of this room undetected and pretend it had never happened. I should've alerted the police. I know now that

I must put right what I failed to do then.'

'I understand, Sam. It wasn't your fault. Whatever took place here happened a long time ago and nothing can change that. This child and his poor, unfortunate mother can rest in peace once we've proven the Bourcher family murdered Rebecca Slingsby.'

'I believe the proof we're looking for is in the trunk under the shutters.' He squeezed her shoulder in acknowledgement of her implicit forgiveness then led her towards the trunk. 'If my memory serves me right, there's not much of value in there other than the documents. A few rotting clothes and some worthless tat.'

Charlotte removed her gloves, opened the rusty latch on the trunk and opened the lid. She stepped back to avoid the cloud of dust threatening to engulf her, then began pulling the items from the trunk. The rotten garments were put to one side, but she picked up a curious red velvet purse and tipped the contents onto the decaying fabric of Rebecca Slingsby's gown. She gasped as she examined a delicate gold necklace studded with rubies and sapphires, then sifted through the gold brooches, lockets and earrings.

'These jewels are fit for a princess. I thought you said it was worthless tat?'

'It was to a boy of thirteen.'

Charlotte smiled and picked up a delicate wedding ring bearing a large glittering diamond at the apex of its gold band. Surrounding the large diamond was a halo of smaller diamonds.

'Would you bring the torch a bit closer, Sam?' she whispered. Her voice was shaking with emotion. 'There's an inscription on the inside of the band.' She turned the ring around in her fingers until the light glinted off the band. 'It says *"Charles & Rebecca. Paris. 10 September 1646"*. It's Rebecca's wedding ring; I'm convinced of it.' She slipped the ring onto her left ring finger and allowed the diamonds to glitter in the torchlight.

'I doubt it would convince the Attorney General,' Faulkner replied. 'We need to find the wedding certificate and establish the paternity of the child in the crib.'

Charlotte pulled more clothing from the trunk and extracted the fragile papers nestling at the bottom of the wooden chest. 'The bottom of the trunk has rotted through.' The disappointment in her voice was palpable. She examined the papers, which had matted together into a single papier-mâché slab. The paper at the top was yellow and brittle and the edges were blackened by mould. The ink had faded and become illegible. Charlotte looked crestfallen at the loss of the priceless documents. 'We're never going to be able to prove anything now,' she said.

But Faulkner was not listening. He had redirected his torch to the four-poster bed and was shining the beam on the headboard. It was carved with an image of the goddess Diana hunting a deer. He walked up to the bed and tapped its headboard with his knuckles. It sounded solid. 'English Oak,' he said.

'What are you doing?' Charlotte asked. She was still holding the solid mass of paper in her hands.

'Something smells familiar.' He bent down to where the old pillow was nestled against the headboard and tapped the wood once more. This time there was a hollow ring to it. He took another deep breath. 'Lanolin. Just like the smell of grease from the old school kitchens.' Faulkner ran his fingers along the bottom of the headboard until he felt a slight indentation in the woodwork. Charlotte had joined him and was looking at the image of Diana on the headboard. She wiped away the dust with a scrap of what once might have been a bed sheet.

'She's beautiful,' Charlotte said.

'It's the image of Rebecca Slingsby. Her father must have ordered the headboard for her.'

'How do you know?'

'I saw her portrait in a locket I found. I gave it to your mother.'

Faulkner pushed at the edges of the groove, seeking a latch, but it remained closed. 'I thought I knew Sir Henry and his confounded hidden latches, but this one is defeating me.'

'You're thinking like a man,' Charlotte said. 'The key would be in her heart.' She indicated an elaborately carved heart at the apex of the headboard. She ran her fingers along the embossed shape, then pushed it inwards, releasing the tension in a hidden spring within the headboard. Nothing happened for a moment as the rusty mechanism behind the headboard seized. Then gravity overcame the resistance of the rusty chain and a heavy counterweight descended towards the floor. The door to the compartment at the base of the headboard slid to one side, revealing a hidden cavity. Inside the cavity was a parcel wrapped in a lanolin-coated material.

Faulkner looked behind the four-poster and gawped in admiration at Slingsby's cunning counterweight device. Charlotte reached into the compartment and pulled out the parcel.

'It needs a can or two of oil and a new chain, but I think I could get Slingsby's mechanism back in perfect working order,' Faulkner said.

'Never mind that, look at this,' Charlotte said, holding up a hefty King James Bible. 'It must have been removed from the chapel to protect it from the Puritans during the Civil War.'

Faulkner opened the front cover of the delicate artefact. 'It's an original 1611 edition, printed by Robert Barker. One in this condition could be worth hundreds of thousands. Unfortunately, it's not what we came here for.'

Charlotte turned the pages until she came to the twenty-fourth chapter of Genesis, which told the story of the marriage of Rebecca and Isaac. Faulkner could no longer hide his impatience. 'It'll be dawn in an hour and this place will be crawling with squaddies. We should get going.'

Charlotte lifted a sheet of vellum lodged between the pages of the bible and held it out to Faulkner.

'It's the marriage certificate,' she said with wonder in her voice. 'It's on French notepaper from the Château de Saint-Germain-en-Laye in Paris. It's dated 10th September 1646 and bears the signatures of Charles Stuart and Lady Rebecca Slingsby. You can see the names of the witnesses, including the priest, Father John Huddleston; the prince's mother, Henrietta Marie; his sister Mary, the Princess Royal; and their brother James.' She stared at a childish signature on the bottom left. 'I can't read that one,' she said with tinge of disappointment in her voice.

Faulkner squinted at the scrawl under the powerful light of his torch. 'It says "Louis". That must be Louis the Fourteenth, the Sun King of France,' Faulkner said. 'He would have been a boy of eight at the time, but he became the most powerful king in Europe.'

'Then there can be no doubt. My ancestor Rebecca Slingsby was indeed the legitimate wife of Charles the Second of England.'

CHAPTER 39

Faulkner put the cumbersome bible back into the lanolin-coated bag and slipped it into his rucksack. He then replaced all the discarded clothing back into the trunk before closing the lid.

'I'm going to replace the broken latch on the shutters,' he said to Charlotte. 'There may be other secrets in here and I don't want Lambert or his goons rifling through the place. I'll meet you down the bottom.'

As Charlotte climbed down, Faulkner retrieved his set of tools and hurriedly replaced and reinforced the latch. He repositioned it on the outside so he could access the room more easily when he returned. As he climbed out of the window, the first pre-dawn zodiacal light peeped over the horizon. An army officer had emerged from Red House and was striding towards an armed Land Rover on which was mounted a Browning M2 fifty-calibre heavy machine gun. Faulkner decided he had no option but to descend the side of the building before it got any lighter. It would not be long before the soldiers would emerge in increasing numbers. Faulkner worked his way down the metal rungs. As he drew level with the old headmaster's study, he was unable to resist the temptation to shift his weight to the right and peer through the window. The curtains were drawn but the window was open about four inches He reached in and eased the curtain aside and was hit by a complex combination of odours that transported him back to his adolescent years.

'Quickly, Sam. Someone's coming,' Charlotte whispered from below.

Faulkner pulled back from the window and continued his descent. With five yards to go, one of the iron rungs detached from the wall under the weight of his right foot. Faulkner hung by his arms while he scrambled to regain a foothold. Loose masonry cascaded from the building as his left foot located another rung, but the broken rung clanged against the wall as it fell and hit the ground. In the pre-dawn silence it sounded like the toll of a bell. Faulkner pressed himself flat against the ivy as a powerful torch beam probed in his direction.

'You, man! What do you think you're doing?' The torch beam had caught him in its glare. The officer strode up to the rose bush where Charlotte was hiding.

'Colonel Clarke suspects there's a listening device on the outside of this window, sir,' Faulkner replied, trying to bluff his way out of the situation.

'At four-thirty in the morning? I don't think so.' The officer's voice was clipped and well educated.

'He only informed me last night and he wanted it done before we leave for the special operation. It was the only time I had, sir,' Faulkner replied.

'That may be the case, but I don't have time to stand here and argue with you. This bloody RWMIK Land Rover has a leaking gasket and needs sorting out. Come down from there and show me what's in your rucksack, then we can both be on our way.'

'Yes, sir.'

'Your face looks familiar,' the military man said as he confronted Faulkner. 'What regiment are you from?'

'Special Air Services, sir.'

'Really?' There was new respect in the lieutenant's voice. 'I didn't realise we had an SAS detachment with us. Nevertheless, I need to see what's in your rucksack. Turn around, man.'

Faulkner felt the burden of the country's future history weigh heavily on his shoulders as his hand reached inside his jumper for his British Army fighting knife. What he chose to do next would either light the fuse for a long and bloody civil war, or allow Britain to slide inexorably towards a totalitarian state.

'Good Lord!' said the army officer. 'You're the saboteur, Sam Faulkner. We've been told to keep an eye out for you. You're under arrest!' the lieutenant said as he unclipped his leather holster containing his pistol. Faulker had a fraction of a second to strike with his knife or succumb to his arrest.

He was interrupted by the metallic sound of a round being chambered into a Glock 19 pistol.

'On your knees, Lieutenant, or I'll blow your fucking brains out,' said Charlotte as she pushed the barrel of the Glock hard against the back of the officer's neck. 'And don't think I won't do it.'

'Yes ma'am, take it easy,' said the lieutenant as he knelt with his hands in the air. 'But I'm warning you, there's no way out of here. The estate is surrounded by General Lambert's patrols. I suggest you hand yourselves in and I'll do my best to make sure you're well treated. Goodness knows we need a bit of compassion in these divisive times.'

Charlotte removed the lieutenant's pistol from its holster. 'You're going to take us for a drive in your Land Rover,' she said. 'You can tell anyone who stops us that we're road testing the new gasket.'

'Yes, ma'am. Now, would you mind removing that pistol from my neck? It's making me very nervous.'

Charlotte eased the pressure on the lieutenant's neck. 'The three of us are going to walk to the Land Rover and you'll do exactly what I say. This Glock will be aimed at your groin while you're driving, so I suggest you smile at the guards and tell them what they want to hear.'

The lieutenant nodded. He rose from his knees, and they sauntered towards the militarised Land Rover. The lieutenant took the wheel while Charlotte sat in the passenger seat next to him. She removed her black sweater and placed it over her pistol hand. Faulkner climbed up to the elevated gun platform at the rear of the vehicle and stood next to the heavy machine gun.

'What's your name, Lieutenant?' Charlotte demanded.

'Castlemaine, ma'am.'

'Now drive as if you're going on a Sunday sightseeing tour, Lieutenant Castlemaine.'

'May I ask where we're going?'

'London. Do we have enough fuel?'

'Yes, ma'am.'

'For goodness' sake, my name is Charlotte. I'm not your bloody schoolteacher.'

Lieutenant Castlemaine nodded and turned the ignition. It fired first time and he pulled away from Red House. A light went on in the old headmaster's study above them, but otherwise no-one challenged them. As they drove past the old playing fields, Faulkner and Charlotte stared at the rows of tents and tank transporters loaded with Challenger tanks and armoured cars. The smell of diesel, damp canvas, gun oil, cigarette smoke and frying bacon wafted across the fields. At least two hundred personnel carriers were parked side by side, waiting to transport the thousands of soldiers to their destination.

'An impressive sight, Lieutenant,' said Charlotte.

'It is indeed, but I never imagined a show of force on this

scale would be used to intimidate our own people. If I had, I would never have enlisted.'

'What's the range on this Browning?' Faulkner asked Lieutenant Castlemaine.

'It's actually an L111A1 fifty-calibre heavy machine gun and it can fire up to two thousand yards. It's deadly accurate. Isn't she a beauty?'

'It sure is. I'd love to give it a try one day.'

'I would be happy to arrange it, Mr Faulkner, if we survive this debacle. It's more accurate than a Browning and has a higher rate of fire.'

They cruised along Red House Lane for two miles before encountering the first roadblock. A sleepy guard jumped to attention as Lieutenant Castlemaine slowed the Land Rover to a stop. The two soldiers exchanged salutes.

'You're out and about early, Lieutenant Castlemaine. Is everything all right?'

'I'm testing the Land Rover's replacement head gasket, Corporal. I need to give it a spin before this morning's operation.'

'There's still a bit of smoke coming out of the exhaust. Would you like me to take a look, sir? I'm an ex-mechanic.'

'Perhaps when I come back, but I'm not sure there's much you can do. The cylinder head is worn and needs to be machine-lathed back into shape.'

'We're setting off in an hour. Make sure you're back before then.' The guard stared at Charlotte and Faulkner. 'May I ask who your passengers are, sir?'

'They're officers from the 22nd SAS regiment working under cover. We have a small detachment coming with us on the operation.'

'They're letting women join the SAS now?' said the guard incredulously. 'This new government never ceases to amaze me.'

'Yes, they are, Corporal,' said Charlotte. 'And I'd keep your neanderthal opinions to yourself, or you'll find yourself on a charge faster than you can straighten that sloppy beret you're wearing.'

'Excuse me, ma'am, I didn't mean any offence,' said the guard as he adjusted his beret. 'I guess I'm still getting used to the idea.'

Charlotte nodded. 'Carry on, Corporal'.

'Yes, ma'am.' He saluted, and then raised the barrier for the Land Rover to proceed.

'You did well,' Charlotte said to Lieutenant Castlemaine.

'It might surprise you, but even though the government has promised to triple the size of the army, not everyone in the forces is thrilled about replacing the king with a Stuart pretender,' he replied.

'Is that the purpose of this morning's operation?'

Castlemaine nodded. 'Nigel Pride's orders. A regiment of tanks and infantry has already secured the Scottish borders to prevent any attempt to extricate the present king from Dumfries House. We're going south to secure London.'

'What's Lambert's role in all this?' Faulkner said.

'He's leading the Royal Yorkshire Regiment into London so everyone will know he commands the British Army now. It might surprise you there are some in the top brass who don't like the prospect of Mike Lambert taking over.'

'That doesn't surprise me at all,' Faulkner replied.

'The legislation enforcing the king's abdication is being debated in parliament today. The Stuart dynasty screwed it up three-and-a-half centuries ago and shouldn't be allowed anywhere near the throne again.'

'Oh, I wouldn't go that far!' said Charlotte, offended at the insult to her distant ancestors.

'Will we encounter any other army divisions on our way to London, Lieutenant Castlemaine?' Faulkner asked.

'The infantry from the 2nd Battalion of the Royal Yorkshire Regiment set off from the Catterick Garrison last night. They're camped just north of Sheffield. The artillery regiment based at Red House will join them at junction thirty-seven of the M1 at 07:15 hours. My advice is we bypass junction thirty-seven, just in case we encounter any early birds from the 2nd battalion.'

'You said *we*, Lieutenant. Do I take it we're now on the same side?' Charlotte asked.

'I think you'll find most soldiers are Windsor loyalists at heart. Nigel Pride has tried to buy our loyalty with bigger military budgets and the promise of a return to empire, but by forcing the king to abdicate in favour of a puppet monarch, he's taken a step too far. Yes, I'm on your side, even though it will cost me my career and reputation. But at least my conscience will be clear.'

'If you can get us to London in time, Lieutenant, we can stop the Abdication Bill from passing through parliament and you'll have done your country a great service,' Charlotte said. She made a show of removing the round from the chamber of the Glock and unclipped the magazine.

'You're not going to shoot up the House of Commons, are you?'

Charlotte laughed. 'No, we plan to make a constitutional challenge to the Abdication Bill. We have in our possession a document that proves Nigel Pride's puppet pretender to the throne, Jimmy Stuart, is not the heir apparent to the Stuart dynasty. The whole parliamentary debate is a charade.'

'When is the bill being debated?' Faulkner asked.

'At 14:00 hours. We'll be pushing it to get there in time, especially with a leaking gasket.'

The lieutenant joined the M1 motorway at Aberford, then looked over his shoulder. He frowned. 'We've got company,' he said, pointing to the sky. A Westland Gazelle helicopter was accelerating towards them from the north at one hundred and fifty miles per hour, its rotor blades pulsating in a rhythmic cacophony of sound. Faulkner turned the barrel of his L111A1 heavy machine gun towards the oncoming helicopter.

'Be careful with that thing,' Castlemaine said. 'It's already primed with ammunition from the belt box. You could knock the Gazelle out of the sky with a few bursts.'

'Hypothetically, of course, how would I fire this thing?'

'Hypothetically, you would need to pull the slider back three times to release the ammunition belt link, release the safety catch and you're ready to go. The trigger is that lever on your left. You've got one hundred rounds in the belt, unless Charlotte can reload another ammunition belt for you.'

They were interrupted by a crackle on the radio. Castlemaine picked up the receiver.

'RWMIK Land Rover. Identify yourself, please,' came the disjointed voice over the radio.

'This is Lieutenant Castlemaine, call sign RWMIK Leader. I'm General Lambert's aide-de-camp engaged on Operation Restoration. Gazelle 030 Pilot, identify yourself please. Over.'

'Lieutenant Johnson from Catterick Garrison. What is the purpose of your movement? Over.'

'We are the advanced reconnaissance unit for General Lambert and have a classified time-critical document to deliver to the prime minister. Over.'

'Has your mission been authorised by HQ? Over.'

'Affirmative. Over.'

'We have no record of your orders in our register. You are advised to pull over and await further instructions. Over.'

'Check again, Gazelle 030. The operation details were filed with my counterpart Lieutenant Coughlan at Catterick Barracks at 19:00 hours yesterday. Over.'

There was silence on the radio for several minutes as the Gazelle continued to shadow the Land Rover.

'You're good at this, Lieutenant,' Charlotte said in admiration.

'I should be. I really am General Lambert's aide-de-camp.'

'What's he like to work for?' asked Faulkner.

'A tyrant with limited intelligence.'

'No change there, then,' Faulkner replied.

'General Lambert mentions you frequently. He's acting like a jilted boyfriend because you've thrown in your lot with the Windsors.'

They were interrupted by another burst of static on the radio.

'We cannot trace Lieutenant Coughlan. Your orders are to pull over until we locate him. Over.'

'Who issued those orders, Lieutenant Johnson?' said Castlemaine, dispensing with radio protocol.

'Umm, I did, RWMIK Leader.'

Lieutenant Castlemaine was unable to hide the scorn in his voice. 'My orders come from General Lambert. Our mission is time-critical, Gazelle 030 and is not to be jeopardised because you cannot organise your paperwork properly. Your request to pull over is denied.'

'RWMIK Leader, I have permission to prevent any unauthorised use of this road by force if necessary. I suggest you comply immediately.'

'Lieutenant Johnson, my orders from General Lambert are to defend ourselves from any attempt to impede our mission. You have been warned.'

There was silence from the Gazelle as Lieutenant Johnson considered the standoff. Then the radio sprang to life once more. 'You may proceed until we have confirmed your orders with

General Lambert directly. Do you copy that? Over.'

'Understood, Gazelle. Out.' Castlemaine turned to Charlotte. 'We've bought ourselves half an hour at most. General Lambert will be tucking into his bacon and eggs right now. Not even the threat of a Russian invasion would interrupt his breakfast. You need to decide your next move.'

Faulkner frowned as he spotted a distant black line that spread across the entire width of the M1 a few miles ahead of them. He grabbed the binoculars from a side pocket and adjusted the focus. 'It seems our choice has been made for us,' he said. 'The entire 2nd Battalion of the Royal Yorkshire Regiment is waiting for us at junction thirty-seven.'

'Can we retrace our way back to the previous junction?' Charlotte suggested.

Faulkner turned around and scanned the terrain behind them. Another line of military vehicles filled his field of vision.

'It appears we've driven into Lambert's ambush,' Faulkner said. As if in confirmation, more soldiers emerged from the long grass at the side of the motorway to block any attempt to drive off-road.

Once more, their radio crackled into life.

'This is Lieutenant Johnson from Gazelle 030. We have a message for the crew of the RMWIK Land Rover. General Lambert is awaiting your arrival at the roadblock two miles ahead of you. He is apoplectic with fury that you have disturbed his breakfast.' There was a slight pause on the radio. 'Good luck, arseholes. Over and out.'

The Gazelle banked to the east and then swooped away to the north in a manner Faulkner could only describe as cocky.

'Keep going, Lieutenant. We'll see if the general really commands the loyalty of his men.'

Faulkner's phone trilled in his pocket. He was tempted to ignore it, but he was out of options and took the call as a welcome distraction to his predicament. 'Faulkner,' he said brusquely.

'Faulkner, this is Colonel Clarke from the Red House detachment. I'm commanding the light mechanised infantry battalion to your rear. I understand you're fighting to preserve the current monarchy?'

Faulkner considered Colonel Clarke's question. He had nothing to lose so he answered truthfully. 'Affirmative, Colonel.'

'My battalion wishes to join your fight. Are you willing to accept our assistance?'

Faulkner suspected a trap, but he continued the conversation, regardless. 'Why would they want to do that, Colonel?'

'Because we're the 1st Battalion of the Royal Yorkshire Regiment, and the present king is our commander-in-chief.' He placed the emphasis on the word Royal.

'The odds are not good, Colonel. Maybe twenty or thirty to one. Are you sure they want to be part of this?'

'I've told my officers and men there's only one person with enough honour to lead the United Kingdom through this crisis and they should trust your judgement. The 1st Battalion has agreed that this ... political lunacy must stop.'

'Then the 1st Battalion of the Royal Yorkshire Regiment are welcome to join me at the next junction, where I'll be reasoning with General Lambert. Be good enough to cover my back, if you will.'

'It'll be an honour, sir,' replied the colonel.

* * *

The RWMIK Land Rover cruised to a stop fifty yards from the massed infantry battalion of the 2nd Royal Yorkshire Regiment. Five hundred high-powered rifles were raised as Faulkner and Charlotte climbed out of the vehicle. Lieutenant Castlemaine stayed in the Land Rover and moved to the L111A1 heavy machine gun platform at the back of the car.

Faulkner squared his shoulders and strode with Charlotte to a point midway between the Land Rover and General Lambert's staff car. He stopped and fixed his attention on the bull-like physique of the general. For almost a minute they stared unblinking at each other until Lambert broke eye contact. He selected two of his military staff and walked towards Faulkner and Charlotte.

'Lambert,' Faulkner said, tilting his head in acknowledgement of his former classmate.

'Faulkner,' Lambert replied.

'I have a document I need to deliver to parliament, and I'm requesting you move your forces aside to allow me to carry out my duty.'

'You can give the document to me.'

'That's not possible. The document is of state importance and must be delivered to parliament by me in person.'

'You're not in any position to demand anything, Faulkner. I suggest you hand the document to me. You will, of course, be arrested for treason, along with Miss Talbot. Nigel Pride told me this morning you've had one too many chances. He'll be demanding the death penalty.'

'One cannot be treasonous against an illegitimate rabble that has not been sworn in by the king.'

Lambert laughed and swept his arms across the array of military forces at his disposal. 'I assume your document is a missive from the current king. How many tanks can *he* call on right now?'

'The mere presence of your tanks is proof of the Cavalier cabinet's illegitimacy. Why would such a show of force be needed if Pride had the support of the British people?' He spoke loud enough so the soldiers in the front ranks could hear.

General Lambert shook his head sadly. 'You had the world at your feet, Sam Faulkner. You symbolised everything that was great about Red House and you became a hero on the rugby field of Twickenham. We promised you everything you could have dreamed of. Did you not realise it was our intention to make you president of the United Kingdom? It may well have been a symbolic role, but it would have been an important one. Now you'll pay the ultimate price for throwing our generosity back in our faces.'

'You want to make Britain great again, yet Britain's greatness came from defending the world against tyrants, not from creating them.'

There were murmurings of assent from some of the soldiers, and a few lowered their rifles. Lambert noticed their unease and drew his pistol. He pointed it at Faulkner.

Fifty yards behind them, Lieutenant Castlemaine worked the slider mechanism of the Land Rover's heavy machine gun. Its unmistakable sound carried to the men on the motorway. It was answered by several hundred rounds being chambered into the rifles of the 2nd Battalion.

'Lieutenant Castlemaine is digging his own grave,' said Lambert. 'You're encircled, and his gesture of defiance is pitiable. In fact, I can hear the 1st Battalion coming from the north to close the trap door now. I'm surprised you fell so easily into my hands, Faulkner.'

The roar of massed engines of Colonel Clarke's mechanised infantry battalion prevented further discussion. Fifty Foxhound and Jackal armoured vehicles arrived in formation, then manoeuvred alongside Castlemaine's Land Rover. A cloud of diesel exhaust hung over the imposing war machines.

'Well, don't just sit there. Arrest the man,' General Lambert yelled to Colonel Clarke.

Only the throbbing of diesel engines answered Lambert's order and it became evident a standoff had ensued. Five minutes passed as both sides faced their adversaries, each daring the other to fire the first shot that would signal the start of a long and brutal civil war.

Suddenly, a small pocket of Lambert's soldiers who had been stationed at the side of the road emerged from the trees. They cleared the rounds from their rifles, pointed them towards the ground and walked towards Colonel Clarke's 1st armoured battalion. They saluted the colonel before taking up position alongside his men.

'Those men will be court-martialled for their insolence,' Lambert yelled.

'You're going to need a very large building for your court martial,' Charlotte said as she pointed to the right wing of Lambert's light infantry division. It too was melting away and heading towards Colonel Clarke's battalion.

'Any of my soldiers who desert their post will be shot for cowardice!' yelled Lambert. He waved his pistol in the air for emphasis.

'Up yours, mate,' yelled an infantry soldier as he rushed to join the throng that were heading towards Colonel Clarke's men.

Order broke down as Lambert's remaining soldiers debated furiously with each other for what seemed like an hour. Eventually Lambert's tank transporter vehicles started their engines, and chaos ensued as seventeen heavy vehicles executed cumbersome three point turns so that the entire mechanised forces of the Royal Yorkshire Regiment formed up alongside and behind the RWMIK Land Rover. A minute later, the remaining infantry of the 2nd Battalion lowered their weapons and joined their colleagues protecting Colonel Clarke and Lieutenant Castlemaine. Cheering broke out among their ranks as handshakes and backslaps were exchanged among the two battalions.

General Lambert stared ashen-faced at the sight of his once-loyal troops standing in opposition to him. His revolver shook in his hands, and he raised it towards his own temple like a man caught in a nightmare.

'I'll take that, if you don't mind, General,' Faulkner said. He gripped Lambert by the wrist and eased the revolver from his hand. 'You can accompany us to London as my guest, or make your own way back to Red House. The choice is yours.'

Lambert's mouth flapped open and closed but no sound emerged. He seemed unable to comprehend the scenes that had just taken place.

'He'd be better off in one of the transporters,' Charlotte said. 'He's going to need psychological help when we get to London.'

They were interrupted by Lieutenant Castlemaine. 'We'd best be off, Mr Faulkner, if you want to get to London in time for the debate. I've taken the liberty of transferring you to General Lambert's mobile command vehicle. It has state-of-the-art communications equipment, laptop computers and printing machines on board. They're also cooking you a hearty breakfast and preparing you a shower and change of clothes.'

'Thank you, Lieutenant. Now that General Lambert is indisposed, would you be so kind as to act as the aide-de-camp to Miss Talbot and me for the rest of the day?'

'It would be my pleasure, Mr Faulkner.'

CHAPTER 40

The House of Commons, London

'Order! Order in the house.' The Speaker of the House of Commons, Jeremy 'Swotty' Sedgwick, banged his gavel in a vain attempt to restore calm.

Nigel Pride uncurled his lanky frame from his green leather seat and propped his left arm on the prime minister's rosewood despatch box. He positioned his body so that his back was turned to the leader of the opposition in a deliberate snub. 'As I was saying before I was interrupted, Mr Jimmy Stuart is not a "Pretender" to the throne, he's the real deal. If those opposite had been taught any history at school, they would be able to follow the debate.' He paused to allow the guffaws to die down before continuing. 'The so-called "Glorious Revolution" of 1688 was a foreign invasion that ultimately led to the illegal overthrow of the Stuart dynasty.'

There was another round of uproar from the opposition benches.

'Had the illegal invasion not taken place in 1688 to overthrow King James the Second, then Jimmy Stuart ...' he pointed to the portly figure in the public gallery '... would be wearing the crown of Great Britain right now. It's clear, Mr Speaker, the Windsor dynasty is illegitimate, and the current king should abdicate in favour of the rightful claimant, his Royal Majesty James the Third of the House of Stuart.'

Once more the House of Commons erupted into chaos.

'And don't get me started on ...' Nigel Pride tried to shout above the hubbub, '... the German interlopers known as the Hanoverians who ousted the Stuart dynasty!'

There were loud cries of 'Shame!' from the opposition bench.

'The so-called Elector George of Hanover couldn't speak a word of English and was only the fifty-sixth in line to the throne. Yes, Mr Speaker, the fifty-sixth! And why did this happen? Because an act of religious bigotry prohibited James the Second's catholic son from inheriting the throne.'

Pride waited for the cacophony of noise to die down. 'This government intends to correct a historical wrong, honourable

Members of Parliament. We're going to pass the Abdication Bill and restore the Stuart dynasty to its rightful place on the throne.' He paused to let his words to sink in and allowed himself a sneer at his opponents. He had the numbers to pass the bill, despite the histrionics from the opposition and the small bunch of Windsor die-hards from within his own party. His chief whip, Bernard Walters, had done an excellent job of intimidating and bribing at least thirty closet Windsor supporters within the ranks of the Freedom League to vote for the bill.

'The Abdication Bill proposes that the rightful heir of the Stuart dynasty, Jimmy Stu... I mean, His Majesty James the Third, by the grace of God, of the United Kingdom of Great Britain and Northern Ireland and of His other Realms and Territories King, Head of the Commonwealth, and Defender of the Faith, becomes king with immediate effect. I commend this bill to the house.'

Jimmy Stuart rose from his front-row seat in the public gallery and bowed to the House of Commons. The sweat glistened on his bald head and his chubby jowls quivered. Stuart turned to bow to the gallery, but no-one was paying him any attention. A commotion had erupted at the gallery entrance as the security guards remonstrated with a group of intruders.

'Sam Faulkner! What are you doing here? You're interrupting the debate. Go away!' Jimmy Stuart shouted at the party of six who were advancing towards him. 'They're about to make me king!'

Faulkner, Charlotte and four armed men in army fatigues marched to the front of the public gallery. 'Sit down, Stuart, and move away from the glass,' Faulkner said. 'I don't have time for your drivel.'

The four soldiers moved towards the bulletproof glass that protected the politicians from the unruly elements in the public gallery. They attached P4 plastic explosives to the glass at strategic intervals and inserted wireless electronic detonators into the centre of the putty-like substance.

'Stand well back, ladies and gentlemen,' Lieutenant Castlemaine said to the guests in the public gallery. 'The explosives will make a bit of a bang.' He produced a device from his pocket that looked like a key fob. He looked at each of his men in turn.

'Sergeant Cook?' he asked.

'Ready, sir,' came the confirmation.

'Corporal Lightfoot?'

'All set, Lieutenant.'

'Private Gordon?'

'Aye, sir.'

'Excellent. Firing in three ... two ... one.' He pressed the button on his fob and six flashes of light lit up the gallery. They were followed by muffled explosions. The bulletproof glass quivered, then fragmented into sections. When the smoke had cleared the glass was lying in pieces in the front row of the gallery. The left-hand section still hung like the broken wing of a seagull and Private Gordon used his pistol butt to detach it from its frame.

Faulkner stepped forward and leaned on the public gallery's railing. He took a minute to take in the scene of ancient wood panelling, green leather seating and the pomp that was the British parliamentary system. Below him was the speaker's chair. The packed government benches were to his right and the opposition to his left. The two main parties were separated by two-and-a-half swords-length's distance. Opposite him on the far side of the chamber were the double doors that the usher of the Black Rod would strike before entering at the start of each parliament. Microphones and cameras dangled from the chamber's roof, and Faulkner knew the events of the day were being transmitted live around the world on television and radio.

He stared at the faces of the shocked and frightened politicians who gazed back up at him. Faulkner squared his shoulders and then ushered Charlotte to stand next to him.

'You are in no danger from me or my colleagues, ladies and gentlemen of parliament,' he said in a clear voice. 'I've come to introduce you to your new monarch, should you decide to pass the Abdication Bill.' He gestured towards Charlotte, who looked commanding but unregal in her black jeans and pink T-shirt. Her chestnut-coloured hair was wild and there were remnants of makeup smudged around her eyes. It was clear she had not slept for days. Her Glock 19 pistol hung from a holster strapped over her left shoulder adjacent to her bicep. In her arms was a large bundle of photocopied documents.

'Allow me to introduce Miss Charlotte Talbot. She is the daughter of the late Rebecca Vavasour and the direct descendant of Lady Rebecca Slingsby, who was married to King Charles the Second on 10th September 1646.'

The politicians gawped in disbelief at the scene in the public gallery. One or two had regained their composure and were snorting in derision at the statement Faulkner had just made. Some remained cowering under their seats while others displayed affected outrage at the affront to British democracy.

Faulkner watched the chaotic scenes below with disdain. 'Show a bit of courage for a change, Sullivan, and come out from under your bench,' he said to his former classmate. 'Sedgwick. Yes, I'm looking at you. The Speaker of the House is supposed to be a leadership role. For goodness' sake show some backbone.'

Faulkner paused for a minute while the pandemonium on the floor of the House of Commons settled, and an uneasy calm returned. Then he continued. 'I would like to address you as "honourable Members of Parliament", but the term does not seem fitting. What I see below me is a cesspit of conniving, duplicitous and self-interested weasels, who have driven Britain to the brink of civil war. The worst culprits, I'm ashamed to say, are the Old Cavaliers of Red House, who have allowed wealth and privilege to go to their heads. You forget your primary role is to serve the people and not treat them as tools for your own aggrandisement.'

Nigel Pride emerged from under the Table of the House near the speaker's chair. He looked around for the sergeant-at-arms. 'Arrest that man!' Pride said in a high-pitched voice, pointing at Faulkner. The sergeant-at-arms gave a shrug of his shoulders and remained in his seat.

'Nigel Pride,' Faulkner said in an exasperated manner. 'Yet again, I must sort out the chaos that follows you around like a black shadow. You'll be pleased to know the country is at peace once more, except for a few gangs of your Darkshirt thugs who seem to revel in the anarchy that you created. The armed forces have returned to their barracks, except for the soldiers of the Royal Yorkshire Regiment, who are keeping a watchful eye on the proceedings here in parliament.'

'Are we going to stand here and let this ... jumped-up travel agent ... tell us what to do?' Pride flapped his arms and looked around at the members of parliament.

'Shame on you, Pride!' said an opposition member.

'Sit down, Pride!' said a member of his own back bench.

Pride's face paled as he realised the House had turned hostile.

Penny Oakton stood up from the front bench and strode towards the prime minister's table. She turned to address the House. 'It's evident the *acting* prime minister, Nigel Pride, has lost the confidence of the House. I propose we take a vote of no confidence in him and that I take his place as prime minister designate until further notice.' She looked up at Faulkner as if challenging him to intervene. Faulkner shrugged his shoulders.

'All those in favour of the motion?' said the speaker.

There was a resounding chorus of 'Ayes'.

'The ayes have it,' the speaker said without asking for the noes.

Nigel Pride looked aghast at his Cavalier cabinet colleagues, who had unanimously betrayed him. His head dropped and his shoulders slumped. He picked up a sheaf of papers from the despatch box and placed them into his brown leather satchel. Then he trudged towards the double doors that led out of the chamber, accompanied by raucous jeers, whistling and scoffing from the opposition MPs.

'Where is the king?' asked the speaker.

'He's flying down from Scotland in an RAF transport plane as we speak. He'll be back in Buckingham Palace by nightfall,' replied Faulkner.

'What do I do now, Mr Faulkner?' the speaker asked.

'Sedgwick, I never knew how someone who was so good at Latin and Chemistry could have such little common sense. You are to resume the debate,' said Faulkner.

Penny Oakton cleared her throat and pulled back her shoulders. She tossed her mane of blonde hair over her shoulder and addressed her colleagues in a commanding tone:

'Charlotte Talbot is no more a direct descendant of Charles the Second than I am. She's the daughter of a school matron and runs a corner shop pharmacy. She can't come into parliament dressed like a female Che Guevara, blow up the bulletproof glass screen and proclaim she's the next Queen of England. Good grief, we'll have the tea lady saying she's the Archbishop of Canterbury next.'

Oakton's display of bravado heartened the Cavalier cabinet, and a few sniggered at her joke.

'Or a backstabbing administrator claiming she's the new prime minister,' countered Charlotte.

'I believe you still have an outstanding arrest warrant for entering the country under a false passport. I'd be careful what you say, young lady, or I'll have you locked up the minute you step out of this place,' Oakton replied.

'If you pass the Abdication Bill, I'll become your new sovereign. It will be me that you'll have to report to, and I'll be your worst nightmare.'

'Your claim is absurd,' Oakton said, folding her arms across her ample bosom. 'Charles the Second had a succession of mistresses and illegitimate children, but no valid heirs. You're a charlatan.'

'I think not. I have here the original marriage certificate of Charles the Second and Lady Rebecca Slingsby. It was dated the 10th of September 1646 and was witnessed by a long list of dignitaries, including Louis the Fourteenth of France, James the Second and the Princess Royal. The marriage took place before any of his dalliances with his subsequent mistresses and the union produced two male heirs. I'm the most direct living descendant of his surviving heir.'

Charlotte leaned over the balcony and flung the large bundle of photocopied marriage certificates she was holding into the debating chamber below. The papers fluttered like confetti towards the curious politicians.

'This document is a forgery and proves nothing,' Oakton said as she examined one of the copies. 'Where's the results of the DNA test?'

'The skeletal remains of one of the two princes fathered by Charles the Second are lying in rest at Red House. A lock of hair from his head has been recovered and was rushed to the Oxford Genetics laboratory. The preliminary results of this sample confirm the prince was indeed the son of Charles II and is a match to my own DNA. Furthermore, in a direct comparison between my DNA and the earlier sample provided by Jimmy Stuart, it shows my DNA is a closer match to the Stuart kings by a factor of four hundred per cent. The DNA test results will be published at nine o'clock tomorrow morning by Oxford University's History faculty.'

'What we have here is an elaborate fraud designed to torpedo the passage of the Abdication Bill,' said Oakton to her fellow MPs. 'If we hold our nerve, we can still pass this bill and unblock our programme of radical reforms that will restore Britain to its former glory. Do not fall for this fraudster's web of deceit.'

'To any of those who still doubt I am indeed the direct heir to the Stuart dynasty, I've invited Dr George Greer, the country's most pre-eminent early modern historian, to examine the marriage certificate. He's on his way here as we speak,' added Charlotte. 'He'll give his opinion on the authenticity of the document within the hour.'

Jeremy Sedgwick rose from the speaker's chair. Without the dominating presence of Nigel Pride in the chamber he carried himself with the genuine authority of his office. 'Honourable members of the House,' he began, 'We have a straightforward choice between Miss Talbot and the present king. I suggest we waste no more time and vote to pass the Abdication Bill, or keep the constitution that has served the country well for a thousand years. Let your consciences be your guide.'

Sedgwick adjusted his robes and cleared his throat. 'The question is: "That the Abdication Bill be agreed to." All those who say aye?'

There was a long silence in the chamber until a solitary voice spoke up. 'Aye,' said Penny Oakton.

'Of the contrary, say no?'

There was a roar in the House as the politicians bellowed their rejection of the bill.

'Order, order!' said Sedgwick, banging his gavel. 'The noes have it. The noes have it. This house has voted to retain the present king and the Windsor dynasty.'

The house erupted as cries of 'God save the king!' echoed spontaneously around the debating chamber.

CHAPTER 41

Red House, 10th September, 9 p.m.

Faulkner climbed the rusty iron ladder until he was halfway up the ivy-clad red-brick building. He cursed as the rung he was holding with his left hand came loose in his hands. He pulled the rung free and allowed it to drop into the soft earth of the rose garden below. He noted with satisfaction that the window to the old headmaster's study was open and the light in the room was still on. He leaned to his right and peered through the glass.

The image he saw was distorted by condensation and the age of the glass, yet the room still retained the grim familiarity of his childhood memories. He took in the dark oak panelling and the solid brass floor lamp with its yellow-tasselled, 1970s-style lampshade. Dominating the centre of the study was a large, polished desk made of sturdy oak. It was the same desk on which several generations of school children had been thrashed till they bled. Faulkner could almost feel his buttocks blazing at the memory of the vicious blows meted out by Bernard Bourcher after the Rebecca Vavasour incident. Behind the desk and facing Faulkner was the rear of an imposing high-backed leather chair.

Faulkner grasped the underside of the sash window and eased it open. He was assaulted by myriad familiar smells, including wood polish, old books, sweat, cheap cologne and stale whisky.

Faulkner swung a leg onto the window ledge and grasped the underside of the study window with both hands. Once he had steadied himself, he eased himself into the study and stood stock still while he contemplated his next move. On the other side of the old leather chair, he could hear the wheezing of an old man and laboured fingers tapping the keyboard of a laptop. He inched his way around to the side of the desk, and then lunged for the laptop.

'Give that computer back to me!' screeched Bernard Bourcher. 'It's not yours.'

Faulkner looked into the rheumy eyes of his old headmaster. They remained as fanatical as ever, but his broad shoulders and bull-like chest had shrunk to skeletal proportions. A walking frame was positioned to the right of the desk, but otherwise the study remained as he remembered it. Keeping a watchful eye on the old man, Faulkner glanced at the screen of the laptop. It was full of computer code, but within the code were references to cybercurrencies and it appeared an illicit drug transaction had just taken place. At the top of the screen was the infamous *Battlefield Z* logo, representing one of the most sophisticated dark web marketplaces on the planet.

'Stay there, Bourcher; I'll deal with you later,' Faulkner said as he pulled out his mobile phone and speed-dialled a number in Sydney, Australia.

'This is Moody,' came the reply.

Faulkner put the phone on loudspeaker and placed it on the far side of the desk, where Bourcher could not reach it.

'Hi, Sean. I'm with our old friend Bernard Bourcher in his study at Red House. He's still alive and trading narcotics on the dark web.'

'Good grief! Did you manage to get hold of his laptop before he closed the lid?'

'Yes, why?'

'Most dark web operators have encrypted their laptop so that if the lid is closed while the computer is still running, it'll erase the hard drive. That way their passwords and the identities of their co-conspirators will not be compromised if their laptops are seized.'

Faulkner clicked an icon in the taskbar at the bottom of the screen and the hardline forum known as the Protectorate lit up the screen. He typed a brief message into the dialogue box: '*You guys are not going to believe what's just happened!*' He waited for about thirty seconds before a response pinged onto Bourcher's message board.

'*Hey is that you, Recusant? Long time no hear. I thought you must've been busted by the feds,*' wrote Ballsov Titanium.

'*It's good to see you back, man. You've been off reservation for too long,*' came a message from a character named Shagmeister.

'*Wassup, Big Dog?*' It was a message from Krypt Kreeper. '*Is the Battlefield Z marketplace still operational? I'm in serious need of some Class A shit, if you know what I mean.*'

Faulkner typed again: '*I'm still in business and will be back in contact soon. Stay cool, guys.*'

Faulkner spoke into his mobile phone. 'Bernard Bourcher's

your man, Sean. He's the Recusant himself. His dark web associates still think he's operational, so we might be able to lure them into the open using his logon credentials to impersonate him.'

'How on earth did you work out Bourcher was the man behind the Recusant?' Moody asked. 'I thought he'd been dead for twenty years.'

Faulkner looked down at Bourcher with contempt. 'I could smell him through the open window the last time I was here. He's a habitual fresh air freak, which means his study window is always open. I couldn't see him, but I caught a whiff of his cheap cologne, whisky and stale sweat. That stench never leaves you once you've been thrashed to within an inch of your life.'

'Even so, it was still a big leap to connect him to the Recusant.'

'Once I knew he was alive, everything fell into place. Nigel Pride was too shallow to pull off a political coup of that magnitude on his own. Someone had to be pulling his strings. Someone who was obsessed with the values of Oliver Cromwell and his Protectorate. The giveaway was his moniker – the Recusant – a throwback to the seventeenth-century religious non-conformist and subversive secret societies.'

'You should take Bourcher's laptop to the National Crime Agency in London. We've so much evidence on the Recusant, our friend will spend the rest of his days behind bars,' said Moody. 'In the meantime, my team in Sydney will hunt down his Russian mafia sponsors.'

'Thanks, Sean,' said Faulkner. 'What I don't understand is why a man who claimed to be so patriotic would accept Russian mafia money to betray his own country?'

'He's right there. Why don't you ask him?'

Faulkner disconnected the call, then turned to face Bourcher and raised a quizzical eyebrow.

'Why should I tell you anything, you snivelling, woke, good for nothing?' Bourcher retorted.

'You don't remember me, do you?' Faulkner said, astonished.

'Why should I?'

'Because you caned me so hard, it took my injuries six weeks to heal.'

Bourcher looked blankly at Faulkner. 'I caned hundreds of boys during my time at Red House. Why would I remember you?'

'I'm the one who captained your precious rugby team to eleven trophies during its three-year unbeaten run.'

Bourcher's face flickered with recognition, then his withered face creased into a scowl. 'Samuel Faulkner! The turncoat who brought down my Cavalier cabinet. You deserve a traitor's death. I'm telling you nothing.'

'Suit yourself. You're the one who took the Russian mafia's thirty pieces of silver and now you must live with your conscience.'

'If you must know, the Russians confused my *Battlefield Z* military antiques website logo, consisting of a diagonal pike crossed at the top by a musket and at the bottom by a broadsword, with a 'zed', and therefore assumed I must be a kindred spirit. If they wanted me to launder their ransomware profits and move a few hundred kilos of cocaine around the dark web for a five per cent cut, then who was I to turn their dirty money away?'

'And you didn't think that it was they who were manipulating you by giving you the means to destroy democracy?'

'It wasn't like that.'

'Suddenly you had access to more money than you knew what to do with. You'd already indoctrinated hundreds of former pupils with your puritan ideology and developed your hardline Protectorate chat forum to poison the minds of the weak and vulnerable. Even better, you had a willing political puppet in the shape of Nigel Pride and his Freedom League poised to carry out a full-blown political coup d'état.'

'I had no choice. Britain was bending the knee to the woke, culture-cancelling zealots and those who would gender-neutralise our youth. Our nation needed to rediscover the origins of its greatness. It was Oliver Cromwell and his major generals who injected the culture of discipline, religion and hard work into the British people, and I had to reignite that flame by any means possible.'

Bourcher pulled a soiled handkerchief from his pocket and coughed in a rattling, mucus-filled symphony. 'I had such high hopes for you, Faulkner. You could have been the leader that Britain needed during these dark days of decline. "Cometh the hour, cometh the man," I said to Nigel Pride. But then that evil bitch Rebecca Vavasour poisoned your mind yet again with her woke ramblings. I will never forgive her for what she did to you.'

'She was murdered by a gullible idiot who was obsessed by

the wild conspiracy theories promoted by the Recusant and his acolytes on your Protectorate forum. You might as well have placed the gun in that young man's hand.'

'You lie! Get out of my house!'

Faulkner noticed the old man was reaching into the top drawer and he dashed around the desk to grasp the ex-headmaster's wrist. In Bourcher's skeletal hand was a Webley & Scott army pistol that had once belonged to Captain McTavish.

'I'll take that, if you don't mind,' Faulkner said as he levered the Webley from Bourcher's grip. Faulkner noticed a yellowing legal document written on early modern era rag paper in the open drawer. The title of the document was *The Last Will and Testament of Samuel Fauconberg*.

'Where did you get that from?' Faulkner asked as he slipped the revolver into his pocket.

'It's none of your business.'

'It's dated 1678. So, Fauconberg did not die on the scaffold?'

'Fauconberg was a deranged killer who murdered my forefather. The Bourcher family was denied justice in 1660 because the murder weapon could not be found when he was arrested. That spineless excuse for a judge, Justice John Holt, accepted Fauconberg's story that my forefather's head could have been severed by a pane of glass that flew from the chapel following a second lightning ball strike. Instead of the death penalty, Fauconberg was demoted to the rank of major, exiled for life to the new English colony of Tangiers and was charged with setting up the military fortifications there.'

'So, why do you have his will in your drawer?'

'To prove Fauconberg was a liar. It contains clues as to the whereabouts of Fauconberg's murder weapon, the so-called Enlightener.'

'So, why haven't you found it?'

'The clues in the will are indecipherable and were probably designed to taunt members of my family into searching for a sword that he had already destroyed. Fauconberg claimed only his son would be able to retrieve the sword once Red House had been returned to the Slingsby family. The will contains nothing but the ravings of a deranged mind.'

'Fauconberg had a son?'

'Yes, but what's that got to do with you?'

'Probably nothing.'

'Then you're done here, and I'm asking you to leave. You may have appropriated my laptop, but I have final stage cancer and won't live long enough to face a trial.' Bourcher managed a smirk. 'So you see, you've wasted your time after all.'

'You might think I'm done here, Bourcher, but I haven't even started.' Faulkner strolled across the study to where he knew there was a small cupboard and opened the door. Inside was arrayed a large collection of canes, riding crops and a long, heavy hippopotamus-hide sjambok whip.

Faulkner whistled through his teeth. 'You vicious old bastard,' he said as he pulled the sjambok from the top shelf. 'You must have bought this whip during our 1987 tour of South Africa. How many times did you use it?'

'Never. Despite Jeremy 'Swotty' Sedgwick's lies to the contrary.'

'No wonder Sedgwick had such deep-rooted issues.'

'Yet look at him now. He's the Speaker of the House of Commons. He owes his success to me.'

'Ex-speaker. The Cavalier cabinet you constructed using your psychological influence and Russian mafia money has fallen. A new election has been called for November.' Faulkner flexed the vicious-looking sjambok and then swished it through the air like a swordsman.

'What ... what are you doing with that whip?' Bourcher stammered.

Faulkner advanced towards Bourcher and tested its flexibility by bending it almost double. 'You need to learn a lesson you won't forget. But rest assured it's going to hurt me far more than it will hurt you.'

'But I'm eighty-five years old. I've got cancer, for goodness' sake.'

'You've broken the rules of democracy that have served Britain for centuries. Bend over this desk, Bourcher. You know the routine.'

'This is monstrous. I'm a vulnerable member of society who can't defend himself.'

'That power imbalance didn't seem to worry you when you caned over two hundred children. Some as young as seven years old.'

'But that was different. They were cheeky little shits who didn't know how to behave.'

'The subtle distinction is lost on me. Bend over, Bourcher, and take it like a man.'

'I ... I ... I ...' A tear ran down Bourcher's cheek. 'I don't want to be beaten, Mr Faulkner. My heart might give way. Can't we work something out?'

'Oh, do stop snivelling, man. A good flogging is character building. You said so yourself when you thrashed me to within an inch of my life.'

'I beg you. Please don't hurt me.'

'Do not try my patience or I'll return night after night to avenge each of the two hundred children you brutalised during your reign of terror.'

'What is it you want? Why did you really come here?'

Faulkner reached inside his pocket and extracted a sheaf of documents. 'I'm surprised you had to ask. I want peace and restitution for the descendants of the Slingsby family. Their spirits have been calling out to me since I was a thirteen-year-old boy.'

'You're mad, Faulkner.'

'You may think so, but I've spent the last three months searching for Lady Rebecca Slingsby's last will and testament. I thought it was in her trunk in the attic room, but then I discovered Rebecca's maid, Helen Barnes, had delivered it to Mary Fairfax at Nun Appleton Hall for safekeeping.'

He pointed to the yellowing documents with the tip of the sjambok. It was written in the neat hand of a seventeenth-century female aristocrat. 'Rebecca Slingsby maintained that if she were to die in tragic circumstances in the days following the drafting of her will, it would be proof of Bourcher's plot to murder her. The date of the document is 30th December 1659, and her death was recorded as the 1st of January 1660. The official cause of her death, according to the York City Council, was lightning incineration during the great storm that hit the chapel that night.'

'Ha! So, you see, she was married to my forefather in the chapel after all, and therefore he was legally entitled to claim her property.' Bourcher smirked at Faulkner.

'Not so. Attached to the death certificate is an affidavit written under oath by Rebecca Slingsby's maid, Helen. It states Rebecca never entered the chapel that night. The document claims Rebecca was chained to the stake in the stable yard and was burned to death in the most vile and cruel way by your forefather. It was written for her by Mary Fairfax and witnessed by Mary's husband, the Duke of Buckingham. But it seems your forefather's cronies in the York City Council dismissed her affidavit as being – and I quote – *"the unworthie fantasie of a sillie servant girl"*. A modern-day court would not dismiss her evidence so lightly.'

Bourcher sighed and his skinny shoulders slumped. He coughed once more into his handkerchief. 'I suppose you're asking me to transfer the Red House deeds to Charlotte Talbot?'

'Of course.' Faulkner pointed to the third document with the tip of the sjambok. It was a deed of sale for Red House.

'I only ask that I be allowed to live out the rest of my days at Red House.'

'Agreed.'

'How much will she pay me for the house?'

'The same amount it was worth when your family stole it from her ancestor.'

'How much was that?'

'Eleven thousand two hundred pounds.'

'Adjusted for inflation, of course?'

'No.'

Bourcher erupted into a coughing fit once more, then spat into his handkerchief. 'What about my laptop? Are you really going to hand it to the police?'

'Once Moody has copied your hard drive and ended the careers of the scum that infest your marketplace, you can have it back. But he'll be keeping a close eye on your online activity.'

'You'll not flog me if I sign the deed of sale?' Bourcher asked, staring at the device Faulkner was still flexing in his hands.

'Not if you keep your side of the bargain.'

Bourcher picked up the weighty Parker Duofold fountain pen that he had once used to sign the initial board in the red passage. He trembled as the gold nib hovered above the deed of sale. For a moment Faulkner feared the old man might expire before he could sign it. Then with a practised flick of his pen, the former headmaster signed over the ownership of Red House to Charlotte Talbot.

CHAPTER 42

Red House, six months later

The Lord Mayor tugged at the gold cord and unveiled the tasteful brass plaque affixed to the stable wall. It commemorated an injustice that had taken place three-and-a-half centuries ago, when an innocent noblewoman had been burned at the stake and her property stolen from her. The excavations in the corner of the stable yard had revealed the charred remnants of a once-sturdy wooden beam, the scorched and misshapen hoops of a gunpowder cask, and links from a thick iron chain. Traces of human remains had also been discovered in the soil, which Charlotte Talbot had placed in a silver urn and transferred to the chapel next to the resting place of Lady Rebecca Slingsby's son Luke, during a short but poignant ceremony.

The mayor gave an emotional speech in which he apologised for the council's role in the persecution of Lady Slingsby. He hoped the many wrongs that had been committed during the brutal English Civil War would be forgiven, and her soul and those of countless others who had suffered the same fate could rest in peace.

Charlotte stepped forward to thank the dignitaries for their act of reconciliation and for allowing the torment, which had festered like an ulcer through a dozen generations of her family, to heal.

The Lord Mayor bowed his head as he shook Charlotte's hand. 'You've demonstrated considerable dignity since the defeat of the Abdication Bill in parliament, Miss Talbot. It might not have been such a bad thing had you become sovereign of this troubled nation.'

'I can assure you, Lord Mayor, the nation would have been much more troubled had the bill been passed into law.'

'And where is the new independent member of parliament for Greater York? I was led to believe he would be here at the ceremony.'

'Mr Faulkner is in the horse paddock preparing the new horses he's bought at the auction. He's not one for ceremonies.'

'Then perhaps he chose the wrong profession by entering

politics?'

'I insisted he ran. He's the one man who commands the respect of both sides of politics. His presence in Westminster will heal the nation, and then we can become a stronger, more prosperous, but kinder society.'

'Your election campaign on his behalf was quite brilliant, Miss Talbot. He was lucky to have you at his side. Did you not think of running yourself?'

'I've a multinational pharmaceutical company to run, your worship. And besides, I owed him. He ran my mother's campaign against Nigel Pride. She would have won had she not been murdered on election day.'

'Yes, that was deeply distressing. Do we know what has happened to Nigel Pride since the election?'

'He was given a role as a political commentator on a populist news channel. His ratings were so disastrous, he was moved to the eleven-p.m. graveyard slot.'

'I wanted to thank you for donating those historical artefacts you sent to the York Museum last month. We've created a fascinating new exhibit based on the history of the witch trials during the Civil War. The exhibit has been a huge hit with the public.'

'I was pleased to get rid of them.'

The Lord Mayor looked up at the grey skies. 'I believe it's about to pour, so we had best be off.'

Charlotte escorted the dignitaries to the mayoral car and waved them off. Then she retreated to Red House's main entrance hall just as a ferocious downpour hit the old house and its grounds. To Charlotte, it felt like the heavens were cleansing three hundred and fifty years of corruption and cruelty from the fabric of the building, in readiness for the return of its rightful owners.

She studied the portrait of her illustrious ancestor, Henry Slingsby, as she waited for the rain to subside. She had once considered his expression dour and haughty, but Charlotte had had the painting restored to its original condition and Slingsby now looked like a contented country gentleman watching over a much-loved daughter. It had been painted when Sir Henry had married his wife, Barbara, and had brought the young Samuel Fauconberg to Red House as a stable lad.

Charlotte unclasped the chain around her neck, opened the locket and looked at the dashing young cavalry colonel who had idolised both Sir Henry Slingsby and his daughter, Lady Rebecca. She could see the uncanny resemblance to Samuel Faulkner and her heart skipped a beat as she thought of him preparing their horses in the stable yard. Her eyes drifted to the other half of the locket and the beautiful image of Rebecca Slingsby stared back at her through time and space. She wore an expression of contentment, as if the manner of her death no longer defined the extraordinary life she had lived.

* * *

The rain eased and Charlotte changed from her formal attire into a white polo shirt, tight-fitting jodhpurs and a warm, fleecy riding jacket. Then she skipped down to the old school boot room and selected a pair of long black riding boots topped with a three-inch band of brown leather. After pulling them on she tied back her hair and donned her velveteen-covered riding hat. Finally, she clasped her riding crop and stepped out into the sunlight.

The wind still carried the remnants of the rain shower, but the grounds smelled fresh, and spring sunlight sparkled against the buildings. She caught her breath at the sight of Faulkner, who was waiting for her by the chapel doorway with the reins of two beautiful horses in his hands. His sandy hair was swept back, revealing a hint of grey at his temples. Charlotte fingered the silver locket at her throat and wondered if this was how the dashing Colonel Samuel Fauconberg of the Northern Horse would have greeted Lady Rebecca Slingsby centuries before.

Faulkner smiled as Charlotte approached, handed her the reins to the chestnut mare and helped her onto the back of her horse.

'She's beautiful,' Charlotte said as she stroked the shining flanks of her mount.

'I took the liberty of naming her Juniper. It was the name of your mother's horse while she worked at Red House,' Faulkner said as he jumped onto the back of his American quarter horse.

'Thank you, Sam. You didn't have to buy these horses for me.'

'I thought we could start a stud farm.'

'*We*? Are you thinking of moving in, Mr Faulkner?' Charlotte asked, pretending to be shocked.

'Umm, I thought the stud farm would be a fitting tribute to the Slingsby family. They supplied hundreds of thoroughbred horses to the royalist cavalry, you know,' he said evasively.

'Let me guess. You named your horse Bullet?'

Faulkner coloured slightly. 'How did you know?'

'My mother told me the story of your race in Red House woods many times.' Charlotte urged her horse forward and they proceeded towards Red House Lane. 'It's touching that you still think about her so often.'

'I didn't mean to spoil the mood. I thought I had got over my grief.'

Charlotte reached out and put her hand on his arm. 'You're very loyal. I like that in a man. But you still haven't answered my question.'

'About moving into Red House? Were you serious?'

'Maybe.'

'Then I can't deny the attractions. It's close to my business and my electoral office. It's picturesque and has wonderful facilities.'

'Are there any other ... attractions?'

'Now you come to mention it, there's one attraction near me right now who has a very special place in my heart. But I feel geriatric in her presence.'

'Come now, Sam. You're younger than my sister's husband, Steve. You're smarter and classier than Vance Messervy ever was, and fitter than most men half your age. And there's no man alive with quite so much charm.' Charlotte manoeuvred Juniper so their legs brushed as they rode towards the woods.

'There's something else,' Faulkner said.

'What is it?'

'I was put on a pedestal by your mother because I bore a passing physical resemblance to the man in the locket.'

'That's not so bad.'

'No, but since the moment I saw Fauconberg's portrait, I've felt the full weight of his expectations on my shoulders. It hasn't been easy to follow in the footsteps of a Civil War hero whose exploits I could never hope to emulate and whose blessing I can never receive.'

'You'll always be my handsome cavalier and you have nothing to prove to me, Samuel Faulkner.'

Faulkner placed his hand over his heart and bowed his head in appreciation of her sentiments. 'Unfortunately, since I've exorcised the Slingsby ghosts, I've developed one of my own. I feel I've incurred Fauconberg's displeasure for failing to prevent your mother's death and it's a heavy cross to bear.'

Charlotte touched the locket at her throat and Faulkner was unsure if her gesture was an affirmation of their developing relationship or an unconscious rebuke at his lack of commitment. Then suddenly she urged her horse into a canter and headed towards the gate of Red House woods. Faulkner took up the challenge and caught up with her just as she was opening the gate.

'The offer to move into Red House has been withdrawn,' she said as she closed the gate behind them.

Faulkner stared at her in disbelief, not knowing if she was serious. He cursed himself for not grasping the proposition she had dangled before him minutes before.

'But I might change my mind if you can beat Juniper and me to the end of the trail and back.'

Charlotte grinned, then urged her horse forward. She was at full gallop before Faulkner could gather his wits. At the touch of his heels, his horse shot forward like a round from a gun. He felt himself lurch to his right and his left foot slipped from the stirrup. She was twenty yards ahead before he regained control of his horse, and he set himself the desperate task of closing the distance between them.

EPILOGUE

The Chapel, Red House

'Sam, what are you doing?' Charlotte said as she closed the heavy chapel door behind her. It was one a.m. and she pulled her woollen dressing gown tightly around her.

'I couldn't sleep,' Faulkner replied. He was in the pulpit and was looking up at the wooden plaque affixed to the chapel's oak panelling. He pulled out a screwdriver and attacked the first screw that fastened the plaque to the northern wall of the chapel. It displayed the word '*courage*' in ornate gold lettering and was one of the four plaques spread around the chapel that made up the old school motto: '*discipline, piety, loyalty, and courage*'.

'I was rather partial to that plaque,' Charlotte said. 'I hope you'll put it back when you're finished.'

'We would stare at these plaques so often as schoolchildren that they almost became invisible to us. But something has been haunting me ever since Bourcher signed the deed of sale.'

'You mean something Bourcher mentioned about Fauconberg's will?'

'Yes.'

'But you said when you read it there were no clues as to the whereabouts of his sword, Enlightener.'

'There weren't. But he did say his son would be able to retrieve the sword once he had returned Red House to the Slingsby family. Why would that be?'

'Because Fauconberg had already told his son where it was hidden?'

'Perhaps. But the will reads like the two had not had any contact since Fauconberg was arrested and exiled to Tangiers.'

'Then the clue would be something deeply ingrained into their family history. Something that is passed from generation to generation,' Rebecca said.

'Like a family motto.'

'Yes. Do you happen to know Fauconberg's family motto?'

'No, but I'll never forget my late father often quoting the only Latin phrase he ever knew: "*De audacia venit illustratio*".'
Faulkner removed the last of the screws from the plaque and

handed it down to Charlotte.

'What does that phrase mean?' Charlotte stared at the beautiful gold lettering that spelled out the word 'courage'.

'"*From courage comes forth enlightenment*". My father was quoting the Faulkner family motto.' He ran his fingers along the wood panelling where the plaque had been, until he felt a small protrusion in the woodwork.

'So, you're suggesting the Fauconberg name might have changed to Faulkner over the centuries, but the family motto remained the same?'

'We'll soon find out,' Faulkner said as he pushed at the protrusion and heard the click of a hidden latch. A second later the sound of a heavy counterweight on a chain could be heard lowering to the ground. As it did so, a section of wood panelling slid open, revealing a recess in the chapel wall that was just large enough to hide a large adult lying prone. 'Another of Sir Henry's confounded priest holes.'

'There's something in there,' said Charlotte. 'It's wrapped in a lanolin bag.'

Faulkner reached inside and extracted the heavy bag, which he handed down to Charlotte.

Charlotte reverentially opened the bag and pulled out an exquisite long-bladed broadsword. She held it by its intricate half-basket hilt and beckoned Faulkner down from the pulpit. 'I believe the honour of unsheathing your forefather's sword must go to you, Sam.'

Faulkner slid the long blade from its scabbard and stared at the Enlightener with wonder. Etched on its blade were the words '*De audacia venit illustratio*'.

'There's a note from Fauconberg in the bag,' said Charlotte. She stared at the old-fashioned cursive handwriting for a long moment as tears welled in her eyes:

To my dearest son.

That you are standing in the Red House chapel with Enlightener in your hand signifies you have corrected an injustice that I was powerless to prevent. You have proven yourself to be the most courageous and enlightened of men, better than ever I could have been and all that a father could have wished for.

I am not long for this earth, and as you read this note –

my last to you – my beloved Lady Rebecca Slingsby and I will be together once more in the Kingdom of Heaven and smiling down at you with pride and joy in our hearts.

One final piece of advice I give to thee as a father to a cherished son. Should you be blessed to find a noble woman who makes your heart sing with joy, as Rebecca did for me, do not hesitate to honour her with your eternal love; for who knows what trials life may put in your path to true happiness.

Your ever-loving father,
Samuel Fauconberg

HISTORICAL NOTE

Britain has faced many perils since the English Civil War ended in 1651, but it has also heralded an era of unprecedented political stability and prosperity. Freedom, resting on the bedrock of constitutional monarchy and parliamentary democracy, was hard won. It evolved after nine years of brutal civil war (1642–1651), the beheading of King Charles I (1649), ten years of strict Puritan rule under Oliver Cromwell (1649–1658) and a year of near anarchy (1659).

Cavalier is a cautionary tale. It starts in 1658, when the three kingdoms of England, Scotland and Ireland were under the brutal heel of a puritanical regime. It ends in 2024, by suggesting how a handful of bad actors, financed by foreign interests, could sabotage our beloved institutions and plunge the United Kingdom back into repression and civil war. The message is clear: democracy is a precious gift that should never be taken for granted.

Sir Henry Slingsby of Scriven, First Baronet, and his beloved home, Red House, are the real heroes of this story. Slingsby was born in 1602 to parents Sir Henry Slingsby and Frances Vavasour. He married Barbara Belasyse (daughter of Viscount Fauconberg), who died in 1641 when she was aged only thirty-one. Slingsby was a kind and gentle man, who had the misfortune to be on the losing royalist side in the Civil War. He was also a man of honour, who remained loyal to his principles to the end. He was beheaded at Tower Hill on 8 June 1658, for 'distributing commissions signed by Prince Charles Stuart among the officers at Hull gaol', where he had been held as a prisoner of war. Had he avoided the executioner for three more months, he would have outlived his tormentor, Oliver Cromwell; there would also have been the likelihood of a return to his beloved Red House.

Slingsby wrote a fascinating diary covering the years 1638 to 1648. It was first published in 1806 and is a valuable first-hand source for the Civil War period in northern England. Even more poignant is his 'Father's Legacy' to his daughter, Barbara, and his two sons, William and Henry, written in the Tower of London in the hours before his death. I have re-imagined his daughter, Barbara, in the heroic image of Rebecca Slingsby. Slingsby's real daughter married Sir John Talbot of Lacock in 1660. She lived a long, happy life and did not die at the stake.

Red House was confiscated from Sir Henry Slingsby in 1651, after he refused to swear the required oaths to Cromwell, but his extended family bought Red House back from the government for £11,200, which they held in trust for his children. Red House was eventually returned to the Slingsby family following the restoration of the monarchy in 1660. The house remained in Slingsby hands until 1916, when Red House and 2,223 acres of land was sold at auction. The black-hearted Benedict Bourcher is a figment of my imagination, and so the theft of Red House by the notorious 'Bourcher family' in 1660 is fictional.

Even amid the horror and bloodshed of the Civil War, real heroes could be found. One such man was the parliamentarian General Sir Thomas Fairfax, who emerged with a proud military record and his reputation for honour without equal. I have taken artistic liberty as to my knowledge, Fairfax did not have an illegitimate son, but otherwise I have tried to remain as true to his life as possible. The historic meeting with his entourage at his home in Nun Appleton is well recorded. His mere presence on the battlefield on New Year's Day in 1660, with a paltry five hundred Yorkshire gentlemen (including Sir Henry Slingsby's eldest son, William, and his fifty horsemen) was enough for Colonel Redman and his Irish brigade to defect from General Lambert's huge army. This was immediately followed by Lambert's remaining 10,800 battle-hardened troops leaving Lambert devastated and broken. Thus, General Fairfax was able to defeat Lambert without a single shot being fired and he secured Yorkshire for General Monck. Monck then marched into London unopposed and in May 1660, Charles II returned to London as King, amid wild celebrations. A fascinating account of the restoration is recorded in Samuel Pepys' famous diary.

The Northern Horse cavalry regiment was assembled from the wreckage of the Royalist cavalry that had been beaten at the Battle of Marston Moor in 1644. They were led by a charismatic Yorkshireman called Sir Marmaduke Langsdale. Described as a 'rabble of gentility', the Northern Horsemen were wild and ill-disciplined, but were also superb fighters. The Northern Horse defeated John Lambert's army at Wentbridge in Yorkshire, played a crucial role throughout the Civil War, and in 1645, in one of the epic encounters of the war, rode through hostile territory from Oxford to Yorkshire and defeated General Fairfax to relieve Pontefract Castle – the last Royalist stronghold in the North. It was only after the Northern Horse was subdued in 1648 that the first English Civil War came to an end. I have based the fictitious character Samuel Fauconberg's war record on the remarkable exploits of Sir Marmaduke Langsdale.

The societal breakdown during the Civil War period and the subsequent Puritan stranglehold on religious values enabled the rise of the witchfinders. Belief in witchcraft during the seventeenth century was universal, and misfortune of any kind would be seen as evidence of diabolic forces at work. The most notorious of the self-styled witchfinders were Matthew Hopkins and John Stearne. These two men were responsible for torturing and prosecuting more 'witches' during their three-year campaign than in the preceding 160 years in England. Their unfortunate victims were just as likely to die under their barbaric interrogations than at the end of a hangman's noose.

Fortunately, there were sufficient men of good conscience to counter the witchfinders. The Puritan vicar John Gaule was so appalled by the methods used to extract confessions that he petitioned against the practice to Parliament, resulting in the premature retirement of Hopkins and Stearne in 1647.

The man credited with ending the prosecution of witches in English law was Justice John Holt. Holt recognised the malicious intent of those who brought forward accusations of witchcraft. In 1701, he acquitted Sarah Moordike of witchcraft. He then ordered her violent and vindictive accuser, Richard Hathaway, to be arrested and locked up in the Marshalsea prison, on charges of perjury for 'pretending himself to be bewitched'. Richard Hathaway was subsequently convicted by Justice Holt at his own trial in 1702 for inciting violence against Moordike, and was ordered to stand in the pillories in the City of London, and then to be whipped at a house of correction, where he would serve a sentence of six months' hard labour. And so ended the persecutions of witches in England. Holt would only have been seventeen years old during the fictional trial of Lady Rebecca Slingsby in 1659, but I was sufficiently moved by his legacy to bring forward the essence of his judgment by forty-two years.

The iconoclast William Dowsing was a historical figure who

visited over 250 churches between 1643 and 1644 and who '*by vertue of a pretended Commission goes about the Country like a Bedlam breaking glasse windowes, ... not only in our Chapples, but (contrary to Order) in our publique Schooles, Colledge Halls, Libraryes, and Chambers*'. He charged each church a noble (one third of a pound) for his services.

The ball lightning scene in which the Red House Chapel was struck and Benedict Bourcher maimed was based on 'the great thunderstorm' of Widecombe-in-the-Moor in 1638. The church of St. Pancras was similarly struck by ball lightning during an afternoon service. The building was packed with approximately three hundred worshippers. Four were killed, around sixty injured, and the building was severely damaged. Curiously, this event was captured in Sir Henry Slingsby's diary.

The English language was going through a profound transformation at the time Slingsby wrote his diary. The use of 'thee' and 'thou' was already obsolete even when the *King James Bible* was first published in 1611. Older members of society, including Slingsby, would still end their verbs with '-est' and '-eth' (e.g. 'wither goest thou' and 'the iceman cometh'), whereas younger members of society had dropped these verb endings by the end of the Civil War. Britain was also in the middle of 'the great vowel shift' (e.g. from 'hoos' to house, 'weef' to wife and 'beet' to bite.) This shift in the way the vowels were sounded did not happen uniformly across Britain, leading to confusion between different regions. Similarly, word order within the sentence was not as rigid as it is now; spoken language was more formal and double negatives were much more common. I have tried to reflect this use of early modern language by making the older characters in my novel (particularly Stearne and Dowsing in Part 1 and the witch in Part 3) speak in an archaic East Anglian dialect. However, for the younger characters I have adopted a more modern but formalised manner of speaking, to give them a distinct seventeenth-century personality.

The Duke of Wellington is alleged to have said that the "Battle of Waterloo was won on the playing fields of Eton". This remark was the inspiration for Part 2 of my novel. Red House was indeed a boarding school of excellence from 1902 to 2001. However, all the characters and events described in this section are entirely the product of my imagination. By 1988, the draconian practices at British boarding schools were thankfully long gone, but there was no doubt that schools like Red House were geared towards the creation of tough, intellectual leaders, destined for service to the Empire and the Commonwealth. Twenty-nine British prime ministers including David Cameron and Boris Johnson, were schooled at Eton, and it is not too much of a stretch of the imagination to suggest that future prime ministers could be drawn from the privileged ranks of a small Yorkshire preparatory school like Red House. Especially if its headmaster was to be a messianic, brutal man funded by Russian mafia money, like the fictional Bernard Bourcher.

Red House is the glue that binds the separate threads of this book together. It has hosted kings and princes, and has been the foundation stone of so many people's lives, from the great and the good to the humblest student. It instilled in me a love of history and English literature, and so it feels only right that I should repay Red House in kind by crafting a tale in which the house plays the hero. If you would like more information on Red House Estate, or would like to sneak a glimpse of the buildings at the centre of this book, you can visit the Red House website on https://redhouse.orpheusweb.co.uk.